Faces in the Fire

Scandinavia in time of Beowulf
(from Osborn 1983 after Klaeber, emended 1993)

Faces in the Fire

BOOK ONE: THE WOMEN OF BEOWULF

"Dee" Rogers

Donnita L. Rogers

iUniverse, Inc.
Bloomington

Faces in the Fire
Book One: The Women of Beowulf

iUniverse books may be ordered through booksellers or by contacting:

iUniverse
1663 Liberty Drive
Bloomington, IN 47403
www.iuniverse.com
1-800-Authors (1-800-288-4677)

ISBN: 978-1-4502-7139-4 (sc)
ISBN: 978-1-4502-7137-0 (e)
ISBN: 978-1-4502-7138-7 (dj)

Library of Congress Control Number: 2010916920

Printed in the United States of America

iUniverse rev. date: 3/29/2012

For D. D. F.

Guide to Pronunciation

DANES

Aeschere	=	ASH-heruh
Freawaru	=	FRAY-uh-WAH-roo

(Initial H before R is sounded)

Hrethric	=	HRETH-rick
Hrothgar	=	HROTH-gar
Hrothmund	=	HROTH-mund
Hrothulf	=	HROTH-ulf
Unferth	=	UN-ferth
Wulfgar	=	WOLF-gar
Wealtheow	=	WAY-ul-THAY-oh

GEATS

Beowulf	=	BAY-oh-wolf
Ecgtheow	=	EDGE-thay-oh
Hygelac	=	HIG-uh-lack
Hygd	=	HIG

Contents

Illustrations

Note: All illustrations are copies of pictures from ancient artifacts, drawn by the author.

Acknowledgments

For inspiration, information, and professional advice, I thank Marijane Osborn, *Beowulf* scholar and translator at UC Davis. She set the standard for "hands-on" research and generously shared her own work with me, most notably her invaluable studies in *Beowulf and Lejre*, John D. Niles, ACMRS, Tempe, Arizona, 2007.

My thanks to California friend Robert Paton for putting me in contact with Dr. Osborn.

I also owe a debt of gratitude to retired schoolmaster Jan Ekborg of Bohuslan, Sweden, who shared his home with me and personally took me to visit relevant historic sites.

For timely assistance in formatting the manuscript, I thank Quaker friend Nell Warnes of Houston, Texas.

For introducing me to the world of Internet publishing, I thank Earlham College classmate Fred Campbell of Williamston, Michigan.

To Jim Finholt and Barbara Henwood in the computer lab at Northfield Community Center, Northfield, Minnesota, I am indebted for their assistance in matters electronic.

To all my students at Kingwood High School in Kingwood, Texas, I say "thank you" for your enthusiastic embrace of a timeless classic and for the moment of epiphany that resulted in this book.

Finally, this novel would never have reached fruition without the support, encouragement, and critical acumen of my partner Don. Thank you for your love and patience.

A Note on Translations
For passages in the novel quoted or paraphrased from *Beowulf,* I have drawn upon three translations: that of Seamus Heaney (Farrar, Straus

& Giroux, NY 2000), Marijane Osborn (University of California Press, Berkeley and Los Angeles 1983), and Burton Raffel (New American Library, NY 1963).

Chapter 1
The Making of Heorot

Voices woke me. *"Hwǽt wē Gār-Dena in geār-dagum þēod-cyninga þrym gefrūnon, hū ða æþelingas ellen fremedon.* What of the Spear-Danes in days gone by? Ancient kings winning glory with their deeds, courageous warriors heroic in battle?"

As these words faded, an image rose before me like a great ship's sail, towering so high it seemed to cover the sky. I blinked at its brightness, golden in the morning sunlight.

When I blinked again it was gone. Eager to find it, I lifted my wings and flew into the night, but the vision had escaped into darkness.

Shaking myself, I slid from the warmth of my fur-lined bed, set my bare feet on the cold, wood floor, and looked around sleepily. Mother's bench was empty; so was Willa's. Pulling a robe from my bed, I ran to the door and used all my strength to lift the heavy bar and squeeze outside. At first, I shivered in the cold, but soon I was skipping over icy patches, joyful at heart to be out of doors, glad to take in the first smells of earth coming back to life after long months of darkness.

Voices, different voices now, drifted down to me, blown on a gust of wind that made me pull the fur robe closer around my shift. Scanning the horizon, I saw two figures against the sky: one tall and regal, the other short and broad. Their backs were turned to me, and they seemed to be deep in talk. Father and Aeschere. They could tell me.

Breathlessly I climbed the hill, soon dropping the heavy robe that dragged behind me.

"Father, Father, where is it? Did you see it? Did you hear the singing?"

The shorter man turned first.

"Child, what are you doing up here in your nightclothes? You should be—"

"It's alright, Aeschere." Father reached down and lifted me, rubbing his rough beard against my face as I dangled in his grasp, giggling. "What is it you want to see, little Freaw?"

"Your hall, Father, your new mead hall." For so it must be.

Aeschere laughed and reached out a big hand to tousle my hair. "Not yet, child, not for many a day. But how did you know of it? Not even Hrothgar's thanes have been told of his plan."

"It came to me last night. I saw it."

Aeschere stared first at me and then at Father, who frowned.

"Another seeing, little one? Then … it must be so." Father now smiled at me in reassurance.

Aeschere drew himself up stiffly and spoke in a formal tone. "Whatever King Hrothgar commands shall be done. If it is his wish, the hall will be built."

"Yes, Aeschere, it is my wish, and it will be built—soon. Our stores and treasury can now support it." Father paused. "We will start it here by this twisted oak … and carry it all the way to … there to the end of the ridge … and back again. Come." He swung me up onto his back, and Aeschere followed in silence as Father paced off the length.

"So big?" marveled Aeschere when we stopped. "You could house a hundred warriors in a hall so big! A grand hall indeed—a fitting place for feasting, drinking, and the giving of gold rings." Aeschere's face broadened in a great grin as if already anticipating these activities.

"Yes, old friend." Father laughed a huge laugh that echoed from the distant hills as I clung to his neck. "Yes, young warriors will find a suitable home with Hrothgar, including those sons of yours. We need strong young thanes here, we old graybeards."

"Father," I cried, tugging at a handful of his whiskers, "your beard isn't gray—at least not as gray as Aeschere's."

Now both men laughed. "Not yet, Freawaru, but soon. Right now, let's go down for hot food. Your little belly must be empty; you're as light as a feather!"

Riding atop my father's shoulders as we headed toward the settlement, I surveyed our world. On one side of the path clustered farmers' huts, pastures, and fields. Beyond them stretched dark hills and forests. On the other side stood a row of sturdy structures, which housed my family, our animals, and our other possessions, including Father's storehouses for food, weapons, and booty. This was our kingdom. Father was king and I, Freawaru, the king's daughter. Safe and happy, I trusted completely in Father's strength and power.

As our breath took shape and hung in the frosty air, I leaned my stinging cheeks into Father's leather helmet. Aeschere, trailing behind, scooped up my fur robe and threw it lightly over my shoulders.

Looking back, I remember that morning clearly—so fresh, so full of promise. In those innocent days we had no hint of what was to come, no warning of the monster, no warning of the darkness that would envelop our world and our lives, bringing unimaginable terror.

That spring our settlement rang with the sounds of work and laughter. King Hrothgar was building a mead hall, the most glorious in the world! Each day new workers and materials poured in from surrounding farms; cargo ships unloaded in the harbor nearby. Month after month, the settlement swarmed with activity. Every hour of our short summer was used to shape Father's great hall.

Bars of iron brought by wagon from distant charcoal smelting camps went to the forge of our blacksmith, Bjorn. Oak, birch, and pine trees felled in distant forests were dragged in behind oxen and delivered to the timber yard where carpenters set aside their shipbuilding to fashion the poles and planks needed for the hall's construction.

Mother was so busy with the additional work of supervising helpers and slaves to feed this labor force that she sometimes let me go off with Father and Aeschere to inspect their progress. I gloried in these outings, in the smell of fresh pine shavings, the noise of Bjorn's hammer clanging on the anvil, and the feel of mud between my fingers as I dipped them into pots of plaster.

"Better not put those fingers in your mouth," Aeschere laughed. "That mud is mixed with straw and cow dung!"

I watched in awe as great deep holes were dug in the ground and heavy oak posts, straight and smooth, were lowered into them. Much swearing and shouting and good-natured jesting accompanied these procedures. Everyone seemed proud to be working for my father. I felt proud too as I looked up at him—so tall, so lordly, so commanding. Hrothgar. My father. The king.

On other days, workmen set pine staves vertically in the ground, lashed them to the open posts already in position, and then applied plaster. This took many days—more than I could have counted even had I known how to count—for Father's hall was to be a great hall indeed, in size as well as grandeur.

Our hall was not to be roofed with turf or thatch like most buildings in the settlement, but with wood shingles laboriously shaped in the timber yard by skilled carpenters with an adz. The floor was not to be formed of beaten earth strewn with straw, but with long wood planking and dry stone imported from afar. It seemed as if the whole world labored to please my father, to turn his vision into reality.

Sometimes, late in the evening while light still glimmered in the west, Father would coax Mother outside to view the mead hall rising like a dream on the edge of the hill. I would run after them, for I loved to see Father and Mother walking together.

"Of course, it will look even better in a few weeks," Father boasted one night, raising his arms as if to embrace the whole building. "I'm bringing in goldsmiths from the Rhineland to cover the gables with gold leaf. Imagine how they will gleam in the setting sun! You'll be able to see this hall all the way from the fjord. It will be a beacon to the world, and warriors will flock to the hall of Hrothgar!"

"As they do already, my lord." Mother took his arm and pulled it around her shoulder. "Your generosity is as renowned as your battle valor. I am fortunate indeed to have such a warrior as my husband. One day, no doubt, your hall will be famous in song and story."

Father beamed at these words and wrapped Mother in his arms, holding her close for a long time. He often bragged that his Wealtheow was slender as a willow, and he would circle her waist with his two hands to prove it.

I believe my mother truly loved my father, even though it was rumored she'd been taken from her tribe as a captive in a long-ago raid. It was said that Father had immediately chosen her as his prize, decking her in gold and the finest garments available. I learned these few details much later, when I was preparing to take a husband myself. As a child, I only knew that Mother came from a distant land and had brought with her one tribeswoman to act as wet nurse for the son she would surely provide. That woman was Willa: her confidante and friend, my second mother.

Willa had always been a major part of my life. It was Willa who coaxed me to take my first steps, Willa who rubbed salve on my hand when I burned it dipping into a cooking pot, Willa who told me stories at night when I could not sleep.

Into this happy world with its four corners—Father, Mother, Willa and Me—came an unwelcome intrusion: Hrothulf, the son of Father's brother Halga, the son Hrothgar did not yet have. He arrived one afternoon as I was helping Mother bring in firewood. Father and Aeschere had just ridden up to the cookhouse door. Surprised that Father was riding his great warhorse, I ran out to greet him. Then I saw it: a small figure sitting in front of Father, on the spot usually reserved for me.

It was a boy, a pale boy who stared at me with no discernible expression. I stared back, astonished at his black hair, black as a crow's feathers, which stuck out all over his head. With his long thin nose and bony chin, he was the ugliest boy I had ever seen. His face reminded

5

me of the wolf faces dangling at the end of pelts displayed on trading days, and his gray eyes were just as cold.

"Freawaru, come here. Meet your cousin, Hrothulf. He is my nephew, Halga's son. He is going to live with us and learn how to be a warrior one day."

I stood with my mouth open, not knowing what to say, but Mother hurried forward.

"Welcome, Hrothulf, welcome. We are happy to have the son of Halga in our home. Come inside for food; later I'll show you where you are to sleep."

The boy shot me a sideways glance as he followed Mother into the cookhouse, but he said nothing to either of us. Then Father bent down to take my hand in his.

"Hrothulf has three winters more than you," he said, "but I hope you will find him a good companion. He'll soon become part of the family. Don't worry," he added, looking at my face, "you'll get used to him."

At bedtime that night, I questioned Mother.

"Who is this Halga, and why do we have to take in his son?"

At first, seeming to ignore my question, Mother smoothed my hair in silence, and then she pulled me close.

"Hrothulf is here to stay, Freawaru, and I want you to be friends. We must all get used to him," she said, almost to herself. "Halga is your father's only remaining brother, and Hrothgar has a responsibility to his son."

I thought she said this with some misgiving, but in the days to come she never openly showed any unease, treating Hrothulf as if he were already an accepted part of our family. From Willa and the servants, however, I heard whispers and rumors about Hrothulf's dubious parentage. I already knew that if someone set Willa's tongue wagging, one could learn a great deal, so I often lay awake to hear her gossip with the other women.

"There's some who say it was the daughter's fault, that she tricked her father into it."

"Into what, Willa?" I couldn't resist asking a question out loud.

"Nothing, child, nothing. I should not have spoken so. But there's dark deeds in that line. I know some call him 'Halga the good'," she continued, turning away from me and lowering her voice, "but what good could come from sleeping with your own ... there now, I'm talking too much again. Freaw, child, go to sleep."

I did not then understand the dark secret of Hrothulf's begetting, nor did I know that noble families often farmed out their sons to relatives to ensure a disciplined upbringing. I only knew that I now had a rival for my father's attention. I also wondered if Mother was worried because she had not yet given Father the son and heir he so often talked about. I wondered if she was sorry that I was not a son. She never made me feel less than loved, but I'd heard Willa tell stories of unwanted baby girls in other tribes left outdoors to die from exposure. Surely, that could not happen in my family?

At first this Hrothulf paid little attention to me; I was only a girl and, at four years of age, still a baby in his eyes. Soon, however, he learned how to torment me, always under the guise of "just playing." His tugs on my braids brought tears to my eyes, and he delighted in tripping me when we were out of sight of my parents. One day he offered me something sweet to eat—or so he said—and then burst into guffaws as I choked on the sticky mass: honeycomb with dead bees inside. I quickly learned to avoid Hrothulf whenever possible.

Father, on the other hand, took this ugly boy with him everywhere and personally undertook his training in the arts of battle. A light wooden sword and shield became Hrothulf's most treasured possessions—and instruments of torture for me.

"Hey, Freaw-Beaw-Weaw, you be a Frank and I'll be a Dane. Try to get away from me!" My body bore the bruises of many such "games."

Except for Hrothulf's presence, this was a happy time in my life and in the life of our settlement. The crops were good that year. Farmers noted with approval an abundance of bees, for that meant a bountiful harvest. We had plenty of wheat and rye for bread and porridge and barley malt for ale. The cows gave buckets of milk for butter and cheese.

Fish and game were plentiful; Father and the earls loved to hunt with bow and arrow from horseback for deer, elk, and even wild boars and bears, leaving the tamer sport of fishing to workers with nets and lines. We ate our fish fresh, or we gutted and hung them in the open air to dry for winter consumption. Fish were also smoked over wood chips and packed in barrels of salt. I loved salt, so these were my favorites.

One day, a huge fish was brought up to the *eld-hus*—so big it took two slaves to carry it. Those nearby dropped their work to come and stare at the creature, as did I. A ridge of bony fins outlined its long, curving back, and bony plates covered the large head. What looked like fangs or whiskers protruded from under the long, rounded snout.

"What is it?" someone shouted, "And how did you catch it?"

The two young thralls who'd carried up the fish puffed out their chests, delighted to be the center of attention.

"I caught it on a big hook baited with part of an oxtail," said one. "Then Karl," he nodded at his grinning companion, "hit it over the head with an axe after we got it to shore." Indeed, blood trickled from a gash on one side of the creature's head.

Aeschere, who had joined the group unnoticed, cleared his throat and looked around the assemblage. "I have seen such a fish before. Some call it a sturgeon. Yes, a sturgeon." He nodded vigorously as if to establish the name beyond question.

"This creature puts me in mind of the story about Thor going fishing, using a chunk of ox as bait. He hooked the Midgard serpent and pulled it all the way out of the ocean. The whole world trembled until Thor restored that monster to the deep."

I stared at the fish—if fish it be—thinking hard. Everyone said that the seas were full of monsters, some much bigger than this one. I'd heard *our scop*, Father's harper, call the sea a "whale-road," and he sometimes sang of the sharp beaks of needlefish. I gazed at this great creature in wonder.

Just then, Willa bustled out and pushed through the crowd, brandishing a carving knife. "Plenty of meat on it, I'd say, and possibly roe if it's a female. Let's have a look at it out here to keep the mess out of the cookhouse."

She knelt, rolled it over, and slit the creature's belly from head to tail. Inside the body cavity, a mass of tiny blackish eggs was revealed.

"What did I tell you?" she asked no one in particular. Scooping out a sample with her fingers, she popped it into her mouth. "*Ummm*, yes! This will be a treat for Hrothgar's supper tonight!"

As she turned back to the eld-hus, I dipped my own finger into the gooey mass. *Umm*, yes, salty and good! I licked my finger.

Aeschere winked at me and dipped his finger too. "Yes, indeed. Sturgeon roe. Good," he confirmed.

We had our own cooking house, the eld-hus, separate from our eating and sleeping quarters, a mark of Father's wealth and status, I later learned. There we cooked in big iron cauldrons over the hearth or roasted meat on spits over the fire. Hot stones, which lined the hearth, were sometimes dropped into bowls of water or milk to bring them to a boil. At midmorning, we took porridge with bread and ale. In our main meal at dusk, we had meat, fish, bread, herbs, fruit, and ale. Ever hungry as a child, I always looked forward to our two daily meals.

As I grew, I began to internalize the rhythms of our daily life by following Mother's routine. All women worked, from the lowest thrall to the king's wife. In summer, Mother got up at sunrise to wake the women slaves to send them to bring water or start the cooking, and she gave orders for the day to male slaves with farm duties. Some might be sent to take cattle and sheep to pasture, drive pigs to new feeding grounds, harvest honey from the hives, or haul firewood for the hearth. She also supervised the cow milking and the feeding of chickens, geese, and ducks. I loved to accompany her on the latter chore to search for fresh eggs in nests scattered about the outbuildings and then lay them, still warm, in my woven basket.

In the dairy, she checked on the churning, sometimes adding precious salt to the butter from the bag tied at her waist. Sometimes I was allowed a sip of buttermilk. Then we might mix and knead bread dough in the big wooden trough, letting it rise before baking it into crisp, fragrant loaves over the fire or in the stone oven outside. How I loved that smell!

We had recently started raising flax to make linen—preferred by Mother for our undergarments. I liked to pick its fresh blue flowers. Our looms sang continually with the weaving of linen and woolen cloth for garments and blankets. During the day, our house slaves washed and then spread clothes on bushes to dry. Our best garments would be pressed on a board of whalebone with a heavy glass ball. At night, we worked by the light of oil lamps.

Father imported glass drinking horns from the Rhineland, as well as glass beads to be made into jewelry for the women. He wanted us to set a good table when entertaining visitors or celebrating a holiday, so in addition to wooden bowls and serving ware, we also used carved soapstone and imported pottery. His fondness for mead kept us busy brewing that liquid made from fermented honey and water with herbs sometimes added. We grew most of our own herbs, but spices were also imported.

Throughout the day, Mother supervised other women at weaving or worked on the loom herself. She was also skilled at embroidery and pattern braids, which she made by passing colored threads through holes in bone tablets. Willa tried to teach me how to do this, but my fingers were clumsy and slow. There was so much to learn! Mother and Willa were patient with me, however, and my skills gradually improved.

Everyone paused in his work or made some excuse to get to the harbor when traders arrived. Oh, what a hubbub then! Traders' tents lined the waterfront, with their wares displayed outside. Willa loved to stroll among them, myself in tow, making mental selections and comparing prices, hefting a pelt, or holding up a necklace of beads to check the sparkle in the light. She also loved to bargain.

I loved to dip into the sacks of spices arrayed on a plank in front of one tent.

"What's this, Willa?" I held up a wet finger coated with brown dust.

"Cinnamon. A rare treat, but expensive. You'd best keep your hands out of that bag or this merchant will be wanting to keep you as payment!"

I knew she was joking by the twinkle in her eyes, but the dark-faced man behind the display scowled at me in disapproval. Hastily I tucked my hands behind my back.

One morning, as we neared the harbor, my eyes were dazzled by bright lights in dancing colors of red, green, yellow, and blue. "What is it, Willa? A rainbow?"

"No, child, just sunlight reflecting off glass—from those beakers over there." She motioned to a tent with a row of objects arranged on a bench in front. "Probably a Frankish merchant. Your father fancies such drinking goblets for his feasts; let's take a closer look." She picked up one of the beakers and held it to the light. There seemed to be a picture painted on the glass of two men struggling. The trader hurried forward.

"Very famous Roman heroes, very famous. Hector and Achilles."

"Huh—never heard of them." Willa set down that beaker and picked up another. "Do you have anything with Sigmund and the dragon? Hrothgar likes that story."

"No, no, only Roman stories here. Very fine. Rare. Valuable. Only the richest can afford these wares."

Willa snorted again. "Hrothgar can afford anything he wants."

"Then he should consider these." The trader almost purred as he leaned toward us. "These would make very fine gifts for exchange— perhaps in an alliance? And, of course, always highly favored for bride purchase." He winked at someone standing behind us, who laughed out loud.

"Too soon to think of that. Farming and fighting will be my lot for years to come." The voice sounded rueful. I turned to see a young man reach out, stroke one of the beakers thoughtfully, and then lift it close to his eyes.

"Now there's a rare animal! Must be one of those beasts the Romans use in their arenas to fight against men." He peered at a long green ... what? I crowded closer for a better look. The creature had four legs, a long body and tail covered with dark spots, and a mouth that gaped with menace.

"I think they're called leopards," said the merchant. "They come from a land far to the south." We gazed at the image in mutual wonder. The young man set the beaker down regretfully and turned away.

Could these leopards be real? I wondered, remembering that Hrothulf had once told me of another strange beast, a sea creature "big as a horse" with hairy whiskers on its face and "two sharp tusks as long as a man's arm." Of course I hadn't believed him; you couldn't trust anything that sly boy said. I'd once repeated something he told me, only to be greeted with laughter at my childish foolishness. The memory still stung.

We strolled on toward the tents of hunters, where I saw a big display of sealskins, wolf pelts, and piles of antlers from deer, elk, reindeer, and caribou. Carvers of soapstone offered cooking and eating vessels and slate whetstones for sharpening tools and weapons. Weavers offered sailcloth. Dark, swarthy men from beyond what Father called "the Baltic" had brought exotic items from even more remote countries: silk fabric, threads of gold and silver, blown glass beads. Silver coins from Arab traders were much in demand both for barter and to be made into jewelry. The different tongues spoken by these men added to the strangeness and excitement of it all.

News of other settlements and other lands was also exchanged here. Men spoke of whaling in icy seas, of fighting among the Swedes, and of new trade routes opening up to the east. I paid little heed to their talk, intent on my own explorations.

Willa had moved on, but I was close on her heels when she spied Torgun, the blacksmith's wife, looking at a rack of dead ducks hung beside a makeshift hut.

"Too rich for me," said Torgun wistfully. "Just feel those breast feathers—what would it be like to sleep on those, I wonder?"

Willa stroked the birds thoughtfully. "Eiderdown, sure enough—must come from the north. We seldom see eider ducks around here. I'll have to tell my lady about these. She might want to buy enough to stuff her sleeping mats."

"Lift me up, Willa, let me touch!" I too stroked the soft breasts, imagining for a moment that I could see the birds in flight, skimming above icy waves.

"That's enough now; we're supposed to be looking at furs for your father's winter cloak." She lowered me gently.

"I saw some fine pelts near the fish smoker's hut, "offered Torgun. "You'll find them worth inspection. I need to get back to the forge and take Bjorn some food. He's been so busy making fasteners for the new mead hall doors that he's hardly eaten all day. Which reminds me—here's a bit of honeycomb I've been saving for the little one." She dug in her basket and held out a sticky package, which I eagerly accepted.

"I do love sweets," I admitted.

She laughed. "Don't they all? Mine were ever after the honey jar when they were little. So, Willa, it's back to work for us both." My teeth were already stuck in the sweet waxy comb, so I did not join in Willa's farewell.

Ana, Aeschere's wife, next claimed our attention. As tall as Willa was wide, she stood in front of the fur hunter's hut, eyeing his wares.

As we approached, my gaze fell on the faces in a stack of seal hides. Their great round eyes caught me and filled me with sadness. I could almost see their sleek bodies gliding through the water, once alive and beautiful. Reaching out, I stroked the coarse hair.

Nearby, draped over a pole, hung the heavy skin of a bear. Its claws dangled, helpless but menacing. I shied away from their sharp tips. A large basket beside it contained deer and elk skins already cut into strips for ropes and bindings. A tall rack displayed the glossy pelts of sable, martin, and mink.

"Fair morning, Lady Ana." Willa spoke formally and dropped her head in a kind of bow. I showed no such restraint.

"Ana, Ana, look what the smith's wife gave me! Want some?"

"Nay, nay, little Freawaru—and don't touch my gown with those sticky fingers!"

She spoke severely, but smiled broadly. "I too have something for you, but you'll have to come to my house to get it."

"Oh yes, yes! Can we go right now, Willa? I want to see what it is!"

"In good time. We have trading to do first." Willa did not look overly pleased by the invitation.

"Of course; it will keep." Ana smiled again, at Willa this time, and the lines of Willa's mouth seemed to soften. "I know why you're here: Wealtheow told me that Hrothgar wants a new robe to go with his new hall. Just look at these pelts over here—good quality, all of them. You can tell they've not been held over from a previous winter. The hairs are tight and soft, not loose and brittle."

Hearing Ana's words, the trader hurried forward. "Yes, yes, you won't find any skins finer than these. This season's catch, all of them. What do you have to exchange?" He paused, sizing up Willa in her everyday gown and apron. "I don't need kitchen goods or cloth at the moment."

Willa proudly held up a small bag and shook it to make the contents jingle.

"Silver!"

The trader's eyes widened. "Silver? Hrothgar must be doing well!"

"You can see his new hall rising up on the hill." We all followed Willa's pointing finger to gaze at the emerging structure, floating like a great proud ship above the trees.

"Aye, yes. Well, of course silver is acceptable. Let me get my scales." He darted inside his hut and returned with a set of balanced discs. As he and Willa began to haggle, I licked my fingers clean and pulled Ana aside.

"What's in your house? Is it something you made for me? Is it good to eat?"

Ana picked me up and hugged me so tightly I couldn't speak. To my surprise, tears glistened in her eyes.

"Something I made once … for my little girl. But she left me a long time ago. I thought another little girl might like to have it now."

As I looked into her eyes, I seemed to see a face, but it was not my own. Perhaps the face of that little girl from long ago? Blue eyes, soft cheeks, long braids. "What was her name? What happened to her? Did she die?"

"Hush, child. I'll tell you more about her when you come to my house. Now I see that Willa is almost ready to leave and may have some furs to carry back with her."

Indeed Willa was smiling broadly as she approached, her arms laden with pelts.

"The king should be happy with these! I can't wait to get started on that cloak."

"Your skill with the needle is well-known in this settlement," said Ana. "And I understand you are equally skilled at the loom."

Willa beamed with pleasure. "I do the best I can—and I'm glad when it pleases."

Aeschere's longhouse lay on the path to our own, so my curiosity about the gift was soon to be satisfied. Willa dropped me off on her way back, after Ana promised to bring me home in a short time. By now, I was jumping up and down in gleeful anticipation.

As soon as my eyes adjusted to the dark interior, I looked around curiously. Ana's house was different from ours. There were the usual benches along the wall and a big open hearth in the middle, but beyond that, in the gloom, I saw movement, heard the nicker of a horse, and sniffed the pungent smell of warm manure.

"Do you keep your animals inside?" I blurted.

"Only this foal at the moment, but he'll go out to pasture with the rest in a day or two. He needs to gain more strength."

"Oh, can I see him?" I loved to touch live creatures. The dogs that trailed behind the boys of the settlement were lank and scary; they looked at me with indifference and never offered signs of affection.

Once Holger, one of Aeschere and Ana's sons, had found a wild forest cat in his traps and brought it to Willa to tend while the broken leg healed. Whenever I came near its cage, the cat hissed and lifted the hair on its back. Still, I thought it beautiful with its long golden hair, yellow eyes, and fluffy tail. Perhaps one day it would let me stroke its silky coat.

"Here he is." We walked past a partition, and Ana pointed into a dark corner. I knelt on the prickly straw and cautiously reached out a hand. Something soft and fuzzy nuzzled my palm and then wrapped its tongue around my fingers!

"Ooh, it's trying to eat me!" As I jumped back, the creature staggered to its feet and wobbled forward. Ana laughed and caught me to her apron as I hid my face.

"He won't hurt you. He's looking for his mother and a mouthful of milk. Right now, I'd say he likes you. Maybe someday when you're both bigger he can take you for a ride."

"Does he have a name?"

"Not yet. He'll need to grow into that."

As we backed out of the stall, the colt followed, but Ana pulled down a bar to enclose him. "In good time, young one, in good time."

"Now we must wash our hands," said Ana, leading me to a stone basin and pitcher. She shooed away the servant who came forward and supervised the washing herself. Washing hands? This must mean something good to eat!

"Sit down on this bench while I pull out my chest."

I sat, legs dangling, while she stooped to pull something from under her bed, a high, carved bed, which looked like the one my mother and father shared. Setting a small wooden chest down beside me, she blew dust from the cover and took a key from her brooch chain and inserted it into the lock.

At first, the lock would not turn, but finally it gave way and the lid opened to reveal … what? All I could see were dark, moldy linens, but they had a sweet smell—some kind of herb I supposed. I wrinkled my nose.

"You're smelling lavender. It prevents moths from eating the cloth." Ana sat down beside me on the bench.

Cloth? My hopes fell. I had expected something more interesting, something to eat—or play with.

"Here she is." Ana carefully lifted a large bundle from the box. "Aeschere carved the face. I made the clothes."

As she laid back the wrappings, I gasped. For a moment, I thought it might be a real child, shrunk by magic to live in the chest, for a little girl's face smiled up at me. I looked at Ana in wonder.

"It's a doll—have you never seen one?" Ana asked. I shook my head.

"We made it for Auda, our firstborn." Ana paused. "Auda was about your age when she died. Aeschere wanted to burn the doll with her body, but I pulled it out of the fire and kept it all these years. See, there's a charred spot on the foot. Here. You can hold her now."

I took it awkwardly and cupped the head in my hands, letting the legs dangle. "Does the doll have a name?"

"I think each girl should name her own doll—so that is up to you."

I closed my eyes. When I tasted a lingering sweetness on my tongue, my eyes flew open. "I know: *Hunig*—I'll call her honey!"

"Ah, very sweet." Ana and I chuckled together.

As we sat together quietly, my thoughts wandered back to a day when Willa and I had stopped to talk to a farmer's wife whose little boy clung to his mother's hand. When he turned his head toward me, I saw two white puckered circles around his eyes. Curious, I'd stared into their milky depths. Slowly an image formed, and when I suddenly understood, my mouth fell open.

"He fell into the fire pit," I blurted out. "No one was watching him, and he fell into the fire and poked his eyes out on the tongs!"

Willa and the farmer's wife had both frozen for an instant, and then the mother pulled her son under her apron and hissed at me: "Little snake! Foreign child! Why were you spying on me? How did you know?"

Willa shook herself and gathered me in her arms.

"Calm yourself, woman! Freaw is just a baby. Of course, she never spied on you! She probably heard some gossip, or … guessed, that's all."

We had left immediately, but Willa had looked at me strangely all the way home. After that day, other mothers kept their children away from me as if afraid of what I might see. Looking down at Hunig, I knew I now had a playmate who couldn't run away. I looked up to see Ana's eyes on me, misty with emotion.

"Won't you be sad to give her away? Maybe you'll have another little girl someday."

"Nay, child, I am too old now—and Aeschere has given me sons aplenty. You may know some of them who serve the king: Harold? Harig? Holger?"

I nodded, sure of only one name—the Holger who'd caught the wild cat. "Thank you, Ana, for the doll." I stroked Hunig's face, running my fingers over her nose and lips. "I'm sorry your little girl died. What happened to her?"

"She took a fever. Many died that year." Ana did not continue, so I fell silent as well. Willa often told me that I talked more than was proper. Had I said too much this time? As I laid my hand on Ana's lined palm, a strange shiver passed through my body. I seemed to see Ana bending over a dead child almost as small as the doll in my hand, but covered with blood. I must have had my eyes closed, for Ana rose and took my arm.

"Come. It's time to take you home."

When she left me at the women's house, Ana said she would climb on up toward the mounds outside the fencing—the place where our dead live—"just to check that nothing has been disturbed," she told Mother.

"Is your Auda there?" I asked.

"Yes, she is. I arranged stones in a pretty pattern around the bottom of her mound."

"I know the one—what a big mound for one little girl!" I marveled, for I had seen this mound many times on my walks with Willa.

"Oh, she's not alone. Her ashes lie in the center, but nearby lie those of Ermlaf, Aeschere's brother. Do you remember him, Wealtheow?"

Mother nodded and Ana continued, but she seemed to be talking to herself.

"One of those raiding parties the men love so much. Died of his wounds, Ermlaf did. Such a young man too, a waste as I see it, and all for an armful of rusty weapons and a skinny slave who died himself a few days later."

"Do the slave's ashes lie there too?"

"What?" Ana stared at me and then gave a brief laugh. "No, child. Such folk are thrown in the ground somewhere; I have no idea where that one was buried."

Ugh! Thrown in the ground and not even burned in the proper way? I was about to ask more, when Mother placed her fingers on my lips.

"Enough questions, Freawaru. It is best to speak few words on such matters. Good-bye, Ana, may the gods be with you." She saw her friend out the door and then turned and pulled me gently into her arms.

"Now tell me: what is it you have under your cloak?"

I drew out the doll, as Ana had called it. "Ana says I can keep it. I named her Hunig."

Mother took the doll, fingering the texture of its tunic.

"May I keep her?" Something in Mother's face made me anxious, but she nodded, handing the doll back to me.

"I had such a thing once … long ago. I wonder if anyone holds it now?" She too seemed to be talking to herself.

"You look sad, Mother. Did you lose a little girl too … like Ana?"

"No, I lost a father and a mother. But enough. Again, it is best to speak few words of such matters." She rose. "Come help me in the garden. You can hold the basket while I harvest herbs. Oh, you'd best put your Hunig in my chest for now, so she won't get lost."

We worked side by side in the evening coolness. I touched each leaf and stem to my nose before dropping it in the basket, inhaling the scent of rosemary, sage, basil, and other herbs whose names I did not yet know. Ah, this must be lavender—the smell in Hunig's clothes. A sudden sadness swept over me.

"Mother, why don't the other children like me?"

Mother stopped picking and straightened to look at my face. "What has happened? Who has been cruel to you?" Her eyes blazed.

"No ... no one, except for Hrothulf, and he doesn't count. I don't want to play with him! I mean the other children in other families— those who live around us. They never speak to me or ask me to join their games. Sometimes they call me names."

"Names? What names?" Mother knelt beside me and pulled me onto her knee.

"Oh, silly names, like *wild child*, *big eyes*, and *bird girl*. And sometimes they flap their arms at me as if they're flying."

Mother sighed and held me close for a moment. "Listen, Freawaru, each of us is different. Each of us has been given different gifts. You have a gift of sight, which goes beyond what others can see. This makes you different. People sometimes fear what they don't understand."

I nodded. "Yes, Mother, but what about the flying?"

She waited a long time before speaking, as if choosing her words carefully. "When you were born, Freawaru, you were perfect in every way, but with something extra. You have a special birthmark behind your right shoulder: a perfectly formed feather. It is a mark of Freyja, the goddess."

"Where? Let me touch it." I swiveled my head and pulled down the corner of my gown, but could not see past my shoulder.

"Here." Mother took my left hand and guided it down over my shoulder to the spot.

"But I don't feel anything at all!"

"No, but the outline is clear, and the color grows stronger each year."

"What color, Mother?"

"A soft blue-gray, like the feathers of the heron."

"And Freyja? Why is the feather her mark?"

"Freyja is said to have the power to change herself into a bird and fly unseen where ever she wishes. Freyja is a powerful goddess. Her mark on your body means that you too may have powers as yet unknown. Your sight is a beginning. What is to come will unfold with the years. Now, I think that's enough for now. Let us take these herbs inside for washing."

Silently we rose, and I followed Mother into the eld-hus, pondering all I'd heard.

One afternoon, at the height of the mead hall construction, Aeschere rode in with a hunting party made up mostly of his numerous sons. They were all in high spirits, for across one packhorse lay the carcass of the largest stag ever brought into our settlement. Men, women, and children crowded around to view the noble beast.

"He gave us a good chase, but Holger's arrow finally brought him down," bragged Aeschere, as proud as if he himself had killed the creature. "Look at that rack: twelve points if I can still count—a stag fit for a king."

At that moment, Hrothgar himself joined the group. "If it's fit for a king, it's fit for a king's hall." He raised his arms and looked around. "Hear me! We will mount this rack above the door of our new mead hall. We will name the hall Heorot,for this hart, in honor of Aeschere and his sons."

Whoops of delight rose from the young men. Aeschere bent his knee before my father and lowered his head. "My lord, you do me honor."

"Stand up, my friend. No man here can equal you in battle or in loyalty to his king and comrades. Take this ring as further evidence of my love." Hrothgar pulled from his finger a large gold circle entwined with serpents and held it out to Aeschere, who rose proudly. Father clasped him about the shoulders. Aeschere returned the embrace and then stepped back, holding the ring high.

"Hail, Hrothgar, giver of gold! Hail, Heorot, home of brave men!"

"Hail! Hail!" echoed surrounding voices. I was thrilled to be part of this moment, proud to have Hrothgar for my father and Aeschere for my friend. Because of them, I need never feel afraid. No one dreamed, in those happy days, of the darkness and sorrow to come.

Sometimes on long summer evenings, I rode out with Mother and Father to the great barrow near the harbor where the ashes of grandfather Healfdane were buried. Our settlement was dotted with mounds and standing stones, most of them so old that no one could remember for whom they were erected. One of them, called Horse Hill, was said to contain the remains of an ancient king, sitting upright on his horse. Such talk made me uneasy, fearful that the dead might rise up and come back to life. Willa had told me a story about an evil woman, a sorceress, buried with three huge stones atop her body so she could never return to harm the living. That thought always made me shiver.

I hooked my fingers in the braided mane of Father's stallion while he held me lightly in front of him. His warmth at my back always made me feel secure, no matter how fast we galloped. Gullifax's mane tickled my face, and I laughed with glee; surely we flew as fast as Odin on his eight-legged horse. Mother followed on a slower steed.

Wildflowers grew all around the earth mound: cornflowers, dandelions, clover, and yellow feverfew. These I loved to pick, avoiding the scratchy leaves of lavender thistles, while Mother and Father walked slowly hand in hand around the great mound.

"Here will I rest one day," I heard Father say, "among my Scylding ancestors."

"But not soon." Mother smiled up at him. "First you have more sons to sire." She took Father's hand and placed it on her belly.

"Has it quickened?"

"Yes, my lord."

They laughed together—a sound I loved to hear. Father seemed more like other men on such excursions. He seemed more like Aeschere, who always had time for me. Father could often be distant and remote, as silent as one of the wooden statues Willa prayed to.

"Father, what was grandfather like?"

"Healfdane? He was a great warrior and generous to his men."

"Did he let you ride with him on his horse?"

Father laughed. "I don't remember. He died long ago."

I hoped my father would never die. He was the most powerful king in the world—everyone said so. I thought nothing could harm him or Mother or me. As we rode home in the twilight, I looked back over my shoulder. Silhouetted above us stood a line of horses, grazing on the mound. On one horse sat a tall figure, mail-clad and helmeted. I raised my arm in a gesture of greeting.

"What are you doing?" asked Father, flicking the reins on Gulifax.

"Saying good-bye to grandfather."

"Oh," laughed Father. Without turning, he added, "Good night, Healfdane, good night."

Chapter 2
Up from the Swamp

When I was a girl of six winters, my childhood came to a sudden end. It was night, the night of the year's turning—the longest and darkest of all nights. Smoldering in the mead hall hearth lay the ashes of a great oak log. Willing hands had hauled it in the day before to be burned at the solstice feast amid great ceremony and rejoicing. We joined together on that night to summon new life, to bring back the warmth and light of the sun.

As was our custom at Yule, great numbers of animals had been slaughtered and preserved in advance of winter: cattle, sheep, goats, pigs, and chickens. For weeks, the settlement echoed with their cries as the axes fell; the smell of their blood still hung in the air. During this time of killing, I hid inside the eld-hus as much as possible. Willa laughed at my squeamishness, but Mother seemed to share my distaste for the butchering, necessary though it was to see us through the dark, cold days almost upon us.

Now the butchering was done. Now we could look about us and take satisfaction in our labors. Smoke no longer rose from the smokehouse roof hole. Hay and grain had been stored for the horses. Cod and herring hung in the rafters. Now it was time to celebrate, to give thanks for the year's harvest, to rejoice in Hrothgar's glorious new mead hall. Now it was time to thank the gods and by our gratitude ensure the return of the life-giving sun.

That night, every freeman in the settlement crowded into Heorot to gorge himself on roasted boar flesh and drink deeply from Hrothgar's golden cups. Even I had been allowed a taste of mead; its heavy sweetness still lay on my tongue and weighed down my eyelids. After singing and carousing late into the night, the last stragglers had finally staggered away, leaving only Father's hall guard inside. All was quiet.

In the women's house, we lay sleeping; I had crept away from Willa's bed to escape her snores and now lay curled close to my mother, her belly big with child. She no longer slept with Father as her time drew near but had withdrawn to join us here. My heart beat in rhythm with her heart and that of the unborn child as I dreamed. I dreamed of swans bearing me aloft on their strong white wings, carrying me over water as I floated in a world of warmth and air.

A sudden shriek tore open this womb of silence. Another cry—and another—a horrible din as if spears and shields were gnashing their teeth in full battle rage (as Aelric, our scop, later described it). Ripped awake by the savage cries, I struggled to free myself from the bed covers.

In her haste to rise, Mother rolled over me, crushing my cheek into the sleeping robe. Other women were springing up, bleary-eyed in the light of the dying hearth fire. I cried out, but no one heeded me. A great roar seemed to shake the very timbers of the house; we froze in our places. Then came a long, triumphant cry, a sound like gurgling laughter from a mouth filled with blood.

Wide-eyed with terror, we screamed and screamed. Then we held our breath, listening for more ... but no sound came. For a moment, no one moved; suddenly everyone turned to Mother, who responded firmly, her voice filled with authority.

"Stay inside. There is danger in darkness. Gyda—see to the door; be sure it is barred! Brita—stir up the fire; we need light. Willa—go to Freawaru. Whatever has happened, Hrothgar's hall guard will deal with it." Her words were strong, but her voice broke as she spoke.

I whimpered as my old wet nurse gathered me in her arms and pressed me to her heaving bosom. I wriggled free to run to Mother and clung to her, shivering; I felt an answering quiver in her thigh. Then a gush of wetness soaked the side of my night shift. Mother inhaled sharply and bent nearly double.

"My water, it has broken! Willa—quick—it is time. Danger or no danger, this baby wants to come out; it is seeking the door into our world. Build up the fire, light torches, and set water to boil. Fetch mugwort from my shelf—and mallow, should it be needed."

Shaking with fear, I watched in confusion as Estrid and Ingeborg hurried to do her bidding. Willa pried loose my fingers and eased Mother onto her sleeping bench. Momentarily forgotten were the terrible cries from the darkness—a darkness now eerily silent.

That night changed my life and my dreams forever. Never again would the swans come to bear me aloft. Never again would I feel safe in my mother's love and secure in the might of my father's hall. Though we did not know it then, our living nightmare had begun. The House of Hrothgar would be plunged into misery and dark despair.

As if from far away, I heard Mother's voice.

"Freawaru? Freaw, listen to me. The baby—it's coming at last." She gasped again. "I may cry out, but do not be afraid. You will soon have a brother ... or sister ... to be your playmate and your charge. Now go to Brita's bench, my dear, and stay there until called."

"Yes, Mother." Pulled between excitement and dread, I crawled up on the now-empty benches and drew Brita's coarse robe over my head. In the time that followed, I tried not to hear Mother's moans, her screams, her calls for help: "Freyja, goddess, come to me now!"

Willa kept talking throughout the ordeal, encouraging Mother to "push," "hold your breath," and "push again." Suddenly Willa exclaimed with delight, "There's the head!"

Curiosity overcame my fear, and I peeked out. The women were crowded around so I could not see Mother, but I heard them laugh with relief and saw Willa lift up a squalling baby dangling a bloody cord.

"It's a boy—and a big one!" she crowed.

A boy? I thought to myself. *Like Hrothulf?*

"Ale—get a dipper of ale," commanded Willa, "and boil the mallow in it; we must give it to the queen to bring forth the afterbirth."

While this was being done, she dipped her fingers in warm oil and rubbed them over the baby, now wailing loudly. Its cries subsided as she wrapped it snugly in a soft woolen cloth and placed it at Mother's side.

"All is well, my queen," she crooned. "It is almost over now. The baby is sound and sturdy; I'd say he looks like Hrothgar! Just drink this and you can rest." She helped Mother sit up and proffered the dipper. Mother drank and then sank back.

I sat up too. "Is it not a sister?" I asked, still hopeful. The women turned in my direction, and Willa came slowly to sit beside me.

"No, dear Freawaru," she said, speaking my full name slowly and seriously, "It is a boy, a fine, healthy boy, thank the gods. Come, see your new brother."

I climbed down and took her hand. Mother opened her eyes wearily; her face was drained of color, but a weak smile played on her lips. Willa lifted a corner of the cloth to show me the baby. My brother. As I gazed at his red, wrinkled face, a feeling of great tenderness welled up in me. My brother. This tiny creature would now be my charge. I would see that no harm came to him—ever.

"Hrethric," said Mother. "His name shall be Hrethric. At the ceremony, three days hence, your father and I will give him his name, a fine name for a fine addition to the Scylding line. Hrothgar, dear husband, you can be glad … a son and heir at last." She closed her eyes and fell into a deep sleep.

Gradually, one by one, the rest of us followed her example, exhausted by the night's events.

When pale morning light sifted through the smoke hole, I awoke, still wrapped in Brita's blanket. She and the other women had gone out to relieve themselves—only Willa remained, bending over my mother and the baby.

"Shall I go now to tell the king?"

"Yes, Willa. Tell him he now has a son of his own blood—news that should bring him gladness. Yet my heart misgives me that some great evil befell us in the night. Bring me news of him."

When Willa left the longhouse, I slipped out to follow her, eager to see my father, hoping that he'd smile at me and lift me up in his arms—but my hopes were to be dashed.

A light dusting of snow lay on the path; Willa's feet left prints, a guide for my own. High above us on the crest of the hill, Heorot gleamed as the odd ray of sunlight caught its towering gables, bright as the golden rings that Father gave to his men. Dazzled, I blinked, and then blinked again. The hall looked … wrong. Its doors hung open, crazily ajar, jagged as a broken tooth. And where was Holger, who always stood guard there?

Willa cried aloud and started up the path, gathering her skirts as she ran. In the doorway, she stopped, so abruptly that I banged into her generous rump. A terrible stench—blood, urine, feces, and something like swamp water—assailed us. Backing up, I stepped on a mound of what looked like guts. At my wail, Willa whipped around, face white, lips twitching.

"Get back to the house, child. This is no place for you."

At that moment, Hrothgar emerged from the hall, his eyes dark with grief and rage. Behind him stalked Aeschere, Saxe, and Sven. All looked stunned.

"Who has dared to enter unbidden the hall of Hrothgar?" asked Aeschere of the morning air. "To seize so many proud thanes and end their lives in this bloody fashion?" He turned to Father, but his eyes were searching for someone he did not see. I thought again of Holger, his son.

"We will seek out this enemy," declared Hrothgar. "We will avenge the deaths of my brave athelings. No man-price will be exacted. Only death can repay this evil deed." His voice was strong, not yet tinged with the despair that would come to him in later days.

Aelric, our harper, now emerged from the yawning mouth of the empty door hole. "My lord, there is not enough left of any one man for a proper funeral pyre—bits of skin and teeth, a few shreds of clothing—but I can gather their swords and shields together."

"Do so. And send for the smith to repair the hinges. We must make fast the door against another raid."

For the first time, Hrothgar noticed Willa and me, down on our knees at his feet.

"What are you doing here? Is anything amiss in the women's house? Wealtheow—?"

"All ... all ... all is well there, my lord," Willa stuttered in her anxiety. "Good ... good news from the queen. She gave birth this night to a son, a healthy boy."

"A son, you say?" My father's face momentarily cleared and his eyes brightened. "The gods be praised. Tell the queen that I shall visit her soon, but now we have a heavy task before us. Aeschere—" he turned away from us, not even acknowledging my presence.

"Come, child; your father has much to do, and your mother will need our help."

I cast a longing look behind me as Willa pulled me down the hill, but the men were already walking away from us.

The house slaves were abuzz when we returned. Some chattered excitedly, some wept. They seemed to know already what had happened in the mead hall.

"Did you hear? Eight men—eight! Who could have killed so many and escaped alive?"

"Was Karl one of them?" asked a trembling voice.

"Aye, he'll never warm your bed again!" For this, the speaker received a slap, which she quickly returned. I could see that hair pulling would come next if no one intervened.

"Stop, you bitches! This is no time for personal quarrels!" Willa's voice sounded high and narrow, as if she could not catch her breath. "Brita, Gyda—fill pails with river water and hurry up to the mead hall. You'll be needed there."

Brita's question made me think again of Holger, Aeschere's gray-eyed son, the one who liked to tease me, tugging gently on my braids, while offering me bits of honeycomb—without the bees. Where was Holger? The house slaves spent the whole of that day scrubbing Heorot's walls, floors, and benches, sometimes emerging to retch as they dumped their bloody pails and returned with fresh water.

Father's thanes searched diligently for evidence of the deadly intruder, but found no imprint of horse's hooves or booted feet. Traces of slime caught the attention of Aeschere; he pondered them thoughtfully, looking off westward toward the great fen.

"Look, my lord, could this be … a track? Yes, I think so—though it is unlike any track I have seen before." He bent low, studying a faint outline on the cobbled path that led up to Heorot. Hrothgar bent too.

"A bear? It has the shape of a bear's claw, but it's far too large." Both men straightened and looked at each other. Aeschere shook his head.

"What wild beast, even a bear, could open these heavy oaken doors, fixed on iron hinges?" He paused. "I wonder … were they properly fastened on the inside last night?"

Alas, no man was left from the hall guard to answer Aeschere's question. Hrothgar rose to his feet and spoke.

"I will send my thanes throughout the settlement and surrounding farmsteads for any clues to this invader. Perhaps someone has seen it; perhaps others have been victims of this midnight marauder. Saxe. Sven." He summoned them, "See to it that riders leave immediately and return with news."

Suddenly Hrothulf appeared at Father's elbow. "Send me too, my lord. I can help."

Father paused, frowned, and then waved a hand. "Go—go with Sven."

Hrothulf hurried off, a grin on his face. As he passed, he gave me a superior look. I wished, not for the first time, that I had been born a boy. I had to admit that Hrothulf sat a horse as well as any man. He'd been assigned a sturdy little chestnut from the common herd and rode it every day. I seldom got a chance to ride.

When they returned, they bore only this news: no one else had been attacked. No one had seen the attacker. That did not prevent panic from spreading quickly, however, for no one knew who might be next.

Once the blood had been washed away, Hrothgar called his athelings into council within Heorot itself. Outside, the younger thanes stood muttering. All held shields and spears. As I watched and listened in silence, I recognized Sven, who always kept his beard neatly braided, and Saxe, a rounder version of Sven. An older, taller man, who wore the scars of many a battle, spoke little but always to the point. The others called him Thorkel.

"No weapons, no armor taken? Whoever came did not come for booty," said Sven, pulling at his beard.

"Aye, that adds to the puzzle," said Saxe. "It's as if whoever—or whatever—it was came deliberately for man flesh." Saxe shook his head at the dire thought and patted his crotch as if to assure himself that everything below was intact.

"No man could eat another man—c-c-could he?" Thorkel growled incredulously, shifting his feet. No one answered his question. No one was in a mood to jest or brandish his spear in a show of bravado. They all looked worried and wary.

By nightfall, the entire hall had been cleansed and its doors re-hung, but no banquet was laid on the long tables, no ale poured into drinking horns. That night, every man stood erect and alert, sword and shield in hand. Those who had chain mail, wore it.

In the women's house, my mother lay wrapped in furs, suckling the baby. I nestled against Willa. Torches burned in each wall socket throughout the night, as we lay rigid on our benches, straining to hear sounds in the darkness. Three men had been placed at the door with swords drawn. That night we slept little, but no horror returned to haunt our dreams or our waking.

Several days of calm followed. We honored the dead on a funeral pyre and mounded earth over the ashes. Gradually we dared to breathe more freely. I noticed, however, that Mother had added a new ritual to her going-to-bed routine: a spell against the night.

She walked along each wall of the house, carrying a bowl of smoking herbs. Into each corner she blew a bit of smoke and repeated these words:

I know a charm, if monsters prowl
At night from swamps or fens.
The spell I sing sends them astray
Lost both minds and skins.
Algiz, Eihwaz, Uruz.
Algiz, Eihwaz, Uruz.

Finally, when there had been no further attacks for several days, Hrothgar gave the long-delayed naming feast to celebrate the birth of his first son. Aelric was told to compose a suitable song for the occasion, heralding the arrival of this new member of the Scylding clan. As a child, I was not expected to attend the feast, but I heard Aelric practicing his song under the big oak beside the river. He paced back and forth, reciting out loud, sometimes striking a note on his harp.

Hear me!
Spear-Danes in days gone by had courage and greatness.
Shield Sheafson, wrecker of mead benches,
Rampaged among foes, this foundling from afar,
Exacting tribute from many lands.
That was a good king!

There was more, with many names. I recognized that of Healfdane, my father's father, who had died before I was born, and of course, Father's own name, but I tired of the endless repetition as Aelric strove to fix the words in his memory. I walked back toward the women's house, wondering: *would Aelric someday sing a song about me?*

When Mother returned from the naming feast that night, she wore a great neck ring of gold, the largest and most beautiful torque I had ever seen.

"A gift from your father," she smiled at me. "He is well pleased with his son and his queen." Removing the heavy torque, she rubbed her neck where the ring had pressed into her flesh.

"Indeed!" Willa picked up the heavy collar, a look of awe on her face. "A rare gift from a rare and generous man." She caressed the shining object, fingering its separate layers braided in an elaborate pattern. The other women crowded around to admire it, their eyes wide. "Very handsome," Willa concluded, wrapping it in cloth and locking it in Mother's chest.

"It puts me in mind of the Brisinga necklace. Do you all remember that story?" She turned quizzically toward the other women, who came forward with expectant faces.

"As I've heard it told, Freyja happened upon four dwarves working in gold. They were fashioning a lovely necklace, the likes of which she'd never seen before, and of course, she had to have it. Freyja always loved beautiful things, you know. She offered them money, but they laughed, as they already had all the gold they needed. She begged, she wept, but the dwarves would not part with it. Finally, they told her, 'The only thing we truly desire is you. If you'll spend one night with each of us, the necklace will be yours.'"

Here Willa paused, laughing so hard she almost choked. The other women looked uneasily at each other, though they too were snickering. Mother appeared to be absorbed with the baby, whom she had put to suck.

"That Freyja! You know her appetites: running after men like a nanny goat in heat. Well, she had to have that necklace—so she did it. She slept with each and every one of those nasty little men! But she got that necklace, she did, and it became her most prized possession."

Willa paused to catch her breath and grinned over at me. "I hope you don't take after your namesake in that way, little Freaw."

"Willa!" Mother's voice cut through the giggles like a knife blade. "Be silent! Hold your tongue, foolish woman!"

Willa clapped both hands to her mouth and fell on her knees before Mother's bench. "Oh mistress, forgive me. I talk too much, I know it. Beat me, I deserve it, I—"

"Silence! Stop your babbling. And the rest of you—get back to your beds."

"Mother, what's wrong? Why are you shouting?" I was terrified. I had never seen my mother look so stern and sound so harsh, especially to Willa, her own clanswoman and best friend.

"Freawaru, come to me."

I obeyed instantly, crawling into her bed as she shifted the baby to make room. She spoke in low tones directly into my ear.

"Listen, child. You are too young to understand some things, but it is foolish to scorn a goddess. Freyja has great power, as may you one day, but it is not yet time to speak of such things. Sleep now. You will stay tonight with me."

"Yes, Mother." Glad for this unexpected favor, I snuggled under the furs, her soft body a welcome change from Brita's sharp bones and Willa's greasy smell. Mother was wrong on one point. I did understand about sleeping with men. I'd seen Brita do it with Karl, and she seemed to like it. They had been wrestling each other and laughing.

Now Karl was gone, and I suddenly remembered that I had not seen Holger's laughing face since the night of that chilling howl and the bloody morning after. Could he have been one of those whose spear was cast on the funeral pyre? I would not believe it, yet shivered at the thought. Mother reached out and pulled me close to her side. So it was that I found myself in my mother's arms when the nightmare returned.

After the naming banquet, after the rejoicing, after the gift giving, after nightfall, it happened again. The man-eating monster, the Heorot-hating night demon, came back to my father's hall. So swift, so silent was its entrance that we did not stir, did not wake, and only shifted uneasily in our beds when the shadow of evil crossed our dreams.

In Heorot, it found thirty men fast asleep after their feasting, oblivious to pain or sorrow. It grabbed them all, butchering as it went, and rushed back into the darkness, leaving only a trail of blood and slime.

"*Aiiee! Aiiee!* Blood! Murder!"

Screams roused us all in the early light of a shrouded dawn. Shaking off sleep, Mother thrust the baby into my arms and reached for a shawl. Hrethric began to howl, but I gave him a finger to suck and he seized it greedily. Brita stood clutching the frame of the doorway, her body heaving, eyes staring. "Heorot!" she gasped. "Blood! More blood!"

Our guards rushed into the mist, swords drawn.

"Brita, what did you see? Tell us," Mother commanded.

"Worse—worse than before," she sobbed, and then sank to the floor in a heap. Willa hurried to the shaking girl, gathered her up, and carried her to the sleeping benches.

"There now, settle yourself. I'm sure we'll find out soon enough what happened."

We did, for this time there was a witness: Aelric. Aelric was found, barely conscious, crouched under Hrothgar's chair. He was drenched not in blood but in his own urine. Two thanes helped him out into the light. I crouched down and peered between someone's legs to get a look at him. At first, he babbled incoherently, but after a time he formed words.

"It was huge, horrible," he began, addressing the circle that now crowded around him. "It was not a man but stood upright on two legs like a man. Its eyes burned with a gruesome light. Rough, scaly hide it had, and great cruel claws." He stopped, as if struggling to collect himself.

"It came of a sudden—burst open the door. It was so enormous that it had to force itself through the frame. Our men sprang up to attack the thing, but their swords left no mark. It—it bit off Hugeleik's head, drank his blood, and bolted him down—swallowed his body whole."

Everyone gasped. I felt sick to my stomach.

"Yes," he nodded, "the grim fiend swallowed him whole. Then it killed our other brave men, though they attacked from all sides. It snapped their necks and stuffed them into a huge sack—a sort of leather bag."

Aelric stopped again, rubbing his arm across his eyes as if to blot out the scene. His voice fell to a hoarse whisper. "I don't know how or when it left Heorot, for I fell into darkness." He shuddered, clutching his stomach, and vomited sour ale. We bystanders shuddered too, dazed by the horror of his tale.

"How did you escape?" questioned Hrothgar sharply.

Aelric wiped his mouth and struggled to stand erect. "You know, my lord, that I have no weapon save my harp. During the night, I moved my blanket under your throne chair to escape the snores of the other sleepers. The monster must not have seen me there—so I was spared to tell this tale."

Hrothgar scowled and pulled at his beard. "You say their swords were useless against it? So, as we feared, it is not man, but a monster."

Then Hrothgar did a thing I had never seen him do: he wept—not silent tears, but a great howl of grief and pain. It shook us like a sudden storm blast. He pulled at his hair and howled, long and loud. "Hugeleik … Hroar … Skudd … Ulf … Gamle—" Here his voice broke, and his shoulders heaved with great sobs. "Brave thanes, loyal comrades, we will have vengeance for your foul slaughter. Hear me! We will avenge your deaths!"

A few days before this, I would have believed Father's words; I would have trusted in his ability to defend us. But now? As I looked around the circle, I saw doubt on many faces. A pale sun emerging from the clouds found Heorot filled with fear and lamentation.

Once again, the hall was cleansed, and this time the doors were reinforced with double planking and hung with bigger hinges, newly forged. The smoke of another funeral pyre billowed up to the heavens. But the monster's appetite was not yet sated. That night it struck again, and another score of men—brave volunteers—fell before the strength of the demon. This time they were not asleep and befuddled with ale, but awake and alert, ready to receive the shadow walker on the point of a spear. Yet once again, no man could prevail against the might of the monster.

Now it became a deadly game. The monster toyed with us, staying away for nights at a time. Then it would strike again, demolishing the animals tethered inside Heorot as a sacrifice, smearing the walls with blood in its rage at being cheated. Sometimes it took a single victim afoot after dark: an old woman foolish enough to go outside to relieve herself, a child sleepwalking. It was no longer safe to traverse the misty moors after nightfall. Death lay hidden in the shadows, ready to ambush the unwary. Always it returned to Heorot, haunting that once-shining hall. All through the winter, the monster held sway in savage isolation, for no one dared tarry there after darkness fell. Folk began to give the thing a name. They called it Grendel.

Thus began a long, dark time in the history of Heorot. Day after day, Hrothgar sat silent on his throne, stricken and helpless. Even my mother's presence and the happy gurgles of his newborn son did not rouse him from his deep distress.

Some of our people made private sacrifices to their personal gods at small structures erected near the edge of the settlement. I saw Torgun, the blacksmith's wife, carrying a length of linen cloth to place on an altar she'd dedicated to Gefion. Torgun had once told me a wonderful story about Gefion, a goddess married to Odin's son, Scyld. Gefion had turned her four giant sons into a team of oxen and used them to plough all the way around our land, thus separating it from our enemies on the mainland. How clever and powerful she must be! Could she help us now?

As for Bjorn, our smith, he sacrificed haunches of meat to Thor. I knew as well as anyone that the dogs would eat such offerings as soon as they were left, but it seemed to give people comfort to perform these deeds. Some erected platforms before their dwellings as a public display of sacrificed animals. Others worried aloud that the breaking loose of monsters might mean that Ragnarok, the end of the world, was near.

Aeschere, like most of the older nobles, worshipped Thor, the good-natured god whose reputed strength and mighty hammer were said to subdue even giants. Some of the younger thanes, like Saxe and Sven, called on Tyr, said to be a fierce ally in battle. Mother and Father never talked much about the gods, but animal sacrifices were made at regular intervals on the stone altar near the mead hall. At such times, different names were called aloud by Hugeliek, who led such rituals: Thor, of course; Freyr, a god of horses and good harvests; Tyr; and sometimes Odin, a name that seemed to evoke dread in both priest and participants.

After one council meeting, Father rode off with Aeschere and a small party of athelings toward the burial mounds. They were gone all day, barely returning in time for the evening meal. At Mother's inquiring look, Father said only that they'd been checking each mound and tumulus for any sign of an opening.

Listening behind Mother's skirts, the possible significance of his words suddenly came to me. Although many names had been given to the Grendel, such as Night Walker and Shadow Walker, I'd never heard it suggested that this thing might be one of our own ancestors, risen from the dead! All my life I had played run-and-hide among the great standing stones and gathered wildflowers on the mounds. Now these things, once so safe and ordinary, took on overtones of menace. If Father thought it possible that the dead could rise, it must be possible.

Mother turned and saw me staring, transfixed. She gave my shoulder a little shake. "What do you see, Freawaru?"

"Nothing, Mother. Nothing."

"That is well. That is very well."

"Father, what did you see at the mounds?" I asked, touching his arm.

"Nothing, Freaw, nothing. We found no disturbance of any kind. Don't worry, little one. Our dead still rest."

But I did worry, and I rested little.

Inside the women's house, we honored Freyr's sister Freyja, who gave us children and aided us in matters of love—or so Willa said. A few spoke of Frigg, said to be the wife of Odin, but she was a dim and distant figure, like Odin himself.

One day in the eld-hus, where we women were grinding meal for bread, Willa tried to lift our hearts by telling a tale.

"This puts me in mind of a story," she said, nodding at the grinding querns. "Long, long ago, old King Frothi went raiding in the north and came back with two female slaves, two giant maidens named Fenja and Menja. He needed their strength to grind on a giant quern—a magic millstone it was, named 'Grotti.' Now this millstone would grind out whatever the grinder asked for, and Frothi wanted riches. He kept the two women busy grinding night and day. 'Keep the stone turning,' he commanded. He gave them no rest lasting longer than the cuckoo took to sing its song.

"'Grind on, Grotti,' they sang as they spun the stone. At first Fenja and Menja were content to grind out treasure for the king: gold rings, down pillows—it could even grind out peace. They were proud of their strength, able to do what no ordinary woman could. But he gave them no rest.

"Fenja began to grumble first and then Menja. Soon they were no longer willing to be prisoners of the king.

"One day, a trader happened by in a great ship and was invited to feast with the king. Now this trader was really a pirate, named Mysingr, who would often return to plunder those with whom he had traded. Now Fenja and Menja changed their song:

Once we two maidens moved bedrock and boulders,
Hurled down this millstone heavy and huge
Now we're held captive by Frothi, cruel king

In this dreary place we're as good as dead.

"Mysingr heard the two women singing at their work and saw them grinding out riches for the king. *I must have that millstone*, he thought to himself. So, late at night, he crept back to the cookhouse and lured the two women onto his ship, promising them their freedom and a return to their home country. 'And of course, you'll want to bring your quern, as you are so attached to it,' he said. This they did, glad to escape from Frothi's constant demands. But after they had sailed away, Mysingr began to make his own demands.

"'Grind out salt. I must have salt for my trading!'

"So they began to grind … and grind … and grind. At midnight, they asked him if he had enough salt. 'Keep the stone turning,' he commanded. 'I need much more salt.' So they continued. But after a few days the ship began to ride lower in the water, and the crew grew fearful.

"'Stop grinding,' shouted Mysingr. 'I have enough salt now.'

"But Fenja and Menja were singing and could not hear him.

"'*Grind on, Grotti, grind on*,' they sang. The ship sank down, down to the bottom of the sea, drowning Mysingr and all his men. Some say that Fenja and Menja are down there still, grinding salt on Grotti, the magic millstone. And that is why, to this very day, the sea tastes of salt."

We sat in silence, staring at the hearth fire, while Willa smiled with satisfaction at her telling. Suddenly I could not stop myself from bursting out: "I wish we had a magic mill and could grind out peace— or better yet, death for the monster!"

Gyda burst out as well. "We should beg Thor to strike it with his hammer; surely Mjolnar would be strong enough to cleave the bone house of the beast!"

Mother rose. "May the gods help us. Our mighty warriors are no match for this demon of the night." Ruefully, we nodded agreement.

After weeks of worry and uncertainty, Mother called a council meeting of her own. She, Willa, Ana, Torgun, and several wives from the settlement met early one evening in the women's house. I was assigned to watch over Hrethric while they talked. Fortunately, he was content to play with his toes and suck on a honey rag, so I could listen to their conversation. Our house thralls, sitting or working near their benches, listened too.

"What is to be done?" asked Ana despairingly. "Holger gone—I do not wish to lose another son! But if our men cannot stop this evil thing, what can we women do?"

Mother began to speak, slowly, as if weighing her own thoughts. "We now know some of the creature's habits. So far it has focused on the mead hall alone, not offering to attack other dwellings."

"We can't trust in that," broke in a voice I did not recognize. "We are all in danger."

"We know it roams in darkness," continued Mother. "We know that spears and swords cannot stand against it. We know it has strength beyond mortal ken." She paused; her tone had been as level as if describing a plant or giving directions for the day, but now she drew herself up and spoke forcefully: "If our human efforts cannot prevail against the monster, we must call on superhuman forces. We must invoke the goddess."

Several women opened their mouths as if to object that they had already done so, but Mother seemed to know their minds. "Nay, not with some bit of food or trinket laid before a statue, but with a true sacrifice: a sacrifice made by all of us at the sacred pool."

The women exchanged worried glances.

"What kind of sacrifice, my queen?" Willa voiced the question on each face. "No offense, but haven't we had enough killing already?"

"Desperate times require desperate measures, Willa, but it won't require your life. It will require your hair. You must sacrifice your hair."

"What?" cried Ana. "Is there nothing else we can do, Wealtheow? A woman without her hair is not fully a woman! Cutting off my hair would be like … cutting off a breast!"

"Exactly. A true sacrifice." Mother looked around the group. "I will lead the way, sacrificing my own locks as an offering to Nerthus, Earth Mother. Since this Grendel creature is thought to dwell in the swamps, we will invoke Earth Mother to bind it there, to hold it fast and bar it from our homes and children." She glanced in my direction as she spoke.

Now Willa reached up with both hands to pat the fat braids wound around her head. "My hair too?"

"Yes, your hair, Freawaru's hair, the hair of Brita, Gyda, and every woman here. We must give it as an offering to the goddess to bring peace to Heorot."

"But it's taken me many years to grow it this long!" Willa was almost wailing.

"Yes, and your life could be snuffed out in a second if the Grendel is not appeased or banished."

"What about mistletoe? Couldn't we use mistletoe instead? It can banish evil spirits and promote peace." Willa was almost pleading now.

"Why, Willa, I did not know you were so well-versed in magic. Mistletoe could be helpful, but it is not the proper time of year to gather it. No, it must be our hair."

After a period of silence, Ana spoke for the rest. "As you see fit, Wealtheow. When shall we hold the ceremony?"

"Tonight there will be a full moon, but we dare not tempt the Grendel. No, we will rise early in the morning and hasten to the sacred pool. There the ritual will be conducted, far from men's eyes, for the mysteries of the goddess must be protected if our efforts are to be successful."

Mother looked up as six thanes entered the house. "Ah, our guards for the night. Welcome!"

To the women she bade farewell, with instructions to assemble at dawn.

That night I noticed Brita and Gyda spent extra time combing their long blond tresses, sighing as they did so. My thoughts turned to the previous summer, when most of the women in the settlement had flocked to the river for a hair-washing day. The younger thralls had stripped to the skin, shrieking and shouting as they plunged into the still icy water and submerged themselves, their hair floating out in long golden strands like rays of the sun.

Mother let me bathe naked, but like the other wives, she did not remove her shift. It clung to her body as she stood, waist-deep in the stream, rubbing tallow soap into my hair. Then, as I held my nose, she dipped me under and lifted me up to sit sputtering on the bank. While I dried in the sun, she washed her own tresses.

My pleasure and excitement in this annual event had clearly been shared by Gyda and Brita who'd emerged, sputtering but smiling, and then raced ashore to chase each other like children, their long locks swirling around their knees. My hair was red-brown, like Mother's and Willa's. Strange, it had never occurred to me before, but now I wondered as I looked around the room.

Why were we three the only ones with dark hair? And brown eyes? Yellow hair and blue eyes were most common in Heorot—though Father's hair and beard had turned white in recent weeks. Curious. I knew that Willa belonged to Mother's tribe, the Helmings, located somewhere far south across the water. How had Mother come to Heorot? Surely those stories about her being a captive prize must be just that— stories. I must ask her one day. I yawned and sleep overtook me.

Even though oak leaves were budding, and a sprinkle of wildflowers dotted the wet grass, it was chilly and damp the next morning when we assembled, a shivering clutch of women wrapped in gray wool. Hrethric was left with the blacksmith's daughter, who was delighted with the honor of watching the king's son.

We walked in single file, Mother in the lead carrying a small bag; I walked behind her and then the other women, with Willa at the rear to prevent stragglers and keep watch. No one spoke as we padded silently across the commons, past the outbuildings, through the oak grove, and then along the river. At last we approached the sacred pool—or so I supposed, as I had never been allowed to visit it before. My stomach rumbled with hunger, but Mother had insisted we take no food until the ritual was completed.

A small wood hut, open on three sides, stood beside the water. There we stopped, and Mother laid her bag atop a low wooden table. As she folded back the wrappings, a shaft of pale sunlight glinted off gold—the blade of a small sickle.

My face must has shown apprehension, for Mother smiled and said, "Don't worry, it won't hurt. The blade is very sharp, newly honed." Then she turned to address the silent line.

"Women of Heorot, attend me. We come before the earth goddess, the Great Mother. We offer her a part of ourselves. We ask for her protection against the dark force that assails us. We ask for peace in Heorot."

She picked up a long branch leaning against one corner of the hut and let fall her cloak. She was dressed all in white.

"With this staff cut from the ash tree, wood of the world tree Yggdrasil, I draw a circle, a sacred space in honor of the goddess. Freawaru, you will be the first to enter. Remove your garments."

Startled, I hesitated. Mother seemed transformed into someone I did not know: beautiful, remote, even—dangerous. It would be best not to cross her. Regretfully, I let fall my warm wool cloak and then undid the clasp of my tunic, finally dropping my night shift. Freeing myself from this puddle of clothing, I stepped warily into the circle with Mother.

"Great Mother, you see your child, naked as on the day of her birth. Bless her and protect her. Shield her from harm. Receive the offering she is about to give you." Mother raised the sickle in one hand and grasped my braid in the other, lifting it high above my head. It was gone in an instant. I felt cool air on the back of my neck, and shivered with relief that my part in the ritual was over.

One by one, the women came forward, disrobed, and stepped into the circle. Soon their long hair, which made me think of the swishing tails of horses, lay in a cloth bag at Mother's feet.

When the last woman had contributed her locks, Mother dropped her white robe, her naked body pale in the thin morning light. She reached for her own dark braid, severed it with one stroke, and dropped it into the bag. She turned, stepped out of the circle, and walked into the pool—or so it seemed to my startled eyes. Then I realized that she was walking along a narrow platform projecting out over the water.

"Earth goddess, Great Mother, receive our gifts. Grant us peace. Take away the dark shadow that haunts our hall. Bind it fast in its lair, never more to journey here. Grant us peace, Great Mother, grant us peace."

One by one, Mother dropped our shorn tresses into the pool. I watched as they floated and sank. Then, slowly, she returned to us, picked up the ash staff, and erased the circle.

"It is finished. Let us return to our homes."

The very next morning, Mother dressed herself in her best garments and headed up the hill to Heorot with Hrethric and me in tow. Aeschere now stood guard at the doorway. He admitted us immediately without the usual protocol. We walked the length of the empty hall, our feet resounding on the wooden floor. Hrothgar, flanked by two athelings, did not take note of our approach but sat staring into space as if to penetrate the darkness into which his men had disappeared.

"My king, hear me!" Mother stood directly before the throne, resplendent in all her jewelry, including the magnificent neck ring he had given her. "All is not lost. You still have many loyal men. Your treasuries are still well-stocked. You still have your queen, your son, your daughter. The tragedy of this house is not yet known beyond our kingdom, from what I can tell. But our humiliation will soon be talked of over the whole world if we do not take steps to check this evil."

Hrothgar raised his head slowly. He did not look like the father I knew. His eyes were dull, his beard unkempt, and his skin sagged.

"We have tried everything proposed in council. Our best men have perished in repeated efforts to vanquish the monster. What else would you have me do?"

"Since human efforts have not availed against this enemy, we must make serious sacrifices to the gods. We must beg for mercy. We must beseech their aid against this fiendish foe."

"You say this, Wealtheow? You who never beg?"

"Yes, I do." Mother lifted her hands in a gesture of resignation. "What else is left? We women have called on Earth Mother at the sacred pool. Now you and your nobles must prepare a formal sacrifice."

Father nodded wearily. "You may be right. But who would lead such a sacrifice? Hugeleik, as you know, was taken in a night of slaughter." He looked away.

"You, yourself, my lord. It must be a sacrifice of horses—yes, it must be so," she added, as she saw Hrothgar wince. "Horses must be given to Freyr, the peace-bringer. Nine horses. We must make it a true sacrifice if the gods are to take notice."

And so it was done. Choosing the horses created considerable difficulty, however. Each thane prized his warhorse as much as his sword, and was loath to lose it in what might be a vain exercise. Yet to select farm horses would be an insult to the gods. It was decided that four young mares and five stallions would be needed.

Then Aeschere suggested that the nine horses be chosen from those whose riders had been murdered by the Grendel. A few horses had been slain and added to their funeral pyres, but many still grazed in the commons, unclaimed by any kin. This solution met with relief and approval. A counter would be made for each horse in the pool, and then lots cast to select those for the sacrifice.

Before the choosing, I walked out to the meadows where the horses grazed, Willa at my side. Though it had never attacked in daylight, with the Grendel on the loose I was no longer allowed to roam unattended.

Red horses, brown horses, pale yellow horses, chestnuts—I loved them all. Willa carried a basket of gnarled apples so that I might feed them. She held me up to rub their velvety noses while they chomped and drooled, apple juice dripping from their muzzles. Baerningfeax and Sweordfeld were two of my favorites. I prayed they would not be chosen for the sacrifice, but Sweordfeld's counter fell face up when the lots were cast. His fate was sealed.

I did not wish to see horses killed, even had I been allowed to witness the sacrifice. I stayed indoors all that day, helping Brita and Gyda wind wool for weaving onto spindles. Gyda claimed to have witnessed such a ceremony before, in her home tribe.

"First they build a big fire on a stone altar," she said knowingly. "Next they blindfold all the horses and lead them up one by one. The priest thrusts a spear in to each horse and catches the blood as it spurts forth."

The priest? But Father was acting as the priest this time! Could he really be putting our horses to death? He loved them as much as I did—a bond we had shared in the old days, when he'd pull me up before him for a gallop across the moors.

"No, they don't burn the whole carcass. The best parts are roasted and fed to those at the ceremony. Later the head, backside, tail, and legs will be staked out in the sacred bog as an offering to the gods."

"Ugh, they eat horseflesh? Sounds disgusting to me."

"Well, Brita, I'll bet you've eaten worse—or have you sworn off man flesh since Karl was killed?"

Brita turned white and then red and then jumped up and spat in Gyda's face, upsetting the basket of wool at our feet.

"Jealous witch! May your breasts dry up and fall off! Then they'll have no further use for you as a wet nurse!"

I backed away, sure of a hair-pulling, teeth-biting fight between the two house slaves. Hrethric, asleep in the wooden cradle beside Mother's bed, awoke and added his cries to the insults flying through the air. Just then, Willa entered.

"What's all this? What's going on here? Get back to your work, you two hussies. If you can't behave like decent women, we'll put you outside after dark tonight—or worse!" Willa's threat had an immediate effect. The quarrel subsided, Brita and Gyda muttering under their breath at each other.

"Willa?" I asked, "What could be worse?" Willa did not look like herself. Her eyes were curiously wide, the whites almost swallowing her dark pupils." Willa, what is it? Why do you look so strange?"

"Human sacrifice." She choked on the words. "They strangled a man at the horse sacrifice and hung his body from a tree as an offering to Odin. I hope the gods are happy." She spat.

"Strangled? Who?" Brita and Gyda spoke as one.

"I don't know his name. That young fellow Ulf captured in one of the raids last autumn, the one who limped. He'd been put to tending pigs, but apparently he was needed today for a higher purpose." Her tone did not match her words; disgust and disapproval were written all over her face.

Why was Willa so upset? Even I knew that the life of a slave meant nothing. No *wergild*, no man-price would be exacted for his life, even if his family in some distant tribe should hear of the sacrifice.

I thought no more about the sacrifice of this slave until a week later, when the putrid smell of rotting flesh came wafting in from the west. Now my nose told me the location of the bog where the man had been hung.

"That's the slave, you know." Hrothulf had slipped up behind me unheard. "His skin is falling off, and his eyes have already been pecked out by the ravens." I whirled in anger and disgust. He leered at me and flapped his arms like a bird.

"How do you know? You weren't allowed to go there!"

"Oh, yes I was—and I saw it all. The whole sacrifice. I even ate horse flesh with the other men!"

"Huh, you're not a man yet," I countered.

He made a face at me. "Hrothgar seems to think so. He lets me do whatever I want."

This stung, and he knew it. I turned, blinking to stop the tears starting in my eyes. As I walked away, Hrothulf's words rang in my ears: "He lets me do whatever I want."

I wish I could say that the sacrifices brought peace to Heorot. But neither horse nor hair nor human sacrifice moved the Grendel to spare our hall. His depredations continued—at irregular intervals—now accompanied by a pile of dung as a parting insult, as if to say, "*That* for your rituals!"

Father's despair grew deeper, his torment unceasing. Sometimes he rode out to Healfdane's mound and sat there alone, desperately seeking inspiration on how to combat the monster. When he returned from these solitary sojourns and met Mother's questioning gaze, he shook his head sadly.

The Grendel was waging war on Heorot—a permanent feud—but there was no way to parlay with this enemy and no force that could stand against it. Heorot, the best of houses, stood empty of its rightful occupants night after night, a bitter woe for Hrothgar and all his band.

Desperate to help Hrothgar, Mother now undertook a new project: to beautify the walls of the mead hall with hangings, and thus divert men's minds from what would happen at nightfall. As the subject of her first tapestry she chose Scef Scylding's arrival on Danish shores, a child sent over the waters to found a great dynasty. She used Hrethric as her model for the baby. She even used gold thread to match his golden hair. Day by day, I watched her nimble fingers at the loom, fascinated with the picture developing before my eyes.

"May I do that, Mother? Will you teach me?"

"Yes, Freawaru, but there is much work to be done before the weaving can start. Ask Willa to show you how the yarn is prepared and dyed. Those are tasks where your help would be welcomed. You need to grow taller before you can weave on this loom." Indeed, the loom was higher by a head than Mother herself, who stood before it to move the shuttle through warp and weft. Looking at her profile, I noticed something else: her belly had begun to grow again.

Hrothmund was born in the dead of winter just as Hrethric had been—another easy birth, thank the gods, as Willa always said. The arrival of his second son seemed to alleviate Hrothgar's sorrow for a time. He gave another banquet and presented Mother with a splendid gold arm bracelet, but seldom did he laugh or take pleasure in carousing with his hall companions as was his wont in former days. I tried to distract him by begging for a ride on his great warhorse, but when he humored me, we rode in silence, at a steady pace. Clearly, a great heaviness had settled on his heart.

Two-year-old Hrethric became my special charge. When Hrothulf tried to scare Hrethric with talk of the Grendel, I was quick to comfort him, but the monster seemed to have little reality for my young brother, who had never known a life free of its evil menace. Still little more than a child myself, I lavished on my brother all the love my father was unable to receive. Aeschere noticed my loneliness; having no longer any daughter of his own, he showed me special favor. That winter he carved several small toys: a swan for me, a horse for Hrethric, and a hammer of Thor for baby Hrothmund. These treasures I kept in a basket I'd woven myself and took them out when Hrethric was fretful.

Mother gave me tasks to perform and skills to master. Her antidote for sorrow was to keep busy. She saw to it that those around her were kept busy as well—a boon to us all, I soon realized. She set me to work at everyday tasks: picking out burs from wool for spinning, gathering plants to make dye colors, stirring the cooking pot in the eld-hus, and taking a turn at churning milk and butter, all tedious tasks that I disliked. Willa began trying to teach me how to hold a needle and thread for simple sewing.

As winter followed winter, we seemed to become accustomed to living with terror. We rarely spoke of the Grendel, but any patch of darkness brought a moment of panic. We carried on as best we could, worked at our daily chores, and dreamed of better days to come.

One night, my dreams took a startling form. As I stood on our headland looking north to the sea, a great white swan flew over the waters with fifteen men on its back. One of them, taller than the rest, turned his head and smiled at me.

Chapter 3
No Visible Weapons

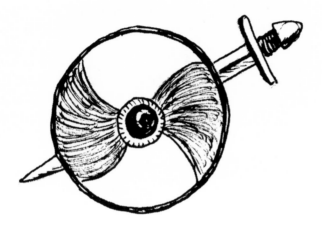

One midsummer morning, a stranger rode into our lives, guiding his horse straight to the door of the mead hall. Hrethric, Hrothmund, and I were playing sticks in the dirt there, as I'd been told to keep the boys out from underfoot while the women prepared the solstice feast.

Since Heorot's nightly occupation by the Grendel, fewer and fewer warriors had arrived to join Hrothgar's band, so I stood up hastily to get a better look at this newcomer: a tall figure atop a dapple-gray horse that looked exhausted. The stranger bore himself like a noble, a man of consequence.

He wore no armor and carried no visible weapons, though a long, leather bag hung beside his saddle. White hair and beard caught the sun, but two dark eyes blazed like hot coals out of a pale face. As he dismounted, his black cloak swirled around him, revealing a thin, bony frame dressed in clothes unfamiliar to me.

"Good day to you."

At first, I thought he was speaking to me and had opened my lips to answer when Thorkel, today's hall guard, stepped forward.

"Halt. Come no further. Identify your-s-s-self and s-state your business."

Despite his speech difficulty, Thorkel's tone was clearly commanding.

"My name is my own business," said the stranger calmly, "but most men call me Unferth. I come from the north, from the court of King Finn, to see King Hrothgar."

As Thorkel digested this information, Unferth turned in my direction.

"Good day to you again, king's daughter."

"S-sir, good day. How do you know me?"

"I know many things—but the gold collar I see around your neck reveals your identity."

Gold collar? In confusion, I pressed a hand to my bare throat. As usual, I wore only my light woolen shift and tunic. Mother had told me I was too young for jewelry—that I must wait until I came of age.

"Sir …?" But Unferth had turned from me to follow Thorkel into Heorot, leaving his horse tethered outside.

I thought no more about the strange man's strange words that morning, for Hrethric and Hrothmund were tugging at my hands. As usual, they wanted me to help them climb into the great oak tree beside the river—one of my favorite play places as well, even though I was "a big girl of ten" as Willa said.

"Put me up first, Freaw—I'm oldest! Hrothmund's too little. He'll just get stuck and cry. He always cries." Hrethric was jumping up and down in his eagerness.

"Now, Hrethric, don't be mean. I'll put you both up, but it is Hrothmund's turn to go first."

At four, Hrethric could almost reach the lower limbs by himself, but two-year-old Hrothmund needed help. I remembered the days when Willa had been the one to give me a boost. Now she spent all her time in the eld-hus supervising the cooking and baking.

"Are you alright, Hrothmund? Hold on tight and don't wiggle so you won't fall." He was only a few limbs above the ground, so I wasn't too worried if he did.

"Freaw, let's go out over the water today. You promised I could do that when I'm big enough, and I'm big enough—look!" Hrethric demonstrated his prowess by scrambling along a branch that arched gently toward the stream below.

"All right, but I'm coming right behind you, just in case." We inched forward, giggling conspirators, while Hrothmund looked up at us enviously from below.

C-R-A-C-K!

Without warning, the limb broke behind us. We plummeted into the stream below, where dark water, still icy from the spring runoff, closed over my head.

I gasped and kicked, the weight of my clothes pulling me down. Something nearby kicked me back—Hrethric! What had I done? We'd both be drowned! Somehow I had to save us. Fighting off terror, I reached out with both hands, searching for Hrethric's body—and found him, thrashing beside me.

Suddenly I felt myself being lifted, pulled free of the suffocating blackness; I was rising above the water in what felt like the grasp of a strong, bony hand. Hrethric surfaced simultaneously in the grasp of a second hand. We hung suspended for a moment, choking and coughing as water streamed from our hair and clothes. Somewhere in the distance I could hear Hrothmund wailing.

"Good day to you again, king's daughter."

The hands lowered us to the ground and released their grip. Hrethric burst into tears, and I followed suit, happy that he was still alive, terror-stricken that I had almost lost him. The stranger stood above us, wet to the waist, shaking with silent laughter.

"Next time you go swimming, check the depth of the water first. You had only to put your feet down to touch bottom." It was Unferth, the stranger, speaking.

Sobbing in relief, gratitude, and humiliation, I stood up, pulled off my soggy outer tunic and turned to help Hrethric remove his wet woolens. In the midsummer sunshine, we'd be warmer without them. Ignoring the stranger a moment longer, I lifted the whimpering

Hrothmund down from the tree and prepared to lead us all back to the women's house.

"Thank you, sir, for your help. I—I'm sorry you got wet." I spoke with as much dignity as I could muster, but my lips were quivering and my teeth chattering.

"One moment, king's daughter. What is that mark on your shoulder?"

My shift had slipped down, exposing the upper part of my back.

"I-I don't know, s-sir." Of course, I did know, but it was surely no business of his.

"A feather? Yes, it could be a feather … which might mean—" The stranger stared at me, much as Hrothulf often did, but there was no malice in this man's eyes. "Come, you need dry clothes—and no doubt a scolding from your mother." We trudged back in silence.

At the door of the eld-hus we paused, the stranger coughing politely. Willa took one look and charged out to drag us inside.

"Freaw, you were in charge of these boys! Can't you do a better job of watching them? Look at these sopping, muddy clothes—what were you playing!"

Willa did not stop for breath as she hustled us along, ignoring the silent stranger who followed us. Mother was working at the loom, but she stopped short at the sight of her three cowering children, a fuming Willa, and the tall stranger.

"What happened?"

"A small error, my lady queen, which it was my pleasure to rectify. Your daughter, though she may be able to fly, does not yet know how to swim." He bowed his head slightly as he spoke.

Mother's face froze at these words. She regarded the stranger intently.

"I do not know what you mean," she said icily, "but words can wait. These children all need dry clothes. Willa, see to it."

All? Indeed, she was right. I noticed then that Hrothmund had wet himself.

As Willa led us away, I looked back to see Mother offering the stranger a cup of ale. When I returned, Mother and the stranger were still talking.

"I must leave you now. There are special plants to be gathered this day," Mother said, rising.

"Ah, yes, my lady—mugwort, fern seed, and mistletoe, I believe?"

Mother studied him again. "You are familiar with these plants and their uses?"

"These and many more. Their magic qualities are not unknown to me. Mushrooms also fall within my ken. If I may aid you in your harvest today, I am yours to command."

"I know where there's mistletoe," I chimed in. "High up in the oak tree beside the stream."

"Ah, yes—the best kind. Your eye is keen, king's daughter."

"My name is Freawaru," I said shyly.

"Freawaru. Yes, you are well-named: one might question the choice of ruler and defender, but you may be a queen one day, called upon both to rule and to defend ... as may you, my lady," he said, turning to Mother with a half-smile.

"Hrothgar is my ruler and defender," she said stiffly. "Now there is work to do. Come, Freawaru, you may assist me."

We spent the rest of the afternoon gathering plants. Mother did allow Unferth to climb the oak tree and harvest the mistletoe using her golden sickle, while she waited below to catch it in a white cloth. As we walked back, I listened to their conversation.

"May I have some of this for my own use?" he asked. At her inquiring look, he added, "as a protection against the Night Walker—the Grendel, I believe you call it."

Mother's face lost its color. She spoke bitterly. "The best protection, as Hrothgar's thanes know well, is to quit the mead hall before nightfall!"

Unferth raised his hand as if to forestall a further outburst. "I have heard that in the far north country," he said calmly, "they are plagued by trolls, giant beings who walk by night but cannot abide the light of day. It may be that your Grendel is of similar kind. If so, one might use light to destroy it."

"Could it be so?" Mother's face showed a glimmer of hope. "What a deliverance that would be after these years of dread! But who would undertake such a task?"

"I would. That is my purpose in coming here, lady. I have already offered my aid to Hrothgar, and he has graciously accepted.

Both Mother and I stared at him in surprise. For many months, no man had dared to challenge the Grendel.

"We will say no more of this at present. I will speak at length tonight before your settlement. Now I go to help prepare the bale-fires."

Bale-fires? My heart leapt for joy. These fires were my favorite part of the midsummer celebration. Hrethric and Hrothmund loved them too. Gathering straw and sticks all day was worth the glorious sight of the fires blazing on every hilltop surrounding Heorot.

Farmers in our settlement often drove their cattle between fires to protect them from disease. Sometimes men and even women jumped over the flames—for what purpose I knew not. Mother would not let us do it, though the boys longed to join in the excitement. They had to content themselves with pulling brands from the smaller fires and running about with them screaming and laughing.

Midsummer was a favorite time for everyone. The long days of sunlight helped alleviate the darkness that weighed down our hearts all winter. With so little darkness, the Grendel's visits had dwindled to sporadic occupations of the mead hall.

Even Father seemed more cheerful, riding out on his warhorse (with Hrothulf beside him on his chestnut) to hunt or lead a band of thanes on a raiding party and return with even more loot to stock his bulging treasury. His generosity in rewarding men with gold rings had only increased since the Grendel's coming, thus his leadership remained strong and unquestioned.

The long light of summer permitted this solstice celebration. Still, all ceremonies were completed before the semi-darkness fell. Then everyone scattered to take refuge from the Grendel. By now we knew that it attacked only Heorot itself, not deigning to enter anything less than the king's own hall.

Soon after his audience with the king, Unferth was called to speak before an assemblage of Hrothgar's men. For this occasion, both Father and Mother sat in their places of honor at the head of the banqueting tables. Of course, everyone was eager to hear what the stranger had to say, so many others, including women, slipped into the back of the hall to listen. I followed Ana; we stood in the shadows, as curious as the rest.

When Unferth rose to speak, he seemed a slight figure, but his voice carried with surprising power.

"I am Unferth; I come from the land of Finnmark to offer my services to this hall, for even in the far North the woes of Heorot are known. I do not come to you as a champion, but I do come bearing gifts."

He knelt to unwrap something at his feet. When he rose, he held a gleaming sword.

"Behold, Hrunting! In all its long history, it has never failed the hand that wielded it!"

All eyes followed the sword as he brandished it aloft. From the front benches came a gruff voice.

"I have heard of this Hrunting. If what you say is true, it is a princely gift."

"Isn't that Aeschere speaking?" I whispered to Ana.

"Yes, but hush. The stranger speaks again."

Unferth's voice dropped slightly. "To my sorrow, I can no longer carry Hrunting into battle; it is cursed for me, but may be used by another."

"What!" Hrothgar rose and seized Unferth by the shoulders. "Why not? Make clear your meaning."

As Unferth turned to the king, he spoke words we could not hear from the back of the hall, but we saw Hrothgar's men exchange questioning looks. Then Father received the sword from Unferth and fingered the edge.

"A fine blade, damascened, I see … and with runes on the hilt. What do they say?"

"It is a charm to protect the one who wields the sword." Unferth's voice had regained volume. "If any here wish to try it against the Grendel, I offer it freely to them."

A buzz of voices filled the hall. Some laughed as if at a jest. Unferth continued, ignoring the outburst.

"This is not all I have to offer. I also bring knowledge of magic, of spells and charms, of herbs and poisons, a knowledge which few here may possess. In my own country, I was accounted a shaman of some note."

Now the buzz rose louder, filling the hall. Father sat down heavily and turned to look at Mother before addressing Unferth again.

"Magic, you say? It may be magic that we need now. The strength of our men and our weapons has not prevailed." He looked down at the blade across his lap. "Even this sword, Hrunting, may be no match for the monster we face. Yet we welcome you and welcome your aid in this unequal battle. You have traveled far to bring us this gift. The hospitality of Heorot shall be yours, and a place made for you on the mead benches."

As the assembly began to break up, Ana and I slipped out the door.

"Help at last," breathed Ana. "This Unferth is the first to come of his own accord to offer aid."

I almost opened my mouth to tell her of the fifteen men in my dream but paused in doubt. Could I have been mistaken? Unferth looked nothing like the man who had smiled at me, and Unferth had come alone. I let it go.

In the days that followed, Unferth moved slowly and systematically about the settlement, talking to everyone. He questioned Aelric about the Grendel's appearance and movements. He conferred with our blacksmith on the composition of the door hinges. He spent much time with Mother, asking about the properties of local plants. I listened one day as they discussed what Unferth called the "baneful herbs."

"Wolfsbane," he was saying. He stood beside the loom where Mother wove yet another hall tapestry. "This poison plant grows in damp woods in the high mountains; the flower is a bright yellow. It is dangerous to handle and fatal if ingested. I wonder …" he stared, unseeing at the pattern unfolding on the loom. "It can be used to reverse shape-shifting spells …" Here he paused for a time and then lowered his voice. "Have you considered the possibility that this Grendel could be one of your own people in a changed form?"

I gave a stricken cry; Mother dropped the shuttle. We both shuddered as if a cold wind had blown over us.

"Do not speak of such things!" Mother blazed at Unferth, pulling me to her side and looking around to see who else might have heard his words. "We have no such evil wights here!" she declared loudly.

Unferth shrugged. "I ask pardon if I have offended, but all possibilities must be considered."

Silence. Finally Unferth picked up the thread of his earlier conversation. "There are other poisons too: hemlock, hemp, henbane—as well as deadly mushrooms. I have a few samples in my pack," he said calmly.

"Of what use would they be against the monster?" asked Mother, who had regained her composure. "We could certainly prepare a poison stew for its dinner, but it seems to relish only raw flesh and fresh blood." Suddenly she looked down at me. "Freaw, you should not be here. Go outdoors and see what your brothers are doing."

Unferth raised a hand. "Wait. Your daughter's presence puts me in mind of a larger issue. Have all the gods been honored as they should? Could this monster have been sent as a punishment for some sacrilege or omission?"

As Mother's face hardened, he backed toward the door. "These are hard questions," he said, "but I wish only to help you find answers. Please consider what I have said." He bowed as he exited, leaving Mother and me to stare at each other.

"Is he truly a seer?" she murmured, "or only a man full of his own importance, come to make trouble?" She sighed. "Yet he is right. We must overlook nothing that may provide a clue."

Unferth's presence certainly did stir up trouble. His questions were soon bruited about the settlement, and an undercurrent of dis-ease spread like a poison. People began to point fingers and assign blame. Whispers circulated. Accusations flew. To our fear of the Grendel was now added a fear of each other, as possible causes of our own calamity.

We came to know more of Unferth in the days that followed. He spent more time with the women than with the men, which I found puzzling. It was whispered among the house slaves that his mother had been a *volva*, skilled in the use of *sejd* and *galder*, prophecy and enchantment. It was said that he had killed men with his magic and brought the dead back to life. Such talk was accompanied by shivers and the shaking of heads.

I heard with my own ears one day the challenge issued by one of the younger thanes.

"Where is your sword and your shield? Have you come to serve Hrothgar or no?"

"I serve only Odin," said Unferth, "but I have come to give Hrothgar such help as I can."

That night in the women's house I asked Willa. "Who is Odin? Does he rule a kingdom like Father does?" This brought forth one of Willa's belly laughs, though she lowered her voice when she answered.

"Some folks believe in Odin as the chief god—the 'all father' some calls him, though a bloodthirsty sort of father he must be. He likes battles and fighting and all that. They says that if you die bravely in battle, you'll end up spending your days in Odin's mead hall, feasting and drinking and fighting forever—just what a man likes!"

"Those that serve 'im," she continued, "are a queer lot—vicious sometimes. They eat or drink something that makes 'em fight like wild animals. Why, they could kill their own brothers when the frenzy is on 'em—'berserkers' they're called. But this is not good talk for bedtime. You'll be screaming in your sleep again, if I don't hold my tongue."

"Me? I scream in my sleep?" Astonished, I had no recollection of having done so.

"Yes indeed, though your mother don't like me to speak of it. It's a wonder we don't all do it with that Grendel lurking in the dark—there, I've gone and done it again. Best to keep my mouth shut. No more talking now."

I lay awake for a while, trying to recall a dream so terrible that it could make me scream aloud. Thoughts of the Grendel had receded into a dim corner of my brain behind a closed door, which I did not choose to open. Another dream emerged, however, a dream of flying.

I was driving a cart pulled by … white swans … yes, my swans were back! We flew high, high above the golden gables of Heorot, high over the harbor, the fjord, and out to the open sea. Icy wind rushed past my face. My fingers grew numb, but the swans kept flying higher and higher until the reins fell from my frozen fingers, and I spiraled into darkness, floating down like a feather.

One afternoon I came upon Unferth seated under the great oak tree, carving something on a branch he'd broken off.

"What's that?" I pointed to his stick.

"A rune," he answered. "Have you never seen one?"

"Maybe." I inspected the marks he'd cut with his knife. "They look like the lines on one of Father's sword hilts."

"Ah, yes, you do keep your eyes open. Yes, those were runes."

"What are they for? I mean, why are you cutting them on this stick?"

"These are to help me when I meet the Grendel face-to-face."

His answer took my breath away.

"Face-to-face? Aren't you scared? He kills everybody—he *eats* them!" Had no one told him the truth about this monster? As a newcomer, perhaps he had not heard the full story. I started to enlighten him.

"Wait, wait, little Freaw." He had never called me by name before. "I know the sad history of Heorot. All the world knows! Lays are sung in many a hall about the woes of Hrothgar. I've come to try something different—to see if my magic can put this monster to flight, if not destroy it."

"How will this stick help?"

"I am carving runes of magic, charms to protect me, to aid me in the fight against this evil. Hmmm, perhaps I'll teach you the meaning of one. We can carve it on a stick for you if you like—perhaps to keep away monsters in your dreams?"

"I don't dream of monsters," I replied haughtily, "only of swans."

"Swans ... do you fly with them?" He looked at me keenly.

"Sometimes." Why did he ask so many questions?

"I'd like to learn how to make a rune," I said aloud. Inwardly I was thinking: this would be something Hrothulf didn't know how to do! "I have my own knife. Aeschere gave me one when he made them for Hrethric and Hrothmund."

"Very wise, very wise. Let me see it a moment."

He took the small knife I handed him, lifted my hand, and brought the blade swiftly across the tip of my middle finger. When bright blood spurted out, he seized the finger and pressed it into the rune newly carved on the oak stick.

"Now it is yours," he said. "sealed with your blood. I will make another for myself."

I was too astonished to cry, though my finger quickly began to throb. Unferth wiped the knife blade on his sleeve, set it down, and took hold of my shoulders. He looked straight into my eyes.

"Tell no one about this, or the magic will not work. Now listen, Freaw. Remember what I say. This is a rune of power, not to be used lightly. A rune is a secret thing, a mystery." He continued, "Odin himself discovered the runes, but not before he had hung upside down on the world tree for nine long nights, wounded by his own blade. You see, Odin bloodied himself as an offering to himself."

Unferth released me, stood up, and closed his eyes. He began to chant, as if he were a scop singing without a harp.

None gave me bread,
None gave me drink.
Down to the deepest depths I peered
Until I spied the Runes.
With a roaring cry I seized them up,
Then dizzy and fainting, I fell.

Unferth shook himself, appearing to return to the present, though his eyes had the look of one wandering in a far place, and his voice was not his own.

"May the wisdom Odin found be our wisdom too. May we be worthy of his sacrifice. To those who would master runes, he gave these instructions:

Know how to cut, know how to read,
Know how to stain, know how to prove,
Know how to ask and sacrifice,
Know how to send and destroy.

He opened his eyes and picked up the oak stick with its branched lines. To me, the marks looked like an outstretched hand, palm up.

"This rune is called 'Algiz.' It is a rune of defense and protection, in some measure a force for preservation in the face of danger. It may serve to keep open space around you, but be mindful: timely action and correct conduct are your only true protection. Each of us is a warrior, Freaw, though we carry no sword or shield."

"Had I not seen the feather on your shoulder, I would not be telling you these things, nor initiating you into the craft of the rune-master. But the gods work as they will. You bear the mark of a goddess upon you. You will have the strength to use that power one day. Now you hold one aspect of that power in your hands. Keep it hidden. Use it only when real need is upon you." He stood up suddenly. "Now I think it is time for you to return to the women's house."

Awed by all that Unferth had told me, I turned to go, but then hesitated.

"Thank you, Unferth, but I have one question: did you really kill your own brother?"

His face froze, his smile melting like an icicle in the sun.

"Who told you that?"

"No one ... I mean, I only heard that Odin-worshippers kill their own brothers in their frenzy—"

What had I done? Unferth's face twisted into a mask of pain; he shut his eyes tight and lifted his chin in a chilling howl—like the howl of a wolf in the forest.

Rooted to the spot, I clasped my hands over my ears and shut my own eyes tight, certain that in the next instant he would fall upon me and tear me to pieces like the wild animal he was. Time stood still. Then I heard low, choked words.

"Brothers, forgive me. You know I bore you no hatred. When the fury was upon me, I did not know you. I cannot avenge your deaths, but I will give my own life to pay for yours. Let the Grendel take me, if that is the will of Odin."

As he sat with head bowed, I slowly began to fit the pieces together. Unferth had come to Heorot to pay a debt—to his brothers, who were owed a life. It would be the life of the Grendel or the life of Unferth himself.

My mind rebelled at this conclusion. I did not want Unferth to die. He had become my friend. He treated me, a girl, with the same respect he gave to my mother and father. I did not want to lose him.

"Unferth, Unferth, let me help you." In desperation, I knelt beside him and took his hand. He lifted his head.

"A self-exiled, kin-killer and a ten-year-old girl who bears on her back the mark of Freyja, goddess of love. A likely pair." He began to laugh, a choking, halting laugh that rose shrilly and then subsided into silence.

I hid my rune-stick in the only place I could think of where it might not be discovered: deep under the roots of the oak tree itself. In the women's house, I had no private possessions larger than a comb or sewing case, for I would not get a chest of my own until I came of age—as Willa frequently reminded me. So the oak tree seemed safest. It was frequented primarily by my brothers and me. Fortunately Hrothulf had no interest in trees.

Lately Hrothulf's attention had been transferred to my two little brothers. He lost no opportunity to tease and torment them. I could not always be present to shield them from harm, but I tried to comfort them at bedtime. Hrothulf, now thirteen, slept with the men, of course, but Hrethric and Hrothmund still slept in the women's house.

One night both boys begged, "Tell us a story, Freaw—about Thor." Hrothmund never tired of hearing about his favorite hero. Fortunately, I had heard enough tales from Willa over the years to satisfy his appetite.

"All right. Which one shall it be? The story of Thor and the sea serpent, or Thor and the three visits, or … wait a minute. I heard a new one from the blacksmith's wife yesterday. In this story a giant steals Thor's hammer, and Thor has to dress like a woman to get it back."

"Ugh … dress like a woman? Thor would never do that!" Hrothmund wrinkled his nose in disgust.

"Not even to get his hammer back?"

"Well, maybe." Hrothmund fingered the tiny replica hanging at his neck. "All right, Freaw, tell us that one." He and Hrethric wriggled under their blankets as I sat down on the edge of the sleeping bench.

"One day, the gods of the Aesir were horrified to learn that Mjolnir, Thor's hammer, had been stolen by the giant Trym while Thor slept. This was a grave matter, for Mjolnir could be used both to destroy and to create."

Hrethric nodded sagely. "Remember, Hrothmund, how scared you were in that thunderstorm when Thor banged his hammer so loud?"

In response, Hrothmund pulled the blanket over his head.

"Don't tease your brother, Hrethric. You too used to shake when Thor banged his hammer."

"Aw ... go on with the story, Freaw."

"Very well. The gods decided to send Loki, that trickster, to see if the giants would give the hammer back. To speed himself on this journey, Loki borrowed Freyja's feather cloak. When he arrived in the giants' world, he found Trym sitting on his high seat twining golden collars for his hounds and braiding the manes of his horses. Loki got right to the point.

"'Have you hidden Thor's hammer?' he asked.

"'Yes' roared the giant. 'I have hidden it eight days journey beneath the ground; no man shall fetch it back again unless he brings me Freyja to be my wife.'

"Loki at once flew back to the Aesir's courts, where he repeated Trym's words. Thor immediately sought out the fair lady and told her, 'Array yourself, Freyja, in bridal gown. We two must go to the giant world.'

"Freyja flew into such a rage that the hall shook, and the Brisinga necklace she always wore shattered, sending gold and jewels in all directions. Since she refused to become the giant's bride, a council was called to decide what to do."

"Just like Father does," interjected Hrethric.

"At the council," I continued, "Heimdal the White had an idea: 'Let us dress Thor in a bridal gown and let him wear the Brisinga mene. Let him also wear a bunch of rattling keys.'"

"Just like Mother," piped up Hrothmund.

"Yes, like Mother ... 'and a woman's garb falling about his knees, upon his breast broad rounded stones, and bridal linen upon his head.' Thor did not like this idea one bit, but he was persuaded by the others that this was the only way to get his hammer back. Loki volunteered to go with him as the bridesmaid, and off they went.

"At his hall, Trym commanded the other giants to strew the benches with sweet-smelling rushes, to bring golden-horned cows and all-black oxen, and to prepare a feast for his bride. At the bridal dinner that night,

Thor ate one whole ox, eighty salmon, all the dainties meant for the women, and he drank three kegs of mead."

"A whole ox?" Hrethric clapped a hand to his mouth. "I bet it gave him a belly-ache!" Hrothmund joined his brother in pantomiming gastric distress.

"Trym, noting this, said, 'When did you ever see a bride with a broader bite? Or a maiden drink more mead?'

"To which Loki answered, 'Freyja ate nothing for eight whole days, such was her longing to come to the giant world.'

"Then Trym bent beneath the veil to kiss the bride, but staggered back the length of the hall. 'Why are Freyja's glances so fierce?' he demanded. 'Her eyes burn like fire.'

"To which Loki responded, 'Freyja slept not for eight whole nights, such was her longing to come to the giant world.'

"Then the giant's sister came in. 'Give me the red gold rings from your hands, if you would win my love and my favor,' she said to Thor."

"Freaw," interrupted Hrethric, "this story is too long."

"Hush, I'm getting to the good part right now. Let me see ... oh, yes ... Trym said, 'Bring in the hammer to consecrate the bride. Lay Mjolnir in the maiden's lap and join our hands with the wedding band.'"

Hrethric jumped up in glee. "I know what Thor does next: he grabs the hammer and smacks all those giants in the head!"

"Well, yes, he does—I mean, he did—including the sister who demanded a bridal gift. Now it's time to sleep. Back under the blankets, you two, or I won't tell you any more stories next time you ask."

I kissed the boys, loving the feel of their soft, smooth cheeks against my lips. Later, on my own bench, I thought about the story I had just recounted. Would I ever be asked to marry against my will? Mother and Willa said that it would be my duty to obey Father's wishes in such matters, that king's daughters were often expected to become peace-weavers, bringing peace where there had been conflict between tribes. That sounded like a big challenge, hopefully one I'd never have to face.

Little did I know what lay in my future.

My immediate attention was focused on Unferth, whose preparations to meet the Grendel were almost complete. I knew this because he drew me aside one day to entrust me with a special gift.

"This is Hrunting ... the sword with which I killed my two brothers. I have not drawn it since that dark day, and I will not draw it against the Grendel. If I should fall, I want you to cast it on my funeral pyre."

Speechless, I nodded. Hrunting was a beautiful sword with a long, damascened blade and runes carved upon the hilt. "What do the runes say?" I rubbed a finger over the shapes but did not recognize them.

"It is a charm to protect the one who wields the sword."

"Then why not use it against the Grendel?"

"Odin has revealed to me that I am to rely on no metal made by man; I must rely only upon my own wits and my magic."

"What is your plan?" I asked breathlessly.

"Wolfsbane."

"Wolfsbane? That herb you spoke of to Mother?"

"Yes. It is a deadly poison. I have obtained its roots and will prepare a decoction to welcome the Grendel."

I was dubious. "How will you get the monster to take this poison?"

He laughed hollowly. "That is the question; the answer has not yet been given to me."

"Is there anything I can do to help you?"

Immediately I felt foolish for asking, but to my surprise, Unferth responded with a sudden, "Yes," as though an idea had just occurred to him.

"I will need a strong fabric, one woven of nettles. You and your brothers could help by gathering them."

For days after that, we used every free moment to roam the fields, farmsteads, moors, and hills collecting nettles for Unferth. Our fingers bled from pulling the prickly stalks, and more than once I had to bribe the boys with honey to keep them searching. At night, I applied thyme and mint leaves to our skin where the nettle hairs had stung us and prepared a hot drink from the leaves as an antidote to the swelling.

When we had gathered several large sacks of the noxious weed, Unferth took them to Mother and explained what he wanted. She immediately set Brita and Gyda to work separating out the fibers in each stalk for spinning. Mother herself wove the fibers into fabric. It took her many hours to produce enough cloth to cover a grown man—part of Unferth's request. Her own hands turned so red and rough before the task was done that she had to bathe them in oat water, but she persevered, even working at night by lamplight.

A cloak of nettles. Who was to wear it?

Soon everyone in Heorot knew that Unferth was planning some sort of magic attack to rid us of the Grendel monster. Derision and despair alternated with admiration for the boldness—or foolhardiness—needed for such a project. Unferth himself gave no clues and answered no questions, seeming not to hear the few who dared broach the subject directly. Only we who were his allies, we women and children, knew a part of his plan.

"When will you do it, Unferth? When will you fight the Grendel?" Hrethric's question echoed my own unspoken thoughts.

"I wait only for the return of darkness. Now the nights are short, but soon they will grow longer. Soon."

I shivered, torn between fear for Unferth and fear of the monster. As summer waned, I watched the sun set lower each day, wondering when "soon" might come. It happened unexpectedly.

Father was giving a banquet in the mead hall to divide the spoils from a recent raid. Gyda and Brita were called to serve it. Shortly before dark, they came back to the women's house in a state of excitement.

"It's tonight—he's going to do it tonight," hissed Gyda. "We'll be mopping up again in the morning."

I did not have to ask who they meant. Instead, I burst into tears. Mother hushed me and demanded information. "What did you hear? What did he say?"

"The other men were taunting him—good-natured-like—about his plan to attack the Grendel, when he pulled a dagger from Sven's belt. I thought there'd be a fight, but Unferth slashed the dagger across his own arm. 'Blood!' he cried, 'blood will be my bait. Who will lend me some of his?'"

"That silenced the boasters, I can tell you. They left pretty fast after that, until only Unferth and Hrothgar were left in the hall."

"Where is Hrothgar now? Surely he did not stay…"

"No, my lady, he did not stay. Unferth asked him to leave, saying he had preparations to make."

"What kind of preparations?"

"I don't know, but he bid us build up the hearth fire before we left—and when I looked back, he was smearing his own blood on the door of Heorot."

Mother's face reflected my own perplexity. "Brita. Where is the cloak of nettles we wove for Unferth? Does it still hang behind the loom?"

Brita lifted a wall torch and peered into the dark corner. "It's gone."

"Then let us pray to the gods to protect him!"

That night we waited in an agony of suspense. Would the Grendel come? Would Unferth be able to kill it or drive it away? Would Unferth himself survive?

Soon , too soon, inhuman screams rent the darkness. We huddled, cowering in our blankets. Howls … of rage, of … fright? More screams and then thudding feet as if an army were tramping out of Heorot. Out? Yes—out! Out! The monster must be fleeing! But what had it left behind?

I sprang from my bench and ran toward the door, but Mother's arms caught me before I could reach it. "Don't be a fool. The monster may still be roaming outside."

"But Unferth—he may be hurt, dying …"

"He took that risk for our sakes. We will not waste his effort. We stay inside until morning light."

My heart ached, though I heard the wisdom in her words. I lay back down, but sleep would not come. Visions of Unferth floated before me: his white face covered with blood, his mouth twisted in a strange …

smile. When could we go? How long must we wait? Unferth needed us!

At first light, Hrothgar and his men cautiously approached Heorot, we women close behind. Its doors were once again wrenched askew, though they still hung on their hinges. Foul droppings littered the path. The air smelled of burnt flesh and hair. Holding our breaths, we stepped across the threshold.

By the light of the smoke hole, I could see a crumpled figure lying beside the hearth. As we approached, it seemed to stir. Father held out a torch.

"Unferth, do you live?" Father's voice was unexpectedly gentle as he knelt and touched the still figure. The head turned. Unferth's face was bruised and bloody, he could only open one eye, and his limbs were twisted—but he was clearly alive.

"He lives! The gods be praised! This man must have special favor in their eyes."

In the wonder of the moment, we shouted with relief and astonishment: "He lives!"

"My lord, don't move him," Mother cried sharply. "He may have broken bones or other injuries inside his body. We women will tend to him."

She too knelt and began slowly to straighten his arms and legs, feeling each one carefully. Unferth groaned, and his eyes closed. Finally satisfied that he could be moved, Mother bade the men lift Unferth and carry him to the women's house—where she put him on her own sleeping bench. In response to Hrothgar's quizzical look, she said, "He will need constant care. We will tell you when he is able to talk. Have patience. It is miracle enough for now that he has survived."

We had to wait many days to hear the full story. All the strength seemed to have drained out of Unferth. At first he could barely whisper, but bit by bit he began to reveal the events of that night. Father, Mother, and several of Father's counselors were seated by the bed one night as

Unferth spoke. My brothers and I had been allowed to join them on condition that we keep absolutely silent.

As we knew, he had used his own blood to signal his presence in the mead hall, and as he hoped, the Grendel took the bait.

Propped up with blankets, Unferth took a sip of ale before beginning his tale.

"I waited with my back against the wall beside the door, knowing the monster must enter that way. On the far side of the hearth I had laid what looked to be the body of a sleeping man, covered with a cloth of nettles drenched in wolfsbane."

"So that was your plan—to trick the monster!" I burst out.

"Yes." Unferth turned toward the sound of my voice. "But I knew he would soon discover the deception. To allow the poison time to do its work, I entertained him with flaming brands I'd made ready at the hearth—throwing them at his face and eyes."

My eyes grew wide at this calm recital of unimaginable courage. "What happened when he saw you?"

"With fire in his eyes, I don't think he ever saw me, but he could still smell me. He struck blindly at me, hurling me against walls and benches. But pieces of the poisoned cloak still clung to his mouth and stung him. Finally he charged wildly out of Heorot to escape the burning." Unferth paused to catch his breath from this long recounting.

"If he never returns, the poison did its work. If not—I have failed."

"Failed? Never! You faced the monster and survived. No other man has done that!" Father's verdict expressed the admiration on every face.

"We shall see. For now, I must sleep."

In a month's time, Unferth had recovered physically, but his mind seemed to wander in dark places. At such times he would not speak—to me, to anyone. His self-inflicted wound festered and left an ugly scar. We all waited anxiously to see if the Grendel would return. A seed of hope began to grow, as night after night passed with no attack. Still, the mead hall remained vacant after nightfall.

Without Unferth to talk to, I sometimes turned to Golden, my cat. Once Holger's cat, and then Willa's cat, she was now my cat. She had long since ceased to hiss at me; in fact I often found her curled in a ball on my sleeping bench when not outdoors preening in the sunshine or hunting in the granary for tiny velvet mice to bring me as an offering. When I buried my nose in her tawny fur and stroked her sides, she rumbled with pleasure.

"Golden, what do you think?" I lifted her face to mine so her whiskers tickled me. "Has the Grendel gone? Will it never come back?"

Her yellow eyes stared into mine; then she arched her back and yawned.

"So you don't know either?" She blinked and then shut her eyes. I sighed. "Nobody knows."

The next morning, however, it was Golden who gave us the answer. Her yowling outside the mead hall brought me running. She stood stiff-legged, back arched, tail up. I called to Wulfgar, just coming up the path to take his turn as door guard. It was broad daylight; surely we did not need to fear the Grendel's presence. Still, Wulfgar listened long before he slowly opened the door.

The stench of manure and swamp water struck us. A mound of dung lay heaped beside the cold hearth. The Grendel was back.

Chapter 4
First Blood

My brothers and I were playing near the granary late one afternoon when Father and his hunting party rode up at a gallop on sweat-soaked horses. I looked up in surprise, for no carcasses hung behind the riders. Rarely did they return from a hunt without game of some kind. As the men dismounted, I heard low murmurs and saw them casting strange glances at each other.

"What do you think it was?"

"Nothing I've ever seen before—neither man nor beast."

"And the water—did you see the color of the water?"

"No, my horse bolted—I mean, there were too many riders in front of me."

"Father, Aeschere, what are you talking about? What did you see?" Hrethric boldly asked the questions swirling in my own head.

Father did not answer, but Aeschere seemed eager to talk. He bent low over us as his horse was led away.

"We were following a deer—a fine stag with a rack much like that which hangs over the door of Heorot—a real prize. It took us far from our usual hunting ground toward the great swamp in the West. Few of us have ventured into that dismal waste, a place of darkness and treacherous terrain, but the dogs were hard upon the deer, and we were almost in bow range. Then it reached the fen."

Here Aeschere paused and shook his head in wonder.

"The stag stopped short at the water's edge and seemed to consider, lowering its head and shaking its antlers. Then it turned to face the dogs, which fell upon it and tore it to pieces."

"Why didn't the deer swim away and save itself?" asked Hrethric, wide-eyed.

"Aye, that's the question I'm asking myself," Aeschere responded. "But there was something else ... some ... thing ... in the water, thrashing just below the surface. It spooked the horses; they reared and bolted for home—and so you see us here."

In an undertone to Hrothgar, he added one more piece of information: "I saw something else on a ledge above the fen. It looked like a head, a human head ... but when I looked again it was gone."

Aeschere glanced at me and saw me staring at him. "What is it, child?"

I could not answer, gripped by a vision that his words had summoned. It was Aeschere's own head on the ledge! I saw wet, tangled locks stuck to his ashen face, eyes rolled back in their sockets, and his tongue dripping blood. Shuddering, I shook my head to clear it of this apparition.

"Don't worry, Freaw; whatever lives there, that swamp lies far from Heorot." Aeschere gave my shoulder a pat and turned to follow Father.

This stag hunt was much talked about for weeks, and then gradually forgotten—by most. Unferth pondered the story, questioned each man for details, and conferred often with Aeschere. Most of the other athelings gave Unferth a wide berth; the men respected his bravery, but felt uneasy in his presence.

"He sees right through you," one man commented. From my own experience, I could have told him that this was indeed so.

Following his recovery, Unferth had gradually assumed the role of priest. Now he led the hall ceremonies at solstice celebrations and presided over public sacrifices. It was also rumored that he and a small group of Hrothgar's younger thanes met secretly in a distant grove of oak trees to worship Odin.

Unferth no longer confided in me. Since his failure to drive out the Grendel, he had become even more aloof, withdrawing into himself. Only in the mead hall did he seem to relax. Brita and Gyda reported that he drank deeply of ale and seemed to welcome the stupor it produced. But he would rouse himself when I approached him outside Heorot to ask for another lesson in rune carving.

Now that I was "almost a woman" as Willa put it, there were fewer opportunities to escape from daily tasks. I resorted to using Hrethric and Hrothmund, now six and four, as my excuse, feigning a need to instruct them in various pursuits.

I was determined to gain knowledge of all twenty-four runes. So far, I knew how to carve Algiz (its memory preserved in a scar on the tip of my middle finger); Fehu, the rune of wealth, which I related to Freya's Brisingamen; Ansuz for Odin/God; Teiwaz for warrior/victory; and Ehwaz, the horse rune. But I was still learning their uses and knew I had not mastered their full meaning. While the boys played in the branches of the great oak tree, Unferth and I worked beneath them.

One day while we were thus employed, I felt a growing pain in my belly, followed by a wetness between my legs. Alarmed, I looked down and saw reddish spots emerging on my tunic. Could it be? My discomfort did not escape Unferth's hooded eyes.

"Do you bleed?" he asked matter-of-factly.

"Yes … I think so. I must go … to see Mother. Boys, come down quickly! We need to return."

"There is no need; your brothers are safe with me." Unferth laid his hand on my arm and looked at me directly. "First blood makes strong magic. Tell your mother it is time to test your powers."

"If you say so … I'll give her your words."

I should have expected this. I was twelve, after all. Mother had begun to bleed at the age of ten, as had Willa. But the day of my "womanhood" had seemed so far off that its sudden arrival found me unprepared. Folding my shift in front of me, I hurried awkwardly away.

In the women's house, Mother helped me make the necessary physical arrangements. I'd seen the women with their moon rags all my life and knew how to tie one beneath my shift, so this was easily done. But Mother had other arrangements in mind as well.

"Unferth is right," she said thoughtfully. "We must prepare a ritual introducing you to the goddess—and see what will come of it."

"What do you mean, Mother? Will it be like cutting off our hair?" I almost added "to no avail." Since that ritual six winters ago—it seemed a lifetime—my own hair had grown long again. It lay in two braids down my back. Mother kept her hair covered by day, as was the custom for married women, but I knew that hers now showed signs of gray. Then a happy thought struck me. "May I wear jewelry now, Mother?"

She laughed at my delight and anticipation.

"You may indeed. In fact, you may expect a gift from each member of our household."

I glowed at this news. For months I had been secretly coveting the adornments of the older women. Even Willa owned one silver ring.

"I will tell your father tonight, and we will arrange a feast. But before that, we must visit the sacred pool."

Willa put my stained clothes to soak and helped me bathe, strewing the water with mint leaves, and then dressed me in a newly woven shift of white linen.

"I can dress myself, Willa," I protested.

"Of course you can, but this is a special day. Let me do this for you."

She combed sweet-smelling oil into my hair and then pulled it up into a topknot, letting its amber waves fall freely to my shoulders. She stood back to admire her handiwork.

"Can it be twelve winters?" she marveled. "I remember the day you were born," she sniffed and blinked back sudden tears.

"Did you say 'thank the gods' then?" I asked to tease her.

"Didn't have to—you were born with the mark of Freyja on you— clearly you had already been chosen."

"Chosen for what?" This "mark of Freyja" business annoyed me. That silly birthmark again. "No one has ever really told me what it is supposed to mean. Can you tell me, Willa? Now that I'm ... a woman?" A woman? Me? The idea brought mixed feelings.

"Best let your mother explain that. Speaking of the queen, she must be ready for us. Let's not keep her waiting. Oh, but first you must drink this, brewed especially for you."

Obediently I drained the cup she handed me, its taste unfamiliar.

This time the assembled women wore light summer clothing, and it was midday when we set forth. But again, Mother carried a small bag; again, I followed her; and again, Willa came last. Farm women nodded to us from their doorways as we passed; one called out a greeting: "May the goddess be with you, king's daughter. May your vision help us all."

I turned to look back at her.

"What does she mean, Mother? What vision?"

"Patience. Keep silent. We will soon know."

This time I recognized the pool, which looked far less mysterious in the sunlight. At the hut, Mother once again picked up the ash staff and drew a circle on the ground—a very small circle this time. From her bag she took a small drum.

"Freawaru, enter the circle."

I obeyed, glad that I had not been asked to remove my clothes and expose my moon cloth. The other women arranged themselves around and outside the circle. When all were quiet, Mother lifted her arms and began.

"Freyja, dear goddess of life and love, we greet you. Here is your daughter, Freawaru. She bears the mark of a feather from your cloak. Now grown to womanhood, she bleeds as we all do. Give her wings to leave this world and fly to greet you. Share with her your wisdom, great goddess."

Into the center of the circle she dropped a white feather and then faced me, smiling reassurance.

"Freawaru, step to the rhythm of my drum, following the circle's edge. Follow it sunwise, keeping Freyja's feather ever on your right. Women, as you pass the cup of blood, begin your song."

Willa held up one of Father's gold goblets and handed it to Ana. Mother picked up her drum and began to strike it slowly.

Cup of blood? Now I realized why Willa had asked me to relieve myself in the basin rather than go outside to the latrine before my bath. Surely they were not going to drink it? But no, as the cup passed, each woman dipped a finger and touched it to her own forehead. At the same time, they began to chant in rhythm with Mother's drum.

Blood of the body, blood of renewal, blood of life.
Blood of the body, blood of renewal, blood of life.

I began to revolve in the narrow space, trying to keep my eyes fixed on the feather, but it soon became a blur. The drum beat on relentlessly. I was sweating, my head spinning. Soon I lost all sense of my body and felt lifted out of myself. Had my swans returned?

Yes! I was flying! I myself had become the swan, for I felt my wings beat the air. Joyously I soared to dizzying heights and then coasted on the currents. As I floated weightlessly, I turned my face to look down. Far below me I saw … what was this? Heorot? Heorot on fire—Heorot burning! With a shriek, I plummeted to earth—hard ground rushed up to meet me.

"Come back, Freawaru, come back to us. Your flight is over. You are safely home. Come back."

I opened my eyes, saw Mother's face, and then sank into darkness again.

When I came back to myself, my head lay in Willa's lap. Mother was bathing my face with cool water from the pool.

"It's all my fault," sobbed Willa. "She fell so sudden; I couldn't catch her."

"Hush, Freaw is awake. The goddess has preserved her. She's taken no harm. Freawaru—my daughter—what did you see?"

"Oh, Mother," I gasped. "Heorot—Father's hall—it was burning!"

A shudder passed through the circle at my words. No further words were spoken as Mother and Willa helped me to my feet. Slowly we began our journey back to the doomed hall.

"Yet it may not be what actually is to come. The vision may have been sent as a warning to help us prevent such a catastrophe."

"Maybe we *should* burn it down—set fire to it with the monster inside!"

My parents' voices woke me from a light slumber. I jerked my head up and looked around. Sated with food and drink, I had nodded off as we sat at the mead hall table.

"Do not despair, my husband. Take heart. Look, your daughter awaits your kiss. Go to her. Welcome her to her womanhood."

A kiss? It had been years since my father had kissed me. Surely I did not deserve such an honor now, bearer of bad tidings that I was. Despite these thoughts, I lifted my face when he came to me. Placing his big hands on my shoulders, he kissed me on the forehead. Then, sighing deeply, Father returned to his seat. Suddenly he sat bolt upright.

"No more trances! No more! I do not wish to know what ill fate the gods may have in store for us! Let *Wyrd*, let Fate, come as it will!"

As we sat gripped in silence, a new voice spoke: "All may yet be well. Welcome to your womanhood, king's daughter. Please accept my small gift."

Shaking my head to clear it, I looked up and down the table. Father sat in his high seat, Mother at one side, Hrothulf on the other. Then came Hrethric, Hrothmund, Willa, and … Unferth? When had he joined us?

As if in answer to my unspoken question, he raised his voice. "I asked to be present on this occasion, and your parents graciously consented."

Unferth rose, walked to my side of the table, and handed me a small leather pouch. Wondering, I felt inside and drew forth two amber drops set in silver.

"In other lands, women wear them in their ears," he said quietly. "Some say they contain the fire of the sun. I say they represent the tears of Freyja. May yours be tears of joy, not sorrow, king's daughter. All may yet be well."

"Oh, Unferth, thank you. I don't deserve them, I—"

"Freaw, Freaw, open ours next!" The grinning faces of my two little brothers appeared at my elbow, holding up another small pouch. This one held a string of glass beads containing all the colors of the rainbow. I held the necklace up to the light.

"Oh, it's beautiful! How did you know I wanted one?"

"We didn't, but Willa said—"

"Shut up, Hrothmund. We helped pick it out, Freaw." As usual, Hrethric sought precedence over his younger brother. I grinned at them both.

Willa then sidled up with something clutched in each hand. She opened them to reveal two oval brooches cast in bronze.

"There's a new pinafore to go with these, but I haven't had time to finish it."

"Dear Willa, thank you for these gifts. You always take care of me."

Next Mother presented me with two silver arm bracelets, sinuous spiral serpents. "May they protect you from evil," she said.

Father turned and glared meaningfully at Hrothulf, who finally roused himself enough to slide a package down the table. "Here—I made it myself."

Suspiciously, I unwrapped the folded cloth. Inside lay an antler comb decorated with iron pins. I laughed inwardly. Made it himself? Any fool knew what time and skill it took to create such an object. I had once stood beside a comb maker on a trading day, watching him cut the side-pieces from red deer antler, fasten in the tooth plates with iron rivets, and then cut the teeth with a fine saw. Such exacting work lay far beyond Hrothulf's capabilities. Nevertheless, I nodded and smiled at him.

"Why … thank you, Hrothulf. It's perfect."

"Good for finding lice and fleas—just joking!" he added hastily as Mother looked over sternly. Then she turned toward me.

"Now, Freawaru, your father has a special gift for you. Something for your dowry."

My dowry? Surely they were not going to marry me off—to some stranger? There had been no talk of marriage heretofore. Surely it couldn't be—Unferth?

Father was lifting something bright and shiny from a small chest, beckoning me to come forward. Around my neck he clasped a golden neck ring—not as magnificent as Mother's, but still a kingly gift. My eyes filled with tears.

"Thank you, Father. I shall always be proud to say that I am Hrothgar's daughter. But … when am I to be married?"

He burst into loud laughter.

"Not for many a day, daughter Freawaru. You may be a woman now, but you are not yet ready to become a wife. I am sure your mother and Willa have a few more things to teach you."

Relief flooded over me. Father's laughter restored our good mood, so my womanhood celebration ended on a happy note—and none too soon, as light was beginning to fade in the west. Time to seek refuge for the night, refuge from the Grendel.

That evening's celebration appeared to reawaken Hrothulf's interest in me; he began to seek occasions to find me alone—to torment me as of old, I supposed. But now there was a difference. One day in the granary, he came up behind me, slid his hand under my pinafore, and whispered sly words in my ear. I recoiled so violently that my head hit his front teeth; he backed away with blood on his lips.

"Little bitch," he hissed. "I'll get you for this. Or … better yet, I'll get Hrothmund."

I knew that he was quite capable of taking out his anger on my four-year-old brother. "What is it you want?" I spoke firmly, but my knees trembled.

"Don't you know? I thought you were a woman now." He almost sneered. "A woman would let me touch her, look at her. Let me—"

I did not stay to hear more, but fled to the kitchen, forgetting that I was supposed to be bringing more grain to be ground into flour. What should I do? Tell Mother or Willa? Would I dare speak to Father? Father might not believe me, I reflected bitterly, for Hrothulf could do no wrong in his eyes. Perhaps Unferth could advise me. Then I remembered Algiz, the rune of protection, the rune stained with my own blood. Could Algiz help me? Could I release its power? I decided to find out.

As soon as I had an opportunity, I sought out Unferth at the oak tree, where he spent much time alone.

"Unferth, to activate a rune, do words need to be said over it—directions given, I mean, to bring forth its power?"

"Why do you ask? Are you in need?" He looked at me closely.

"Yes, though I'd rather not say why." I looked up into the tree and then back down at Unferth, who regarded me intently. Was he seeing right through me?

"If it is a curse you're after … but wait, you've not been shown such runes as yet. So it must be protection that is needed. Am I right?"

I nodded, not looking him in the eye.

"Then you'll want Algiz. Keep it upon your person, hidden in your clothing." He sighed, as if a heavy duty had been laid upon him. "Keep it with you at all times. Tell the rune who or what it is to protect you from. Imagine the rune creating a space around you which evil cannot enter. Then believe in your own magic."

"Thank you, Unferth. You always have an answer for me." I turned to go.

"You honor me by asking, king's daughter. And perhaps," he added, "it is time to teach you other runes—now that you are a woman." Before I left, he gave me one of his rare smiles.

How was it that Unferth made me feel good about becoming a woman, while Hrothulf's words filled me only with disgust and dread? That same afternoon I unearthed my rune sticks from beneath the oak tree roots and selected Algiz. Brushing off the dried leaves and dirt, I held up the stick and addressed it as if it were my doll Hunig.

"I need your help, Algiz. Keep Hrothulf away from me and prevent him from harming Hrothmund. This is Freawaru who asks for your aid."

Not knowing what else to do, I kissed it. Then an anxious thought crossed my mind. I didn't know if the rune could protect two people at once—I'd forgotten to ask Unferth that detail—but I fervently hoped it could.

I took out my knife and cut a small hole in the stick and then strung it on a strip of deer hide I'd brought with me. Lifting my shift, I tied the thong around my waist. Just putting it there made me feel more secure, but the real test would come the next time I encountered Hrothulf.

Such a confrontation came the very next day. Willa had sent me out to gather fresh herbs for drying; I was alone with my harvest basket when Hrothulf rode by on his chestnut pony. He slowed, glanced at me with a twisted smile, and then kicked his horse into a gallop, leaving me in a cloud of dust. It worked! I was exultant: Algiz had protected me! Joyfully I went about the herb gathering, proud of my newfound power.

It was many months before I learned the real reason for my deliverance: Unferth. He had threatened to shrivel Hrothulf's genitals if he ever bothered me again.

Since I had now become a woman, Mother decided it was time for me to begin a serious study of medicinal herbs. Of course, I already knew how to prepare many herbs, having helped Willa over the years. I could steep leaves and roots to make tea, mash herbs into a paste for poultices, and even mix oils and beeswax to create salves. One evening, after our meal, Mother led me into the herb garden next to the kitchen.

"Freaw, since you have started your bleeding, I will first show you plants that are helpful to lessen the problems it may bring. Flaxseed you already know: it will help regulate your times. Motherwort controls excessive bleeding."

She paused and reached down to pluck a blossom. "Notice the pink and purple flowers and the outer leaves which are spiny and toothlike. Many herbs that aid digestion can also be taken as a tea for stomach pain, such as chamomile, valerian, and cramp-bark. Use only the dried roots of valerian. Cramp-bark comes from those small shrubs with white flowers sometimes called viburnum."

My brain was already reeling, but she kept on talking, taking no notice of my confusion.

"The best antidote for nausea is ginger, but that must be obtained by trade—it does not grow in this country. Before your cycle begins, a time when you may feel irritable, burdock and dandelion tea can be drunk. Yarrow is also an excellent medicine for many women's problems, but the yarrow must be made into a tincture. Now mallow …"

So much to learn! I knew that someday I would be expected to know how to treat all sorts of sickness and injury, just as my mother did now. A heavy weight seemed to settle on my shoulders.

"What if you make a mistake, Mother? I mean, what if I make a mistake?"

She looked at me with sympathy in her eyes.

"There is much to learn. I will oversee your work as you practice. Mistakes can be dangerous—even fatal. For example, if you confuse mugwort and wormwood, which look much alike, it could cause the death of a woman in childbirth. I do not tell you this to frighten you," she said gently, "but so that you will be attentive to details. Take heart, my daughter. Remember that Willa is also here to help you."

But two days later, Willa was gone.

I was the first to miss her. That morning an uneasy dream had awakened me, a dream of loss; I had risen on one elbow to look about and clear my head. Willa's sleeping bench was empty, but that caused me no alarm. She'd probably gone early to the kitchen to build up the hearth fire. Quietly I rose, careful not to awaken other sleepers. Our guards were gone, so I knew it must be light enough to go outside safely. As I pulled on my tunic, I wondered when Willa was going to finish the pinafore she'd promised me. I couldn't wait to fasten its straps with the new bronze brooches. Maybe I'd help her in the kitchen this morning. Sleepily, I stumbled over to the eld-hus, but no smoke rose from the roof opening.

"Willa?" I peered inside. No stir of life. Perhaps she'd gone out to the garden to pluck herbs for a poultice—Father had been complaining lately of a rash on his back.

I walked along the wattle fencing, humming a melody to match the birds in the nearby trees. I drew in a deep breath, savoring the scents of each plant: pungent, fragrant, sweet. Bees buzzed above the blossoms. Even the stiff, dried carcasses of ravens hung along the fence to scare off crows could not disturb me on such a fine, fresh morning. It promised to be a good day.

"Willa?"

On the far side of the garden, my foot slipped on something slimy. Ahead of me a cloud of flies—not bees—buzzed over a pile of ... guts. In their midst shone a silver ring, still circling part of a finger.

"Willa? Willa!" I gagged and choked as my stomach rose into my throat.

"W-Willa? Willaaaaaaaaaa!"

My cries brought men and women running from their quarters. Ulf, one of Father's hall guards, reached me first.

"Stay back, my lady, go no further. There is evil here."

I stood frozen, rooted in shock. The house slaves rushed past me in a flock, chattering like magpies.

"Willa, is it? Why would she go out in the dark?" cried Brita.

"Foolish woman!" barked Gyda. "Surely she knew the danger. Now it may come back for the rest of us!"

The sound of a resounding smack broke my trance. Mother, her face contorted with fear and fury, towered over a crumpled Gyda. Our eyes met, and she strode forward to gather me in her arms. As she held me to her bosom, I shook with great, gasping sobs.

When she spoke, however, it was not to me.

"Death must come to us all, but I would not have wished such a death for you, dear friend."

She looked past me to the knot of men examining the ground. Raising my head, my eyes followed hers. Little could be found. I saw them hold up Willa's shredded cloak, a few strands of her gray hair, and one mangled finger with a silver ring. This was all that remained of my Willa, my lifelong friend.

Ulf spoke solemnly to those assembled.

"She was attacked, fought her attacker, was gutted, and dragged away. This much can be told from the remains and marks left on the path. Poor woman."

"Poor woman," echoed someone behind me. "What could have caused such a vicious attack?"

"Surely we are beset by a fiend." Mother's voice choked as she led me away, guiding me back to the women's house.

Inside I rushed to Willa's bench, threw myself on it, and pulled her robes about me, shivering uncontrollably. Willa's warmth was gone, but her smell, achingly familiar, remained. Willa, where are you?

I had always gone to Willa in times of emergency, but now Willa was no more—Willa was dead—killed—eaten by a monster. Monster? Yes, for surely the Grendel had murdered her. Exhausted with grief and crying, I fell into a light doze. Hardly had I closed my eyes than I saw her; Willa, not dead, but alive and smiling at me! She held out her hands, but as I reached to take them, she disappeared.

When I woke, the horror of her death returned to me full force, slamming into my stomach like a fist. I vomited, over and over, until nothing more remained. The image of Willa being eaten alive—bitten—chewed—and swallowed—consumed me.

"Freawaru—child—drink this."

Mother was holding me up, wiping my face, and offering me a drink. Catnip. I recognized the smell. Only yesterday Willa had taught me the several uses of catnip, including its power to soothe the stomach. I turned my head away.

"I can't. I can't eat or drink—ever again!"

For the moment Mother let me be, struggling with her own sorrow.

In the days that followed, I recognized the depths of my father's despair, for I now shared it. Opening my eyes in the morning was an effort too great to make. I could not eat, though Mother coaxed me with my favorite oat cakes flavored with honey. I could not lift my hand to the simplest task. Hrethric and Hrothmund begged me to go with them to the oak tree, once our favorite spot, but I barely understood their words. Sealed in a gray world without light, without air, without color—without Willa—I grieved and turned my face to the wall.

One morning, the ordinary bustle and stir of women rising was interrupted by a visitor. Brita and Gyda, who had been arguing as usual, stopped talking abruptly. In the sudden silence, I heard Father's voice.

"Freawaru? Daughter? How fare you?"

He lifted my hand and brushed it against his cheek, rough with stubble. He smelled of ale and horses. I lifted my eyelids and tried to smile.

"Come for a ride with me?" His tone was gentle, almost pleading.

"To the mounds, Father? No, I'll go there soon enough."

Why bother to rise? Father could not save Willa from the monster. He could not save me now. He was powerless, and we were all doomed. I closed my eyes.

With a sigh and a squeeze of my hand, Father rose to go. Faintly, I heard muffled words and Mother's voice as I drifted off to sleep—my only refuge.

That evening, collapsed and feverish on my sleeping bench, I closed my eyes to shut out the waning light. Darkness suited me. Suddenly my body convulsed, as darkness greater than I had ever known seized me and pulled me under.

Was someone calling my name? Father? With a great effort I raised my head—and found myself riding on his shoulders, a little girl again. We strode toward the harbor in clear sunlight. But something was amiss: where were Father's ships? Where were my swans? Without warning, the ground gave way beneath us. I lost my grasp, and Father ... let me fall—fall—fall. I screamed, but could not hear my own voice.

Strong fingers clutched at my wrist ... a disembodied hand. On the middle finger shone a silver ring. Willa? Willa! Where are you? I can't see you! Alas, the hand dissolved in blood, slipping away.

With a jolt, another pair of hands, rough and scaly, seized my ankles, piercing skin and bone with sharp nails that bit and burned. "Let me go!" I twisted desperately, struggling to break free, but they pulled me down relentlessly.

Now a terrible stench filled my nostrils and a great, gaping maw rushed up to meet me, a bloody mouth with jagged teeth. It opened wide to swallow me whole.

"Freawaru, daughter, open your eyes! Look at me! Come back to us!"

From a great distance, I heard my mother's voice. With a shudder, I swam to the surface and opened my eyes. Her face came into focus and then the face of another—perhaps—Unferth?

"Unferth? Why are you here? Go away. You have no magic to bring the dead to life. You would only fail—again."

Bitterly I turned my face away. No force could stand against the Grendel. We would all die. I should die now, not wait for the darkness to seize me and crush out my life. I must have been speaking out loud, for Unferth seized my shoulders and shook me fiercely.

"King's daughter! It is not your time to die!"

"Why not, Unferth?"

"Because I am going on a journey—and you must come with me."

A journey? What journey? Wondering, I opened my eyes and looked into his, dark and deep as the fjord. "When? Where? How will we go?"

"Now—by boat—to the edge of the world."

The idea was so ridiculous that I began to laugh.

Chapter 5
Journey to the Moon

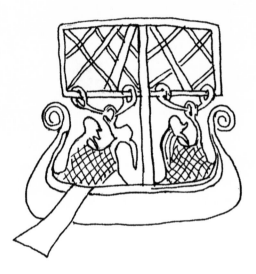

As it turned out, we did not go to the end of the world, but certainly much farther than I'd ever traveled. That day, I let Mother feed me a bowl of broth before I slept again. When I woke it was light, and she sat beside me, stitching a patterned braid to the bottom of a pinafore.

"Yours," she said, when my eyes opened.

"Is it the one …?"

"Yes. You may wish to wear it on your … journey. Willa wove her love for you into the fabric."

"Am I really to leave this place?"

Suddenly I was not so sure that I wanted to go anywhere at all. Yet I felt the darkness hovering over my head, ready to descend at any moment. Perhaps it would be good to leave Heorot.

"You'll be gone only for a short time—to gather herbs and plants along the coastline. Unferth will be your guide, and such of our people as can be spared will accompany you."

"But what will you do without me, Mother? I mean, with all the work to be done, now that Willa is ... gone." I choked on the word.

"Torgun, the blacksmith's wife, has consented to come to Heorot. Her daughters are old enough to take her place at home." Mother smiled. "Now ... we have preparations to make. Even for a short trip you must go forth as the king's daughter—never forget that!"

Gradually I began to take an interest in the trip as we selected items for my travel chest—once Willa's chest. I could have requested one much grander, but I wanted something of hers to hold onto. Her silver ring, I was told, had been added to the meager possessions on her funeral pyre. I was not sorry to have missed that burning.

Now, what should I take for my first journey away from home? Warm clothing, a few pieces of my jewelry ... a small tent and cooking pots ... what else would I need? Packets for gathering herbs, my knife ...

Hrethric and Hrothmund hung about looking dejected.

"Why don't *we* ever get to go anywhere?"

"Who's going to tell us stories now?"

"I'll come back with new stories of our trip," I promised. "And I've heard that you boys will soon be getting sailing lessons. One day you'll be able to go anywhere you want in the whole, wide world!"

Indeed, their instructor in the art of navigation was to be Hrothulf, who now accompanied Father and his men on raids along the coastline as far north as the land of ice and snow. Father felt that Hrothulf should take a hand in the instruction of his young cousins. This made me uneasy, but my worries were lost amid happy thoughts of my own upcoming adventure. Part of me longed to escape from Heorot, to leave behind the pall of evil that hung over it, blighting our nights, snuffing out lives.

To sail on an open boat, with the wind in my hair—that prospect brought joy to my heart. As a child, I had sometimes been allowed to sail within the harbor's boundaries, but never out into the open sea. I could almost smell the heavy scent of tar, a thought that made me remember something else as well.

"Sea sickness?" Mother nodded. "Ginger is the answer—or its preventative; you should take a bite of ginger each day before setting sail. I can send only a small bag with you, for our own supply is not great."

Olaf, Sven, Gorm, and Saxe were selected from the younger thanes to join Unferth on the boat. Ana volunteered to be my guardian on the trip. She said it would do her good to see new places. Unspoken was the fact that she would take the place once occupied by Willa. When I chose Brita to be my attendant, Mother approved.

"She is most level-headed of the house thralls and young enough to be good company. Both of you, however, need some practice rowing; you will be needed when the winds are calm."

Brita and I were equally unskilled at rowing, a circumstance which gave us common ground and much cause for laughter as we set our hands to the task. At first, we dragged our oars clumsily across the water's surface, unable as yet to dip deeply. Unferth sat at the helm, guiding us.

"Together—you have to pull together!"

Swans in the harbor fluttered off in alarm as our boat lurched in zigzag fashion through the water. Normally a larger craft designed for a crew of twelve or thirteen would be used for a sea journey, but so many could not be spared with harvest time close at hand. Brita and I would complete a crew of seven on a smaller boat. Ana was to be exempt from rowing; she would "add weight," as she put it.

"Don't worry," said Unferth, "you'll get the rhythm when the men are rowing too. You'll also build muscle, which will make the task easier."

"Build muscle? How long is this trip going to take?" I paused to wipe sweat from my eyes and looked up in alarm.

Unferth cast his gaze at the horizon. "That depends on the weather. We'll be sailing south, keeping the coastline to starboard; we'll always be in sight of land."

"How do you know the way, Unferth?"

He turned back in surprise. "I have explored many islands and many coasts in my day." He looked at me with a speculative smile. "Do you know that you live on an island?"

I shook my head in disbelief.

"It's true. We are surrounded by water, though it is sometimes far distant. This land is like a great ship floating in the sea."

A great ship—I liked the idea. A ship could carry you to places you'd never been, places that had no ... Grendel. My thoughts must have shown in my face.

"All may yet be well, king's daughter. You will live long and visit many lands in your time. For now, let's get back to rowing. Lean forward from the waist when you push against the oar, and keep your back straight as you return it—yes, that's better."

After a time our efforts came together, and Unferth nodded approval.

"Listen," he said. "I will tell you a tale while you row." Brita and I brightened in anticipation, and leaned into our work.

"It is said," he began, lifting his eyes to the horizon, "that in former days when Odin walked the earth in the guise of a man, he kept his seat at Othinsey on the island of Fyn. There he gave lands in the South and West to his many sons. Gefion he sent north to seek her own land. She went to Sweden where King Gylfi gave her a ploughland. Then she went to Jotunheim, land of the Giants, and bore four sons to one of them. She transformed her sons into oxen and attached them to the plough."

Here I wiggled with delight, knowing what came next, as I'd already heard part of this story before. Unferth paused and his voice changed pitch.

Gladsome Gefion, steeped in glory,
Pulled up Gylfi's patrimonial lands.

Unferth smiled—a rare thing to see—and continued the story.

"With that team of oxen, Gefion pulled her ploughland out of Sweden and over the sea until it was facing Othinsey." He paused, as if marveling at this feat. "That land is the very island where we now live. Some call it Sealand."

"It is said that Skjold, a son of Odin, took Gefion as his wife and made his seat where Hrothgar's hall now stands. It is also said that where the land was taken out of Sweden, a lake was left, now called Logrin."

"Unferth, are you teasing us? Can that story be true?"

Questioning Unferth? I was surprised at my boldness, yet why not? I am the king's daughter, I told myself, and a woman preparing for a journey!

Unferth seemed not to notice my challenge, for he answered calmly.

"I myself have seen Lake Logrin, and I have sailed the coasts of Sealand. The bays in that lake match the headlands of this island." Here he fell silent.

Emboldened, I asked another question.

"I'm not sure I understood about Gefion. Was she Odin's daughter?"

"No, Gefion is one of the gods—one of the Aesir who dwell in Asgard."

Eager to learn more, I was about to ask another question, but Unferth leaned forward.

"Focus on your rowing and pull together. We have almost reached the harbor."

Brita and I nodded, bending to our task. But inwardly I wondered: what became of the four oxen? Did Gefion change them back into human form? Did she not care for her own sons? Don't be foolish, I told myself. It's only a story—like those I tell the boys at bed time. Anyway, no one has the power to change a human being into an animal—do they?

An icy chill gripped my heart as a new thought struck me: shape shifters! I'd heard talk of such beings: men by day and wolves by night—or worse. Worse? Like … Grendel? A horrible possibility took shape in my mind. Could the monster be living among us as a human, transforming only at night? With a gasp, I dropped my oar. The boat lurched sideways.

Unferth looked up and pinned me with his gaze. "Freawaru, king's daughter, all is well. Do not let your mind wander in dark places." His tone was firm and reassuring. "You will live long and visit many lands in your time. For now, turn and row for the landing."

Brita had not spoken a word while we rowed back, but she was all talk as we walked up from the harbor.

"Ooh, that man makes me shiver. His eyes see things, I tell you. Gyda says—"

"Since when do you trust what Gyda says? I thought you didn't like her!"

"Oh … she's just bitter because she'll always be a house thrall. Not like me—I'll be getting my freedom when Ivar takes me to wife."

Ivar the one-eyed? Taking her to wife? I'd heard nothing of this, not even in the whispered talk shared among the women at night.

"Are you sure…I mean, has he asked you to marry?"

"Not exactly, but he always reaches for me after the mead-hall drinking, and he tells me that one day I'll have a fine new gown to wear."

She looked down in distaste at her worn, stained tunic. Like most thralls, she wore cast-off clothing. I wondered: was Brita pretty enough to make a man buy her freedom? I said nothing as she chattered on, feeling in my heart that she was blinded by her own desires.

Finally the day of departure arrived. I'd been anxious lest fog delay our leaving, but a fresh breeze blew from the West as we stowed our gear and climbed aboard. We would cast off on a fair morning—a good beginning.

"Don't forget to search for scabwort," called Mother. "I need to give the boys a dose of it, I fear—and it makes the best blue for dying wool. Oh, and bilberries if any are still to be found."

I had the list in my head, but nodded cheerfully, proud to be entrusted with these tasks. Brita looked apprehensive. She had little experience of the sea, though like every grown-up in the settlement she knew how to swim. Ana settled herself in the back of the boat, looking as comfortable as if seated at her own hearth. The men matter-of-factly picked up their oars, ready to row.

As we skimmed out of the harbor, swans followed in our wake. I looked back over my shoulder for one last glance at Heorot, shining high on the hill.

When we had rowed out far enough to raise the sail, I recognized Willa's work in the diamond-patterned wool. Many days of weaving had gone into the square sail that now billowed above us. A pang for my lost friend smote my heart, but sorrow could not long endure on such a bright, sparkling morning. The water danced before my eyes, reflecting sunlight and shadow.

Gulls wheeled above us, their raucous cries a celebration of life and freedom. Salt spray stung my face, but left a pleasing tang on my lips. The boat's undulating motion as it surged forward bore me along, riding the swells. I glanced across at Brita. She too seemed to be reveling in the rhythms of the sea. We grinned at each other like children who had fled their chores. With the oars stowed, we could now look about freely. My first adventure! All seemed new, yet somehow familiar. As I pondered this, it came to me: my dreams—dreams of flying with the swans. Sailing felt like flying!

As we sailed south, the coastline gradually changed. At first dense forests lined the shore, but then the trees thinned, and the shore was dotted with an occasional rocky or sandy beach. Brita and I exchanged glances at the latter: what a fine place for a swim! We did not voice our thoughts to the men.

By nightfall, my cheeks were wind-stung, my rump numb from sitting on hard wood, and my belly rumbled with hunger. Unferth directed us to a sheltered cove where we drove the boat up onto a gravelly shore. It was a relief to stretch my legs and help the men unload and set up camp. Brita and I erected a tripod and started a cooking fire, while Gorm and Saxe set up our tent. Then we lugged water from the sea in wooden buckets to fill the iron cauldron hung over the fire. Ana opened our food stores. Soon the hearty smells of boiling beef and vegetables filled our nostrils.

Later, sated with food and ale, we sat around the fire telling stories— at least the men did. I looked around the circle at these strong young men with wind-tanned faces and sun-bleached hair. I laughed with delight at their stories of Thor and Loki, their bragging accounts of raiding parties, their boasts of brave deeds. Ana had shut her eyes, as if lost in her own memories.

Without knowing that I was going to speak, I blurted out a question. "Why does Ivar have only one eye?"

In the sudden silence, I thought I might have given offence, but the men soon burst into loud laughter.

"Family feud," said Gorm matter-of-factly.

"Ivar didn't move fast enough," chortled Sven.

"He told me that he lost it in a fight," volunteered Brita.

"He might have told you that," began Saxe, "but the truth is—"

"It was gouged out by a woman!" Olaf finished the sentence gleefully.

"One of our women?" I asked breathlessly.

"No, no, though I'm sure many have wanted to." Olaf winked at Brita before going on.

"Some farmer's daughter he got with child—then forgot to marry. When he rode off headed for Heorot, wanting to change his luck you might say, her whole family came after him. The girl's father was cut up in the fight—got his nose chopped off, according to Ivar, but the girl's mother stabbed Ivar in the face with a spindle. That did it for the eye."

All the men chuckled, except Unferth. Ana rose and stretched, yawning a great yawn.

"Time to turn in," said Unferth. "We have a long day's journey tomorrow to reach our destination."

"What is our destination, Unferth?" I had thought we would be stopping frequently to search out the plants on Mother's list, but Unferth seemed to have other ideas.

"Moon Cliff—a great chalk cliff higher than anything you have ever seen, including Heorot." He smiled. "Rare plants grow there, and rare birds nest there." He patted the woven wicker cage on which he sat. "Falcons. It is my intent to bring back hunting birds for Hrothgar and his athelings."

The other men grinned at each other as if they'd known this all along.

"So, are we women to have no help in gathering these rare plants?" I inquired with some asperity.

"Worry not, king's daughter. We will aid you as we can."

He said no more, signaling the men to fetch their sleeping sacks from the boat. We women laid out our sleeping robes inside the tent, Brita and I giggling like children. The fire had been left to burn itself out on the rocky beach, and its dying light cast our shadows on the tent walls. Shadows? I realized that something felt different.

Of course! No Grendel to fear! No marauding monster to haunt our dreams! I could barely remember a time when I had gone to bed with no fear of the night. Now I wanted to stay awake, to relish this new sense of freedom. As I lay unsleeping, questions rose in my mind, and I turned to the person most likely to answer them.

"Ana," I asked quietly, "why doesn't everyone leave Heorot to escape the Grendel? Why do we all stay and suffer such terror each night?"

She was silent a long time.

"That is a hard question, Freawaru—one I have asked myself and Aeschere. He says the king refuses to surrender. Hrothgar believes that abandoning the mead hall to the monster would mean the Grendel has won the feud." She shook her head ruefully in the shadows. "You know how men behave in a feud. Neither side will give up. I believe your father still believes he can find a way to avenge the deaths of his warriors and end the feud—but that hasn't happened yet, as we all know." She shook her head again and sighed. "I hope Wealtheow never has to endure what Hildeburh endured."

"Hildeburh, who is she?"

"Surely you've heard of the Finnsburg feud?!"

"No," I shook my head to the contrary. "What does it have to do with us?"

"It's too complicated to go into all of it tonight, but I'll tell you the basic facts. It involved an unexpected battle during a family visit. Hildeburh, a Dane, had married Finn, a Frisian. At their stronghold, a fight broke out between Danes and Frisians in which their only son was killed, as well as Hildeburh's brother Hnaef. Hildeburh and Finn tried to restore peace by paying *wergild*, the man-price, for each warrior killed. They burned uncle and nephew on the same funeral pyre and imposed a truce on the visiting Danish warriors, which lasted through a winter of exile. But come spring, the remaining Danish leader, Hengest, killed Finn and brought Hildeburh back to her own people."

"Poor Hildeburh," sighed Ana. "She lost everyone she loved— husband, son, and brother—although some do say that Hengest had it worse, caught between oaths of loyalty to his old lord Hnaef and his new lord Finn, but of course the duty of revenge came first."

95

I had followed the tale with difficulty, but this last idea seemed strangest of all.

"Why? Why is revenge so important?"

"Why? Ana sounded shocked. "Because the honor and reputation of your people depend upon it! You should be old enough by now to know that!"

Stung by her rebuke, I spoke no more, but wriggled under my robes and closed my eyes.

We rose at first light, broke camp, and reloaded the boat. A light mist lay over the water, but Unferth pronounced visibility sufficient for navigation. Now I noticed the many wicker cages wedged between the men's sea chests. If we filled all of them, we'd have a noisy cargo on our homeward journey.

For some time we rowed in silence, hugging the shoreline and waiting for the wind to rise. Instead, it began to rain, gently at first and then harder, dropping a solid sheet between us and the shore.

I was alarmed, but the men seemed unperturbed. They lifted their heads occasionally to sniff the air, and turned their ears to listen, but kept on rowing. Brita and I had no choice but to do the same, after donning sealskins to keep our woolen capes from getting soaked. Soon my fingers began to cramp, and then the muscles in my back started to ache, but I kept rowing. *You're a woman now*, I told myself, *you must do your part*. Still, I envied Ana, sitting motionless behind me.

By mid-morning I was having second thoughts about this adventure—especially when I pictured my family back in Heorot enjoying hot porridge and bread fresh from the hearth. Unferth took notice of my distress.

"Take heart, king's daughter," he called from the front of the boat. "This will soon pass. We have no time to stop now, but you and Brita may help Ana distribute the food packets; we'll all feel better with something in our bellies."

Glad to set aside our oars, Brita and I climbed over the chests and cages, handing each man a portion of bread and cheese from the stores at Ana's feet. Eating did help me feel better, and as Unferth predicted, the rain stopped soon after. A fresh breeze sprang up, filling our sail and lifting our spirits.

"To Moon Cliff!" cried Unferth, as exuberantly as if he were Hrethric or Hrothmund.

We spotted the cliff from a great distance. At first, I thought it a cloud low on the horizon. Then the sun came out to illumine a headland almost blindingly bright against the dark sea. As we drew nearer, it became a white mass, crowned with dark fringe against a gray sky. Soon it loomed above us, towering and immense. Leaning back to look up, I grew dizzy at the height.

"Unferth, how will we get to the top?"

"We'll sail around to the lee of the island; there's a natural harbor on that side."

He was right, as usual. As we worked our way around the headland, we came upon a flock of ducks feeding quietly along the shoreline. Suddenly the whole group came to attention, veered straight toward the boat, and then reversed—zigzagging madly as if to escape an unseen enemy.

"What are they doing?" cried Brita.

"Look up!" shouted Unferth.

As we did so, something exploded out of the sky, plummeting down in a blur of motion. When it rose again, feathers fluttered from its talons.

"That," said Unferth with satisfaction, "is a falcon."

This time we unloaded everything from the boat, including tents for the men. Ana, Brita, and I spread our wet cloaks over nearby shrubs before building a fire. This took some time, as most of the wood we gathered was still wet. Seeing our difficulty, Unferth pulled flint and a bag of wood chips from his sea chest.

"Here. Use this."

"Always Unferth to the rescue!"

"Not always. But neither do I always fail," he said, his face impassive.

I stared at him, uncertain how to judge his tone. Was he reproaching me for the words I'd once spoken? Unsure, I kept silent.

That night, Unferth favored us with a story as we sat gazing at the fire.

"Men say that in olden days a certain god, one of the Aesir, left Asgard and came down to Midgard, our middle world. There he rode along the seashore until he came to a homestead, a miserable hovel whose door was closed. 'I am Rig,' he called out. An old couple, Asa and Edda, let him in and served him simple fare—soup and bread. That night he lay in bed between them, great-grandfather and great-grandmother. Nine months later, Edda gave birth to a son named Thrall. He had dark, wrinkled skin; thick, rough fingers; a bent back; and a misshapen face. But he grew to be very strong and exerted his strength to bind osiers, prepare burdens, and haul wood. Later, he mated with a sunburned woman named Tir, and together they laid out farms, fertilized fields, bred swine, and dug peat. From them are descended the race of thralls."

I was listening intently, but I noticed that Brita had bowed her head and was rubbing her eyes, as if in pain. Unferth continued his tale.

"On his journey, Rig next came to a comfortable hall where the door was ajar. Here he was welcomed to their hearth by Afve and Amma. Grandfather was whittling a loom, while grandmother spun yarn at a spinning wheel. That night he lay between the two of them, and nine months later Amma gave birth to a son named Karl, pink and pretty with sparkling eyes. As he grew, he learned how to tame oxen, make plows, and build timbered houses and tall barns. He married Alert, adorned with a veil and a kidskin skirt. Together they erected a home and united their possessions. From them, all free men's races had their source."

One by one, our men lifted their heads and nodded to each other.

"Finally," Unferth intoned, "Rig came to a hall where the door was open. Inside sat Fader and Moder, their fingers entwined. Fader was making a bow and arrows. Moder was pressing her fine, starched linen. They fed Rig white bread on silver platters, fish, pork, and wild fowl, and wine in costly cups. That night Rig lay between Fader and Moder, and nine months later Moder gave birth to a son named Jarl, fair-haired and rosy-cheeked, swathed in silk. Jarl grew up in that hall. Soon he swung shield, bent bow, hurled spear, harried hounds, rode horses, and swam the waves.

"Rig himself came striding from the concealing woods to teach the boy runes and to call him 'son.' He gave him his name, and he gave as his inheritance his possessions, farmlands, and ancient cities. Jarl found a bride in Arna, soft-fingered, white-skinned, noble-minded. Together they increased their race and gained age. They were the race of nobles."

Here Unferth fell silent, staring into the fire. Then, as if speaking only to himself, he added these words in a low voice:

He gained that which was his lot:
To be named Rig and to know runes.

Later that night Brita and I lay awake talking in low voices, though we could scarcely have been heard over the snores coming from the men's tents—and from Ana herself.

"Thank you for choosing me, my lady. I love this sea journey. I've never been so far from Heorot before, not since the day I was brought from my village."

"Where do you come from, Brita?" I knew that many house thralls had been captured in raiding parties, sometimes as young children. Brita had been part of our household for as long as I could remember, but I had no idea of her age or background.

"I'm not sure—somewhere in the south. When I heard we were heading south on this trip, I thought maybe ..." She fell silent.

Surely she was not thinking of running away? Horrified, I hurried on with another question, equally ill-chosen.

"Do you remember your family?"

"No, but I remember my dog. Isn't that strange? It was a little brown dog named Tore. If I gave him bones from the cooking pot he would lick my face."

"Hmm, my brothers like dogs too, but I've always preferred cats."

"Of course, you being marked by Freyja and all."

That again! This time I was determined to get more information.

"What does Freyja have to do with cats?"

"I don't know myself, but Willa always said that Freyja's wagon was pulled by cats, and they could fly."

"Really! Flying cats! Very likely!"

"I'm just telling you what Willa said."

Willa, dear Willa. Suddenly the tears began to flow, and I forgot to keep quiet.

"Hush, hush, my lady. You won't get better if you go back to crying again. Then this whole trip will be wasted."

Better? Wasted? I sat up abruptly, shaking the tears off my nose and eye lashes.

"What do you mean? Tell me the truth!"

Brita sat up too and wrapped her arms around her knees.

"They were afraid for you—your mother and father, I mean. You were fading away after Willa died. Then Unferth suggested this trip—to get you away from Heorot and turn your mind toward other things, he said. I was serving at table when they had the conversation." She paused.

"And it's done you a great good already. Look at yourself: the picture of health, talking and laughing—with the men even. Willa would be happy, she would. She doted on you like her own child. I hope I haven't said too much, my lady, but you wanted the truth and there it is. You're lucky to have so many people care about you—even Unferth loves you, and he's not exactly the loving kind."

Unferth ... love me? Of course Brita must mean like a father—though he was much younger than Father.

"Thank you, Brita. I didn't know. You're right. I am very lucky. I can see that I've been selfish." I pretended to yawn. "Let's go to sleep now."

I really wanted to think about all this new information, but once again fresh air and fatigue pulled me down into darkness—a darkness free of monsters, free even of sorrow. When I awoke refreshed, Brita was already up, and I smelled hot porridge. Ana brought me a bowl in the tent before I dressed and emerged into the light of a fresh new day.

"Good morning, king's daughter." Unferth walked over from the circle of men squatting around the fire. "Today we go hunting: for plants in the ground and birds in the air."

Unferth looked as eager as a child. Even if he had invented this journey for my benefit, he was clearly enjoying it.

"How will you catch them—these falcons?"

"They nest in the chalk cliffs. We will gather their eggs if unhatched, but we also have nets with which to ensnare the birds themselves. Patience is the primary skill required. Olaf and Gorm will aid me this morning, while Saxe and Sven help you women After a midday meal, we will switch. Agreed?"

"Agreed." I grinned. Unferth always had a plan.

We women spent a glorious morning roaming the high, open meadowland. While Ana foraged under scrubby undergrowth for low-growing herbs, Brita and I scrambled up and down steep clefts in the limestone rock, where we found bilberries growing in protected pockets. Our bags were full when the sun told us it was time to return to camp.

Unferth and the other men were still not back when our meal was ready—a delicious stew of dried fish.

"I hope there has been no mishap—" I began, when we heard a shout. My heart froze—but melted with relief when Olaf and Gorm ran up, each bearing a swinging cage, Unferth behind them.

"Don't get too close," he warned as we ran to meet them. "Falcons are meat-eaters with strong beaks."

"What lovely, long tail feathers!" I marveled. "They're the color of the sky before a storm."

"Yes," he agreed, "they'd make a beautiful cloak, wouldn't they? And look at the eggs—reddish and spotted." He held out an egg for me to touch.

"You're spotted too ... is that blood on your face?"

"It could be." He reached up to touch his cheek. "Their talons are sharp as a sword edge. Now, ladies, how was your morning's gathering?"

In answer, I pointed to the wooden pails heaped with berries and the bags of plants.

"We still need to dig some scabwort roots, if we can find any. Do you know if it grows on this island? Horse-heal is another name for it—a tall, hairy plant with yellow flower heads?"

Unferth reflected. "Yes, but it grows on the far side of the island. I'll have to take you there myself, and let Gorm and Olaf go back to the cliffs with Saxe and Sven. Agreed?"

"Agreed."

Brita and Ana stayed a short distance behind us as Unferth and I set off that afternoon. The day was still fine and my heart felt as light as a falcon flying high above the cliffs.

Along the way, Unferth pointed out flowers I had never seen before. One especially caught my eye: a pretty plant with black shiny berries and purple, bell-shaped flowers.

"Don't touch it!" Unferth's voice rang out as I leaned forward to brush the strangely hairy petals. "Deadly nightshade: belladonna. Every part of it is poisonous."

Hastily I drew back my hand. "How do you know so much about plants, Unferth?"

"I watch, I listen, I remember. In northern magic, this plant is used for an ointment that is said to make people fly." He looked at me as if to see whether I believed him.

"Mother told me that certain plants can affect the mind—that's one reason I must be careful to identify them correctly."

"Your mother is wise; she is a very skilled woman, though I doubt she makes much use of hemlock, henbane, and hemp."

"Hemlock, henbane, and hemp?' I seemed to remember hearing those names. "What are their uses?"

"Primarily to induce a state of trance—though there are safer methods."

My thoughts flashed to the women's circle in which I had seemed to fly, a memory that brought anxious thoughts of home. Seeing my expression, Unferth changed the subject, pointing out other flowers—innocent of evil he said—which charmed me with their long white throats tinged with delicate pinks, purples, and golds. 'Orchids' he called them.

"How glorious! Do they have medicinal value?"

"Not that I know of. Some things exist only to give pleasure with their beauty." He turned to stare at my face. "Like you, king's daughter."

"Unferth, you're making fun of me." My face grew hot, and I laughed to cover my confusion. Just then Brita called out.

"Here they are—I think I've found those hairy plants you're looking for, my lady."

Indeed she had, and we four set to work digging up a large quantity. On the way back to camp, we spoke little.

Saxe and Sven were jubilant with their afternoon's success: three more birds to bring back to Heorot, six in all.

"Who will get them?" I asked Unferth.

"One goes to your father, of course, and one to Aeschere. I expect these young fellows will each want to keep a bird for himself, as they've gone to the work of capturing them."

"But that leaves none for you!"

"I will help train each falcon, and if any of the eggs hatch, I'll try to raise the young birds."

"Unferth?" I lifted my hand to his face, and then let it fall. "Thank you for bringing me to this place. I will never forget it."

The look on his face suggested that he would not soon forget it either, but whether he was thinking of the falcons or something else, I could not tell.

Our journey home took longer, working against the current, but time flew by as if in a dream, with cloudless skies by day and starry skies at night. Whenever we went ashore, I still felt the boat's motion and stumbled as if unaccustomed to my own feet. I wanted to stay suspended, floating forever on rolling seas. I wanted to sail to the edge of the world, as Unferth had once promised. Some day.

We came in sight of Heorot late in the afternoon. As we rounded the headland leading to our fjord, one of the men shouted.

"There it is, gleaming in the sun."

Gleaming? Yes, it was gleaming, but there was also something else rising in the air—something like fog or ... smoke? Smoke!

"Fire! Heorot's on fire!" I screamed. "Just as I saw it in my vision! Hurry! Hurry! Heorot is burning!"

Chapter 6
Courting the Enemy

"Everyone row! Row straight for the landing!" shouted Unferth.

We put our muscles into it, straining to send the boat hurtling through the calm waters of the inlet. Tiny figures on shore ran in opposite directions—some toward Heorot, some away from it, almost as if they were—fleeing.

"Who are those men?" I shouted.

"Not ours," replied Unferth grimly. "It must be a raid."

I gasped. "Raiders?"

It was inconceivable that Heorot could be under attack. Yet the evidence rose before my eyes: a long, smoky plume spiraling into the sky.

At Unferth's command, we beached the boat abruptly and jumped out, short of the harbor but closer to the long hill crowned by the mead hall.

"You women stay here at the boat! Stay out of danger."

Unferth did not wait to see if we obeyed, but took off at a dead run, the four thanes right behind him. Ana, Brita, and I looked at each other and then scrambled after them.

Fearful thoughts flashed through my mind. Mother, Hrethric, Hrothmund, are they hurt, captured? Who has dared attack in broad daylight? Where are the hall guards? Is nothing safe in my world? Suddenly the place I had wanted most to leave became the spot most precious on earth. Choking back tears, I picked up my skirts and ran, Ana puffing behind me.

When I finally reached the crest of the hill, I saw Unferth standing outside the mead hall talking with Father, several of the nobles—and Hrothulf. Other men were tossing water on the mead hall roof, but no one seemed in a panic. Relief swept over me. As Unferth so often said, all must be well.

Ana, out of breath, greeted Aeschere warmly, but he waved her toward the women's house. She and Brita hurried in that direction. Boldly, I joined the men around Father, choking as a gust of wind blew smoke in my face. Thorkel emerged from the mead hall with a damage report for Father, and—to my surprise—praise for my cousin Hrothulf.

"Good work, lad! If you hadn't r-r-raised the alarm, Heorot might now lie in ashes. As it s-s-stands, only one end of the roof will have to be replaced. My lord," he said, turning to Hrothgar, "this n-n-nephew of yours used his wits today. You have trained him well."

"Indeed," boomed Hrothgar, "and he shall be rewarded!" Hrothgar clapped Hrothulf soundly on the back. Hrothulf beamed proudly and looked around as if to assure himself that everyone was aware of his leading role. I stared at him standing beside Father and noticed for the first time that he was almost as tall as the king.

"But...what happened here? How was Heorot set afire?" At my question, the circle opened to include me.

"Freawaru, daughter, your return is welcome."

After this brief acknowledgment, Father turned to Thorkel. "Did you recognize any of the raiders?"

"No, but it m-m-must have been Ingeld," replied Thorkel, "or some of his men. The Heathobards favor those dap-dappled horses we saw galloping off." He turned to gaze speculatively past the mead hall. "They must have hidden their boats along the c-c-coast and made their way overland to Heorot from the west."

As the men continued to talk, I pulled Hrothulf aside, curiosity overcoming my dislike.

"What happened? Did you really save the mead hall? How did you sound an alarm?"

Hrothulf took a deep breath and puffed out his chest, clearly enjoying the situation.

"While you were off picking flowers with your nurse maids, I've been working with bow and arrow to perfect my aim. This morning," he continued, ignoring my indignant snorts, "I was searching behind the mead hall for a lost arrow when I noticed smoke coming off the roof—not from the smoke hole. Then I heard a horse whinny where no horse should be. It didn't take me long to realize that this meant trouble."

By now he had the attention of everyone nearby.

"When the raiders came swarming out of the trees, both on foot and on horseback, I ran to the front of the mead hall and blew the lur horn as loud as I could. That brought our men running, and we soon put the attackers to flight."

Lur horn? What was that? I'd never heard of such a thing. Nothing had hung before the mead hall when I left … what else had happened while I was gone?!

At this point, several thanes rode up, and one jumped down to report to Hrothgar.

"No sign of them now, my lord. They left so fast we barely had time to draw blood, but I did get part of one!" He brandished a severed arm, still dripping.

"Hmph," grunted Father. "Did you check the storehouses, Nils? It's hard to believe they came only to fire the mead hall. We'd better search the settlement to check for losses and damage." He turned his head and raised his voice. "Saxe—Gorm—drop those buckets, and let the women finish the job. You take horses and ride to the western shore. Find out what happened to our coast guard." He added to himself, "We should not have been taken unaware. Clearly there is a weak spot in our defenses."

"Sven, Olaf—go with Aeschere and check the storehouses—all of them. Report back to me immediately. The rest of you walk house to house. Find out who's been hurt, what's been taken. Go!" The men scattered.

Women were now emerging from the eld-hus, Mother in the lead.

"Freawaru! Daughter! Welcome home!" She hurried to meet me, her eyes bright. "Ana told me you'd all returned safely—returned to this!" She swept an arm toward the mead hall, still slightly smoking.

"Mother, I'm so glad you're alive—and safe!" Tears sprang to my eyes as we embraced.

"The raiders came and went so quickly we hardly knew they were here," declared Mother reassuringly. "Where is Hrothgar going, and Unferth?" She looked around to see them heading for the settlement.

"To check for losses," I answered.

"Then let us join them. I am concerned for those who were outside their houses when the raiders passed through." Mother turned and called toward the eld-hus. "Come out, boys. It is safe now, and we have work to do."

My brothers came tumbling through the door like puppies let out to play and dashed to join Mother and me. As we walked, I asked Mother about the lur horn. Before she could answer, Hrethric burst out with "You missed it, Freaw, you missed it! We had our own adventure while you were gone!"

"I was there too, Freaw, I helped find it." Hrothmund was pulling at my sleeve.

"Found what? What are you talking about?"

"The lah—the loo—that horn you asked about. We found it!"

Their faces were jubilant. Mystified, I looked to Mother for an explanation.

"Yes, they did find it," she confirmed, "in a peat bog, which they'd been forbidden to visit." She shook her head, but not in anger. "After they pulled it partially out of the bog and found it too heavy to remove, they came back for help. Ivar joined them to work it free and bring it home."

"Wait'll you see it Freaw! It's really really long—and all gold-like, and *loud*!" Hrethric's face was glowing as Mother continued her explanation.

"Aeschere remembered hearing of such horns in ancient lays. He gave it a name and suggested your father hang it outside the mead hall as a way to rouse the settlement in an emergency. We had no idea it would be used so soon!"

Well! Clearly I was not the only one who'd been having adventures! I gave each boy a squeeze and assured them that they could show me their treasure when we got back from our survey of the settlement.

At the blacksmith's forge, we found Torgun angrily surveying her vegetable garden, its plants trampled into the earth.

"Rode right through it, the devils!" She picked up a smashed cabbage and dropped it in disgust.

"Anyone hurt or carried off here?" Aeschere seemed to be making a mental tally.

"No, thank the gods. My Bjorn grabbed a ploughshare off the anvil and threw it at one of the riders. He missed, but they gave us a wide berth after that—looking for easier game, I guess." She smirked, but Bjorn looked embarrassed, still holding a lump of metal in his grimy hands.

At each doorway we heard a similar story. No one hurt, no one taken captive. A few horses had been driven off, but little else of value taken. The brunt of the raid had been focused on the mead hall itself.

"Where was Father when they attacked?" I asked. Mother replied in low tones.

"Off hunting with Aeschere and a party of earls. Fortunately they returned in the middle of the raid. Apparently at about the same time you and Unferth returned from your expedition to Moon Cliff."

She turned an appraising eye toward me. "Was it successful?" Her words hung in the air, many questions contained within them.

"Yes, I think so. Father will be pleased with the falcons we captured, and I have several new plants to show you—also bilberries!"

Assured of my family's safety, I was now eager to share details of my own adventure. But one question troubled my brain.

"Who is this Ingeld they spoke of, and why would he want to harm Heorot?"

"Why? Probably because your father killed his father."

Mother's tone was so matter-of-fact that it took a few minutes for her words to sink in.

"K-killed? Why? How?"

"The full story would take long to tell. It goes back to a long-standing feud between the Scyldings and the Heathobards. First Froda, Ingeld's father, killed Healfdane, your father's father. Then Froda himself was killed in a battle against Hrothgar and his two brothers. All this happened before you were born. Is that enough for now?"

I nodded, speechless. Although I knew that Father and his warriors frequently went on raids, I had never really thought about people being... killed. Of course they often returned with injuries that needed attention, but we'd never lost a warrior on a raid. Suddenly Willa's death smote my heart again, this time with the knowledge that it was a fate shared by many. Had Ingeld mourned for Froda as I mourned for Willa?

That evening Saxe returned bearing a body across the back of his horse: our coast guard. His throat had been cut, his clothing stripped off, and his body thrown in the sea. Saxe had found him washed up on the shore.

The reality of death struck me again: this time the evidence lay literally at my feet, impossible to ignore. I stared at the pale body, wrapped in Saxe's cloak, trying not to see the gaping wound on its neck, now washed clean by the waves. I knelt to touch him, but Saxe pulled me up, firmly and respectfully.

"This is not for you, my lady."

"Who was he, Saxe? I don't recognize him." Indeed, his face had been ground against the gravel and rubbed raw.

'His name was Magus—a newcomer, eager to join Hrothgar's band. He hadn't yet earned his first gold ring. Now he never will. At least we have a full body to burn this time." Saxe smiled a grim smile.

"Come, Freawaru." Now it was Unferth pulling me away. "Your Mother has need of you in the women's house."

As we walked in silence, I wondered about the family Magus might have left at home. Surely they would mourn the loss of his life, just as I mourned for Willa.

The sound of horse's hooves drew my attention back to the mead hall. Gorm was pulling up with something slung behind him: another body.

"One of them Heathobards, sure enough," he said calmly, dismounting to pull the corpse from his horse's back. As it fell to the ground, blood flowed from the stump of an arm.

"By the gods! The same man who tried to take my head off!" It was Nils, who'd earlier hacked the arm from an attacker. "Must have bled to death—or his mates left him to die!"

" "I finished him off," announced Gorm calmly. "He was still alive when I found him, down by the shore where their boat had put in."

"So … which of us gets the credit?" wondered Nils aloud. "We'll have to let Hrothgar decide."

"Unferth, what are they talking about?" I pulled at his elbow like a child.

"Gold rings," he answered. "Whoever kills an enemy is rewarded with a gold ring by your father, the king."

I stared at him, open-mouthed. Most of Father's warriors wore gold rings. Did that mean each of them had killed a man?

"What do we do with this one?" Gorm pointed down at the dead Heathobard, who looked to be about the same age as our dead coast guard.

"Burn them on the same pyre—as they did at Finnsburg." I heard my own voice speaking with authority. Everyone stared at me.

"Hrothgar will decide," muttered Nils. I nodded and turned away. Of course, it is Father's business. He is the king.

The damage to Heorot took only a few days to repair. During that time, Hrothulf strutted about as if he personally had fended off the raiders. It did not help that the lur horn hung in front of Heorot, a daily reminder of the raid. Aeschere found me looking at the long, twisting instrument one day and added new information about it.

"It is said that such a horn will be blown by Heimdahl when Ragnarok begins, to awaken the gods so they may prepare for their last great battle."

"Heimdahl," I echoed. "I have never heard that name. Who is he, Aeschere?"

Aeschere cleared his throat.

"Heimdahl is said to dwell beside Bifrost, the bridge between Asgard, home of the gods, and Midgard, our own world. He guards the bridge against possible invasion by giants. Heimdahl's senses are said to be so sharp he can see over mountains, hear grass growing, and sleep less than a bird. A good watchman, don't you think? We don't have Heimdahl, but fortunately we do have Hrothulf."

"Yes," I echoed, "we do have Hrothulf."

One day I asked Hrethric and Hrothmund for a report on their sailing lessons with my cousin.

"Hrothulf is strict but fair, Freawaru. He lets us both put the sail up and down, and in a few days he's going to let us sail our boat out of the harbor." Hrethric's face glowed with anticipation. "Will you come down to the shipyard with us? They're building a new boat for Aeschere there. Hrothulf lets us watch the log splitting."

Hrothmund had other ideas.

"No, let's go see those birds that came back with Freawaru. What did you call them?"

"Falcons," I said, rumpling his sweaty hair. It amused me that since I'd come into my womanhood my brothers now called me by my full name. "Unferth will train them to hunt ducks and other seabirds—after he tames them."

"Ooh, I want to see how he does that."

"Me too," chimed in Hrethric. "I wonder if he'll talk to them like he talks to the ravens."

"Talks to ravens? Are you teasing me?" Hrethric liked to play jokes on his brother and me, but he seldom told outright lies.

"No, he really does—I've heard him."

"What does he say to them?" I asked, amused.

"Well, first he calls them by name. His two favorites are Huginn and Muninn. They—"

"Stop right there!" I stared at the boys in astonishment and alarm. "Are you sure you're not teasing? You must know that Huginn and Muninn are the names of Odin's two ravens!"

"I don't know nothing about Odin," said Hrethric solemnly, "but Unferth's ravens are his messengers. He tells them to go places and bring back news."

"And do they?" I asked, my heart beating faster.

"I guess so. He strokes their feathers and feeds them strips of dried meat."

"Hmm. They … they must be pets that he's trained with food."

"Oh, maybe he'll let us feed the falcons! Come on, Hrothmund, let's go see." Hrothmund jumped to his feet to join his brother already running toward the mead hall.

"You boys go on. I must unpack the herbs I brought for Mother." I turned and then remembered to add, "and tonight I'll tell you a new story before bedtime … about dragons!"

Later, hanging herbs to dry in the rafters of the eld-hus, I reported Hrethric's story to Mother. At the names given to the ravens her eyes narrowed.

"It seems unlike Unferth to be so … open."

"What does it mean, Mother? Do you think he really can talk to birds?"

Mother drew me aside to a quiet corner, away from the bustle of meal preparation.

"First let me explain the names. 'Huginn' means *mind*—the ability to ponder and analyze, the ability to understand the significance of what you see and hear. 'Muninn' stands for *memory*, the ability to recall and draw from the past what might be useful in the present."

I nodded earnestly, proud to be having such a grown-up conversation with my mother.

"Both mind and memory are guides to action. Unferth must be using his two ravens as extra eyes and ears. You too, Freawaru, must use these tools—mind and memory—as you grow into womanhood." She lifted my chin with her finger and looked into my eyes. "Question all that you see and hear. Use your mind to separate the true from the false. Then remember what you have learned when faced with new situations."

"But Mother, won't you always be here to help me?" My chin quivered as I recalled that Willa, my other mother, was already gone.

"Freawaru, there are times when each of us must stand alone. You were born with a special gift, the mark of Freyja, and you may call upon her for guidance and strength. But the gods are fickle and not always available. You must find the courage to be yourself, Freawaru, alone."

She dropped my hands and drew me close. I felt the beating of her heart as I nestled against her like a child.

"This report of Unferth's ravens—do not repeat it to anyone else. A shaman has many powers we don't understand; he may be using animals to help him. Now, tell me about your journey to Moon Cliff."

"You don't have to worry, Mother." I straightened with a sigh. "Brita told me the real reason why you sent me away. I am all right now. I'll always miss Willa and cherish her memory, but I can … I can go on living. It was very good to be free of the Grendel for a while."

"I must speak to Brita about her loose tongue," snapped Mother and then sighed.

"Your father and I have talked of sending Hrethric and Hrothmund into fosterage—to remove them from this atmosphere of evil—but there is no tribe or family that seems suitable. I've had no connection with my own people for many years. On your father's side there is no one left except his sister Yrs, married to the Swedish king Onela, and I would not send my sons so far away."

"Don't do it!" I blurted. "I mean no disrespect, Mother, but please don't send my brothers away! Why, I haven't told them half the stories they want to hear and—" I stopped in confusion, aware that I sounded like a child, not a newly anointed woman. "And I would miss them so much."

"As would I. Do not fear, daughter, nothing has been decided. I should not have spoken of it had I not been thinking about the future— of all my children. Freawaru, what would you say to marriage?"

"Marriage? To what man?"

She did not answer immediately, seeming lost in thought.

"As the daughter of a royal house, it is expected that you be allied to the ruler of another royal house, or at least a tribal leader. Such unions are important for the stability of our culture. They can bring peace where there is conflict, heal old wounds and cement friendly relations, and even bring an end to ancient feuds." She paused. "Like the feud with the Heathobards."

I stared at her. "You don't mean with … that Ingeld?"

She nodded. "I do mean Ingeld. You are near in age—I would judge he is only a year or two older—and your union could put an end to the ever-festering enmity between our peoples. The recent raid on Heorot was an example."

"But Mother, why would he want to marry me? You said yourself that my father killed Ingeld's father."

"You may not know it, Freawaru, but you are very beautiful. That is one reason. Another is the dowry that would accompany you. Hrothgar's storehouses hold many treasures, to which I would add … my golden neck ring."

"What?" I could not believe my ears. "You would part with Father's gift—for me?"

"Yes, my daughter. You yourself are a treasure of great price, but it does not hurt to dazzle a man's eyes with gold. Besides," she laughed, "the necklace is far too heavy to wear except on the highest ceremonial occasions. I have other collars that would suit me as well."

I knew she was making light of the matter, for I had seen with what reverence she donned the great ring on high feast days, and how she shone with pride while wearing it.

"Won't Father be upset it if you give it to me?"

"I think I can convince him of the wisdom of such a move, especially if it helps bring peace between the two tribes. Each year Ingeld gains strength as a warrior. It would be to our advantage to have him as an ally rather than an enemy."

I marveled inwardly at my mother's astuteness.

"But … I've never even seen this Ingeld."

"You shall. I will advise Hrothgar to invite him to Heorot for the next solstice. Then we will see what we will see."

That evening, I was so preoccupied thinking of Mother's words that I almost forgot the story promised to my two brothers—but they did not forget.

"Dragon tale, dragon tale," they chorused.

"Actually the hero of the tale is Sigmund, the Dragon Slayer."

The boys wiggled in anticipation. "Start at the beginning, Freawaru, and don't leave anything out." They nestled into my sleeping robe, pulling it up to their chins.

"Of course not. There was once a dragon so old, so strong, and so rich, that many thanes had tried to conquer it and take its treasure hoard for themselves. One day, over the sea came Sigmund to the shore where the dragon lay deep in its cave. Sigmund had killed many a giant in his time and many a sea monster, but never had he tackled a beast such as this dragon. All alone, he entered the dragon's cave, where he found the beast asleep, guarding its hoard."

I looked down on my brothers, who shivered in dread and delight.

"The dragon reared up, huge and horrible, scales glistening all over its body, and opened its great mouth to wrap Sigmund in deadly flames." I paused for breath as my brothers listened, their mouths agape.

"Sigmund drew his sword and plunged it straight through the dragon's body, pinning it to the wall of the cave. The beast roared and writhed, but to no avail. Its blood gushed forth, flooding out of the cave in a torrent. Slowly that dragon melted, consumed by its own heat. Then Sigmund loaded its treasure into his boat and sailed away victorious."

After a long, satisfying silence, Hrethric cheered, "Good for Sigmund! I'm going to kill a dragon some day."

"Me too," echoed Hrothmund, "but Freawaru, are dragons real? Are they like … the Grendel?" His voice dropped to a whisper at the last word.

"I don't know," I replied truthfully. "There are many creatures in the world we know little of. Some are dangerous, evil, like wolves … bears and … things in the swamp," I added, remembering the aborted deer hunt.

"Did Sigmund have a magic sword? Is that how he killed the dragon?"

"Again, I don't know. The story doesn't say. Right now, it's time for you two to go to your own beds. Tomorrow we'll visit the shipyard—if I have time. Good night; may the gods keep you safe."

The boys slid down and padded over the cold floor to their own benches. Wrapping myself in my bed robes, I drifted off to sleep, imagining a tall atheling on a dappled horse. His hair was gold, his eyes were blue, and his name was Ingeld.

I don't know how the invitation was carried, but one day a band of Heathobards rode up to Heorot. At their head, on a dappled horse slightly larger than the rest, sat Ingeld.

It was the time of year when hours of daylight were balanced by hours of darkness, shortly after the fall harvest. Mother and Father had decided that this time would be more appropriate for entertaining guests than the autumn solstice, when secret rituals were enacted.

The arrival of the foreigners had been signaled by the watch guard, so a band of our thanes stood ready to meet them. I noticed, peering out from inside the women's house, that both Danes and Heathobards wore full armor, their swords ready at hand.

"Hail, men of Hrothgar. We come in peace. Announce us to your king."

Ingeld spoke with authority, his voice deep and powerful for one so young—I reckoned him hardly older than Hrothulf. He turned in my direction, and I drew back quickly from the opening, though I knew he could not see me. His hair was golden beneath his helmet, but his eyes burned like dark fire. They stirred an answering warmth within me.

"Freawaru, come here. It is time to make preparations. You must bathe and rest before the feast. Tonight you will help me carry the mead cup among our guests—wearing your jewelry." Mother smiled at me, and I smiled back.

As I bathed—in the same tub I had used before my womanhood ritual—I looked at my own body. The breasts that had once been so small and round, annoying me with their itching, had begun to swell. Why, I would soon be as big as Brita! She had shown me her breasts inside the tent at Moon Cliff, boasting of them as her best feature—much appreciated by Ivar. I flushed to remember what Ivar reportedly did with them. Would Ingeld want to put his mouth on me? Curiously, the thought did not offend me.

Washing between my legs in the soapy water, I touched the special spot that always made me quiver. Ah …

"Freawaru, aren't you finished yet? We still have much to do."

Mother's voice broke my reverie, and I rose, splashing water on the floor as I reached for a drying cloth.

While I rested, servants were sent scurrying up to Heorot, some to set out tables next to the sleeping benches and others to hang tapestries—including my first completed piece depicting Thor fishing for the Midgard serpent, as requested by my young brothers. Straw was strewn on the paved floor to absorb grease and spilled liquids. Barrels of ale were rolled up from the storehouse. All day, cooking smells wafted from the eld-hus. As the day wore on, my excitement grew.

Never before had I carried the cup at a high feast, an honor usually reserved for the king's wife, my mother. Of course I'd heard reports from Brita and the other serving girls of what went on in the mead hall at ordinary times: men feeding bones to their dogs or throwing them at each other; men drinking so much ale from their drinking horns that they passed out or fell asleep at the table; men singing bawdy songs, or, at calmer moments, listening to lays sung by Aelric the scop. Sometimes arguments and fights broke out, but as long as no serious harm was done, Father tolerated it with good humor, nay even encouraged it, as if eager to see his thanes test their mettle against each other. As Gyda observed, "Who could deny them their pleasure by day, with that Grendel monster destroying all joy at night?" Well, not all joy. I'd seen the men lying with Gyda and the other girls. Tonight, however, was to be a more formal occasion.

I wondered how much Ingeld knew about our affliction. Did he think us weakened by this scourge? How would he and his men be received in the mead hall? What would he think of me—if he noticed me at all? My presence as cup bearer would surely attract attention. Most of Father's men had known me since my childhood, but now I was no longer a child. They would see that tonight. Would Ingeld see it?

As if reading my mind, Mother gave me instructions as she wound my hair into a top knot and bound it with a circlet of silver.

"Don't look directly at Ingeld. Let him do the looking. Hold your head high and speak little."

"Am I to wear the gold collar tonight, Mother?"

"No, I think we'll keep that in reserve. Wear the amber ear drops that match your hair and the gold arm bracelets. Those will set off your fair skin."

For a fleeting moment, I felt like an offering being prepared for sacrifice, but shook off the thought. And despite what Mother said, I wanted to take a good look at Ingeld.

Mother loaned me one of her best pleated shifts to wear as an underdress. It was too long, but we belted it at the waist so I would not trip. Over that went the pinafore Willa had woven for me, dyed with woad to a beautiful shade of blue. Her gift of bronze brooches on the straps completed the outfit.

"There. You look every inch a king's daughter. Now here is what you are to do …"

Mother would precede me into the hall, bearing the mead in a glass pitcher of Frankish design. She would first serve Father in his high seat between the decorated pillars and then serve each Heathobard guest in turn; next she would serve Father's athelings and finally the thanes. I was to follow her path exactly with a second pitcher, filling the men's drinking horns as needed.

Banquet food—great quantities of roast venison, fish stew, cheese, and bread—would be served by Brita, Gyda, and the other house servants. After the ceremonial drinking, we would change to ale for the remainder of the feast, which Mother told me might last for hours. Only the necessity of leaving Heorot to avoid the Grendel would bring an end to festivities.

That night, my cheeks felt hot as I stood near the doorway, awaiting Mother's cue to enter. I could see Father at the far end in his high seat, flanked by Unferth on one side and Hrothulf on the other. Aelric sat below Unferth, with Hrethric and Hrothmund nearby. Aelric was now standing and raising his lyre to perform, which brought a shout from the tables. I soon recognized his tale: the same old story of Scyld Scefing, the founder of our line. Father must want to impress Ingeld and his followers with our glorious past.

Just then, Mother looked pointedly in my direction and nodded her head. I took a deep breath, lifted the pitcher, and entered.

Strong smells assailed me: smoke, sweat, dog—these were familiar. What I had not expected was the sudden silence as the hall became aware of my presence. Even Aelric faltered momentarily and broke off his song. Ivar broke the spell.

"King Hrothgar, you honor us! Even with one eye I can see that Freawaru the fair is the jewel of your kingdom!" Others roared their approval as I approached Father's chair.

"Well done, daughter," he murmured. I bent forward to refill his cup—not a common drinking horn but a fine clear cup of glass. Unferth smiled a silent greeting, but Hrothulf looked away when I approached him. I turned toward our guests, my heart beating rapidly. As I approached Ingeld, I felt his eyes upon me.

"Your name, my lady? I did not hear it clearly."

"Freawaru." I dared to lift my eyes to his.

"You are fair indeed, with a fine low voice for a woman." He drained his horn and held it out to me. I wanted to speak, but found no words. Nodding, I filled the horn and continued down the table to serve his companions. When I reached the doorway again to take a fresh pitcher from Brita, Mother was waiting for me.

"You may retire now, Freawaru. Your work is finished for tonight."

"What? But Mother, I wanted—" What did I want? "I wanted to hear the end of Aelric's tale."

Her eyebrows lifted. "Surely you know it ends with a funeral—the burial at sea of Scyld Scefing; there is no need to hear more of such stories. We've had enough of burials in our own time."

"Yes, Mother." Regretfully I glanced at the group of Heathobards, laughing and talking together. Their presence had apparently created no tension in the hall. All was well.

Back in the women's house, I removed my fine clothes carefully, loosened my hair, and locked my jewelry back in the chest that had once been Willa's. "My lady" he had called me, as if I were a grown woman. Of course, I had come into my womanhood, but I did not feel any different. I still loved to climb the big oak by the river and share stories with my little brothers. When would I feel truly grown up? Ingeld's image floated into my thoughts. A finely shaped head, a jutting chin, a strong face but not an unkind one. His eyes were deep, dark as a winter night, but not cold or frosty like Hrothulf's. Could I live with such a man? Could I love him?

What would it be like to have a husband? Never had I seen Mother and Father quarrel, though I knew they sometimes disagreed. Each respected the other, and they wielded power in their own domains. Mother took charge of the settlement and court when Father and his men went off on long raids or trading trips. In his absence, her word was obeyed without question.

A few men in the settlement kept more than one wife, usually bringing in a younger woman when their first wife grew old or if she had given them no children. Sometimes babies were born to thralls, but such children grew up as thralls themselves, regardless of the Father's rank. I thought of Brita's deluded dream of marrying Ivar. It would never happen. Thank the gods, I'd been born into a king's family.

Ingeld and his company were still present the next day, riding out to hunt with Aeschere and a band of athelings at midmorning. I noticed that they headed in the opposite direction from the swamp. Unferth rode with them, one of the new falcons hooded on his wrist. It was to be Aeschere's bird, but Unferth was still training it to hunt on command.

Mother did not appear until after the hunting party's departure. I supposed she had spent the night with Father, her custom of late. As she drew me into the women's house, now empty, her first words matched my own thoughts.

"Ingeld. Is he not a fine man?"

"So he appears—though I have seen little of him."

"You will have a chance to set up your own household," she said as if she had not heard my reply, "free of the darkness that hangs over Heorot."

In the bright morning sunshine, one could almost forget about the Grendel—almost. I realized that I had given no thought to the monster last night, my mind focused instead on Ingeld.

"Your father and I have talked. He will make the proposal today to Ingeld and establish the dowry to be offered. We will weave a bond of peace between our tribes and lay to rest this long-standing feud."

"Do you wish it, Mother, that I marry Ingeld?"

"I would see you safely settled and provided for, my daughter. Ingeld can protect you—and no doubt give you many fine sons and daughters. You are such a little mother to Hrethric and Hrothmund, I am sure you would one day like to have a family of your own."

But I have one now! I wanted to cry out, but kept silent. Clearly my parents had already decided my future.

"What if Ingeld does not want to marry me?"

Mother laughed. "He kept looking for you after your departure last night. We definitely captured his attention."

We? Yes, we had.

"When will Father speak to him?" I held my breath.

"As soon as the hunting party returns. If Ingeld agrees to the dowry, we will announce your betrothal tonight."

Tonight? My head whirled. I must have looked stricken, for Mother suddenly gathered me into her arms and held me close.

"Do not worry." She spoke softly into my hair. "There will be many months of preparation before the wedding actually takes place. We must weave cloth for clothes and blankets, assemble cooking utensils, and do a great deal more to provide you with all that is needed to establish a new household. You will have time to settle your mind."

She held me away from her with one hand and lifted my chin to meet her gaze.

"We will also have time to speak of your powers and time to instruct you in their use." Lightly she touched the back of my shoulder, where lay the mark I could never see. "I think it possible that one day you may be a great practitioner of *seithur*."

I gasped. "*Seithur*? But isn't that about laying curses on people and seeing into the future?"

"Partly; tell me: who was it foresaw the burning of Heorot?"

I hung my head, remembering the vision in the circle.

"Who can say? That warning might have helped Hrothulf detect the fire as soon as he did and thus save Heorot. *Seithur* can be used for good or ill. You have been given a gift, Freaw. You cannot escape it. You can learn how to use it wisely. I will share what knowledge I have of magic. Unferth will also guide you. He sees great strength in your spirit—one reason he's been willing to teach you the runes."

"You know about that?" I had thought this a secret between Unferth and myself.

"Of course. I cannot see as far as Unferth sees, but I know what is happening under my own nose. Now, go see what your brothers are doing. They wanted you to come down to the shipyard, but I told them to wait."

My thoughts were in turmoil as I headed for the harbor. Today? Father was talking to Ingeld today! By nightfall, I would know my fate.

"Freawaru, where are you going? You walked right past us."

Hrethric's high-pitched voice broke my reverie. I turned. He and Hrothmund were collecting wood chips dangerously close to the flying axes of shipwrights splitting logs.

"Freawaru, do you want to go out on the water today? Hrothulf said he'd take us when he got back from hunting."

"Hrothulf? Uh—no, I don't think I'll have time. You two go without me."

"Why don't you like Hrothulf?"

"Who says I don't?"

"Hrothulf. He says you're jealous, and that's why you're so mean to him."

Inwardly I screamed: *Jealous? Mean? How dare he say such things? And to my own brothers!*

"Don't believe a word he says—about me, I mean. We just don't get along, that's all."

"But Hrothulf likes you. He says he's going to marry you some day."

"What!" Was this another of Hrethric's jokes?

"Yes, he says he's going to marry you and make you behave like a proper wife—just like Offa did when he married Thrith."

My mind reeled. What sort of poison had Hrothulf been spewing on these children? I tried to keep my voice calm.

"What else has Hrothulf been telling you?"

Now Hrothmund opened his mouth.

"When I cry, he tells me to be quiet or he'll tie me up and roast me on a spit."

"Oh, he's just trying to test you and make you tough," interrupted Hrethric. "And anyway, we didn't mean to leave you tied up for so long."

"What? When did Hrothulf tie you up? Where?"

"On the boat. He said he'd tie me up so I wouldn't fall out. Then he and Hrethric left me there—for a long time."

"Hrethric, is this true?"

Hrethric squirmed, avoiding my eyes.

"Aw, we were just playing. Hrothmund was a Frank and we were the Danes—so we had to torture him."

"Torture him?"

"Not really—just scare him a little."

I did not know what to make of all this, but I did not like it. I could remember an earlier version of "Franks and Danes" played with Hrothulf, my childhood tormentor. But Hrothulf was almost a grown man. What was he doing playing such games with these children?

"I thought Hrothulf was supposed to be giving you sailing lessons!"

"He does, sometimes, after our game."

"Another game? A different one?"

"I'm not supposed to tell. It's a secret game, and if I tell … bad things will happen …" Hrethric's voice trailed off.

"If it's a secret, you don't need to tell me," I assured him, at the same time wondering what this new game might be. "Why don't you show me the boat they're building for Aeschere."

"Good idea! Come with us!" They were off at a run.

I followed the boys past stacks of oak planks, wooden buckets full of iron rivets, buckets of tar, and ropes of wool string. On a wood frame near the water's edge, two shipwrights were fitting long planks into place, overlapping them carefully, and then stuffing tarred string in the gaps before riveting the planks together. Augurs, scrapers, and hammers lay strewn on the ground nearby.

"Don't touch that tar, Hrothmund! It will burn your skin and be hard to wash off."

"Good morning, my lady," a worker greeted—who? Me! I still wasn't used to this title.

"Will this be a fighting ship?" asked Hrethric.

"No," the workman laughed, "not this one. See how low and wide she's going to be? No, this one is for trade, for holding cargo."

"Oh." Hrethric sounded disappointed.

"We've plenty of fighting ships already, don't you think?"

The workman waved a brawny arm toward the beach, where I counted thirty-six long, graceful ships pulled up on the sand. Each prow was slightly different. Some were coiled like snakes, others carved to resemble animal heads or the fierce faces of monsters.

"My father has more ships than anyone in the whole world!" boasted Hrethric.

"Can't say as to that," the man responded. "We just provide what is asked for."

"Come on, boys. I need to get back, and it's almost time for morning porridge. You two must be hungry."

"Right!"

Without a moment's hesitation, they turned toward Heorot. I envied them their ability to change focus so quickly, to forget any trouble the instant something new presented itself. I, on the other hand, seemed to ponder and mull over each problem at length. Was that a part of growing up? Or part of being a woman?

Late in the afternoon, Aeschere, Ingeld, and company returned from their hunt—a successful one judging from the deer and other game that hung over the horses' flanks. Unferth held aloft a duck, brought down by the young falcon on his wrist. Clearly his training was bearing fruit.

I busied myself at the loom for what seemed hours, working on a new tapestry. Mother had allowed me to pick my own subject, so I had chosen to represent swans flying above the harbor. Around me women chattered as they wove blankets, dress fabric, or sailcloth. But my mind was focused on only one conversation: that between Father and Ingeld, possibly taking place right now in the mead hall. Father transacted all his important business there during daylight hours.

Finally, Mother entered, but her face gave no clues.

"Freawaru, someone wants to speak to you. Come with me."

I felt myself trembling as I followed her out; was it from fear or anticipation? Both, I decided. Walking toward us were Father and ... Ingeld!

As they approached, Mother moved away with a last admonition: "Listen to your head as well as your heart. You are a woman now."

Wordless, I advanced to meet my fate.

"Freawaru, let us walk together."

Ingeld's voice was low, deeper than I'd remembered it from last night. He took my hand and turned to face the mead hall, but I held back.

"Let's walk toward the river—I have a special place there."

"So, this maiden has a mind of her own!" He frowned momentarily. "To the river then."

We walked in silence, my hand enveloped in his. The smells of hunting still hung upon his clothes: horse and sweat and blood, but they were not unpleasing to me.

How many times had I walked to this oak tree? Played there with my brothers? Sat at Unferth's feet as he taught me rune lore? Now here I was walking hand in hand with a tall stranger who might one day be my husband. His hand gripped mine with almost painful firmness. Glancing down, I noticed scars on his knuckles, some fairly new. Had he taken part in the recent raid on Heorot? Did I dare ask him? No, best not. A peace-weaver must learn to guard her tongue.

Ingeld cleared his throat.

"Lady Freawaru, though not now decked in gold and amber, you are still most fair to me."

"Today was a working day; I've been working at my loom." Suddenly I began reeling off my accomplishments: "I can spin and weave, cook and bake. I know the uses of many herbs, I know—"

"Nay, nay, I have women at home to do all those things. Your father proposes you to me as wife." He stopped and turned me to face him. "Freawaru, I would not have you unwilling. You are so young ... what is your desire?"

What was my desire? Was I ready for this new role—of wife?

"I am woman grown," I declared, suddenly sure of my answer. "I will take you for my husband."

This reply seemed to amuse him. "It is I who will do the taking— but I am glad to see such spirit in the future wife of Ingeld. You will have need of spirit." He gave a wry grimace.

"What do you mean?"

"My mother is also a strong woman. She may not welcome a rival, but she will obey my wishes." He nodded as if reassuring himself.

So … competition even before the wedding!

"Nor can I give you a hall as grand as Heorot, though my own is quite … adequate." He paused, seeming to consider a new thought. "Perhaps I will build a new hall for Freawaru the Fair. Yes, a new hall." He glanced back at Heorot, gleaming in the sun.

By this time we had reached the great oak. I motioned for Ingeld to join me on one of the roots, which extended like a shelf. He sat and then extended both hands before him, covered with gold rings. From the little finger of his left hand, he removed a circlet of twisted gold.

"Take this, Freawaru, as a pledge of my intention to take you as my wife."

As he held it out to me, I stared at the ring, wondering if a man's life had bought it. But Ingeld was leader of his own tribe; no doubt he had gold rings aplenty at his disposal.

Shyly, I accepted the ring, trying several fingers of my own left hand until I found one big enough to fit it. Then an idea struck me.

"Wait a moment—I have something for you." Jumping down, I scrabbled among the tree roots, feeling for the rune I had recently carved under Unferth's tutelage.

"Here—this is Gebo, rune of union. It is my gift to you."

Ingeld's eyes opened wide.

"A rune-mistress? You are indeed a woman of many accomplishments!" He did not sound altogether happy.

I wondered if I should tell him about the mark of Freyja on my shoulder, but decided this could wait. One day he would see it for himself.

"Ingeld, I … I have never been with a man." As I spoke, I looked him full in the face.

"Good!" He smiled now. "I will teach you all you need to know— starting now."

He drew me close and pressed his lips against mine. I stiffened and then relaxed as warmth spread through my body. It felt ... good to be with this man. When he released me I gave a little sigh and smiled, both outwardly and inwardly.

As we strolled back toward the mead hall, my tongue seemed to come loose. I began to name all the wildflowers that we encountered: "bluebells, cornflowers, clover, shepherd's purse, vetch—and this is yellow feverfew, good against fevers as you might guess, and yarrow—which I'm told increases the effects of drinking ale."

"Better yet would be an herb to treat the aftereffects of too much ale," laughed Ingeld.

"Oh, there is such an herb: wormwood."

"Someone has taught you well." He smiled, as if humoring a child.

"Yes, Mother and Willa." Suddenly my eyes filled with tears, and my shoulders began to shake. Ingeld looked at me curiously.

"Why do you weep?"

"I weep for Willa. She was killed by the night monster, the creature we call the Grendel. I miss her every day."

Another thought struck me, a thought that left my mouth before my mind could stop it.

"Do you miss your father?"

"My father?" He frowned, his face clouding. "I have no memory of him—only of the stories told about his killing—by Hrothgar and his brothers."

Instantly, I regretted my foolish question. To change the subject I asked another question.

"What is Hrothgar including in my dowry?"

This seemed to have the desired effect. Apparently the minds of grown men could sometimes be led as easily as those of little boys.

"Gold rings, armor, horses, weapons—a generous dowry. I can well afford to build a fine new hall for you."

His good-humor restored, we continued hand-in-hand toward Heorot.

Our bethrothal was announced that evening at the mead hall as Mother had predicted, but not everyone received it with approval. Hrothulf practically hissed at Father: "Why was I not told of this?"

"Because it does not concern you," said Hrothgar in some surprise.

There were murmurs among the Heathobards as well. One grizzled old thane looked at me with daggers in his eyes, the word "Frodo" on his lips. To my relief, Ingeld ignored him. The time for our marriage was fixed at one year from the present day.

"I will come for you when our new hall is ready," said Ingeld. But it was to be two years before the summons came.

Chapter 7
Beowulf the Geat

The excitement of Ingeld's visit and our betrothal gradually faded, but our workload increased immediately. Besides the daily needs of the court, we now had the added labor of preparing my household goods. Mother recruited women from the settlement to help with the extra weaving, and we lighted whale oil lamps to work at our looms as the days darkened.

Hrothulf remained a dark cloud hanging over me; his very presence made me anxious and depressed. As soon as possible, I told Mother what I had heard about the "game" he played with my brothers and then left the matter in her hands. I don't know if she spoke to him, but Hrothulf's attitude toward me did not improve.

I caught him watching me at odd moments, with a strange expression on his face that made me shiver. I sometimes felt as if I were a deer, and he was stalking me. Although I tried to avoid him, he had a way of appearing suddenly, as if he'd been lying in wait for me. I spoke to no one about his behavior, but always kept Algiz, my rune of protection, somewhere on my person.

From time to time, Mother and I slipped away from the settlement and walked quietly to the sacred pool. This place became a welcome source of refreshment for me—refreshment for the spirit as well as respite from physical labor.

Here she taught me the rituals I must know to lead the women of my future home in worshiping the goddess. One day in the poolside hut, Mother gave me a small drum, fashioned by Unferth, she said, from the hide of a red deer. On one side, he had drawn Thurisaz, the rune of openings, the gateway between worlds. On the other, I recognized Dagaz, rune of breakthrough and transformation.

As I examined this new treasure, my thoughts flew back to the day when I had soared above my body, lifted by the beat of Mother's drum.

"Why is it necessary to go into a trance, Mother?"

Mother was silent for some time before answering.

"A trance is a way to travel deep within yourself and listen to your inner voices. A trance may be used for many purposes—to solve problems, for example, or to discover the cause of sickness, and above all, to connect with forces beyond our human control." She gave a rueful smile. "As you know, a ritual does not always bring the resolution we hope for, but it can be a powerful aid."

"Is that what you use for healing, Mother? You seem to know how to cure anything." I thought of the many people over the years who had come to Mother for help with a sick child, a wound that would not heal, or even for darkness of the mind.

"Part of what I know has been gained from long experience—and of course the study of herbs. But when I am quiet inside myself, I can feel the energy in another and sometimes find the cause of blockage—or send my own energy into their body." Her face was calm as she said this, her eyes brimming with love.

"Is that what happens when you lay your hands on someone? Your touch feels so warm." I gazed back at her, my heart in my eyes. Soon I would be leaving Mother, traveling far beyond the reach of her warmth and her wisdom. How would I survive without her?

"Teach me, Mother!" I cried. "Teach me all you can. I am ready to learn."

She took the drum from me and placed it on the table. With my hands in hers, she spoke.

"Do not be desperate, my daughter. You already possess powers beyond my understanding. I cannot see into the future as you do. I have not been marked with the sign of a goddess. Now," she released my hands and stood to lead me outside, where she picked up her staff of ash wood. "Let's begin with the basics. First you draw a circle of protection …"

That day I was instructed in rituals of protection. On another, I practiced rituals of healing and purification. There was so much to learn: chants, invocations, the raising of power—but with each day I felt closer to the Great Mother and a part of all living things.

Unferth had finished his instructions in rune-carving; now I knew the names and properties of all twenty-four runes, albeit in a rudimentary way. He assured me that I would grow more adept as occasions required their use.

Day by day, the light faded and the time of darkness drew near. The coming of winter meant more time for indoor games and storytelling, but it also meant more time for the Grendel to travel abroad under cover of darkness. When people grew careless and did not seek shelter before nightfall, their scant remains would be found the following morning, mixed with the creature's foul reek. Heorot remained the focus of its attacks. Night after night, Hrothgar's hall stood empty save for the demon who had made it his second home.

Winter passed—and then a summer and another winter. My breasts had grown full, and a patch of red-brown hair grew between my legs. Now I knew I was a woman indeed. Yet no word came from Ingeld, and I despaired. Had he forgotten me? Had he changed his mind? Had he met with some mishap? Or taken another woman to wife? I twisted the gold ring on my finger, but it gave no answers.

Except for the lessons at the sacred pool, my life settled into a dull, repetitive routine. Rise, eat, work at the loom, eat, work, fall into bed. All of Heorot seemed burdened with the same heaviness of spirit— almost a sickness. For twelve long winters we had borne the weight of the Grendel, twelve long winters with no hope of relief.

Life inside the mead hall grew increasingly formal, with set patterns of speech and behavior. It was as if Father wanted to exert control where he still could. He now referred to Heorot as his "court," and to his men as "courtiers." We all acquiesced, willing to contribute to any semblance of control over the chaos that was the monster.

One day a message arrived at court, sent up from the guard on the coastline: "A ship approaches, making openly for the harbor, carrying fifteen men, sail unknown."

Could it be Ingeld? My wedding goods were long since ready, packed in chests and barrels in Father's storeroom along with the promised dowry. Who else could it be? It *must* be Ingeld! I was seized by a giddy happiness.

Soon the coast guard himself appeared on horseback, leading a band of fifteen men on foot. At the door of the mead hall, the guard leaned down to address Wulfgar, now Hrothgar's herald and captain.

"Wulfgar, as you can see, these men are not exiles come to beg for aid, but men of boldness and courage. They would speak with Hrothgar. I myself must return to my post."

Before riding off, he bowed to the leader of the strangers, who nodded his head in return. Who were these men?

The stranger who marched at their head was taller than all the rest. To my chagrin, he was not Ingeld. His men wore clanking chain mail and golden helmets on which the image of wild boar heads gleamed. They carried long swords, thick shields, and ash wood spears. They looked powerful, confident, and—handsome. Still, Ingeld was not among them, and my heart sank.

As soon as the great doors of Heorot closed behind them, speculation began, but no one had a clue who these men might be. Wulfgar had led the company into a separate chamber at the end of the mead hall, where he began to question the men. One voice rang out, so loud and strong that we listeners clustered outside could hear every word.

"We are Geats, men who follow Higlac. I am Beowulf, son of Ecgtheow. Our message is for your king alone, great Healfdane's son."

Geats? Who were the Geats? No one outside seemed to recognize this tribal name. I ran to tell Mother, whose eyes lighted at the mention of Ecgtheow.

"I've heard that name before. Let me think. Yes, it was many years ago, when I was newly married to Hrothgar. Someone came seeking sanctuary: he had been exiled from his own country for starting a dangerous feud. Hrothgar took him in and paid the price to bring peace. I think that man's name was Ecgtheow."

She turned to Unferth, who had come to consult her that morning about an herbal cure for hives.

"If this man is Ecgtheow's son, perhaps he has come to repay the debt incurred by Hrothgar's kindness," Unferth observed.

"Perhaps. You'd best go join the king. He will want your council if this stranger has a request."

"Gladly, my lady." Swiftly Unferth disappeared into Heorot. It would be some time before he re-emerged to deliver his news.

Our first hint of the Geats' reception was a command from Hrothgar to prepare an immediate feast for the visitors. Every servant in the house volunteered to serve. It seemed I was the only one not consumed with curiosity. The man was not Ingeld. Where was Ingeld?

Everyone set to work, Mother and I supervising. By now, I too had become accustomed to giving orders and expecting them to be obeyed. After we set preparations in motion, Mother drew me aside.

"Tonight, Freawaru, we will both carry the mead cup. If Hrothgar wishes to give these men special honor, your presence will be appreciated."

"Thank you, Mother." Our eyes met and we laughed.

From Unferth we discovered that the stranger had indeed arrived with a request. This Beowulf had asked for permission to kill the Grendel!

That night, Mother and I were waiting at the door when we heard the young man's voice ring out again.

"My people have sent me to the Danes, great king, saying it is my duty to use my strength against your evil foe. They have consulted runes. I have been tested by experience. I have driven giants from the earth, killed great sea monsters, and oft survived the darkness of war. Now I come to rid you of this menace, this Grendel. I will use no weapons, since he has none, but with my bare hands will I extinguish his life. If I should fail, return my armor and weapons to Higlac, my lord. Let the outcome be as fate decides."

I was so amazed at this speech that I almost dropped the mead pitcher. Everyone else in the hall was likewise spellbound by the man's bold declaration. Who was this Beowulf? What made him think he could succeed where so many brave thanes before him had failed? Even Unferth's magic had failed. I stared at this stranger as he stood before Hrothgar. He looked to be taller even than Ingeld, and—I had to admit—more noble in appearance.

Hrothgar, ignoring the widespread looks of disbelief and disdain, welcomed Beowulf like a son, recalling aloud the visit of his father Ecgtheow and the friendship begun long ago.

Then he lamented: "Ah, Beowulf, my heart is too heavy to recount the damage done by the Grendel to this hall, the brave thanes taken down to death by the monster's lust. But let us eat and drink a toast to your future victory. Give way, men—make room for our guests."

Danes moved down to make way for Geats, and Mother and I entered with the mead. As we moved among the men, I had time to study this Beowulf more closely: his eyes were blue, his hair blonde—nothing unusual there—but he had massive shoulders and huge hands that looked capable of crushing the life out of an enemy. Yet no one had survived a direct encounter with the Grendel; Unferth's experience was a special case. Presumably, this Beowulf had no magic powers, only great physical strength. Would that be enough? I glimpsed a familiar smile on his face that reminded me of something—perhaps a dream?

By the time we began pouring ale, the noise level had risen considerably. But silence fell when Unferth's voice rang out. He had staggered to his feet and leaned over the table with both hands to address Beowulf directly.

"So, you're the great Beowulf are you? The same boastful young fool who once challenged Brecca of the Brondings to a swimming match? Yes," he sneered, "I have heard of you—a man so full of pride he recklessly risked his life to fulfill a boast. I have heard too that Brecca won that contest, outswam you, and left you behind. You may have been lucky in the past, Beowulf, but your luck may fail if you dare to remain in this hall tonight!"

Beowulf seemed to take no offense at this taunt. In fact, he grinned, and raised his drinking horn.

"Ah, friend Unferth, it is ale that speaks with your tongue, not sense. And you have heard the story wrong. Granted, both Brecca and I were young and boastful, but I won that swimming match and fulfilled my boast. We were carried far out from land, beset by sharks and whales and stormy seas, but our chain mail preserved us. Swept off course, we swam for five nights. My sword slew nine sea beasts before I was cast up on Finmarken, victorious. No man has done more, no strength is a match for mine." He paused to drink deeply and then continued.

"What about you, proud Unferth? I've heard no such tales of your feats—unless you count the killing of your own kin—a deed for which you will surely find punishment one day."

In shock, I looked from one man to the other. Beowulf had spoken with the genial tone of one good friend sharing tales with another, but Unferth's face was white with fury. I feared he would attack Beowulf in his rage. Beowulf was still speaking, now to the whole assembly.

"If you Danes were as brave as you say you are, there would be no need of my aid. But you allow this demon to do as he likes, sparing no one. Let him test the strength and courage of a Geatish warrior! Tomorrow morning, the sun will rise on a Heorot cleansed of evil."

Did Father actually believe this boasting Geat? I, for one, did not. But even Mother seemed taken in. She raised her hands for silence and walked to stand beside our visitor.

"Thank the gods for you, Beowulf! You are an answer to prayer. How happy I am to offer mead to one who has come to help my afflicted people, come to bring relief from our long siege."

Beowulf rose and bowed to her.

"I am here, lady, to win the praise of your people or to welcome death. If I cannot live in greatness, let me die in this famed hall."

As Mother beamed at Beowulf, Father stepped down from his high seat and embraced the man.

"I give you full command of my hall tonight, Beowulf. Take it and hold it, you and your men. If you come through this night alive, you shall want for nothing, but sail home with a ship full of treasure!"

A great deal of cheering and drinking followed these speeches. I made my way up and down the tables as if in a dream, pondering what I had heard. Unferth spoke no more, seeming to drown his anger in ale. The Geats kept their faces blank as they ate and drank with their new companions, though I saw their eyes occasionally glance at the spears and shields ranged close at hand against the wall. Beowulf, however, seemed as relaxed as a man in his own hall.

Father and Mother left the hall together, soon followed by the rest of our people. As I made my exit, I saw Beowulf stripping off his mail shirt, his helmet and sword set aside. So, he really was going to trust to his two bare hands! I shuddered violently, thinking of the blood and guts that would be smeared on these benches before morning. One of the Geats caught my eye before I walked out the door. He looked like a man staring into the face of certain death. Before my eyes, he seemed to dissolve into a pool of blood. Reluctantly, I left him to his fate.

That night I did not undress, though I lay wrapped in my sleeping robes. I did not sleep, but listened intently for what I knew must come. The face of the hapless Geat swam before me. How could Beowulf lead his men into a house of death? Had he no love for them—or himself? Yet be he fool or hero, I had no wish to see him torn to pieces and devoured by the monster. No one deserved such a fate. Through a crack in the boards, I peered out toward the mead hall. The moon was beginning to rise, low in the sky. Brita and Gyda, awake as well, were whispering nearby in the dark.

"I heard he has the strength of twenty in his grip—or was it thirty?"

"He'll need it. Thirty was the number killed in Grendel's worst raid—remember?"

"Don't speak of it. Of course I remember. Oh, it's too horrible. Those poor, innocent men—and so handsome—such a waste!"

"Without weapons too, I heard. He won't have a chance barehanded! We'll have another bloody cleanup in the morning. Yes, I predict—"

"Hush! What was that?" I sat up in bed.

Harsh sounds rent the night air: the groan of twisting metal, the crack of splintering wood. We all knew the meaning of such sounds.

"It's the monster!" screamed Brita. "He's tearing off the doors! They'll all be eaten alive!"

"Hush! Listen!" I commanded.

Sudden silence. What was happening? Were the men not awake? Then—a roar—not animal, not human. Another roar! I shook with terror, surrounded by screaming women—awake now, had they ever slept.

Great shrieks in the night, booming blows like thunder fell again, again, again. The very ground seemed to tremble. From the mighty mead hall, we heard crashing benches—battle cries—battle cries? Someone was fighting back! A spark of hope leapt up in my chest.

The roars and cries gained in frenzy. Then—a sudden change—a wail, torn from a throat shrieking with pain and defeat, a long, terrible, last song in the darkness.

Pandemonium in the women's quarters. Pandemonium outside. Running feet raced past the walls. I found myself outside running with the rest, irresistibly drawn to the mead hall, caution thrown aside. Torches glinted off sword blades, kitchen knives, daggers, axes, whatever had been grabbed up in the rush to Heorot—as if we were mad to attack the Grendel ourselves, mad to drive it from our home regardless of the cost.

We met men streaming from the mead hall door, men shouting, exulting—men alive! Underfoot, a slippery trail of blood ran off into the night. Pushing inside, we gaped at the destruction: support columns buckled, mead benches torn from the walls—but in the midst of it all, silhouetted by the hearth fire, stood Beowulf, brandishing something huge and bloody: the arm and shoulder of the Grendel!

"I meant to kill him outright," he stated calmly, "but he tore loose, running off to his den to die. That fiend will bother you no more."

Hysterical shouts greeted this announcement. Before our eyes, the Geats hoisted Beowulf and his trophy aloft, that he might hang it from the rafters, clear proof that his boast had been fulfilled. I searched their faces for the man I'd seen earlier. I did not find him.

Beowulf turned somber, pointing down at a bloody stain soaking into the planks beneath his feet.

"Here I lost one of my men," he said simply. "The monster came in so quickly I only had time to rise from my bench. It grabbed Hondshu, bit off his head, drank his blood, and bolted him down, hands and feet."

We bystanders shuddered, all too familiar with the Grendel's manner of feeding.

"Then what happened, Beowulf?" It was Aeschere's voice; he stood as if in a trance, mouth open, one hand grasping a huge axe.

Beowulf spoke firmly.

"The monster approached me next, reached out to rip me with its great claws, but I seized him by the arm and held fast. Struggle as he might, he could not free himself. I fastened his claws with my fists and squeezed until they cracked. Then he desired nothing but escape!"

Beowulf smiled grimly and wiped sweat from his brow.

"We battled across the hall, over benches, down the aisles, my men hacking at the monster's hide, but their swords made no dent. I twisted and twisted until the Grendel's shoulder snapped, muscle and bone. Then he fled, leaving behind his arm and his life in my hands."

Beowulf slumped momentarily and seemed as if he might fall, but he quickly drew himself erect. A different voice spoke next.

"Beowulf, we owe you our lives. You have fulfilled your boast."

It was Unferth.

"You and your men can now take your rest without fear of disturbance. We will track the monster in the morning."

"Yes," added Aeschere, "and I think we now know where to find his lair."

Exhaustion from the suspense and terror of the night finally sent us all back to our beds. Could it be true? Was the Grendel, at long last, vanquished? It seemed like a dream—or rather the end of a nightmare.

At first light we were awakened by the lur horn, blast after joyful blast. Everyone in the court and settlement gathered to gawk at the huge bloody footprints left by the monster and stretch their necks in awe at the bloody trophy dripping from the ceiling. All day a train of warriors, nobles, and neighboring farmers walked or rode up to Heorot to view the evidence of the beast's defeat.

At Hrothgar's command, Aeschere quickly assembled a party to track the Grendel to its lair. They set off in high spirits, later returning to report that the water of the fen boiled and steamed, welling with blood and clotted gore, further evidence of the monster's doom. Its carcass had no doubt sunk to the bottom of the swamp.

In due course, a more formal viewing took place. Father and his courtiers were joined by Mother and her women, myself among them. We walked together across the meadow and up the path to Heorot. Beowulf and his men stood inside, waiting.

As he stared up at the Grendel's great claw, dark and alien above him, Father exclaimed: "The gods be thanked! Grendel's anger hung over our heads too long. I had given up hope—knew no way to end this unequal war of men and monster. Our house stood humbled by horrors. Now, one man has come to Denmark and done what the Danes could not do themselves. Blest be the mother who bore you, Beowulf. Let me claim you as a kinsman, make you my son. Glory is now yours, and your fame will live forever."

Bowing, Beowulf replied: "We did what we came to do. I wish I could show you the Grendel's entire body stretched out on the floor of Heorot, but I could not hold him long enough—he was too strong. Yet he fled with death pressing at his back, pain splitting his panicked heart."

Unferth stepped forward and pointed to the monster's claw.

"See how each finger ends in a spike, a nail hard as steel? No sword could have cut through it. You were right to use the strength of your bare hands."

The two men stared at each other and nodded. Apology accepted.

Hrethric and Hrothmund, although now big boys of ten and eight, squealed with delight at the grisly trophy and clung to Beowulf as if attached. Hrothmund broke away when he saw me and ran to exclaim, "Freawaru, did you see, did you see? He did it! Beowulf killed the monster!" His face glowed with the excitement and wonder of it all.

"Yes, I see it. I doubted him before, but there can be no doubt now."

Beowulf must have heard my words, for he turned in my direction. In his eyes I saw no reproach, only a kind of question. For a moment he held my gaze and then turned back to the boys.

"Sons of an illustrious father, may you grow to be worthy of your sire and fight to win fame when your time comes. The future of Heorot lies with you."

Someone in the crowd gave a snort. Who was being so rude? As I sought among the faces, Hrothulf's sour visage revealed itself, frowning at my brothers. His face blurred and dissolved into another image: skulls crackling on a funeral pyre. I shook my head, striving to clear it of this unwanted vision. Surely my imagination was playing me false—but my heart misgave me.

Father ordered Heorot to be cleaned for a banquet—no small task. The whole structure was bent and broken, iron hinges cracked and sprung, furniture smashed to bits. Only the roof remained undamaged. Willing hands set to work; everyone wanted to help. I even saw Torgun, the blacksmith's wife, sweeping out rubble. By evening the hall had been made usable, the worst damage covered with tapestries, lengths of fabric, and even sailcloth. As we labored, an idea worked its way into my brain. I pulled Mother aside to broach it.

"Mother, has the great gold collar been promised to Ingeld as part of my dowry—or is it still being held in reserve?"

She looked at me in surprise.

"Your father and I did not include it in the list, but my intention is still to give it to you, if—"

"*If* Ingeld ever sends for me, yes." I swallowed, striving to keep my voice steady.

"I've been thinking. What if we gave it to Beowulf instead—and asked for his protection for Hrethric and Hrothmund? Did you see how they followed him everywhere today? And he treated them with such kindness—as if they were his own kin."

Mother stared at me, not speaking.

"And there's Hrothulf," I continued, pressing on. "I can't ignore this sense I have that he means to do harm to the boys … sooner or later. We may not always be here to watch out for them, and Beowulf would be a strong friend, if we ask for his friendship."

Mother nodded.

"I should no longer be surprised by what you see, daughter. But are you giving up the collar because you think Ingeld is not coming? In all the excitement, I forgot to tell you. He has sent a message, asking for patience. He still wants to take you as his wife."

"A message from Ingeld? When? What did he say? Why didn't you tell me?" Joy and anger swept over me simultaneously.

"Calm yourself, Freawaru. There has been no time. The message came while we were at banquet, and it was as I have said, no more, no less."

My heart swelled within me, a knot burst, releasing some of the pain I'd been carrying.

"That is good news indeed, but it does not change my proposal: that we give the neck-ring to Beowulf—to buy safety for the boys."

"You put it bluntly, but I think you are right. I will do it tonight, after Hrothgar presents his gifts to Beowulf. Freawaru," she touched her hand to mine, "thank you for your generous heart. You are truly a king's daughter."

That night when Father presided over the banquet, he looked every inch a king. With the weight of twelve winters lifted from his shoulders, he seemed to have grown taller. His eyes were bright, his face flushed with joy. When he spoke, his voice was strong; he sounded like the father I knew of old.

That evening formalities were relaxed in the general rejoicing. Mead flowed freely, as well as ale. Even Hrothulf seemed at ease, lifting his cup again and again to toast Hrothgar and Beowulf. No victory was ever better celebrated.

At a signal from Father, our thanes began to carry in the treasures that Beowulf was to receive: first a golden standard topped with the image of a stag, a frost-gray *byrnie*, a mail-coat that gleamed in the torch light, a wire-ridged helmet incised with boar-heads, and a sword of patterned steel, its hilt inlaid with gold and jewels. Then eight fine horses were led into the hall, each with a golden bridle—save one. On it, I recognized Father's own war saddle, carved and encrusted with gems. With a jolt, I realized what this meant. He would no longer be riding to battle with the younger men.

Each new object was greeted with shouts of pride and appreciation by Danes and Geats alike. Next came treasures of ancient swords and armor for each of Beowulf's men, including a set for the man who had been killed and eaten by the Grendel—Hondshu, the man whose face I had noted just minutes before his death. Should I have spoken to him? Warned him? Would it have made a difference?

When Beowulf held up the silvery mail shirt against his own massive chest, the men roared approval and Father beamed.

"That corselet belonged to my brother, Heregar, king before me. He never bequeathed his war gear to his son, loyal though he was, for the boy fell into evil practices with Odin-worshippers. Enjoy it well, dear Beowulf."

(When I asked Mother about this later, she said only that some young men practiced rites that their elders considered shameful.)

The evening wore on with no thought of its end. Now that the Grendel had been destroyed, we could celebrate until morning if we pleased. Aelric began to sing what seemed a sad song for such a happy occasion. It told of treachery and betrayal, of Danes and Frisians killing each other.

I recognized the story when I heard the names Finn, Hnaf, Hengest, and Hildeburh, the woman who had put both brother and son on the same funeral pyre. Grisly images assaulted my brain as I listened to our scop detail the story that Ana had once told me in outline.

"Wounds split and burst, skulls melted, blood came bubbling down, and the greedy fire-demons drank flesh and bones from the dead of both sides until nothing was left."

Apparently the men found the tale quite acceptable, for they laughed and shouted. Of course, the tale ended with the Danes triumphant. It had been so long since we'd had a triumph to celebrate!

Following this song, Mother approached the hall-seat, where Hrothgar and Hrothulf sat side by side, and raised the mead cup.

"Take this cup, my lord and king. May happiness come to the Dane's great ring giver and gifts flow freely from your open hands. Bright Heorot stands cleansed. I have heard that this greatest of Geats now rests in your heart like a son. Hand out the kingdom's treasures while you still hold them, but leave to your own kinsmen folk and rule, that they may succeed you after your decease."

Father wrinkled his brow, as if trying to make clear her meaning, but she had now turned to Hrothulf.

"Friend of the Scyldings, gracious Hrothulf, I know you will protect the sons of Hrothgar should he depart before you, repaying in kind the goodness we have shown you in your early days."

Her gracious smile elicited no answering smile from Hrothulf.

Mother walked further to where Beowulf sat between Hrethric and Hrothmund, motioning for me to step forward. She offered him the mead cup, which he took and from which he drank ceremoniously. Opening the chest I carried, she removed two arm rings, a corselet of steel rings—and the golden torque. One by one, she held them aloft.

Those nearby cheered to see this great treasure, the torque, displayed again. Thanes further down the row jumped up and craned their necks to see what was causing the stir.

"Wear these bright jewels, beloved Beowulf. Enjoy them and grow richer; let your strength and your fame go hand in hand. Grant your favor to these young Scyldings, lend these two boys your wise and gentle heart. I will remember your kindness, as your good fortune warms my soul. Spread your blessed protection across the king's sons."

She paused and then lifted her voice to be heard clearly by the whole assembly.

"Here, each warrior is true to the other, disposed to generosity, loyal to his prince, all are harmonious and courteous men. Having drunk from my cup, they do as I bid."

She turned back to Beowulf for one last admonition: "May your heart help you do as I ask!"

That night, I went to sleep satisfied with the evening's events. How could I or anyone in Heorot have known that all was not yet well? No vision came to warn me.

Chapter 8
A Mother's Revenge

That night, Hrothgar's thanes and athelings joyously prepared to bed down in the hall that had missed their presence for so long. Amid talk and laughter, benches and tables were cleared, feather pillows fluffed, sleeping robes spread. They hung their shields on the wall above their benches and laid helmets and byrnies and spears nearby as was their custom of old. At long last, Heorot would house a host of men at night as it was meant to do.

Beowulf and his band were given beds in another house. Hrothgar and Wealtheow retired to their quarters. I, as usual, slept among the women and servants of our household. I suspected that not all of our women remained there that night, for I heard stifled giggles in one of my drowsy moments. No doubt they had gone to congratulate Beowulf's men in their own way.

My rest was unquiet, beset by ominous images. When I awoke in the darkness, I was not sure if the cry I'd heard was my own or another's.

I sat up, sensing danger as one recognizes an old friend. What could be amiss? Surely the Grendel was dead—surely it had long since bled to death?

Shouts and cries echoed down from the hall—men's voices filled with anger and fright. Were they too having evil dreams? I shuddered and drew my robes close, unwilling to consider more tragedy. Rushing feet passed the women's house, as if Heorot were being emptied by some malignant force. Fire? I sat up again and sniffed the air, but smelled nothing.

Silence. Then the tramp of more feet, this time running toward Heorot. I heard Father's voice, moaning with grief, and hot anger filled me. He did not deserve more anguish! Somehow our brief peace had been broken.

"Send for Beowulf," cried Hrothgar. "At once!"

In the gray light of early dawn, Beowulf and his men marched into Heorot a second time, followed by many of our household—myself among them. At once I noted something missing: the Grendel's cruel claw no longer hung from the rafter.

Beowulf greeted Hrothgar courteously, though clearly half-awake.

"Hail, Hrothgar. Have you passed a pleasant night, as you planned?"

Father's answer was bitter.

"Ask not about happiness. There is none for the Danes! Aeschere is dead—my most trusted counselor and oldest friend. Another wandering fiend has found him in Heorot, murdered him, and fled with his corpse."

My stomach rose into my throat. No, not Aeschere—let it not be Aeschere!

"He will be eaten—his flesh a feast for monsters!" Hrothgar almost sobbed in his anguish. "Some kinsman of the beast has come to take revenge—and to give us more sorrow."

Beowulf looked nonplussed at this new turn of events. "What manner of fiend can it be, my lord?"

"Our country folk once reported seeing a pair of huge creatures wandering the moors and marshes walking like men, but mightier than any man. One was formed in woman's likeness, the other in a man's. We called the man-monster Grendel—that same beast with whom you grappled."

Father's voice shook as he continued and tears streamed down his face.

"It is difficult to believe that a female could attack our hall, but the arm is gone. She must have been a mate, or even the mother of the Grendel, come to seek revenge for his death—a hard revenge. Oh Aeschere, Aeschere, my friend!"

Now Father sank to his knees, sobbing.

"Dear Beowulf, you alone can avenge this death. We will lead you to the place where the pair were thought to dwell—a terrible place—a lake whose waters burn like a torch at night. If you dare to seek it and slay the Grendel's kin, I shall honor you with heaped-up treasure beyond what any man has seen. Save us once more!"

All of us stood frozen in silence, not daring to hope that Beowulf would step forward a second time, but at a loss for any other remedy. Beowulf showed no such hesitation. Advancing to Hrothgar's side, he spoke with confidence.

"Let your sorrow end! It is better to avenge our friends than to mourn overmuch. Arise, great king. Let us go and seek out this lady monster. I promise you this: she will not escape, go where she will. Be patient for one more day of misery—I ask for no more."

Hrothgar rose to his feet and embraced Beowulf, calling for horses. Within minutes, all were mounted, following the king as he led them toward the distant mere. At the last minute, Unferth joined the procession, carrying something I had never seen him wear before: a sword.

The morning crept slowly on as we waited in an agony of suspense. Long past midday, the sound of horses' hooves alerted us, and we dropped whatever we were doing to rush out of doors. Father and his men, grim-faced, dismounted.

Father spoke heavily to Mother. "The Geats have stayed behind, loyal to their leader, but I fear Beowulf is lost."

"How can you be sure? Tell us what happened!"

We women joined her, crowding close to hear.

"Beowulf plunged into the lake wearing his chain mail as a defense against the claws of the fearsome sea beasts and serpents that infest it. He wore my helmet and took the sword given him by Unferth—both famous weapons, which have always preserved their owners from harm."

"We waited for hours and saw the waters surge with blood. When the sun slid past midday, we despaired of his life and returned, bringing—this."

From his own cloak, wet and bunched on his saddle, he gently lifted out a head—Aeschere's. We gasped and drew back in horror.

Hot tears scalded my cheeks: tears for Aeschere, for Beowulf, for all of us still alive in this doomed kingdom.

"We found it on a ledge above the water—all that remains of the noble Aeschere." Father choked, and could speak no more.

Unferth now stepped forward and held out a weapon. "This is Beowulf's sword, exchanged for mine. I fear it is all we have left of him."

Then Hrothgar spoke again.

"The fiendish female—the Grendel's dam, if that is what she be—had positioned Aeschere's head on the cliff like a warning, perhaps designed to repel her enemies. I fear she may have overcome Beowulf with her powerful magic, despite his great strength."

Time seemed to stop as grief and sorrow overwhelmed us. Our bodies were numb, stripped of feeling or sensation. We could not speak or cry—not even Hrethric and Hrothmund, who stared transfixed at Aeschere's pale, bloody head, the eyes now forever closed.

Wealtheow recovered first. "Take that away. I myself will tell Ana what has happened. We will honor Aeschere at the funeral pyre—as we will Beowulf, if any part of him can be found."

Without a word, two thanes stepped forward to receive the bloody offering and bear it away.

Mother ordered the evening meal for everyone to be served in the mead hall—with no limit on the ale. Her face was drawn and white, but she spoke with authority, and we obeyed automatically. Thus it was that we sat, trying to eat and drink, when a strange procession wound its way up the hill toward Heorot.

"By the gods!"

A thane dropped his drinking horn and hurried to the door.

Up the path, staggering under the weight they carried, came four Geats, two on either side of a long spear shaft driven completely through the skull of a giant head. Behind them strode … Beowulf! He grabbed the huge head by the hair, pulled it off the spear, and marched through the open doorway, carrying his trophy straight to the king and queen—a weird and wonderful sight! Mother did not flinch at this ghastly apparition, but I did.

"Grendel's head?"

"Grendel's head!"

"The gods be praised!"

By now, everyone had jumped up to crowd around the dripping trophy, all ceremony forgotten. The size of the skull was astonishing; it exceeded my wildest imaginings. Several thanes tried to lift it by the hair, once Beowulf let it thud to the floor. A few could move it slightly, but no one could raise it.

The long, lank hair was coarse and gray—almost like Aeschere's hair, I thought with a fresh pang of grief, but the monster's hair was streaked with greenish slime. The Grendel appeared to have no proper eyes, only dark, deep depressions where eyeballs should have been. Beside me, Mother pondered this aloud.

"So, evil, like death, is blind … it takes what it finds without thought or mercy."

She reached for my hand as we stared at the monster head together, still held fast by its capacity to induce terror.

As if to compensate for its lack of sight, the creature had immense, flaring nostrils, bigger even than those of a bull or ox. The skin on the face—if one could call it skin—was pale and leathery-looking. Hrothmund reached out a finger to touch it, but Mother sharply pulled his hand away. Then she laughed nervously at her own caution. Clearly, the Grendel was dead.

At Hrethric's urging, Beowulf pried open the creature's once-powerful jaws. One of the Geats handed Beowulf a sword with which to prop open the mouth. Holding our noses at the stench that came forth, we leaned close for a better look. Now we could see for ourselves the huge, slashing tusks, the cruel teeth that had snapped shut on many and many a thane, cutting life short. The mottled grinders, stained green and brown, were worn in places; shreds of flesh still clung to rotting molars.

"Could have swallowed you whole, Hrothmund!"

This sally from Hrothulf brought a squeal from my brother, who faded back behind Mother. She reached around to pull him forward.

"There is no need to fear, son. The monster can't hurt us anymore."

Silence fell over the group as we pondered this amazing truth. Then shouts and cheers erupted throughout the mead hall as we celebrated in happy abandonment. This time the roar came not from a monster, but from our people, set free.

Father now asked the question on all our lips.

"Beowulf, how did you survive? Tell us your story."

"My story is a long one. Perhaps some ale before I tell it?" He sank onto a bench.

Servants rushed to bring him a drinking horn; Mother herself poured the ale and signaled for silence as he drained it. Beowulf now stood and shook his head as if clearing it from a bad dream.

"After entering the lake, I sank for hours, battling sea monsters during my descent. Then the mighty sea-witch, Grendel's dam, saw me and drew me down to her air-filled cave beneath the water, into a giant's battle-hall. We fought savagely. She ripped and clawed at me, tearing holes in my helmet. Unferth's noble blade was useless against her. Only my mail shirt preserved me from her stabbing dagger as she straddled my chest."

Hrethric and Hrothmund caught their breath, as did every person in the hall.

"Then I saw, hanging on the wall, a heavy sword that must have been hammered by giants. Angry and desperate, I pulled it from its scabbard, breaking the hilt-chain. Savagely I lifted it high over my head and struck with all the strength I had left."

He paused, panting, as if reliving that mighty effort.

"I caught her in the neck, cut through bones and all, and left her there, lying lifeless on the floor."

A universal intake of breath among the listeners. Beowulf drank another horn of ale, clearing his throat.

"I searched the cave for Grendel's corpse and found it lying in a corner. With a single blow, I struck off its head and then swam back up with it to the top of the lake."

Now he laughed. "There is more. Herelick, bring in the other prize."

We turned our heads to see what new wonder might appear. Beowulf's countryman brought in something wrapped in a cloak. Beowulf reached in and pulled out a massive, jeweled sword hilt. Holding it aloft, he shouted, "Behold, Hrothgar, this sign of victory! With this giant sword, I hacked the head from the sea-hag. With this sword, I took the trophy from the Grendel's body. I meant to bring you the whole sword, Hrothgar, but the monster's blood—still boiling in its veins—dissolved the blade."

Open-mouthed, we gazed at each other in amazement as Beowulf continued.

"I carried off all that was left—this hilt. Now," he paused, extending the hilt to the king, "now I have avenged the crimes of both monsters. Now anyone in Denmark, old or young, may sleep without fear of either monster, mother or son."

Cheers filled the mead hall again and again. Men lifted their cups in spontaneous salute to the Geat, to Beowulf. Joyfully, I did the same, yet felt reluctant to rejoice too soon. Could there be other monsters in that den of evil? A sudden image came to me of the fen, its waters calm, reflecting sunlight. Ah, all must be well.

Hrothgar took the hilt, examining it with awe. Clearly it was an ancient relic; I could see runes carved on it—perhaps the name of the owner or maker.

"Hear me, Danes!" All fell silent as Father rose to speak.

"This Prince of the Geats was well born! Beowulf, my friend, I see your fame spreading through the whole world. You will hold it in your heart wisely, patient with your strength and our weakness. But beware of pride, my son, guard against such wickedness as overcame Hermod."

Hermod? Who was Hermod? I must ask Mother later.

"Hermod was a famous ruler," said Father, as if answering my unspoken question. "Like you he possessed greater strength than anyone alive in his day, but he turned dark and bloodthirsty in spirit. His pride brought destruction to his own people. Be taught by his lesson, learn what a king must be, for I say that the Geats could do no better, find no man better suited to be king, than you, if you take the throne they will surely offer you one day."

A sudden smile lightened Father's features.

"For now, take the rest you have earned, and then we will feast and be happy. When morning comes, we will speak again of treasure."

Beowulf cheerfully obeyed. That night I once again saw Geats and Danes feasting together as brothers. When darkness fell, they rose, Beowulf still heavy with exhaustion. I managed to catch his eye as a hall thane led him toward the visitors' quarters.

"My lord, I celebrate your safe return, though I fear you will leave us soon for your own country. Where does it lie?"

He looked me up and down before replying.

"Lady Freawaru, I am honored by your interest. My country lies two days by water to the north and east, on a rocky coastline. There I serve Higlac, King of the Geats, but I would willingly serve you in any way."

Not sure what his words imparted, I hastened to make my situation clear.

"It is for my brothers I speak. I myself am betrothed to Ingeld, chief of the Heathobards. We are … soon to be married."

"Then Ingeld is a fortunate man, my lady."

He smiled, his eyes holding mine, and then bowed and disappeared into the night

That smile … had I seen it before? Then it struck me: the man on the swan's back, the man in my dream vision. It was Beowulf. He had come to our rescue, as I had foreseen.

At the leave-taking next morning, the Geats were clearly eager to board their vessel and depart, but first they trooped up to Heorot to make their final farewells to Hrothgar.

Beowulf sought out Unferth and returned Hrunting, calling it an excellent weapon and thanking him for its loan. He graciously made no further mention of its failure to save him in the sea-witch's cave. This raised Beowulf even higher in my estimation. The feats he had accomplished still seemed too miraculous to grasp, but simple kindness I could understand.

Next Beowulf hailed the king.

"Great son of Healfdane, we have been royally entertained in your hall. If there is any way I may earn more of your love and esteem, my lord, you need only call on me and I shall answer. If I discover from across the sea that neighboring tribes make war upon you, I shall bring a thousand thanes to help you in your need. If Hrethric, your son, should wish to visit the home of the Geats, he will find friends there. It is good to visit faraway lands if a man has valor."

I glowed to hear these words, which confirmed for me the wisdom of giving him the golden torque. Hrothgar, too, was pleased.

"Beowulf, I have never heard a young man speak more wisely. You are strong in prowess and presence of mind, and your courage pleases me better the longer I know you. You have performed so nobly that our two peoples, Danes and Geats, shall have peace together—no more feuds or conflicts—as long as I hold this land and guard its coffers."

Then he loaded Beowulf and his men with more treasures, bidding them safe return to their king and kinsmen. I watched as Father laid his hand on Beowulf's neck, blinded with tears. All of us present in the hall knew it was unlikely he would live to see Beowulf again, for age now sat upon him like a permanent guest.

Turning, Beowulf strode proudly out of the mead hall, decked in glittering armor, shining like the sun. My own eyes filled with tears, blinded by the golden light of his great neck ring. Father, Mother, Hrothulf, Unferth, and I stood together before the doors of Heorot watching the Geats as they descended to the harbor. I wondered if we would ever see Beowulf again.

"Now to more painful matters," said Father, "a funeral pyre for Aeschere's remains. Hrothulf, direct the men in its construction."

Nodding stiffly, Hrothulf headed in one direction, as Unferth headed in another. Mother took Father's arm.

"Let us walk in the meadow, my lord, and let our hearts be comforted."

Her tone was gentle, as if she were speaking to one of the boys. The boys? Where were they? How had they missed our farewell to Beowulf? I need not have worried. They soon appeared, climbing up from the harbor where they had gone to "help" with the loading of Beowulf's ship.

"Getting the horses on board was really hard," they reported. "We helped tie them down in the center of the boat and then carried armor and weapons for Beowulf's men to load. He took the place of the missing man when they rowed out to sea, but they soon put up the sail—it was white with red stripes. Do you know what is carved on his ship's prow? A dragon head! I'm going to use that on *my* first boat!" Hrethric paused. "Freawaru, do you think we could visit Beowulf some day?"

All of this came out in a breathless tumble. I gave each of them a quick hug.

"I don't know, boys, but I am sure you'd find a welcome there. Right now you can help gather wood for Aeschere's funeral pyre."

Hrethric grimaced. "I hope that's our last one. I like fires, but I'm sick of burning people."

His words made me think of the gruesome song sung by Aelric at Beowulf's feast. I must ask Mother what she knew about the Hildeburh of the story.

A light rain began to fall at midday, delaying the lighting of the funeral pyre. But a more ominous problem soon arose. Aeschere's head could not be found! Father said he'd handed the bag to Hrothulf, who said he'd handed it to Unferth, but Unferth seemed to have disappeared. He was missing from his accustomed place in the mead hall that night, though his horse still grazed with those of the other athelings in the settlement enclosure. Where could he be?

Hrethric and Hrothmund knew. With long faces, they pulled me aside to whisper, "Freawaru, Unferth needs help."

"What's happened? Where is he? Is he hurt?"

"No, but something is wrong. He doesn't know we're telling you this—I don't think he saw us, but we saw him. Freawaru, he has Aeschere's head ... and he's talking to it."

A chill swept over me. First the ravens, now this. "Take me to him—but quietly."

We melted into the shadows along the wall and slipped out of Heorot, hoping to avoid notice. The boys led me to one of the storehouses where dried cod hung in the loft. As we stopped outside and listened, I heard mumbling from above. It was Unferth's voice.

"Aeschere, I command you, speak to me! As Mimer once spoke to Odin, speak to me now. Reveal what you see on the other side."

We lifted the heavy oak bar and pushed. A shaft of light shone on the ladder and the square above it. I could make out a figure holding something aloft. A fetid smell of swamp and decay met our nostrils. We pushed again and the door groaned open. Above us the figure whirled.

"Unferth?" I spoke calmly but firmly, as if calling one of my brothers to eat.

"Come down, Unferth. Aeschere cannot speak to you. He is dead."

A face appeared at the edge of the square, eyes glaring. A long, low laugh emerged from its lips. For one terrifying second I could not tell if it was Unferth or Aeschere.

"Foolish woman—leave me! Do not interfere in a rite to Odin, for he deals in blood, and those who would gain knowledge from him must pay. Go! Your interruption may break the spell!"

"No, Unferth. We need Aeschere's remains for the funeral pyre. He deserves the rites of a warrior. Release him. Let him join the ranks in Valhalla."

Silence. Then I heard the striking of a flint. A radiance lit the interior. Outlined above us loomed Aeschere's head, its tangled locks clutched in Unferth's bloody hands.

We stared at each other, frozen in the light. I clutched my apron to my throat. Behind me, I heard my brothers making strangling sounds. As we waited, hearts pounding, I suddenly knew the truth. Unferth was both more and less than a shaman. Unferth was mad.

"Take it! The spell is broken!"

With these words, the thing came hurtling down at us. Instinctively I caught it in my apron, almost ripped from my hands by the force of the blow. I gasped and staggered backward through the doorway, both boys clinging to me.

Outside the world was illuminated as if it were day.

"What is this?" I marveled.

Hrothmund tugged at my elbow; Hrethric pointed up.

"The moon, Freaw, the moon!"

I gazed up in wonder. The moon? Round, full, and luminous, it hung low in the sky above us. The moon. For twelve long winters, we had not stood outside under the light of the moon, our lives made dark by the Grendel.

Now we stood mute, our faces bathed in moonlight. Finally I drew a deep, shuddering breath, and wrapped my apron around all that was left of my friend.

"Come, boys, let us go home. Beowulf has set us free to see the moon again. Now Aeschere is free to sleep in the fire."

Chapter 9
A House of Wolves

Aeschere's head was placed atop the funeral pyre next morning, and the burning went forward. Father sacrificed his own warhorse in honor of his lifelong companion, adding its body to the pyre. Mother stood beside Ana, one hand on her shoulder as the flames consumed the remains of Aeschere.

I wept alongside them, sharing the loss. With Aeschere's death, I felt that my own past—my girlhood—had come to an end, consumed in the flames. Beowulf was gone. The Grendel was gone, along with his fiercesome mother. My future still lay in darkness. What might come next? What of my betrothal to Ingeld? Would he ever return?

Disposal of the Grendel's head presented a new problem. At Mother's request, Beowulf had taken it out of the mead hall before his departure. Now it lay in a nearby pasture exposed to the elements, to carrion feeders, and to the gawking examination of the whole settlement. Our village dogs gave it a wide berth, snarling or whining anxiously when a whiff of it came to their nostrils, for it was rapidly rotting away.

With Aeschere dead, Father now conferred with his remaining athelings, who proposed various methods of disposal. Burn it, bury it, drag it back to the swamp, cast it in the sea—behind each suggestion lay the unspoken question: how can we destroy any lingering power the creature may possess, both now and in the days to come? Finally, it was decided to push the skull into a rock cleft near the sea, drench it with buckets of boiling lye, drop huge boulders in the hole to shatter the skull, and then cover the top with enormous stone slabs dragged to the site by oxen

That afternoon I sat on my bench color-sorting a stack of braided bands for my wedding chest. As I thought back over Beowulf's struggle in the monsters' cave, two details stood out: his use of the giant's sword for decapitation and the melting of the sword blade. On previous raids, the Grendel's hide had deflected every sword stroke of Hrothgar's men. Why had Beowulf been successful? Did the sword he'd found possess powerful magic? Even so, the Grendel's blood had dissolved the blade. Why not the mother's blood?

An image of the monster's mother began to form in my mind: huge dugs, menacing fangs, tears ... tears? Yes, she must have been consumed by bitter grief as she watched her son die, a grief that turned to burning rage—a rage so strong it propelled her out of her cave and into the world of men, where she dared to enter the mead hall alone, seize the Grendel's missing arm, and exact a vicious revenge on the unlucky Aeschere.

Ironically, she had done only what any man in Father's band would have done: taken revenge, a life for a life.

I sat, staring at my lap, heedless of the color and richness in my hands. Grendel's dam had also tried to stab Beowulf with a twisted dagger, and she had come within an inch of taking his life—that man of incredible strength. What a powerful water-witch she must have been! I felt for my own small knife, hidden beneath my tunic. Would I ever need to use it to kill a man?

"Freawaru, what is it? What do you see? More ... darkness?"

Mother's face came into focus, pulling me back into the present.

"No, Mother, I was just thinking … the Grendel's blood dissolved the giant sword blade, while the mother's blood did not affect it. But she almost killed Beowulf. Which monster was more powerful?"

Mother eyed me curiously. "Have you received a vision?"

"No—yes—oh, I don't know! Images come to me, but I can't tell which are true and which are not. Whether dreams or visions, I don't know how to understand or interpret them!"

"Be comforted, daughter. As you grow in confidence, you will learn to trust your special powers."

Unferth avoided everyone for several days but seemed more like his usual self when he walked into the eld-hus where Mother and I were weaving. First, he reported a personal visit to the monster's fen.

"I wanted to inspect the place myself … for any remaining signs of evil. But it is as Beowulf reported: clear, calm, and free of the sea monsters that once infested it." He shook his head in wonder.

"That gladdens my heart, Unferth. Thank you and thank the gods!" I cried. Indeed it was a great relief. Surely our long ordeal was finally over.

"There is something else I must say to you." He turned to Mother. 'You know I have your best interests at heart, my lady queen. Forgive me, but I advise against the proposed marriage of Freawaru to the Heathobard. I have seen omens of disaster in the union."

Mother opened her mouth to respond, but I flared up immediately.

"How can you say that? What omens?"

"Blood on the neck ring that is part of your dowry."

Had the head of Aeschere spoken to him after all? Had it revealed secrets of the future? If so, it had spoken in error. My laughter echoed off the walls and then stopped abruptly. Mother quietly explained.

"It is no longer part of her dowry. We gave it to Beowulf. You were there—do you not remember?"

Unferth's eyes clouded. "But I saw it spattered with blood. I saw its owner fall."

Somberly, I spoke. "May it not be Beowulf's blood, but he is the owner now."

"May it not be Beowulf's blood," echoed Mother fervently.

Without a word, Unferth turned and strode out of the house.

Why had I not told Mother about the scene in the drying shed? Somehow, I felt reluctant to expose Unferth's part in the delay of Aeschere's funeral. He had been my friend and teacher for many years and was still a trusted adviser to both king and queen. Perhaps my fears for him were unfounded?

I tried to watch him closely in the days that followed for evidence to confirm or dispel my suspicion, but Unferth disappeared more and more often. He was missing when a band of men on dapple gray horses rode up to Heorot, their shapes almost ghostly in the fading dusk. I could not be sure they were real.

When Brita burst into the room, I was standing at my loom weaving an image of the goddess Freyja receiving the Brisinga necklace.

"The Heathobards! It's your betrothed!"

"Ingeld?"

I dropped the shuttle of flaxen thread, my fingers suddenly numb. "Are you sure?" I did not think I could stand more disappointment.

"Freawaru, come quickly! Ingeld is calling for you!"

Mother's face appeared in the doorway, beaming. I could no longer doubt the truth: Ingeld had come at last to claim his bride!

His face looked thinner than I remembered it, and his chin was fringed with stubble, but his eyes glowed at the sight of me. I realized he was tracing the contours of my now womanly form. He still sat his horse as he spoke.

"We meet again, my lady Freawaru. Are you ready?"

"I am ready, Ingeld, though you are late in coming." My unfortunate tongue! Ingeld's face darkened.

"The wife of Ingeld must know when to speak and when to keep silent."

"I have kept silent for many months, my lord, but now I greet you with joy and bid you welcome." I gave him a smile full of unfeigned happiness.

Mollified, Ingeld dismounted and strode toward me. I extended the hand that bore his golden circlet, a gesture which bought a smile to his own lips. As we embraced, he whispered in my ear: "You please me well. There were reasons for my delay."

That night, as we were raising our glasses in a toast, Unferth staggered into the mead hall. I rose involuntarily, but Ingeld pulled me back to my seat and growled.

"What is this man to you?"

"He is my rune-master. I fear he is … ill."

Haggard and wild-eyed, Unferth made his way up to the bench where we sat, just below Father and Mother on the raised platform. Strange—Hrothulf, too, was missing. I had been too distracted to notice his absence until now.

Unferth stopped before us. Placing both hands on the table, he leaned forward, bringing his face close to ours. His breath was foul, though it did not reek of ale.

"Heathobard, son of Froda, killer of Healfdane, your presence pollutes our court. You—"

A shower of mead cut short his tirade. In wonder, I realized that I had flung it in his face.

"Unferth, come to your senses! You are not well!"

He swayed, staring at me, and then crumpled to the floor. All around us men were on their feet, shouting. Ingeld's companions had drawn their swords. Wulfgar lifted Unferth to drag him from the hall. I put my hand on Ingeld's arm as he too rose.

"Do not take insult from a madman, my lord. Some other being inhabits Unferth at this moment—I swear it."

Ingeld's eyes were cold, but he hesitated … and signaled his men to put up their weapons. He turned to Father.

"A strange entertainment you provide for your guests, lord Hrothgar!"

Father, who clearly had not heard Unferth's words, looked around in surprise. He raised his golden cup.

"Friends, let us drink to the union of Freawaru and Ingeld!"

Automatically hands reached for drinking horns. Hrothgar signaled Aelric to recite a lay, and he launched into the story of Thor's false marriage to the giantess Thrym—the same story I had once told my brothers at bedtime. For once, I found Aelric's choice appropriate, for its humor restored peace in the hall.

Ingeld squeezed my hand under the table.

"Soon Thor's hammer will be laid in your lap, and you will become my lady in fact."

"Yes, my lord," I replied mechanically. My thoughts were still on Unferth, wondering what had provoked his outburst.

Beside me, Ingeld was getting drunk. By the end of the banquet, he needed the support of his men to get to the visitors quarters. I could not help but compare his weakness with the behavior of Beowulf, who seemed always in control of his strength and his wits. Yet Beowulf had walked out of my life, and Ingeld was here beside me.

The next day we met in Father's chamber to transact the *Morgengifu*, the morning-gift, which Ingeld offered to me as his bride. It was a generous one: ten slaves, ten horses, five weights of gold, and five hides of land. I smiled to think of myself as a landowner.

Father and Mother made no attempt to conceal their pleasure; only Hrothulf, who had been summoned to witness the contract, behaved in his usual morose fashion. While Ingeld conversed with Mother and Father, I faced my cousin.

"What do you think of Ingeld's gift?"

"Generous indeed—if delivered as promised," he hissed. "Let us hope the Heathobard keeps his word."

I shot him a dark look. Why could he never be happy for me?

"You will be happy to see me gone, Hrothulf?"

The vehemence of his reply startled me.

"Never! But I predict you will return to Heorot soon enough."

I tried to make light of his dire words.

"Predictions are Unferth's business. Where is he, by the way? Both of you were absent from the feast last night—though Unferth came late and created a disturbance. Is he well?"

Hrothulf looked at me, a mocking smile on his lips.

"We have business that concerns us alone."

We? When had Unferth and Hrothulf become a "we"?

"Tell him that I hope he is well. I ... I fear for him."

Hrothulf positively snorted at this.

"Unferth can care for himself—he is skilled in the use of herbs ... and of poisons."

"Poisons? What need has he of poisons?"

"You will know in time. Good day, 'my lady.'" He left the chamber without a backward glance.

His words were a taunt, delivered in the petulant tone of a child unable to get its way. Even so, dire thoughts flooded my brain. Poison? For whom? Surely not Ingeld? I must be on guard to protect him—yet not reveal possible treachery. Already, it seemed my role as peace-weaver was in jeopardy!

Ingeld now turned to me. "Why do you frown, Freawaru? Do my gifts not please you?"

"They please me well, my lord. They bespeak a generous heart and your knowledge of what befits a king's daughter."

"Ah, ever the proud lady. You will be an adornment to my court, which could use a little ... polish. Come, let us walk again in the meadow, and I will tell you more of my homeland—soon to be your land as well."

I took his arm as we left the chamber, aware of his skin's warmth against my hand. Outside, a light breeze cooled my brow. For a time we walked in silence. Then my tongue spoke a thought that had long lain on my heart.

"How fares your mother?"

"Ah, you have touched the very spot. Indeed, she is one reason for my long delay. At first, she would not hear of a Scylding bride. You know as well as I the story of our two families!" He shot me a sideways look, to which I nodded assent.

"Many in my hall were likewise against such a union. Your father's gold helped persuade them, for he sent part of your dowry ahead that I might prepare suitable quarters for you. We built a noble hall ... only to have it burn to the ground on the day of its completion."

At my gasp, he nodded grimly, but continued. "So we built it again, from our own coffers this time. I would not go back on the word I gave to Hrothgar."

I halted and seized his hands to turn him toward me.

"You did all this … for me?"

He laughed. "Partly for you. Partly for me. Partly to show my mother and the rest of the hall that my mind is my own, and it is set on Freawaru!"

He embraced me then, seeking my lips. I did not turn away.

Given the lateness of the season, it was arranged that our marriage be celebrated in Heorot after the usual nine nights of waiting. Then I and my attendants would set forth with Ingeld and his men for my new home, far to the south across land and water. Selecting those who would accompany me proved to be a difficult task. Although Mother and I had discussed several names, she left the final choices to me. At last it was settled. Wulfgar agreed to lead our contingent, along with the thanes who had previously accompanied me to Moon Cliff: Olaf, Sven, Gorm, and Saxe—high-spirited young men eager to see new lands and make names for themselves.

To my surprise, Ana, now Aeschere's widow, volunteered to become my companion. She and Willa had been friends for many years, she explained, and Willa would have wanted her to go with me. I suspected that she also wished to leave behind the place of Aeschere's death. Had Willa been alive, she would, of course, have been my first choice as a companion; her loss still echoed in an empty chamber of my heart.

From among Mother's women, I chose Estrid, Ingeborg, and Ragnhild, at the last minute adding Gyda to the list. Despite her sharp tongue, she was a good worker, and she made me laugh. Brita I spared, not having the heart to separate her from the man she still dreamed of marrying.

Our horses, chests, and household gear were loaded on board Aeschere's just-completed cargo vessel. Dear, dead Aeschere—he had no need of it now. Thinking of Aeschere turned my thoughts to Unferth.

Where was he? What was happening inside his head? Would he appear at the bridal feast? Would he bless or curse me?

From time to time during the waiting period, minor quarrels broke out between Ingeld's men and our own—especially after heavy drinking in the mead hall. Serious blows were often averted by Aelric, ever ready to recount in detail the adventures of Beowulf in our court, a tale that always found eager listeners. Each day, I made offerings to Freyja and the earth goddess, asking for their blessing on my coming marriage.

After the high emotion of the great banquets celebrating Beowulf's victories, my wedding feast was a relatively quiet affair. I could sense mixed feelings among both Danes and Heathobards, though Ingeld himself never wavered in his attention and respect to me.

For the first time in my life, I sat between the carved pillars of the raised platform, Ingeld and I flanked by Hrothgar and Wealtheow. Below us sat Hrothulf and Unferth on either side of Hrethric and Hrothmund.

I wore a finely pleated shift of white linen overlain with a blue silk tunic embroidered with flowers around the hem. Willa's brooches fastened the straps. A circlet of twisted gold crowned my upswept hair, and my arms glowed in the torchlight from many golden bands.

Looking out over the rows of tables and benches, I swallowed and choked back a sob, my heart filled with sudden love for this hall and its inhabitants. Would I ever lift a cup again in this place, among these people?

Below me Hrothulf and Unferth sat immobile, ignoring the squirms and jests of my brothers—still boys for all their recent spurt in height. Over the last few days, the boys had been alternately teasing me and mourning my departure.

Too old to beg for "one last story," they shared with me their treasures: Hrothmund pressed a small amulet into my palm—a silver hammer of Thor. He hesitated and then whispered, "To keep you safe."

Hrethric gave me his oakwood game board and all his playing pieces, beautifully carved of whalebone. "So you will remember me when you're playing Hnefatafl this winter."

"Maybe I'll have a chance to win without you as my opponent," I grinned and then sobered as I saw tears gather in his eyes.

"Will I ever see you again, Freawaru?"

"Of course," I assured him, though my heart misgave me.

Others sought me out that week with parting gifts. Mother presented me with a silver chain from which hung scissors, knife, and tweezers, as well as a fine linen head cloth to cover my hair after the marriage.

"Freawaru, I have also prepared a salve of lemon balm to use when you go to bed with Ingeld, should it prove difficult for you. I know you have not yet slept with any man, and the first time can be painful—but only for a short time."

"Thank you, Mother," I was grateful for her thoughtfulness. I had heard the cries of women coupling with men and could not always distinguish pleasure from pain.

To my surprise and relief, Unferth also appeared one afternoon as I was gathering greens in the salad gardens and motioned in the direction of the great oak. I followed him silently to my old special place, the place where he had rescued me from the water and taught me all I knew of rune-craft.

"So ... king's daughter ... you are to leave Heorot."

He looked weary, his face marked with dark lines, but his eyes were the eyes of the Unferth I knew.

"My friend—" I began, but he raised a finger to his lips.

"Listen, Freawaru. All is not yet clear to me, though I have traveled far in search of the truth."

"Traveled? How? Where? You have not left Heorot these many days," I protested.

"Not in body, but in spirit," he answered.

My mind flashed to Aeschere's head and the two ravens, Huginn and Muginn.

"What I have learned troubles me, for I see dark days ahead: blood and fire, screams of pain and terror, which bear the sound of your voice. I ask you again to reconsider this union with the Heathobard."

I waited long before I spoke.

"Unferth, it is my father's will—and mine—that this marriage take place. It is important to unite our tribes. Besides ... I love Ingeld."

Until the words were spoken, I had not been sure of this. Now I acknowledged it to myself: *I love this man, this Heathobard, and I believe that he loves me.*

"Love is not the issue here, king's daughter!" Unferth exploded in exasperation. "Your safety, that is the issue—perhaps your very survival!"

"Why should that matter so much to you?" I asked, coldly.

He hesitated. "You have great power within you. I would not see it wasted—or lost."

"Oh." Somehow I had expected—hoped—for something more personal from him. Suddenly another thought struck me.

"Unferth, what are you doing with poison?"

His eyes narrowed, but he answered freely.

"Do not be alarmed. It is for myself alone. Administered in judicious quantities it is not fatal but brings visions one could not otherwise obtain. The lowly mushroom is my aide in this quest." He smiled a rueful smile.

"Then you're not going to poison Ingeld?"

Now he laughed outright. "What put that idea into your head? No I am not going to poison Ingeld—especially if you are as fond of him as you say."

A wave of relief rolled over me. I jumped up, laughing, and caught Unferth by the hands.

"Let's not quarrel. I'll be gone soon, and I will miss you."

"And I you, king's daughter. Here …"

He reached inside his cloak and pulled out a small dagger, holding it forth for my inspection. Below the silver guard, the blade extended the length of my hand. The handle was carved with runes. He pointed to three on the front.

"Uruz: strength, Algiz: protection, and Sowelu: wholeness—and on the back, Inguz, for new beginnings. May they aid you on your life's journey. This is my parting gift."

I took the dagger, still warm with Unferth's body heat, and touched the tip to my finger. Bright blood sprang forth.

"This weapon must be sheathed carefully," he observed. "Do not hesitate to strike when need calls. It may mean your life! Now, I must leave you."

In a second, he had slipped away, noiseless as a shadow.

At last, the moment had arrived. Ingeld and I were to be married! All the events of the previous nine days and nights passed through my mind as Ingeld and I sat waiting inside the walls of Heorot: our talks and walks, the feasting, final details of packing. Finally Father and Mother rose. Father spoke first.

"We are gathered here to witness the union of Freawaru, daughter of Hrothgar, and Ingeld, son of Froda. As evidence of his good faith, Ingeld has promised to the bride ten slaves, ten horses, five weights of gold, and five hydes of land in his own domain."

Murmurs of approval rose across the hall.

"For our part, we give in dowry five suits of chain mail, five saddles of gilt and leather, five Frankish swords with damascened blades, five helmets, ten horses, ten cows, ten sheep, and ten weights of gold."

Danes roared their approval of Hrothgar's generosity.

"Now for the oath-taking. Ingeld?"

We both rose, and Ingeld turned to face me. He looked proud, serious, and ... handsome.

"Before the gods, I swear to honor you, Freawaru, as my wife, to provide for your comfort, and to make you keeper of my household. I further swear to keep peace between Heathobards and Danes. That is my pledge."

"Daughter?" coached Mother. I seemed to have lost my voice, but soon found it.

"Before the gods, I swear to honor you, Ingeld, as my husband, to provide for your comfort and keep your household. Your enemies shall be my enemies and your friends my friends. That is my pledge."

"Bring in the hammer," commanded Mother.

While Ingeld and I sat down, Hrethric and Hrothmund jumped up and hurried to the back of the hall. They returned carrying between them a large hammer of Thor—recently fashioned by our blacksmith for this occasion.

Mother took it in both hands, raised it high for all to see, and then laid it gently in my lap.

"May the gods hallow this union," she intoned. "Bring in the bridal ale!"

Serving girls entered swiftly to pour the mead flavored with woodruff and juniper berries. I had helped to prepare it myself—later testing it on one of the dogs to be sure it contained no poison. Cups, glasses, and goblets were lifted in the toast.

"To Ingeld and Freawaru!"

"To Ingeld and Freawaru!"

Then Ingeld raised his hand for silence.

"To my bride Freawaru, jewel of the Scyldings, I give these precious gems: garnet, pearl, and lapis."

Into my cup, he dropped three stones: one blood red, one snow white, and one sky blue. The hall resounded with cheers and shouts as we drank to each other, now man and wife.

Feasting and drinking would continue throughout the night, but Ingeld soon took me firmly by the hand to lead me from the hall—to the hoots and jests of the assembly.

"Hail, Freawaru," shouted one already drunken thane. "I have a riddle for you. What grows in its pouch, swells and stands up, and then lifts its covering? A proud bride may grasp this boneless wonder, a king's daughter cover this swollen thing with clothing." He belched and then shouted, "What is your answer?"

"Bread dough," I shouted over my shoulder, not lingering to hear the laughter of his comrades at his expense. Ingeld had my arm firmly tucked under his, and I almost ran to keep up with him.

"Do you know more of such riddles?" questioned Ingeld in surprise.

"My brothers have kept me informed, my lord."

"No more of this 'my lord'," he gave me a squeeze, "at least not when we are alone together, my Freawaru, as we are now."

He pulled me into the chamber prepared for us, strewn with sweet rushes, a lamp flickering on the wall. We fell onto the bed, Ingeld on top, pulling at my clothes.

"Wait!" I fumbled at my breast for the brooch-pins, releasing them and the shoulder straps of the silk tunic. Ingeld's hands slid up my thighs, pushing my petticoat up to my face. Laughing at his eagerness, I struggled free to slip the pleated linen over my head.

Exposed, my flesh quivered as I watched Ingeld strip off his tunic and trousers. Golden hairs covered his broad chest, darker hairs curled further down. His eyes and teeth gleamed like a wolf in the half-light as he lowered himself onto me.

"Freawaru—mine at last."

I gasped as he pressed his swollen member between my legs and bit my lip to keep from crying out. Was pain, not pleasure, to be my lot? He held my hands down with his own, palm to palm, and began to move—slowly at first but then harder as my woman juices began to flow.

As I closed my eyes, the room contracted; the world now contained only this man and me, hot against each other's flesh. I seemed to be sinking into an abyss. Fainting and dissolving. Flooded with sweetness. From a distance, I heard my own voice cry out: "Yes, oh yes!"

With a roar, he thrust his spear, pinning me to the bed. A fountain erupted within me, watered with his seed. Ingeld gave a long, shuddering groan and collapsed on my body, spent. Tears streamed down my face as I tightened my arms around his back, my legs around his waist, and held him close. Now I was truly a woman! Ingeld had made me his bride, and I gloried in his love.

"Ingeld, do you ... Ingeld?"

He was already asleep, snoring lightly. I held him quietly, until his weight made my limbs grow numb, and then rolled him aside and pulled a robe over his body. I rose to grope for my wedding clothes, and my fingers found the small wooden box of ointment Mother had given me, forgotten in the heat of the moment. I did not need it after all.

When we woke next morning, Ingeld reached for me again. I responded eagerly, my desire matching his own. This time he did not fall asleep afterward. Instead he laid me against the sleeping robe and traced the lines of my body with his fingers—hard, calloused fingers.

"You are beautiful, my wife."

He stroked my belly and caressed me between the legs. "Even redder than the hairs of your head," he grinned. "What a shame to keep them covered—but only I will have the pleasure of seeing them."

I blushed, turning my head. Was this how husbands love-talked with their wives?

After we dressed, I tied a white silk kerchief around my head, knotting it at the back. Ingeld tucked in a stray curl and kissed me on the lips.

"It is time, my wife. After these long days of waiting, it is time to leave for my homeland. You must say good-bye to Heorot."

The moment had come. Once I had longed to leave this place, haunted by the all-consuming monster. Now the Grendel was dead. Beowulf had killed him—and his dam. Dear Beowulf ... despite the treasures given, how much we owed him still. I shook myself, adjusted my head cloth, and stepped forth with Ingeld, my husband.

The morning was gray, the skies full of clouds that promised rain. The entire court had gathered to witness our departure. Even Hrothulf was present; his face wore a knowing smile, as if it kept a secret. Unferth stood silent, a hood pulled low over his eyes.

I looked at each face intensely, burning the images into my brain: Hrothmund, still pink-cheeked and round-faced as a child; Hrethric, as tall as Hrothulf now, though slighter of build, his eyes full of life; Mother, regal, composed, gentle in demeanor but tough at the core— the touches of white at her hairline only added to her aura of wisdom; Father, bent under the burden of years, but still strong, still kingly. My eyes misted as I surveyed my family.

"Here—you'll need this. I pulled it out of your chest before it was loaded on board the ship." Mother held out a large wool shawl. She wrapped it around me, murmuring in my ear: "You are the peace-weaver. Never forget that. Watch your tongue lest it lead you into difficulties. But do not fear; all will be well."

Louder, speaking so the whole assembly could hear, she spoke ceremoniously, "May the bonds of friendship between our peoples hold fast, bringing peace and prosperity to all."

Father slapped Ingeld on the shoulder. "Treat her well, my son. She will be an ornament to your hall and a wife who gives good counsel—like her mother. May the gods grant you a safe journey."

I longed to embrace him, but Father made no move to initiate such contact. He had embraced Beowulf ... did I mean less to him than the visiting Geat? Resolutely, I walked forward and kissed him on the cheek.

"Good-bye, Father. May the gods protect you."

Even as I spoke curtly, I saw tears standing in his eyes and was comforted by his sorrow.

"Let us be off! The wind is up, and we have many days at sea before us."

As Ingeld led me away, I resolutely did not look back—alas for my pride! No vision came to warn me that I would never see Heorot at peace again.

On the first day of our journey, we sailed against the wind around the northern tip of the island—as Ingeld informed me, for I was eager to learn the landmarks and boundaries of my expanding world. The breeze grew stiffer and the day grew darker. As our boat bounced through the waves, I was glad that I had nibbled one of Mother's last remaining pieces of ginger!

I could have ridden in Aeschere's boat with the rest of my attendants, but I chose to accompany Ingeld and his men, a choice that seemed to please him immensely. We wedged a sea chest into the bow as a seat for me directly under Ingeld's gaze.

"So—you will brave the sea at my side? A good omen for the wife of Ingeld. There will be many dangers to face together."

Was he still referring to his mother? I laid the thought aside, wishing only to experience the surge of the water as it carried me—us—to our new home. I pulled the shawl closer around me and looked down the row of unfamiliar faces. In the days before the wedding, I had tried to learn each man's name; now I wanted to match names with faces.

Inches away from me sat Gunter, the man whom Ingeld treated as his lieutenant; his deeply scarred face stood out under a shock of white hair. When he caught my eye, he scowled. My heart sank. If my efforts at peacemaking were to succeed, I needed to win over these men.

The next face bore a more cheerful aspect. Hans, was it? Yes, Hans, a younger thane who had laughed loudly during the bridal feast. Even now, he was sharing some jest with the man across from him. Perhaps he could recount to me those stories that were favorites at—hmmm, what did Ingeld call his mead hall? He had never told me.

At my inquiring glance, Ingeld bent down to talk over the wind. "What is it you need to know now, my wife?"

"What is the name of your hall?"

"Wulfhaus—for it is a den of wolves!"

Startled, I looked into his face for some clue. Was he serious? His eyes danced with mischief, yet truth lay behind his words, as I would discover for myself.

I returned to my review of faces. First, on the starboard side, sat Ulf, a thin, lanky fellow with a patch over one eye and a missing ear; he looked exactly like a dog who'd gotten the worst of a fight! Even so, when he saw me looking at him, he opened his lips in a gap-toothed grin. Perhaps I would have one friend, after all, among these men.

Behind him sat Johan, his face blank, expressionless. His attention seemed to be focused on some inward matter. He reminded me a bit of Unferth. The thought brought a pang of regret and longing. We had not even spoken at my leave-taking.

My review was interrupted by a shout from Ingeld.

"Oars out, men! A storm approaches from the west. Pull hard for the channel after we pass this next spit of land."

In my reverie, I had not noticed the menacing clouds, but soon saw raindrops pelting the waves nearby and drew out my sealskin covering. Ingeld's men did not bother to don any protection but sent the boat surging ahead, cleaving the way like a plowshare separating the earth. At some distance behind us, Aeschere's boat also leapt forward. A wave of exhilaration swept over me. Once again, I was flying!

The clouds brought rain and cold and fog. By the time both boats had been run ashore on a sandy beach, it was difficult to see anyone more than a few feet away. Ingeld and Gunter directed the Heathobards, while Wulfgar led the Danes in setting up camp.

I was glad to see the erection of several tents for the use of my women and myself. We busied ourselves setting out food for the wet and famished travelers. Starting a fire was out of the question in the steady rain, so we contented ourselves with cold goods: bread, cheese, and herring, washed down with quantities of ale to provide some heat for the belly.

Good-natured laughter rang out when one person bumped into another in the fog. Shared difficulties seemed to neutralize our differences—at least for the moment. I felt a hand on my rear and turned into the arms of Ingeld.

"My Freawaru—our tent is waiting. Shall we spend this unexpected delay wisely ... together?" Not waiting for an answer, he parted the flap and pulled me inside.

Much later, I awoke from a deep sleep to the sound of knocking on the tent frame.

Ingeld roused himself.

"Who is it?"

"Gunter, my lord. The fog has lifted."

The storm had passed to the east, leaving the wide channel beside us calm in the pale light of waning day. I too felt calm, even serene, basking in the afterglow of Ingeld's lovemaking.

"I judge that we could reach the end of the Great Belt by nightfall, if you wish to proceed, my lord." Gunter's voice sounded gruff.

Ingeld did wish to proceed. So, people, horses, and gear were once again loaded into the boats, and we set sail for Wulfhaus. Ingeld seemed more relaxed now—ready to answer all my questions.

"It will take us another day at least to reach the mainland and then half a day to ride inland to my hall. The Great Belt? It is a wide channel running between two large islands—one of them houses your people. At the southern end, we turn west, making our way through many smaller islands until we reach the mainland. There we will mount horses for the ride to Wulfhaus. It is located on a bluff above a great river that flows into the northern sea."

Speaking of his homeland seemed to inspire Ingeld, and he truly unlocked his word-hoard for me.

"Who will be waiting for us?" I asked, somewhat anxiously.

"The rest of my men—and my mother, Hrun." He paused. "She and her women will no doubt have prepared a suitable welcome for us."

His words were more prophetic than he knew.

Fair weather accompanied the remainder of our journey. On the second day, we stopped alongside a precipice, which Ingeld's men called Flint Cliff. It reminded me of the chalk cliff where I had collected herbs and Unferth falcons in what seemed another lifetime. But here, the prize to be collected was flint: hard nodules of rock, which could be cracked off in sword-sharp shards for use as arrow tips or fire starters—a useful commodity indeed. Another oddity of the place was a strange, toad-like creature, which some of Ingeld's men chased down and captured as surprises for their children.

"We call 'em firebellies," Ulf told me. Hrothmund came to mind, but I told myself that I must stop looking back. Soon after this stop, a long, low shoreline emerged to the west.

"Home," announced Ingeld succinctly. "Hall and hearth and Hrun."

Hrun … what was Ingeld's relationship with his mother? I reached up to touch his hand, but he did not respond.

The land of the Heathobards appeared to be not unlike my own homeland—sandy beaches and marshland rimmed the coastline. Above us wheeled a multitude of seabirds. I recognized bitterns wading along shore and cormorants diving beneath the waves. I heard a loud, raucous cry as something flew high over our boat.

"What bird is that?" I asked Ingeld.

"Too high to be sure—either an osprey or a sea eagle. Don't you see those at Heorot?"

"No … but we have swans," I replied, a lump in my throat.

Strong wind from the west made us row hard to get the boats ashore. Ingeld jumped out first, shouting orders. Unloading the horses took some time, and several at first refused to leave the boat after being unhobbled. The livestock, however, stampeded madly ashore, eager to escape their cramped quarters. My women were loud in their relief as well.

"By the gods, I'll never get the smell of horseshit out of my nose," declared Ingeborg bluntly.

"Can't tell which is worse: cow or sheep," laughed Ragnhild.

"You shouldn't complain; you didn't have to clean it up!" grumbled Gyda.

Estrid made no remark, looking pale.

"Come, women, let us help our lady. There'll be time for talk later."

Ana took charge, directing Olaf and Sven in the unloading of our chests and barrels, while Wulfgar and the other men saw to their disposition on the carts. By the time we were able to mount our horses, it was past midday, and no one had yet eaten.

"We will eat only cold food now," declared Ingeld cheerfully. "Meat and drink await us at my hall. I've sent one of my men ahead to announce our coming."

So we set forth with cold stomachs. My head was full of questions: What lay ahead? How would we be received by the Heathobards? Especially by Ingeld's mother, Hrun? Above all, would I be able to weave a peace, as I had been charged?

Chapter 10
Weaving the Peace

Light rain began to fall as we plodded across sand and heath, picking our way around fens and marshes—riding, riding endlessly. I bowed my head over my mount to shield my eyes from the wind.

Ingeld and his men were leading the way. Wulfgar rode on one side of me, Ana on the other, our people and wagons trailing behind. I had started the journey at Ingeld's side but fallen back to join my own people as we drew close to Wulfhaus … for what? Comfort? Courage? I suddenly felt a distinct lack of both.

Ana must have sensed my mood, for she reached over to touch my shoulder.

"Have no fear, my lady Freawaru. You are the queen's daughter too. You are Wealtheow's daughter."

I straightened in surprise. Wealtheow's daughter? Accustomed as I was to hearing "king's daughter," with all that it implied of position and duty, I rarely thought of myself as the queen's daughter. Turning, I flashed a grateful smile at Ana. Yes, my mother's teachings and example would be a welcome guide for me in my new situation.

Finally—or all too soon—we smelled the smoke of peat fires and saw clusters of low buildings through the mist. A lone figure, whom I recognized as Wilhelm, one of Ingeld's men, rode out to meet us.

"My lord Ingeld, your mother sends greetings and bids you to a welcoming feast in the mead hall tonight—along with your bride and her retinue."

"Give her our thanks. We will soon attend her." Ingeld circled back to bring me to his side.

"Now wife, prepare yourself. Remember who you are—Ingeld's wife—and do not speak the name of Hrothgar in my mother's presence!"

Astonished, I opened my mouth to protest, but said nothing. Clearly, I must proceed carefully with Ingeld's mother. Then another thought struck me: would Ingeld be *my* ally ... or hers?

Perhaps it was my exhaustion or the gray weather, but Ingeld's mead hall appeared to me a long, dark, cheerless structure, not at all like the shining beacon that I remembered as my father's hall. Over the door, in the spot where deer antlers decorated Heorot, hung a grinning white skull: the head of a wolf.

Ingeld saw me looking up at it.

"From the Black Forest in the mountains to the south—where we also hunt deer and wild boar. Don't you like it? I killed it myself!"

He was grinning, so I chanced the truth.

"If it is meant to frighten, it has not succeeded. I have seen the head of the Grendel—a sight more terrifying than any wolf."

He frowned. "Ah yes—the famous monster—dispatched by the famous Beowulf. Was this Beowulf also a pleasing sight?"

"I ... I seldom looked upon him." I paused, as if trying to remember. "He was very large, with strong hands. But we can speak of that another time. Will you direct me and my women to our chambers that we may prepare for the banquet?"

"Of course. Gunter! Lead our guests to their quarters! You, Freawaru, will come with me!"

He lifted me off my horse, took my hand, and led me toward a timbered house opposite the mead hall. He ducked under the low door opening and pulled me inside.

"Now we'll see who is ... large ... with strong hands!"

As he pressed himself against me, I could already feel the strength of his desire.

Ingeld and I were the last to enter the mead hall that night. Ana had helped me dress in the same white pleated shift and blue silk embroidered tunic I'd worn at my wedding feast in Heorot. I also wore all my jewelry. Ingeld had donned a fine scarlet tunic with embroidered borders and then thrown an elegant cloak over one shoulder, fastening it with a silver brooch. I gazed at my husband with pleasure, knowing that we made a handsome couple.

As we entered hand-in-hand, the drinking Danes and Heathobards fell silent. Only one figure rose: an old woman. She'd been seated in the place of honor between two smoke-darkened pillars. For a moment, I saw the white, grinning skull of the wolf—but this face held two glowing eyes, eyes fastened upon me.

"Greetings, my son. Greetings, Ingeld. So ... the Danish princess has come. Welcome to Wulfhaus."

Her voice sounded forced, hoarse, and weary. I judged her to be older than my mother, perhaps even older than Father. Her years did not sit well upon her.

"Greetings, Mother. May the gods be with you. This is Freawaru, my bride, come to honor you."

"May the gods be with you," I echoed, kneeling momentarily. "I have brought you gifts."

At my signal, Estrid and Ingeborg stepped forward with small chests. From one, I removed a length of silken fabric, dark red with golden threads, and offered it to Hrun. She took it, reluctantly I thought, and stroked the fabric with claw-like fingers.

"Very fine, very fine—too fine for an old woman like me."

"And this," I said, opening the second chest, "is a tapestry I wove myself. May it please you."

She took it and held it up, peering close to make out the design.

"What is the story?" she asked, with what seemed genuine interest. I hoped I had chosen well.

"Freyja receiving the Brisingamen."

"I see …" She studied the tapestry and then dropped it on the floor. "Hardly a suitable topic for public display. Freyja played the whore to get what she wanted!" Her lips hissed and her eyes blazed at me accusingly.

"Mother! I rejoice to find you well again!" Ingeld's voice boomed forth, but not before I heard guffaws behind me and half-whispers. Adroitly, Ingeld strode to the central chair, seated Hrun and me on either side of him, and signaled for ale.

"Let us drink, friends and comrades, to my bride … the lovely Freawaru!" In an undertone he added, "who pleases me well."

Hrun lifted her cup but did not drink. Our first meeting was not going well. I leaned across Ingeld.

"My lady Hrun, I have brought a cask of Frankish wine as part of my dowry. If that would please you, I will send to have it opened."

"What? Our ale not good enough for you? Think we can't afford wine if we want it? Nay, I'll have none of it!"

"Mother has not been well," offered Ingeld. "Wine adversely affects her stomach. But opening that cask is an excellent idea—let us taste it tonight!"

I nodded and summoned Olaf to bring in the cask. Ingeld offered me the first cup. I had seldom drunk wine but knew how it went to my head—how else to explain why I opened my mouth to antagonize Hrun further? Following several servings of meat and wine, I tried again.

"My lady Hrun, I have herbs with me that may mend your stomach, should you wish to try them. My mother …"

"Your mother? I hear she still has a husband. Not I! I lost my husband to a man-killing Dane—your father! Ingeld never had a chance to know his father; I have been both father and mother to him all these years."

"And a fine job you've done, Mother." Ingeld laid a restraining hand on each of us. "When Freawaru and I produce a child, you'll have a fine grandson to raise as well."

This thought stopped Hrun's tongue momentarily, though I could see she still simmered with barely suppressed rage. Would this banquet never end? After the long day's journey, I ached to find my bed. I sighed loudly, but Ingeld did not take the hint. He seemed never to tire—in bed or out of it.

"Max! Let's have a song!"

"What shall it be, my lord?"

"Give us 'Waltharius'," shouted a voice from the benches.

"Aye, 'Waltharius' will do," assented Ingeld.

Men pounded the table in glee and anticipation. It caught my attention as well, for Aelric had never sung a lay of that title at Hrothgar's court.

I followed the story with horrified amusement as Max told of two warring parties lopping off body parts: hands, fingers, ears, noses, arms, legs—then finally making peace and settling down to a feast together.

"And how will you wield a sword, brave thane, without a hand to grasp it?" sang Max, telling how each man twitted the other on the disability his wound imposed.

"And how will you find the salt sea air without a nose to smell it?"

But the line which drew the most applause and laughter was this one: "And how embrace your Hiltgund, Walter, without an arm to hold her?"

"Don't worry, Walter," chortled one of Ingeld's men, "as long as you don't lose your personal weapon, you'll fare alright with the women!"

I did not hear the rest of "Waltharius," for Ingeld was apparently thinking along similar lines.

"Let us go, my wife. It is time to start that babe I promised Mother!" He shot her a grin.

But as we rose to leave, I heard a hiss from Hrun: "Son, beware of treachery. This woman may bring your doom!"

Before I could protest, Ingeld had hustled me out of the hall.

"Why does she hate me so?" I cried.

"Take no notice. She does not see you—she sees a Danish princess. You'll win her over in time. You may even become the daughter she never had."

Little chance of that, I thought. Not only does she despise me on sight and reject my gifts, she seems determined to poison her son against me. What a hateful old hag! How can Ingeld put up with her?

"She has been ill for several winters ... and knows her time may be short," he offered apologetically. "Be kind to her."

I swallowed the protest that rose in my throat. "I'll try."

We found a welcome surprise upon reaching our chamber. The carved wooden bedstead, which made part of my dowry, had been set up and lined with down-filled pillows and fine woven blankets, ready for its first occupants. Ingeld whooped and threw a pillow at me. I threw one back. Soon we were pelting each other and laughing so hard that all thoughts of Hrun were forgotten.

Our wedding celebration continued for days. Ingeld seemed determined to show my companions that his hall could equal the hospitality offered at Heorot. I grew weary of eating and drinking. I longed to set my fingers to a loom or walk in an herb garden releasing the scent of each plant as my gown brushed past it.

An awkward moment occurred one morning when the chests were opened, which contained more of my dowry. Gunter was unpacking Frankish blades when he stopped, held aloft one sword, and brandished it menacingly.

"Wilhelm, do you recognize this sword? I swear by the gods it was your father Wethergeld's favorite weapon. He carried it on his final day, when he fell to the Danes!"

His face grew dark as he continued. "One of the princess's people here might be the murderer's son—boasting of treasures which should be yours by right!"

All eyes were riveted on Gunter, all ears filled with his harsh accusation. I held my breath waiting for an explosion—and found myself walking forward, arms outstretched.

"All are equal in war, Gunter. To die in battle is to die with honor. Let this sword be given to Wilhelm if it was his kinsman's treasure. Its value is clearly acknowledged in the gift." I took the blade from the open-mouthed Gunter and presented it, with a bow, to Wilhelm. Then I returned to Ingeld's side.

"Well done, wife!" he murmured. "Your dowry is yours to dispose of as you see fit." Now he raised his voice. "Wilhelm—your queen honors you."

Wilhelm bowed his head briefly, but left without a word. I feared that the thoughts planted by Gunter still rankled in Wilhelm's brain. I feared also that Gunter was not finished fomenting trouble. I was right.

Ana came to me each evening bearing news from the women's quarters and providing a much needed connection with home. Wulfhaus still felt alien and unwelcoming to me. The other women felt it too.

"Now Helga and Inga … by the gods, I swear those two are a pair of icicles. Makes me shiver just to walk past them," declared Ana.

I knew the pair she referred to. Privately I compared them to Odin's ravens, for they acted as Hrun's eyes and ears—missing nothing, reporting everything. Words whispered in private had a way of getting back to Hrun, who received every imagined slight as a gift to nourish in silence until it festered and erupted. Ingeld's reference to me as his queen had sent her into a tirade, according to Anna.

"I asked her a simple question—where the grinding querns were kept—and she actually threw a cup at me. 'Ask your Queen,' she shouted. 'Apparently I'm not the queen here any longer.'"

Ana paused and then looked me in the eye.

"This can't go on, my lady. If you're to be the mistress here, you must take a stand. The sooner you do it the better it will be for all of us. Right now, no one is sure who's in charge—among the women, I mean. Everyone respects Ingeld, but I notice he doesn't meddle in women's matters."

I sighed. Ana had a point, but openly assuming authority might antagonize Hrun further, and Ingeld had asked me to be kind to his mother. Hmmm. Slowly an idea began to take shape in my mind.

"Ana, I think it's time to consult the goddess. We will gather the women for a ritual, a ritual of healing."

Although I had been spending most of my days and all of my nights with Ingeld, I had charged my companions to make friends as soon as possible with Hrun's women and to learn all they could about their daily routines. I had neglected, however, to seek information about their rituals and sacred places. Now I would find out for myself. First thing in the morning, I would talk to the two "ravens."

As expected, I found the two women together. They were preparing mead; apparently our enthusiastic consumption of that drink during the wedding feast had reduced the supply.

"Good day to you." I smiled brightly at the pair.

Startled, they eyed me with a mixture of surprise and distrust.

"That's a fine drink you make. Do you add herbs to it? I thought I tasted a touch of mint in the mix."

"Yes, there's mint," Helga admitted grudgingly.

"And woodruff," added Inga.

"Ah, a pleasing combination. I have also used angelica occasionally, though juniper berries will work as well and are easier to come by."

Helga straightened, planting both hands on her hips.

"So ... the Danish princess is mistress of herbs?"

"It's Lady Freaw, and yes, I have some experience. My chests contain many roots and dried plants—as I did not wish to use up your own supplies," I added hastily, seeing Helga frown. "I will be glad to learn of the plants you grow here that perhaps are not available further north," I continued, "when you have time to show me your herb gardens— perhaps later this morning?"

"I could show you," Inga offered, ignoring Helga's glare.

"Very good—you will find me at the looms."

Indeed, my fingers itched to pick up the shuttle and yarn, but I contented myself with making a survey of the work already underway, complimenting each weaver on some aspect of her work.

"Do I see a dragon?" I inquired of one woman. "What story is being told?"

She gave me a pitying glance. "Sigmund the dragon-slayer. Do you not know of him in your foreign parts?"

I laughed easily. "Of course—our scop sang of him often—that lay was a favorite in our mead hall, and my little brothers never tired of the story."

This seemed to set well with all the women.

"I have golden thread in my chest that would make those scales glisten—would you like to try it?"

She hesitated only for a moment. "Yes, thank you ... Lady Freaw."

Ana was unpacking a few cooking pots when I entered my chamber to search for the thread.

"You are smiling," she observed. "What has pleased you?"

"I am cracking nuts, making a start at winning over Hrun's women."

"Does that mean you are ready to lead the ritual?"

"Not yet—but soon."

During my tour of the garden with Inga, I brought up the subject of Hrun's illness.

"What is the nature of her complaint? Where is it located"

Inga's face sagged. "Something is eating her from the inside. She takes little food or drink, for it pains her stomach. We've tried all the usual remedies, but nothing seems to help." She spread her hands in a gesture of despair.

"Do you think she would let me treat her?" I asked casually. Immediately Inga's guard came up. She spoke stiffly.

"Hrun wouldn't touch anything you prepared for her."

"I wasn't thinking of food or drink. A healing of the spirit was what I had in mind. Tell me, how often do you sacrifice to the goddess? She needs your offerings."

Inga's mouth fell open, and she paled as she gaped at me.

"Are you a *volva*—a sorceress?" she croaked.

"Perhaps." I let that thought sink in before continuing. "If your skills have not sufficed to help your mistress, it might be well to call upon the goddess for healing." My tone now grew severe. "Show me the place where such rites are held."

Dumbly, Inga led me out of the settlement. Only a few clusters of trees relieved the barren landscape. As we drew near one of them, I saw the sparkle of sunlight on water. We pushed through reeds and rushes to reach the edge of a small pool.

"Here. We used to come here. Hrun has been too sick of late to lead us."

"Then we must now help her."

Inga nodded assent. "Yes, it may be time."

That night, I lay awake long after Ingeld had rolled off my body, fallen asleep, and begun snoring lightly. I tried to recall all that Mother had taught me. Much depended on how I handled the ritual—my future, Hrun's future, perhaps even the future of my family back home—for I sensed that the need for revenge still rankled in Hrun's heart. Ingeld loved me, but would his love be enough to save us all? I was the peace-weaver. I must act. In the morning, I would ask Ingeld for a wolf-skin.

When Ana arrived to receive instructions for the day, she reported good progress in befriending a few of Hrun's women.

"That Gudrun, now she's got more sense than the rest. Not afraid to learn new ways. They were grumbling that the porridge had cooled, but they were too lazy to heat it up again. When I suggested they take a hot rock from the fire pit and drop it in the cauldron, they acted as if I'd suggested throwing in a toad!" Ana chuckled at the recollection. "But Gudrun did just that—and we were soon eating warm gruel! Another one—Ursula, I think—said it even tasted better. My lady, it's clear that standards have fallen in that kitchen with Hrun too sick to oversee matters, as they tell me."

She paused to catch her breath, and for a fleeting moment, I felt Willa's presence, comforting and reassuring.

"Ana, today I want you to drop a few hints that I'm planning a special ceremony for Hrun. Soon daylight and darkness will stand in balance, a time well-suited for establishing balance between Danes and Heathobards. Now it's time for me to show myself in the kitchen. Come."

Ana followed without question.

Our entry was not noted at first. Hrun sat on a low bench near the fire. Her women were gathered about her, offering food and drink. She waved them off, accepting only a bowl of porridge.

"Good day, Mother Hrun."

She jerked upright at the sound of my voice, flinging porridge from her spoon onto her already greasy tunic. I pretended not to notice.

"So, you've decided to show yourself have you?" Her voice was a raven's croak. "Maybe turn your hand to some work? You bring all these extra mouths to feed and then spend all your time shut up with my son!" She leaned forward, leering. "Started that grandson yet?"

Heat rose to my face, but I bowed slightly to hide the flush.

"My lady, we have much to discuss. Our women can tend to matters here. Let you and me walk in the gardens while the morning is fresh." I held out my hand, my eyes fixed on hers. To the surprise of everyone she rose, but did not take the proffered arm.

"Inga—my cloak!" Inga hurried to bring the garment and drape it about Hrun's bony shoulders.

"Hot young blood," she muttered, "you'll come to this one day."

Once outside, her strength and haughtiness both sagged. I caught her arm as she slumped against me, feet stumbling. Alarmed, I led her slowly to the nearby chamber I shared with Ingeld and eased her down on the edge of the bed.

"Here, take a sip of this chamomile tea—it may refresh you."

She shook her head at first, but after a sniff convinced her it was indeed only chamomile, she drank deeply from the cup.

"Why do you care what happens to me? The sooner I die the sooner you take over—in charge of everything."

As I took the cup from her, I touched her hand.

"You are Ingeld's mother. I love and honor you as I love and honor my husband." The words were almost true—could be true if she would allow it. I took a deep breath.

"Ingeld brought me here to be a daughter to you. Let me ease your labors, Mother."

She closed her eyes. A long silence stretched between us. When she spoke again, her voice was so low I had to kneel down to hear her words.

"Two things I want before I die—two things only: revenge for Froda's killing and a grandson to carry on his line. Death and life." She peered up at me. "Which will come first?"

I did not broach the idea of a healing ritual that morning. After Hrun had rested enough to walk again, I escorted her to the women's quarters, where Helga and Inga took over, fluttering about her officiously as if to reassert their authority.

At midday, Ingeld appeared with a fine, glossy wolf pelt. He tickled my nose with the tip of the tail.

"Is this what you want, my wife? It's the hide of the very wolf whose skull guards the mead hall. I—"

"Yes, I know. You killed it yourself. Perfect!" I gave him a kiss on the tip of his nose.

"You're not a shape-shifter, are you? You're not going to run away from me one night to howl at the full moon?"

He spoke in jest, but my answer sobered him.

"Not as a wolf, no. Flying is my specialty."

He was silent. When he spoke again, his tone had changed.

"Freawaru, there is a question I have wanted to ask. On your shoulder there is a mark like … a feather. What does it mean?"

Now it was my turn to be silent, as I turned over words in my mind.

"I do not fully know," I said at last, "but there are times when I seem to leave my body and … fly. Then I see things as if from a great distance, but whether those things are real or only visions I do not know." I thought of my vision before the attempted burning of Heorot, but judged it wiser not to speak of that.

"Ingeld, I want to lead the women of Wulfhaus in a ritual of healing—for your mother. In order to be successful, I may have to leave my body again. That is why I need the wolf skin: to pull me back to this place, to Wulfhaus."

Wordlessly Ingeld folded me in his arms, pulling my kerchief off with his teeth and nuzzling my hair against his chin.

"My wife, my Freawaru, never, never leave me."

Seeking guidance, I decided to consult my runes privately before undertaking a public ritual. All twenty-four runes, carved by my hand and stained with my blood, lay nestled in a deerskin bag at the bottom of my clothing chest.

In the past, I had occasionally cast a single rune to help clarify my thinking. This time I must be more ambitious: a three-rune spread would be called for. Unferth had shown me how to arrange the three face down as I drew them. Then they were to be read from right to left as I turned them over: the first would reflect the present situation, the second suggest some action required, and the third reveal a possible outcome.

I did not eat all that day, and drank only water in order to clear my mind. I must be open to the gods if I wanted to receive the runes' message and interpret it correctly. "Freyja help me," I breathed silently. "You are the goddess of love; it is for love of Ingeld and love of my family that I do this thing." Finally I felt ready to begin.

Choosing a time when I could be alone and undisturbed—Ingeld had gone off to hunt with a small band of his men—I spread a square of white linen on the floor of my chamber. With trembling fingers, I knelt and drew one rune from the bag, placing it on the square. As my fingers reached for the second, the trembling ceased. On my third foray, the rune seemed to reach for me rather than I for it, and I laid it confidently beside its companions on the white cloth.

Eihwaz revealed itself when I turned over the first piece: the rune of defense. I laughed inwardly. Yes, I was certainly on the defensive at Wulfhaus—but what was the message here? Eihwaz counseled patience, the necessity of foreseeing consequences before acting. A defensive position meant waiting, persevering. Yes, I had done that. Now, what of action?

When I turned over the second rune, Jera looked up at me—the rune of harvest. In the cycle of time, harvest would be mine, yet the right timing was essential. Again, waiting was called for ... perhaps a year's span. What new situation would this produce?

My fingers lingered on the third rune and then turned it over to reveal ... Algiz, the rune of protection. In the face of challenge and adversity, it told me to retain control of my emotions. The words of Unferth returned to echo in my mind: "timely action and correct conduct are the only true protection."

Unferth ... where are you now? Are you talking of herbs with Mother? Or ... with a shake, I pulled myself back to the present.

Algiz also indicated a time of transition, a shift in life course. That had already happened to me. I paused. Had I lain down the runes in the proper order? *Focus, Freawaru. Be mindful. Knowing may be your only protection.*

Hardly had I returned the bag of runes to my chest, when an urgent voice at the door sought my attention.

"My lady Freawaru—come quickly!" It was Wulfgar, looking very serious.

"What is amiss?"

"Sven has been stabbed by one of Ingeld's men. He may be dying."

"What? Where is he?" I grabbed several bags of herbs from my shelf.

"In the mead hall—we laid him on the table."

Wulfgar gave me a few details as we hurried to the hall.

"One of Gunter's sons—Gunnar I believe—took offense at a story Sven told about Heathobards. They exchanged words and then daggers were drawn. Sven didn't take the boy seriously—a big mistake."

"Where is Gunnar now?"

"Disappeared. He ran as soon as Sven fell." Wulfgar's face was grim.

My heart raced with dread, and my head buzzed with questions. Would I be able to save Sven? If he died, how would the rest of the Danes react? What would Ingeld do?

Inside the mead hall, Sven's still form betrayed no sign of life, but when I laid a hand on his forehead, he opened his eyes in recognition.

"Don't speak. Save your strength." As I lifted his blood-soaked tunic, more blood pulsed in waves from a deep gash in his belly.

"Vinegar—I need vinegar!"

One of the serving girls scurried out and returned with a small pitcher. Mashing a handful of dried mint leaves in one of the drinking cups, I filled it with vinegar. Into this mixture I dipped the cloth still in my hand—the same square I'd used for rune-casting—wrung it out, and pressed it against the wound. The cloth crimsoned immediately, but slowly the flood receded. Sven's face was ash-gray, but his lips moved inaudibly. I bent low over his face.

"Don't try to talk!"

Still his lips struggled to speak.

"S-s-send ... Val ... hal ..."

"Wulfgar, what is he trying to say?"

"He knows he is dying, and it's not in battle. He wants us to send him to Valhalla."

"How?"

"Like this." Wulfgar reached for a spear on the wall and pointed the tip at Sven's throat.

"No! Stop! I may yet save him!"

"I'm not going to cut his throat. I'm going to mark him so that Odin can claim him for his own." Carefully Wulfgar pieced the skin on Sven's neck. A look of satisfaction spread over his face—his dying face, as I now feared.

"Hang on, Sven, hang on!" I implored.

But Sven had already left us. I bowed my head and wept hot tears, which splashed down on his cold face and set lips. Someone pulled me up.

"Do not blame yourself. It is the Heathobards who must pay for this!" Anger blazed in Wulfgar's eyes as he brandished the spear above his head.

"But Wulfgar ... we were sent to be peace-makers."

"Not me, my lady. I was sent to protect you and our people."

"So you have, and shall. Ingeld will surely give satisfaction for this death—*wergild* or the life of Gunnar—I know he will." Wulfgar only stared at me as I continued. "This Gunnar was young and rash. We have found hospitality here ... and may yet make it our home "

I was interrupted by the entrance of Ana, rushing in to the hall with Estrid and Ingeborg at her side. They threw themselves on Sven's body and wailed aloud.

When Ingeld returned at nightfall, jubilant from a successful hunt, he found Wulfgar and me and all our people assembled at the door of the mead hall. Gunter was one of the hunting party. Wulfgar addressed them.

"Lord Ingeld. Inside your hall lies the body of Sven, slain this day by Gunnar, son of Gunter." Before Ingeld could speak, Gunter leapt from his horse and strode forward.

"My son? Where is he? Let me hear him speak."

"Fled. He and his horse are both missing."

Now Ingeld took charge. "Wulfgar? You saw this thing?"

"Aye, lord, as did all my men and many of yours. There is no mistaking the killer."

At the word *killer* Gunter stiffened and let out a great howl. I froze to hear such grief and anger mingled.

"My son—you'll never find him, never—nor shall I ever see him again. He is lost to me!" Then he lashed out at Wulfgar. "Murderous Danes! You provoked him to it! Sven got no more than he deserved, by the gods!"

"Gunter, enough! I will handle this." Ingeld's voice was low but firm.

"Wulfgar, we will fix the man-price to be paid and give the Danes every satisfaction. But now, it is time to eat and drink after this long day—your Sven would do the same. Come."

Our group did not move away from the door.

"We would have the funeral pyre tonight, before food." This time it was my voice.

"As you wish, my wife. I will instruct my men to prepare it."

"No," I said, "let *our* men prepare it—Danes and Heathobards together."

At his nod, the work began.

Watching sparks ascend into the night sky, I found myself thinking of the Finn story sung so long ago by our scop in Heorot. In that song, Hildeburgh the Dane had placed both son and brother on one funeral pyre. Later she lost her husband to the same conflict between warring tribes. Ultimately, she had returned to her father's hall, a failed peace-weaver. Would I be able to avoid a similar fate?

A price in gold was agreed upon as payment for Sven's death, to be carried back to his parents by our men at the first opportunity—probably not for many months with winter approaching. Wulfgar and the other Danes had committed to a year's stay with me at Wulfhaus. After that, I would be on my own with whomever of my women chose to remain with me. Wulfgar kept his face impassive, but I sometimes caught Olaf, Gorm, and Saxe casting dark looks at their Heathobard companions; there was a definite increase of tension in the hall.

In the days that followed, both Ingeld and Hrun seemed subdued, almost distant—out of consideration for our grief I thought—but soon Hrun confronted me directly.

"When are you going to perform this ritual I've been hearing about?" she rasped.

"As soon as you are ready," I answered in surprise.

"Me? What does it have to do with me?"

"You are the leader here. I would only act with your permission."

"Hmmm. You are a clever one. Perhaps it is time to see what you can do. You couldn't stop a man from bleeding to death," she shot me a wicked look, "but maybe you'll have better luck with the women."

I bit my tongue and smiled at her.

"The turning of the year is almost upon us. Shall we visit the goddess then?"

Hrun nodded assent.

"By sun or by moon?" I asked.

"I'm too old for nighttime travel. We'll go in daylight, "said Hrun.

"So be it."

Chapter 11
Revenge or Dishonor

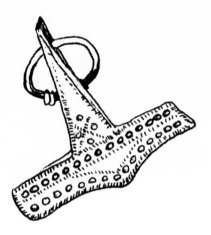

The prospect of attending a ritual seemed to spark new life in the women of Wulfhaus—Dane and Heathobard alike. Ana reported that even Helga and Inga were excited.

"They're preparing some special brew to be drunk before the ceremony—as a purification, they say. More likely it will give everyone the runs!

"We'll be sure to let them drink it first, then," I chuckled.

My instructions to the women were only that they bathe and dress themselves in clean garments. I myself would fast beforehand as an aid to entering a trance state. The necessity for doing this troubled me, for in the past I had often needed the aid of others to return to my body. As a precaution, I would station my own women nearest me and trust to the goddess—and the wolf skin—for the rest.

On the morning of the chosen day, Ingeld lingered in our chamber. He placed his hands on my shoulders and searched my face with his eyes.

"Must you do this thing, my wife? You look pale—and you spoke in your sleep last night."

"Oh? What did I say?"

"You called on your mother ... and someone named Willa."

"That is good. Their presence will be a help. Do not fear for me; I will be but a channel for the healing power of the goddess."

"*You* are the goddess," declared Ingeld, tilting my face to his lips. He kissed my eyelids softly. "Do not fly too high, my Freawaru. Come back to Wulfhaus. Come back to me."

"I will—I swear it by the goddess."

Ana entered to help me dress and arrange my hair. Ingeld left briskly, striding out like a god himself. Ana turned to look back at him.

"A rare one, that man. Do you know how much he dotes on you?"

"I do. Now Ana, we have work to do. Bring me my jewels—I have something to show you."

"Ah ... this must be it," she crooned, lifting a narrow band of embroidered silk from my small chest. Into its threads, I had woven the three gems given to me by Ingeld at our betrothal: the single pearl now formed the head of a white swan, the glowing garnet that of a redbird, and the deep blue of lapis lazuli perfectly fitted the jay.

"Bind it about my temples ... there, what do you think?"

"Ah, my lady, you are lovely as a goddess."

"Two people this morning have now made that comparison! But let us not tempt her anger. I need her help today."

"Surely you can summon her if anyone can."

"That's not what Hrun thinks! But I doubt that she herself has made the attempt in many a year. How else could she have turned so hard and bitter? Her heart is as shriveled as her breasts!"

I was taken aback at my own outburst. This was no frame of mind in which to approach a sacred rite! Ana kept silent, though her face mirrored agreement. *Freyja, forgive me*, I breathed inwardly. *Help me find the path to your realm of love.*

"Ana," I said aloud, "what name do women here give to the goddess?"

She paused to reflect. "I have heard Earth Mother, Great Mother, and Great Queen, sometimes Nerthus or Modron—and once, Brig, from a foreign slave. None here call her Freyja, as we do."

"No matter. She will know herself when I call upon her."

I donned the white robe and tunic I'd saved for such an occasion. Ana fastened my brooches and helped me tie a kerchief to obscure the headband. Thus arrayed we set forth. I held an ash wood staff in my hand and Anna carried the wolf skin. As we emerged, the sunlight struck me a blinding blow; a wave of dizziness washed over me.

"My lady! Are you ill?"

"A ... a momentary weakness. I have recovered."

Hrun sat waiting in the mead hall, which was generally unoccupied by Ingeld and his thanes during the early hours of the day. Helga and Inga were dipping up their special brew. I sniffed at the cup they offered me.

"Garlic? And dill? This should be good for Hrun's stomach."

Privately I thought it needed a touch of marsh mallow to remove the bitter taste, but did not wish to criticize their efforts. I swallowed it down.

More women were entering the mead hall, some chattering excitedly. Each drank a draft of the hot herbal mix. When all had gathered, I rose.

"Women of Wulfhaus. We go to worship the goddess and to ask for her aid in healing Hrun. We will walk together to the sacred pool. There I will prepare a space for our ritual."

A hush fell on the group at these words. Wordlessly, Helga and Inga helped Hrun to her feet, supporting her on either side, and started for the door.

We walked slowly, unhurried, giving Hrun all the time she needed. Out in the open air, away from the buildings, I felt some release from the heaviness and unease that had oppressed me of late. The smell of wood smoke blended pleasantly with the wet grasses we trod underfoot, still spangled with dew. As we neared the oak grove, acorns added a crunch beneath our feet. A hint of winter hung in the air, though the sun had burned off the mist and now shone warmly on our necks.

I did not look back at the procession of women winding behind me, but I knew that Ana would be faithfully walking at the end of the line, positioned just as Willa had been in my first ritual. The memory stung my eyes; I straightened and looked ahead, hoping I looked as confident as Mother always did in her role as leader. Mother—Willa—Ana— where would I be without them? But even should I lose them all, there would always be the goddess.

Wrapped in a cocoon of thought and silence, I called to her now. *Great Mother, be with me this day as in all days. Help me find the space I need to channel your healing power. Reveal yourself to us.* A moment of dizziness made me pause. I leaned on the staff for support, breathing deeply, and then lifted my face to the sun. *Give me strength*, I added.

On my earlier visit with Inga, I had noticed a sandy clearing at one side of the pool. I headed for that spot now.

"I will draw a circle," I announced, halting. "Stand silently within its boundaries while I prepare the center."

With my ash wood staff, I dug into the sand, drawing a large circle to encompass the group. Then I drew four long lines within the circle, crossing them to form nine squares. I beckoned to Ana, who handed me the wolf skin. I spread it in the center square and stood beside it.

"Hrun, I invite you to sit in this place of honor."

Hrun dropped the supporting arms of her women, stepped proudly into the center square, and settled herself on the glossy pelt.

"As guardians and protectors, I summon the four directions. North … Ana, East … Inga, South … Estrid, West … Helga." As I pointed to the squares with my staff, each woman came forward and took her place.

"I now summon the four elements: earth … Raghnild, air … Ursula, fire … Gudrun, water … Ingeborg." Again, I directed each woman to her spot on the nine-square pattern.

"Women of Wulfhaus. We will now call upon the goddess. Let our chant be 'mother of all, great goddess, hear us.' Join hands. We circle sunwise."

To start the dance, I stepped onto the edge of the wolf skin and began to revolve, turning slowly to my right. "Mother of all, great goddess, hear us. Mother of all ..."

Raising my arms to the sun, I shook off my head covering, letting the three gems woven into my head band catch the light. Whispering to myself, "Feathered friends, lift me on your wings," I closed my eyes and gave myself up to the chant.

At first I felt earthbound, unable to free myself from its confines. Slowly, and then more swiftly, I began to rise—lifting, floating out of my body. Looking down I saw three circles in motion: the women at the outer edge, the eight women in the inner circle, and then at the heart, myself, revolving next to a still figure ... Hrun. She looked upward, but I avoided her gaze.

Heat enveloped me as I spiraled closer to the sun. Sweat ran down my face, dripping off my lips as I gasped for air. "Goddess, hear us ..." Suddenly the sun went out and I fell into blackness.

Hrun's cold eyes bored into mine, though it was Ana who held up my head, putting water to my lips.

"What has happened?" I struggled to sit up.

"You failed. That's what happened. We had barely begun the chant when you fainted, like a—" Hrun stopped in mid-sentence, reaching a bony arm to touch my belly. "Like a woman with child," she finished, a slow smile starting on her lips. "Yes!" she crowed, "and you didn't even know it! Our great seeress cannot see into her own womb!"

"What? How can you be sure?"

"In that area, I have more experience than you, Freawaru."

Freawaru! She had spoken my name! But what of the ritual?

"Where are the other women? We must erase the circle, we must release—"

Hrun laughed, not unpleasantly. "I may be old, but I'm not a fool. I have done what needed to be done. Now we must get you back to Wulfhaus. Can you stand?"

This time it was I who walked between two supporters. Hrun seemed to have found new strength and energy—despite the dismal failure of what I had meant to be a healing ritual for her.

As we approached the mead hall, Ingeld emerged to greet us. He stared in alarm and then moved swiftly to take me into his arms.

"What has happened? What have you done to Freawaru?" He glared at Hrun and Ana alike.

"You mean what have *you* done to Freawaru?" Hrun cackled with glee. "She is with child—your child—my grandson."

With a whoop, Ingeld lifted me up and circled crazily, dancing like a drunken man.

"Stop! I am already dizzy," I protested. "What I need most right now is food—I have not eaten since yesterday morning."

"Helga, Inga," Hrun was calling, "some porridge for Freawaru—and make sure it is hot!"

I could hardly believe the change that came over Hrun in the weeks that followed. The prospect of new life seemed to energize her even as it weakened me. She vied with Ana in sharing her knowledge and gave me her constant attention.

"The sickness of a morning will pass, and you'll be able to eat more. You are too thin. Try some of this venison."

After I had retched and cleansed my mouth, she tried again. "A mess of greens? Oat bread?"

"Not now—perhaps some mint or chamomile tea with a little honey?"

"I will prepare it myself."

One night I confided to Ingeld that I did not know which Hrun was worse: the old one or the new one. He beamed.

"She just wants to share our good fortune. Don't begrudge her the opportunity. Freawaru, you have given her something to live for!"

He kissed me tenderly and cupped his hands around my belly.

"My son—you will be a strong warrior one day—I know it."

"Ingeld, what if it's a girl? Can she too be a strong warrior?"

He frowned slightly. "It will be a boy. Hrun has said so."

While a few warm days yet lingered, I delighted in helping with the herb harvest. But as leaves fell from the trees and strong winds swept across the marshes, I spent more time indoors. At first, I tried my hand at the looms, but standing for long hours gave me back pains. Ingeld rubbed my back at night—before lowering himself cautiously onto my growing belly.

"Don't worry, you won't hurt him. He floats in his own watery world."

"Freawaru, my queen, little mother." He nuzzled my ear and then sank into me, sending shivers of bliss throughout my body.

Ingeld—Ingeld—hold me always as you do now.

For a time that winter we were happy—all of us, Danes and Heathobards together. Ingeld and Hrun were happy about the child growing in my womb. I was happy to be accomplishing my mission as a peace-weaver. Sven's death seemed a distant memory, though Gunter seldom appeared in the hall

As winter solstice drew near, we readied the mead hall for nights of feasting and drinking, bringing in holly and sacred mistletoe. A potion from the leaves was brewed to bring fruitfulness to all who drank of it. Ingeld laughed that I had no need to drink, my fertility being evident. Indeed I had grown very large—so much so that Hrun feared there might be twins.

Hrun fussed over my diet, claiming that I must have nothing too salty or too sweet—though I craved both. She prevented pork or other fatty meats from being served to me. And when one day I sought to go horseback riding with Ingeld as a change from the tedium of indoors, she absolutely forbade it.

"What can you be thinking? You'll bring on the baby before it is time!"

Sheepishly, I retreated to the fireside.

Occasionally I roused myself to play a game of Hnefatafl with Ingeld, using the board and pieces Hrothmund had given me. Ingeld always chose the attacking side, as he liked to make the first move toward capturing the king. Sometimes I was a match for him, but usually he succeeded in surrounding my king with four warriors, thus winning the game. At the court of Hrothgar, I had seen men come to blows if they lost, but I accepted defeat gracefully. It gave Ingeld so much pleasure to win.

Ingeld no longer lay with me, though my time of delivery was not yet near. Both Ana and Hrun judged it best that I move to the women's quarters where I could have attendance as needed. I missed Ingeld, sometimes waking at night to reach for his strong, warm body. By day, I grew lazy, content to be waited on, sitting long hours near the hearth fire, talking softly to the child within my womb. A great oak log had been dragged into the mead hall to burn each night of our celebration—just as we used to do in Heorot.

Heorot. My life there seemed a long-ago dream, a tale told to a child at bedtime. As I peered into the fire, the faces of my family rose before me: Hrothmund, Hrethric, Wealtheow, Hrothgar ... I longed to touch them, to tell them of my life with Ingeld, to tell them about the baby.

"What do you see there, my lady? You look sad."

I looked up. Ragnhild had paused beside me, carrying a pitcher.

"Do you ever miss them, Ragnhild? Your family and friends back in Heorot?"

"Aye, my lady, but I can wait until spring."

"Spring? What then? Do you think of leaving me? I will need all my women after the baby is born."

"You are well cared for here, my lady, and there are many who can help you as well as I—Ursula for one. She is good with children."

I looked at Ragnhild in astonishment.

"What of the other women from Heorot? Will they desert me too?"

"I have no wish to upset you, my lady. I speak only for myself. Back home, Thorkel and I had a mind to marry—if he hasn't already gone off with another woman."

She said this was such resignation that I roused myself to reassure her. "Surely Thorkel would not do that—if he loves you?"

"That don't count much with men, my lady. If there's not one woman at hand, they'll find another." She paused, looking suddenly flustered. "Of course I'm not talking about men like Ingeld." For some reason she reddened, and hurried away.

I pondered her words and later that night repeated them to Ana.

"Do you think Ingeld would ever take another woman?"

"It happens. Not all that unusual. Aeschere had another wife before me. She died in childbirth—oh, forgive me, my lady, that was thoughtless."

"No, speak your mind, Ana. But I didn't mean a second marriage, I meant—"

"I know what you meant." She paused, stroking my hair as she unbound the braids. "It's not the same for them—more sport than anything, I'd say."

"Do you think Ingeld had other women before he married me?"

Ana laughed outright. "Sometimes you talk like a child. Of course he did—though if you really want to know, you'll have to ask him."

I did want to know, but I did not want to ask him. Instead, I began to examine the faces of the younger women at Wulfhaus. Could Ingeld have slept with Sigrid? Brunhild? Ingeld noticed my preoccupation one evening at meat. We only saw each other now at meals.

"What is it, wife? You are strangely quiet of late."

I could not bring myself to speak of what lay on my heart. For the first time, I lied to my husband. "I've been thinking about … what to name our son."

"Why, 'Froda' of course, after my father."

This brought me to full attention. "Froda? That would please you? I had thought …" Nay, better not say what I had thought—of my father's brother, the one they called Hergar. He had died long before my birth, but was always spoken of with admiration and affection. It would have been a noble name; but of course, Ingeld would want to honor his father—the father my father had killed.

"Freawaru? Wife? Are you ill? Should I call someone?"

"Nay, my lord, do not alarm yourself. It's just that this … this ale does not sit well with me."

"Hrun told you to stop drinking ale. Why have you not obeyed her?"

"Because she is not my mother, and I am not a child!"

I rose suddenly, bumping my belly against the table. To Ingeld's consternation and my own chagrin, I burst into tears.

"What is it? Can I—"

"Leave me alone! I can take care of myself!"

Heads were turning in our direction. Neither Hrun nor Ana was present in the hall, but I caught the eye of a serving girl, who hurried to my side.

"Help me to the women's house," I muttered, steering for the door. Together we stumbled out into the darkness.

Ana put me to bed and sat beside me, humming a tune I had once sung to my little brothers. I missed them ... I missed Mother ... I missed Ingeld.

"Why did I shout at him, Ana, why was I hateful?" Tears trickled down my cheeks, and I could not stop them.

"Hush, child. It's just your condition. It's natural to be moody when you are carrying a child—and spats are normal between husband and wife."

That word *child* again. Had Ingeld married a child or a woman? Too exhausted to ponder the question, I fell into deep sleep.

When the dream came, it found me unprepared, vulnerable, tears still wet on my cheeks. Two figures revolved in a watery mist. Their hands reached for each other. Fingers locked on throats. They squeezed.

Gasping, choking for air, I sat upright. Was it the monster? Grendel? Where was Beowulf? Frantically I searched the darkness. My cries brought Ana with a hastily lighted torch.

"Hush—you'll wake the house! It's just a dream—a bad one, from the looks of you."

"Is it dead, Ana, is it dead?"

"What are you asking? No one's dead."

"The Grendel—are you sure it's dead?"

"Of course it is. Don't you remember? Beowulf killed it long ago. Dead and burned, what was left of it. What put that fiend into your head?"

"I don't know, but something feels ... wrong. Ingeld—perhaps something has happened to Ingeld! I must go to him!"

"You're staying right here. I'll fix a cup of tea to help you sleep— valerian should do it. No more nightmares tonight!"

She wrapped blankets tightly around my body and stirred up the fire. Still I shivered.

"Will it be morning soon? I need light! I can't see."

"Hush, hush, you'll stir up the baby next, and when it starts kicking you won't be able to sleep at all."

But the baby did not kick, and I did sleep.

Early morning light found me still exhausted, but I was determined to go to Ingeld and make it up to him for my childish behavior of the night before. I slipped out of bed as noiselessly as my weight and girth would allow and pulled on a fur robe. Steadying myself with my ash wood staff, I hobbled to the doorway. It struck me suddenly that I now moved like Hrun used to.

Clammy cold touched my face as I slipped outside, peering through fog to get my bearings. The mead hall's bulk pointed the way to Ingeld's chamber. I reviewed in my mind what I would say to him, imagining his surprise and delight at such an unexpected visit. I would slip under the down comforter and nestle against his warmth, breathing in his ear to wake him.

But Ingeld was already awake. And he was not alone. Low laughter drifted out from under the door, stopping me as I raised my hand to the latch. A woman's laughter—then Ingeld's deep voice.

"Don't go yet. I haven't had my fill of you."

My heart stopped, the blood froze in my veins. I flattened myself against the outer wall, no longer breathing.

"Another time, perhaps? I must go now or Ana will scold."

That voice was so familiar: it was the voice of ... Gyda! My own woman! How dare she? How dare *he*? How could they shame me so? Trembling now with more than cold, I staggered away from the wall, blindly feeling my way back to the women's house. Ana met me at the door and pulled me inside.

"Sleepwalking too? Oh, my lady!"

As I sank into her arms, I felt the bleeding start.

Hours, days might have passed as I drifted in and out of consciousness. I dreamed: of the girl doll Ana had once given me, but it was missing—what had become of it? Faces appeared and disappeared: Ana, Hrun, Ingeld ... Gyda. Voices spoke to me: "my lady ... my wife ... Freawaru, come back to us." Is that you, Mother? Yes, I'm coming, but I'm so weary ... let me sleep awhile longer.

It was dark when my eyelids flew open, and I knew myself to be in my own body—which felt ... different. Lifting my arms, I circled my belly. Its fullness was gone.

"Ana? Ana!"

A figure nearby roused and stumbled toward me in the hearth light.

"Here I am, my lady."

"Ana, the baby—where is my baby?" I bolted upright and then sank back as pain seized my lower body.

"It came too soon, my lady, it was not yet ready to live in this world."

"Where is he? I want to see him!"

"Ingeld, you mean?"

"No, the baby—my son. Where is my son?"

Ana was silent, stroking my hands, her eyes full of pity.

"It was ... it was a girl child, my lady, not a son. It lived only a few hours. We nearly lost you—but Hrun knew what to do to stop the bleeding."

I lay still, absorbing the words I'd just heard. They could not be true.

"But Hrun said it was a boy; Hrun said—" My voice was rising in a shriek.

"Hush, don't excite yourself. You're still weak from the ordeal."

She was right about the weakness. I felt hollow, empty, a husk without a core. My son—my baby—gone.

"How long have I lain here? Where is the baby now?"

"The better part of two days. We wrapped the little thing in skins and laid it in a wooden box awaiting your instructions. Ingeld wanted to bury it, but I said we always used fire to honor the dead."

Burying? Burning? Was he really dead then, my son?

"Froda must have a funeral pyre, of course—we'll build it immediately. We'll give him swords … and horses … and slaves … maybe Gyda."

"My lady!" The shock in Ana's voice penetrated the fog in my brain. "You're raving! You are not yourself! Best we speak of this in the morning. Here—I found Hunig in one of your chests. It may be a comfort to sleep with."

Into my arms she placed the girl doll she'd given me so long ago.

When I woke again it was daylight. Both Hrun and Ingeld stood beside my sleeping bench.

"Dear wife, you've come back to me."

Ingeld seemed to be looking down at me with genuine concern and affection, but like an echo I heard the words he'd spoken to Gyda that night—and turned my face away from him. He mistook the meaning.

"Be consoled, Freawaru. We will have another child. Hrun says you will recover—"

"But not soon," Hrun's voice broke in. "You need time to gather strength. You lost much blood—as well as the baby."

Something in her tone of voice flashed a warning. She sounded almost like the Hrun of old. Was she suggesting that it was my fault? I opened my mouth to retort, but did not speak. Nothing seemed worth the effort just now.

In the days that followed, I dully followed commands: eat, drink, sleep … but my spirit had left my body. It flew high above Wulfhaus, winging over land and sea to Heorot. How I longed for my mother, my real mother, not this aged creature who hovered over me pressing me to eat red meat, not even dear Ana with her attentive ministrations.

We burned the baby's body according to my directions, though not on a great pyre and not with Gyda on it. Instead, I placed the girl doll given to me by Ana next to the small bundle of my infant … daughter … and carved a rune of protection to accompany her on her journey to the other world. I took the handful of ashes that remained and folded them inside a silken cloth, which I buried deep in my great chest. Ana disapproved; she thought the ashes should be buried in the mound begun outside the settlement after Sven's death—a mound for Danish remains. But I could not bear to leave any part of me in this alien land. Now I knew that this place could never be my home.

Winter solstice passed without my participation. Even as my body healed, my spirit lay wounded, for eating away inside me lay the poison of Ingeld and Gyda together. I had spoken of this to no one. Nothing could lighten the double weight I carried: the knowledge of Ingeld's infidelity and the loss of my child. I never spoke to Gyda and avoided her gaze but sensed that we knew what lay in the other's mind.

With the first signs of spring came the arrival of Heathobards from the South who had been exploring and trading in other regions. One man stood out. His name was Starcartherus, and he looked to be as old as Hrun, a grizzled veteran of many battles. I soon learned that he had no love for Danes.

Ingeld planned a feast to welcome the new arrivals and urged me to be present in the mead hall as a signal of honor and respect. That night Ana dressed me in my wedding clothes. I had regained some color, and she brushed my hair to a luster before placing the jeweled circlet on my head.

"There—every inch a queen! Ingeld will be proud of you."

"It does not matter," I muttered to myself—but Ana heard.

"Doesn't matter? Of course it matters! What's wrong with you? You've been sulky as a child ever since … better face up to it, my lady … you've lost a baby, yes, but many women have lost babies, myself included. You will have other children—if you don't drive away your husband with your coldness and hard looks!"

Her sharpness jarred me from my usual lethargy.

"So you think it's all my fault too? I could tell you some things …"

"What's done is done. Best to put it behind you. Ingeld is a good man."

I wondered: did Ana know of Ingeld's—betrayal? Yes, that's what it felt like—betrayal!

"Men are men. This one is your husband. You seem to have forgotten that. He's waiting for you right now."

Ana almost pushed me out the door of the women's house, for I had long delayed returning to Ingeld's chamber, using my need for recovery as an excuse. In truth, I could no longer look at Ingeld without seeing him suspended over Gyda, and my stomach turned at the thought. Flushed with anger and resentment, I entered the mead hall where Ingeld waited to lead me to my seat. His eyes sparkled as he surveyed the gems in my hair.

"So, wife, you value my gifts. That pleases me! It pleases me also to see you looking so well. Tonight ..."

I brushed past him, but he pulled me back.

"Freawaru, I want you. Do not turn away. Tonight you sleep with me."

All eyes followed us as we entered the hall. I forced a smile and took Ingeld's arm. At least Gyda was not among the women serving the feast. It had been many weeks since I'd appeared in the mead hall, and many seemed genuinely glad to see me.

"Hail Freawaru the Fair—we drink to your beauty!"

At first Ingeld scowled at the young speaker, but then he himself led a toast in my honor: "To Freawaru, queen of the wolf tribe."

It's lucky Hrun isn't here tonight, I thought. Ingeld's mother seemed to be suffering of late from a malady that oppressed her mind; she often kept to her bed.

Under the good-natured shouts of the assembly, I relaxed somewhat, even basking in their praise. Turning, I gave Ingeld a real smile, which he returned with an embrace that almost crushed my ribs.

"Careful, my lord. I'm not a common woman to be tumbled like a slave!"

The smile left Ingeld's face, but he showed no trace of displeasure to the men eating and drinking below us. He rose.

"Comrades! Guests! Ingeld, son of Froda, bids you welcome! Enjoy the bounty that Wulfhaus has to offer."

The warrior Starcartherus, sitting in a place of honor, rose to reply. His unexpected words took my breath away and silenced every man in the hall.

"Ingeld, son of Froda, why have you delayed so long to avenge your father? Here you sit, taking pleasure in honoring your bride—laden with gems and golden vestments—while grief and shame torment us, we who were Froda's comrades. Has lust for this woman blinded you to your duty? I recall the fashion of an earlier day, when those guilty of murder were made to pay the penalty for such a crime. Here I see you arm in arm with our foes: the Danes who slew Froda. How long will you patiently endure the slaughter of your sire?"

All eyes stared at Starcartherus. No one spoke. Ingeld himself seemed turned to stone, frozen in the act of raising a cup to his lips. Suddenly he brought it smashing down on the table.

"Enough! It is my place to decide such matters! Freawaru is my chosen queen, a pledge of peace between our peoples."

Several men had jumped to their feet, Danes and Heathobards, their hands reaching for weapons.

"There will be no blood shed in this hall!" roared Ingeld.

"No," Starcartherus roared back, "The blood that should be shed lies in Denmark—at the hall of Hrothgar!"

I shuddered violently, spilling the wine cup clutched in my hand.

"Friends, return to your seats," growled Ingeld. "These matters can be discussed later, in council. For now, let us take our fill of meat and drink. Women: bring in the mead!"

This distraction helped to calm the men, though growls and mutters still rippled through the hall. I sat speechless, turning over Ingeld's words in my head. Would he seriously consider another attack on Heorot? What could I do to stop him?

Chapter 12
Blood, Bones, and Fire

Through the rest of the banquet, my face wore a set smile, but my mind was in turmoil, pulled in opposite directions. I still loved Ingeld—I had to admit that to myself, despite his sleeping with another woman—but I loved my family too. They had sent me to be a peace-weaver; now the threads, so painstakingly woven, threatened to come unraveled. If only Starcartherus had not appeared, as adamant in his desire for blood vengeance as Hrun had once been. Hrun? Hrun! Where would she stand in this struggle? I must speak to her immediately.

During the recitation of a lengthy story about Heathobard victories in battle, I leaned toward Ingeld and whispered in his ear.

"I will come to your bed tonight, but first I must see your mother. She is ill and was asking for me just before the banquet." The half-lie rolled easily off my tongue.

He looked at me in surprise and then nodded. "Your thoughtfulness pleases me, but do not be long; you must spend tonight in my chamber … wife."

"Yes, my lord, I will not fail you."

The irony of the words smote my heart, for had not Ingeld failed me? With worse perhaps to follow? As soon as custom permitted, I left the mead hall and hurried to the hut where Hrun had taken up residence, accompanied by two of her women. When I entered, both rose swiftly—as if to defend Hrun rather than do honor to me.

"I've come to speak to Hrun—alone."

"Ah, the Danish princess wants to see me! Why so sudden, Freawaru? You have not shown your face to me in days—hoping I'd crawled off into a corner to die, perhaps?"

My heart sank. It was the Hrun of old who stared at me from under her robes, one scrawny fist clutching the fur to her neck. She waved off her companions, who scurried out into the dark.

"I heard you were not well, Mother Hrun. I came to see what you might need—and to thank you for your care of me when I was ill."

"Hmph! What I need is a daughter who can give me grandsons—something you'll never do!"

Stung, I blurted out words I had not meant to say.

"Why don't you ask one of your serving girls to do that? Ingeld likes them well enough!"

Hrun laughed, a nasty cackle.

"So you've discovered his taste for female flesh—found out you're not the only woman in the world. Quite a shock, was it?"

Involuntarily I nodded, tears springing to my eyes, and I fell to my knees, clutching my empty belly. I felt Hrun's bony claw on my shoulder.

"So that's part of the answer is it? I wondered ..." She was silent so long that I finally looked up. Her eyes were not unkind.

"Don't be a fool, Freawaru. Any child born of a slave is still a slave! Ingeld needs a son recognized by law. I placed all my hopes on you—a foolish thing to do, for you'll never be able to give birth. Your frame is too small, your hips too narrow. You would die in the attempt. Having this baby come early while it was still so small probably saved your life." Hrun's voice was low, matter-of-fact. "And now Starcartherus comes to stir Ingeld to revenge!"

Startled, I jumped up. "How did you know?"

"I am not entirely forgotten here in my bed. Though you have not seen fit to visit me, others do."

"Mother Hrun, what is to be done? If Ingeld goes off to attack Heorot, he himself may be killed. How does that help either of us?"

She stared at me, her lips set in a stubborn line. "Starcartherus is right. Ingeld must do his duty as a son. He must avenge his father's death."

"Yes, of course," I rose, almost shouting. "That's what Hrothgar was doing, remember? Froda killed Hrothgar's father, Halfdane, so Hrothgar killed Froda. Where is it to end? Must we women always end up like Hildeburh—burning our loved ones on the same funeral pyre?"

"I do not know of Hildeburh, but I know Ingeld." Hrun grimaced, rising on one elbow to peer up at me. "Once his anger is roused, he will take action!"

Despairing, I fled her chamber, almost trampling the two women listening outside the door. When I entered the women's house, Ana met me with a look of such grave concern that I knew she'd already heard what had been said in the mead hall.

"Oh, Ana, what is to be done?"

"That's what you must decide, my lady. You are Ingeld's queen, and you have more influence with him than anyone else."

"I hope you're right. Help me change now. I'm going to his bed tonight."

Her face beamed approval.

Ingeld's chamber was empty when I entered. Only the armor on the wall bespoke his presence. Would those weapons soon be used against my own family? I reached up to touch the scabbard of his sword, graven with symbols my fingers recognized: Teiwaz, rune of warriors, protector in battle. Runes ... an idea began to form in my brain.

Just then the door swung open, and Ingeld staggered in. He usually held his wine well, but tonight appeared to have drunk more deeply than usual. I wondered what might have transpired after I'd left the mead hall.

"By the gods, Freawaru, you are a woman fit to be queen!"

He pulled me to him in a rough embrace; we fell heavily on the bed. There were few preliminaries on his part. Fortunately I had earlier applied the salve designed for my wedding night and did not shrink from his initial thrust. His lovemaking was savage—more a punishment than an expression of love after our long separation. When he finally fell back, shuddering, I curled up like a wounded animal and wept quietly into the fur robe beneath us.

I had hoped to talk to him after our union, relying on the sweetness of reconnection to sweeten his mood, but he already lay snoring. He stank of ale and his own rank juices. How could I ever have loved this man? I started to slip from the bed, but a brawny hand gripped my leg.

"Stay—stay with me."

Wordlessly I slipped back beside him. Once again, he enfolded me in his arms, but gently this time, pulling my body against his so that I felt his breath on my hair.

"Ingeld, my lord?"

He was snoring again. Any talk would have to wait until morning.

By morning Ingeld was gone, along with all but a handful of the Heathobard men. I knew at once where they were headed: Heorot. Ana was already up when I burst, half-dressed, into the women's house.

"We could not stop them, my lady. Saxe tried, but they were too far away. They drove off the horses and took all the ships in the harbor. That Starcartherus, he—"

"What do you mean? Where is Saxe now? We must gather our people together and decide what to do."

"We had the same thought. Most are in the mead hall, waiting for you."

Ana matched my rapid pace as we hurried to the hall, our women close behind. Ingeborg was sobbing; Gyda looked stony-faced.

"What's going to happen? Will they come back and kill us too?" wailed Estrid.

"No one's been killed yet," I started to say and then turned abruptly to Ana. "Have they?"

"No, my lady. Apparently the men left during the night in small groups so as not to awaken our people. Saxe saw a band of them driving off our horses when he got up early to relieve himself. He gave chase on foot, but had no chance of stopping them."

Inside the mead hall we found Wulfgar and the rest of our men counting their weapons. Wulfgar looked rueful and abashed.

"What happened?"

He cleared his throat. "When we left here last night, Ingeld and his men appeared to be ready for sleep. He dismissed us early, saying he was eager to bed his wife. Starcartherus and his men were assigned to sleep in the mead hall. Obviously sleep was not the only thing on their minds." He laughed harshly. "We were completely fooled, taken in by Ingeld's words of peace."

"Do not blame yourself. You were not alone." I looked at the angry faces before me. "Have they taken any of our weapons?"

"No, nothing is missing, since each man sleeps with his own war gear."

I shuddered at the words "war gear." "How long would it take them to reach Heorot?"

"Not being weighed down with women and household goods this time, I'd say no more than four to five days, if the wind is good."

Ana could no longer restrain herself. "So we can know nothing of the outcome for at least ten days?"

"It would seem so," I answered, "but wait!" The idea that had begun to form the night before now returned to me. "To help us see into the future, I shall cast runes. They may help to guide our actions."

Wulfgar nodded. "We can do little else without ships to pursue them."

"I will go and prepare the ritual. Right now, let everyone fill their bellies—if there is still food for us. What is the mood of the Heathobards who remain?"

"Speaking for the women, my lady, they seem to be as shocked and surprised as we are. No one saw this coming."

Ragnhild and Estrid nodded agreement with Ana's words.

Saxe now reported. "The only men left behind are thralls, the very old, or the very young; all of Ingeld's thanes have gone with him."

"And what of Hrun?"

My women looked at each other blankly. No one had seen her this morning.

"We will summon her to observe the rune-casting. As Ingeld's queen, I will take charge of Wulfhaus in his absence."

Wulfgar and the men exchanged looks, but bowed briefly.

"Yes, my lady."

"Set a watchband at the perimeter of the settlement, in case Ingeld's departure is a ruse to put us off guard."

"Yes, my lady."

"And Wulfgar," I paused. "You have served me faithfully; you shall be rewarded for it."

"Yes, my lady."

While the others broke their fast, I prepared to travel over land and sea toward Heorot. From my chest, I selected a white cloth and a clutch of feathers plucked from the swans in Heorot's harbor. How often had we flown together, looking down on the golden gables of my father's hall. We had once seen smoke rising from it, but found it safe after all. Might it yet be so!

Once again, I bound my hair with the circlet of gems given me by Ingeld, though I wore only a plain blue cloak over my gown this time, not my wedding finery.

At the appointed time, we gathered in the mead hall. Hrun and her women were seated on benches to my left, the Danes to my right, for I took Ingeld's high seat as my altar.

"What is this—some of your northern magic?" croaked Hrun.

"Yes, Mother Hrun. I'm surprised you did not think of it yourself before you let Ingeld rush off, perhaps to his doom. It has often been our custom to cast a rune before embarking on any serious undertaking."

"Ingeld did not need any woman's permission for a man's job!"

I ignored her response.

"Since some of you may not be familiar with rune-casting, I will explain what I am about to do. In this bag," I held aloft a deerskin pouch, "lie the twenty-four runes which Odin won from his ordeal on Yggdrasil, the world tree. Today, given the gravity of the situation, I will draw three runes in sequence and lay them before me on this cloth. The first rune, reading from right to left, will comment on the present situation. The next will indicate a course of action. The last will predict an outcome."

I could hear Hrun's labored breathing in the silence. Everyone seemed to be listening intently. Quietly I spread my white cloth on the table before me and then arranged swan feathers around the edges. Rising, I held the bag aloft.

"Gods, reveal your will to us. Speak to us through the runes I draw."

Closing my eyes, I reached into the bag, withdrew a rune, and placed it on the cloth—then a second—and then a third. As I opened my eyes, I saw those in the hall lean forward as one body. Two runes lay face up; the third was hidden. I picked up the first.

"*Hagalaz*. Does anyone know its meaning?"

"Battle!" crowed Hrun. "Disruption. Forces which cannot be controlled."

"So you *do* have some rune-craft, Mother Hrun! Yes," I acknowledged, "Hagalaz, interpreted literally, means 'hail'—a natural force. It signifies destruction and threatens the loss of order. Radical change is taking place. This is the situation in which we find ourselves this morning."

Heads on both sides of the hall nodded in agreement.

"What is to be done in this situation? For an answer, we look to the second rune, *Raido*. What does this signify, Mother Hrun?"

"A journey!" she declared triumphantly. "Ingeld is traveling north to avenge his father's death."

"Right again, but it can also signify reunion at the end of a journey—and joy at achieving one's goal. Could it be that Froda and Ingeld, father and son, will be reunited in death at the end of this journey? Would that bring you joy, Hrun?"

Her face twisted. She hesitated. "Reveal the final rune!"

I knelt, turned over the rune, and stepped back.

"Victory! I knew it!" Hrun's face shown with joy.

There for all to see lay *Teiwaz*, rune of victory, the same rune carved on Ingeld's sword holder.

"Victory for Heathobards—or Danes?" I mused aloud and then took another look. "Wait! This rune is reversed. Its position reveals the opposite of victory. The hoped-for outcome may not be within reach!"

A babble of voices rose along the benches. Hrun half-rose from her seat. So did Wulfgar.

"It's the spear rune of the god of war!" he shouted. "We all know its use to protect the thrower from harm. But … if Tyr turns against you—" He sat down, a grim smile spreading across his face.

Hrun's face turned purple. "This means nothing! It is all a trick to bring us grief! I'm leaving this hall right now. Cast all the runes you like! Ingeld will return victorious!"

With these words she rose, collapsed, and had to be carried out by her women. The remaining Heathobards trailed after them, confusion in their faces. I remained standing at the altar until only we Danes remained.

"What does it mean, my lady?" Ana was the questioner.

"It means there is hope for Heorot. That much I am sure of." I sank down in my seat, suddenly drained of energy.

Each morning, I rose early, wrapped myself in a woolen shawl, and picked my way over patches of still frozen ground to the river's edge. Occasionally a crane flew up from the mud flats, lifting its great wings in slow retreat. I gazed to the north, feeling the west wind cold and damp on my cheeks. Wulfhaus was always cold and damp, so unlike the warmth of Heorot—my home. Each morning I returned to the women's house with nothing to report, and my heart grew heavier.

"They'll come when they come, my lady. Your waiting and watching won't make it happen any sooner."

"I know, Ana, I know."

"Have you had any … dreams … lately?"

I knew what she meant, but again I had nothing to report. My inner eyes were dark, unable to penetrate the mist of unknowing. My thoughts were constantly with my family—and Ingeld. Who would survive their clash? I thought of Ingeld's raid a few years earlier, foiled by the alert response of Hrothulf. Ruefully I prayed that my cousin's vigilance had not flagged, that the attack would not find Heorot unaware and unprepared. I wondered … would Unferth see it coming? Would his ravens at least reveal the approach of a large body of men?

Ingeld—Starcartherus—who was actually leading those men? Much as I rued the knowledge, I knew that it had to be my husband, urged on by that implacable old Heathobard.

In public, I acted with more confidence than I felt, assigning the men who remained to daily, mundane tasks, such as pulling cod and herring from the sea, gutting the fish, and hanging them to dry on racks in the sun. I oversaw the work of the women as well, instructing them to plant herbs and turn over soil as if life would continue as usual. I even spent time with Hrun. It was evident that only a few days were left to her. She was clinging to life, waiting for her son to return … victorious.

"Mother Hrun?"

Her woman held a finger to her lips, indicating sleep, but Hrun lifted one eyelid.

"Still here? I thought you'd have run away by now. You're not needed anymore. Ingeld has left you. When he returns, his mother will be queen again."

This speech, delivered with difficulty, seemed to amuse her. As a thin smile stretched her lips, her toothless mouth opened on gaping emptiness that released a fetid smell.

"Mother Hrun, I have something to ask. Your words of several days ago have just come back to me. You said I would not be able to bear children. Why?"

"You failed. You'll always fail. You're not built for childbearing."

She closed her eyes as if to signal an end to our conversation, but I was not finished.

"You have failed too. You said the baby would be a boy, but it was not. You were wrong about that. You can be wrong again."

She lifted her shoulders in a feeble shrug. "It doesn't matter. You'll never sleep with Ingeld again."

This time she set her lips resolutely and spoke no more. Hrun was right about one thing. I never slept with Ingeld again.

One evening, Ingeld's scop tried to lift our spirits with a lay. He sang the tale of Walter and Hagen, taken hostage by Attila the Hun, in whose prison they swore oaths of friendship with each other. Hagen had also sworn an oath of obedience to his liege lord Gunther, who mounted an attack on Walter, forcing Hagen to fight his friend. This conflict of loyalties ended only after all three were wounded so severely they could not continue the fight.

Ingeld is caught in a similar predicament, I thought to myself. He has a sworn duty to avenge his father's killing on the killer—Hrothgar, but he has also sworn to keep the peace—in an oath to Hrothgar. If only that hateful Starkartherus had not shown up to re-kindle the flames of revenge!

"Come," shouted Wulfgar, rising from his place, "give us another lay! Do you have any local heroes worthy of song?"

Max nodded eagerly, clearly pleased to get such a response from a Dane. "Of course! I will now sing 'Dietrich of Berne' about a renowned giant-killer and battle-warrior, once aided by that same Attila to regain his own kingdom."

In the early days, King Dietmar's pride
In young son Dietrich, bold and fearless ...

Having no stomach for more tales of heroes and fighting, I did not stay to hear more, but slipped out to find my bed. Besides, I had never heard of Attila the Hun.

On the twelfth morning, I woke to heavy fog. In the eld-house I stirred up the hearth fire and started water boiling for porridge. Ana kept saying I was thin as a bird and urged me to eat, but I found it hard to swallow. A thick lump of fear had grown in my throat and choked me.

The fog clamped a wet hand on my face as I emerged, but I shook it off, pulling my shawl tighter. Somewhere in the mist I heard the screech of sea eagles and the loud, clear whistle of an osprey. Strange, so close to land … could it be? I hurried toward the river. Wulfgar was there before me, peering into the blankness.

"My lady Freawaru? I thought I heard something—oars scraping, maybe. Listen."

I listened. Yes, the sound of wood on wood. As we watched, a shadowy shape emerged through the mist: a ship.

"Get back to the mead hall. Alert the men on guard there. We must prepare a suitable welcome!"

I did as Wulfgar bid, running heedlessly through melted snow patches, slipping on mud, my heart pounding with dread and anticipation.

"Saxe, Gorm, they're coming—on the river! Wulfgar and I sighted a ship! Prepare yourselves!"

I noted with grim satisfaction that the men had slept in their armor. Now they grabbed spears and swords, shaking off sleep.

"Ana, they're coming!"

I burst into the women's quarters, rousing Danes and Heathobards alike. Hurriedly they threw on heavy garments against the morning's chill. The fog had thinned when we emerged, blinking like owls. For the first time I thought to wonder why Ingeld had risked a night-crossing over water. What need had driven him? Ana's hand on my shoulder made me start in surprise.

"Let our men take care of this, my lady."

"I am still queen of Wulfhaus. I will meet my husband as befits a queen—boldly."

"Yes, of course, but let's see which way the wind is blowing first. Let's wait at the mead hall."

"All right, but outside."

We arrayed ourselves outside the mead hall door, a shivering clutch of women in gray wool. Gradually we were joined by some of

Ingeld's thralls, who'd also got wind of their master's return. I heard the chattering of teeth and a whisper or two.

"Silence! Stand strong and wait!"

We waited … and waited. As the fog lifted slightly, thin shafts of sunlight warmed our faces. Still no one appeared from the direction of the river—neither Dane nor Heathobard. Ana looked at me quizzically.

"Are you sure you saw a ship? In this fog—"

"Hush! Someone is coming!"

I was wrong. Two someones were coming, leaning on each other: Wulfgar, supporting Gunter. We stared in astonishment.

"Don't stand there with your mouths open. This man needs help— and there are more on the ship. Bring wagons—quickly!"

Gorm and Saxe moved to catch Gunter as he sank to the ground, white-faced. His tunic was stained with dried blood, his helmet missing. Wulfgar had already headed back toward the river.

"Ingeld! What about Ingeld? Is he on the ship? Is he alive?"

Wulfgar glanced back. "I cannot say yet, my lady. There are both dead and dying on board. I don't know how they made it back to Wulfhaus." He disappeared in the fog.

"You, men, take Gunter to the mead hall and lay him on a table. Ana, take these women and fetch my herb bag. You know what to do. I'm going down to the ship."

Not waiting for a response, I hurried after Wulfgar. The spectacle that met my eyes almost brought me to my knees. I gagged at the stench of rotting flesh. Some men hung limp over the oar locks, others lay sprawled on the bottom in grotesque postures. In the midst of the bodies lay one figure stretched out over sea chests and sacks of grain, its golden hair hanging loosely from a face strangely deformed—as if it had melted in the sun.

"Ingeld!"

The figure stirred as if to rise and then relaxed.

"Ingeld—it's Freaw. I'm here, here to help you."

Tears streamed down my face as I beheld this wreckage of a man.

"You two thralls, over here! Carry your master to that wagon!"

Ingeld groaned as they lifted his body. Dark blood trickled from a gash in his chest.

"Careful—you'll reopen that wound. It may be a deep one."

Indeed it was. The back of his tunic was soaked as well. And something was wrong with his eyes: the skin seemed to be sealed over them, as if seared by hot iron.

"Oh, Ingeld, my husband, what has happened to you?"

Wulfgar laid a hand on my shoulder.

"Time for questions later. If you value this man, tend to him now—his thread of life has almost unraveled."

Nodding, I stumbled after the cart as it wheeled toward Wulfhaus, leaving deep ruts in the mud and sand.

In the eld-house I prepared a poultice of comfrey for the burns on Ingeld's face. Fortunately my women and I had gathered a quantity of this plant along the river marshes before winter's onset. Ana gently washed his wounds with water of thyme, her face grave as she probed their depth. When his agony became great, I dug to the bottom of my medicine chest for a precious root of mandrake and brewed tea to press to his lips. Eventually he fell into a drugged sleep, but his breath came rough and uneven, as if he were climbing with difficulty a very steep cliff.

All day we moved from man to man, doing what we could to lessen pain and lengthen life. Slowly some of the men who had used their last bit of strength to reach Wulfhaus began to revive. As food and fluids entered their bodies, they were able to sit up, jest weakly with the serving women, and even share an exchange with a fellow warrior. Others lay still as life faded from their bodies.

Of the twenty-four men who had gone forth with Ingeld, twenty had returned, but only ten still lived—including Ingeld and Gunter. Starcartherus and his men were nowhere on the ship. Again the questions: What had happened? Where were the others? Had Heorot survived?

Near evening, Ingeld awoke briefly. His eyes did not, could not open, but he spoke my name. I leaned forward to whisper in his ear.

"I'm here, my lord, your wife is here beside you."

"Freaw ... mistake ... women in mead hall ... fire ... fire in eyes."

I could see that he paid for each word with great pain, but I had to ask.

"Hrothgar? Does my father live?"

His mouth twisted strangely. "Saw ... saw him ... his spear ... in my belly." The effort to speak drew beads of sweat to his face. I recoiled in anguish.

"My father's spear gave you this wound?"

"Old man ... still fighter ... mother too."

"Mother? How was she involved in the battle?"

A sound that could have been a laugh came from his throat. He lifted a hand to his face. "Trick ... tricked us ... a trap." He fell silent, panting, and then began to cough frothy red blood.

"Ingeld, my love, speak no more. Save your strength to get well. We'll talk of this later."

My words belied my intuition that there would be no "later" for us. I held his hands as the coughing subsided. Then he made a final effort.

"Freaw, wife—my jewel."

"Yes, Ingeld, my husband—my joy."

Tears coursed down my cheeks unchecked, splashing on to his. Leaning over, I kissed them softly.

Ingeld died that night. He spoke no more, though I continued to talk to him as I held him in my arms. Hrun had been brought in and knelt beside him, crooning lullabies as if he were a baby. She rocked from side to side, a boat bobbing in the wind. When his breathing stopped, our breath stopped too.

I heard myself join her in a high, keening wail. All my love and grief were pulled out of me at that moment, leaving me utterly empty. Not so with Hrun. She clung to the body and wept through the night. I sat dumb beside her. At some point I must have slept, for I woke to find Hrun poised over me with a dagger. I looked up with mild interest.

"Strike if you want. It will not bring him back. He followed your wishes—and see what it brought him. Are you satisfied now? Have you had your revenge?"

She stared at me wordlessly, her mouth working—and then plunged the dagger into her own wrinkled breast. Figures around me sprang up; I realized we were not alone. Ana's face appeared above me as Helga and Inga caught their mistress's sagging body.

"So ... we will have two bodies on the funeral pyre: mother and son."

Was it Ana who spoke ... or I? I did not know or care.

It took two days to find wood and build a funeral pyre big enough to hold all the dead: Ingeld, Hrun, and ten of Ingeld's thanes. Gunter was well enough to join Wulfgar in directing the work. He would not yet speak of what had happened at Heorot, saying that the dead must be honored first, and time allowed for wounds to heal. He wore a look of stoic misery as he laid out stones in the outline of a great ship, refusing any aid.

Within this shape, a platform of wood was erected, with more wood stacked nearby. The bodies were placed on top: Ingeld in the center, his mother beside him, his men arranged around them. I had washed his body in thyme water and dressed him in his wedding clothes, watching my hands at work as if they belonged to someone else.

All the dead men's armor—swords, helmets, mail shirts, shields—were heaped on top. Gold was brought from Ingeld's hoard: rings, armbands, and collars, and drinking horns and goblets for feasting in Valhalla. It had been in my mind to add the jewels he'd given me at our wedding, but something stopped me. Instead, I placed a bucket of apples—the last of the winter store—at Ingeld's feet, that he might enjoy eternal youth in the afterlife.

Hrun's women brought out fine linens, combs, and adornments to accompany their mistress to her new home in the house of Freyja. I worked a gold and silver circlet from my wrist and slipped it over Hrun's gnarled and twisted hand.

"Farewell, Ingeld's mother."

I fell afoul of the Heathobards over two funeral customs: sacrificing a female slave to accompany Ingeld and sacrificing his favorite horse.

"No, no slave shall die." In my mind I added, *not even Gyda*. "We've had enough of death and killing. Ingeld will surely not lack for female attention in Valhalla."

Ingeld's men overruled me on the horse. I had to watch as they led out Goldbleoh, cut its throat with one quick sword stroke, and then strained to lift it onto the pyre. Never again would Ingeld ride his spirited golden mount over the lands of his kingdom.

It was almost evening when the pyre was lighted. As smoke billowed, I breathed a mute farewell to my husband. He looked calm, at peace, as though he were sleeping in the fire. Its heat seared our faces as we stood in a ring of silent grief. Flames licked the flesh, bones burst, blood boiled—a savage spectacle. Its awful beauty held me and then released something caught inside. I lifted my head in a keening wail, picked up by the other women, Dane and Heathobard alike. Our death song rose to the heavens.

That night I could not sleep, tossing on the bed I once shared with Ingeld. Finally I rose, pulled a fur robe about me and stepped outside. As it did so often, a mist hung in the air. I leaned against the rough wood, gazing up with unseeing eyes. Gradually the mist began to clear. High above me emerged a pathway of stars, like a great road to Valhalla.

Ingeld, my husband, are you treading that path to glory? It soothed me to think so.

By morning, the fire had burned down to ash and embers, strewn with shards of bone and melted lumps of metal. All able-bodied men were called to the task of hauling earth and heaping it up to create a great mound higher than the mead hall—that all might know where Ingeld, chief of the Heathobards, had lived and died. Then and only then did Gunter consent to tell the story of the battle at Heorot.

We assembled in the mead hall on the third day after the funeral. Those who could not yet walk were carried in by their comrades. Unaccustomed quiet hung over the hall as Gunter took his place—in Ingeld's chair at my request. I sat beside him to reinforce my position as queen of Wulfhaus, but would have preferred a seat with Ana and my women. For this telling, no one of rank or importance had been excluded; as usual, the serving women would hear what transpired anyway as they worked.

Gunter's face worked strangely as he cleared his throat to begin.

"The gods were against us in this undertaking."

Several grizzled heads on the benches below us nodded agreement.

"Only the will of Odin could account for what happened at Heorot. Our plan was sound. We sailed north with the current along the coastland of the Jutes and then made the turn and dropped down to the land where Hrothgar held his court. The first part of our journey was successful."

"We beached our ships on his northern coast, far from the sight of any watch guards, and rode overland, taking care to keep our movements hidden. We planned a surprise attack by night in order to catch the Danes sleeping in the mead hall. We planned to set fire to it and burn it to the ground, cutting down any who tried to escape the flames."

As he paused for breath, I shuddered inwardly, envisioning the scene.

"Ingeld and I were to lead the first attack and set the fires. Starcartherus and his men would come behind us and kill any resistors not inside the mead hall. It did not happen as we had planned. Somehow the Danes knew of our coming. They laid a trap for us."

My heart leapt at these words. Had Unferth forseen it? Had ...

"They baited the trap ... with women!"

Disgust filled Gunter's voice; he rose and pounded the table before him. Wulfgar too was on his feet.

"What do you mean? What women?"

Ingeld's tortured words came back to me: "Old man ... still fighter ... mother too."

Gunter was shouting now.

"Ingeld cried, 'Revenge for Froda! Father, we come!' as we charged forward, casting our brands to fire the mead hall. It caught quickly, began to smoke, but as the great door swung open, it was not a warrior who stood in the opening but a woman—Hrothgar's queen—Wealtheow!"

Shocked cries filled the hall.

"She was dressed all in white, her hair loose and flowing about her shoulders. She appeared to be unarmed but held aloft a torch. At first, I thought she was a valkyrie, sent by Odin to carry us directly to Valhalla. Then she spoke, with venom in her words. 'Ingeld, son of Froda, you have broken your pledge of peace. Unfaithful man, take this for your treachery!' She thrust her burning brand into Ingeld's face, blinding him. As he staggered back, I rushed to cut the woman down, but she had disappeared into the darkness. Magic must have come to her aid."

Gasps of surprise and disbelief filled the hall. How could a woman, however strong and determined, dare to take the role of a man? My mind flashed to the Grendel's mother who'd come to avenge her son. I exhaled the breath I'd been holding. Mother might yet be alive.

"Now the Danes swarmed out from their hiding places, surrounding us, pinning us against the mead hall, all aflame. I pulled Ingeld down, defending his body, for he could not see to fight."

"What about Starcartherus? Did he not come to your aid?"

"Yes, but it proved to be Ingeld's undoing. When he heard Starcartherus shout, he leapt up—straight into Hrothgar's spear. Hrothgar ... or Odin in Hrothgar's guise!"

Gunter shook his head bitterly at the recollection.

"Seeing what had befallen our leader, Starcartherus boomed an order: 'Get him back to the ship. My men and I will stay and fight to the death.' So we parted, battling our way back to the edge of the settlement, back to the place where we'd hidden our horses."

Gunter slumped in his seat, reached for a cup of ale and drank it down.

"None of us escaped injury, but we all worked to save our lord. We rowed most of the way home, for the gods withheld wind from us." He paused, drawing a deep breath. "Now ... our leader is gone. We have been ... defeated."

He spat out the last word as if to discharge a bitter taste from his mouth and then turned toward me with a mocking smile.

"What happens next, queen of the Heathobards?"

I rose, fighting to control my voice, to steady the trembling in my limbs.

"You, Gunter, who defended your lord to the end, are fit to succeed him, if that is the will of your people. I would not stand against it. As for me and my people," I glanced at them, tightly packed together on one side of the hall, "we will return home to Heorot."

Glad cries and sudden smiles lit the faces of my countrymen. Gunter stared at me thoughtfully.

"There may not be much to return to. Heorot was burning when we left—and Starcartherus would have taken many Danes to the grave with him—of that I am sure."

"So be it. We will go as soon as preparations can be made."

I gave to Gunter the land and slaves promised to me by Ingeld and the livestock from my dowry. To each of Hrun's women I gave gifts of silk, finely worked brooches, and herb seeds for planting. To my surprise, Gyda asked to stay behind with the Heathobards. I suspected she had found a lover among the male servants of the house, but did not question her. Instead I granted her her freedom and gave her an amulet in the shape of Freyja.

We decided to ride our own horses overland to the coast where our cargo ship lay moored and retrace the route used on our initial trip to Wulfhaus. With spring already advanced, we could hope for mild weather on the seagoing leg of our journey home.

Home: the very word thrilled me! How I longed to see once again the dark tilled earth, the fields of grain, and our settlement perched high above the deep blue fjord—so different from the marsh and heath land, the broad low rivers of Ingeld's country.

Ah, Ingeld. I cannot find it in my heart to blame you. I can even forgive Hrun for her part in the disaster. You both lie sleeping now in your mound of earth—a monument to revenge.

"My lady?" Ana woke me from my reverie. "Shall I pack this?" She held out the wolf skin we'd once used in a ritual.

"Yes, pack it. Perhaps one day Ingeld's son will lie on that skin, kicking and cooing." Smiling, I patted the soft roundness of my tender belly.

Chapter 13
Waning of the Day

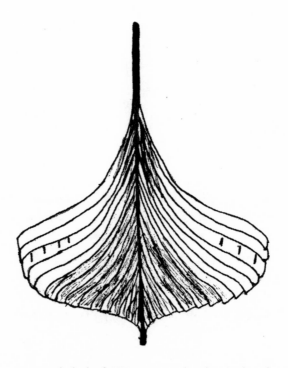

Ana stared at me in disbelief. "How can this be? It has been less than a moon since that night you went to Ingeld's bed. Have you already missed your course?"

"Yes." I smiled triumphantly.

"But my lady, this puts you in a dangerous position. If you bear Ingeld's heir, without his protection, both you and the child will be vulnerable to attack, perhaps from this very Gunter you've put in charge at Wulfhaus."

I frowned. "All the more reason for us to return to Heorot as quickly as possible. No one yet knows of the babe's existence except you and me. I will be careful to conceal the signs ... and you will help me."

"Of course, just as you say." Her face lightened and then clouded over. "Do you feel well enough to travel?"

"Of course," I echoed her, "and don't start sounding like Hrun!"

Ana chuckled softly. "What a witch!—not to speak ill of the dead— she was wise in her way." She glanced around as if expecting Hrun to appear before us. "Sometimes I almost liked her." Ana wrinkled her brow. "She had ten times the sense of her witless women. I remember what—" she broke off suddenly.

"What? What do you remember?"

Ana shifted uneasily, the wolf pelt still clutched against her breast.

"Hrun knew things. When you ... when the baby came too soon ... she said, she said—"

"That I'd never be able to have a live birth? Yes, she told me ... later."

"Oh, I didn't know!" Ana looked stricken.

"But you just said—"

Suddenly Ana was blurting out a stream of words. "Hrun said that you were cursed by the gods...that no mortal child could come from your womb...that you bore the mark of Freyja on your skin...that you were a snare to men, but could never become a mother."

In the ensuing silence, I stared at her. Finally I found my voice.

"Surely you did not believe such nonsense? She also predicted I would bear a son, but it was not so. The child was a girl—we both know that."

"My lady, forgive me. You were so sick; we thought we would lose you. It seemed best to soften the truth."

"Truth? What truth? Tell me!"

"It—they—there were two babies ... both boys ... both dead, strangled with the cord around their necks."

I was on my feet, shaking Ana by the shoulders.

"No! Tell me the real truth! It was a girl child! I saw her myself!"

"Calm yourself, my lady." Tears were running down her cheeks, but fear glimmered in her eyes. "Yes, it was a girl child you saw, but not yours. One of the kitchen slaves had given birth to a dead child. Hrun substituted that infant for your twins. She did not want Ingeld to see what you had produced. She was repulsed by the double death and considered it a sign of evil—a warning even—an omen of future disaster."

Stunned, I sank to the floor, pulling the wolf pelt from Ana's grasp. Two sons? Strangled in the womb? It could not be! But Ana had no reason to lie. Then a new thought struck me.

"The bodies—where are the bodies? What was done with them? My sons, Ingeld's sons, where are they?"

Jumping to my feet, I looked about wildly as if I might find their tiny remains in the chamber itself. Ana took me by the shoulders and looked deep into my eyes.

"They lie in the mound where Sven's ashes lie. Hrun burned the bodies at night in the hearth fire, and I buried their ashes."

Speechless, I stared at my old friend and supporter and then burst into tears.

"This is an evil place. Let us leave it at once!"

Our party set off at dawn; we turned our horses' heads to the east, our backs to the sea and Wulfhaus. As we rode forth, my free hand strayed to my belly, but I brought it up quickly and grasped the reins. Urging my horse forward, I galloped ahead of the group. I was the leader now.

Our ride to the ship took fewer days than when we first had journeyed to Wulfhaus. Urged on by my desire to leave the past behind, I set a fast pace. Even Wulfgar had to spur his mount to come up with mine.

"Slow, slow my lady." He shouted the words over the clatter of hooves. "The rest cannot keep up. It would not be wise to let them become separated—open to possible attack from any who may follow us."

I glanced behind: indeed my retinue trailed out over the heath in a broken line.

"Right! Take the lead for awhile; I'll go back and round up the stragglers."

He hesitated and then moved ahead as I had bid him. Heads turned as I passed, perhaps wondering if I had experienced a change of heart and was returning to Ingeld's house.

"To Heorot!" I shouted and pointed toward Wulfgar. Inwardly I wondered. What did that mean? What would we find when we reached my father's hall?

Ana and my maid servants were riding with the pack animals, watchful lest we lose any of our possessions. They were already sweating, squinting into the morning sun.

"Once we're home, I'm never getting on a horse again," grumbled Ana. "My bones feel every bounce!"

I nodded in sympathy. "We'll all feel better when we reach the ship."

But when we finally reached the place where we had left our cargo vessel moored, our hearts sank. Wulfgar was the first to notice something amiss. He spurred his horse and surged ahead and then sank out of sight over the low ridge before the beach. When the rest of us reached the crest, we looked down in wonder. No ship met our gaze.

Dismounting, we hurried to the water's edge. A few signs of our previous mooring could be seen, along with traces of horse hooves in patches of still-frozen mud. Our men began to search the shoreline to the south, where the sea carved out a shallow bay. We women hobbled the horses and pulled tents from the pack. A stiff breeze from the North had already begun to chill our fingers. We soon had a cook fire started and hot porridge bubbling in a cauldron beneath the iron tripod.

"So, my lady, what do you make of this?" At my elbow, Ana was setting out bread on a makeshift table. "Do you think Ingeld's men stole the ship or sank it to spite us?"

I paused, straightening to face her. "They had other matters on their minds. If you'll remember, they took the North Sea route to Heorot, not this overland route to the western passage. Something tells me that all may yet be well."

Indeed the words had barely passed my lips when Gorm and Saxe burst onto the beach, shouting gleefully. "We found it! Drifted and damaged a bit, but we can make it sound again."

Estrid and Ingeborg ran up to the men, clamoring for details.

"The mooring ropes had frayed from constant rubbing. The boat evidently bumped along the shoreline and finally lodged in a shallow inlet. Lucky there are so few rocks here and no wind strong enough to blow it out to sea!"

I strode forward. "What is the damage?"

"A few planks need to be replaced and the hull re-tarred. It should not take more than a day, as we left extra supplies on board."

Inwardly I breathed a sigh of relief. Outwardly I addressed the women: "This means one more overnight camp. Let's get busy!"

That night as we squatted around the fire, avoiding the damp cold of the beach, I stared into the flames. Faces rose before me: Ingeld, Hrun, Gunter, Starkartherus ... I blinked to shut them out, shook my head and closed my eyes, focusing on Heorot.

After a time, my mother's visage floated into view. Her lips were open, and she seemed to be calling. Was it my name?

"Mother, I'm coming!" Had I spoken aloud? I opened my eyes and glanced around the circle. No one seemed to have noticed. Relaxing, I closed my eyes again.

Mother's face came back to me and then a second face. Father? Is that you? No—a younger face, yet strangely old. That twist in the lips ... it must be ... yes, Unferth, his eyes glowing like coals. "What is happening in Heorot, Unferth? What can you tell me?" My lips moved, but I made no sound.

His lips wavered, melting, reforming and then stretched far apart in a hideous grin. My eyes flew open as I sat up straight. Only Ana's eyes were on me. At her questioning glance, I shook my head and stared again into the firelight. Suddenly three white faces rose and floated above the flames. Pale specters, they seemed drained of all life, but I recognized them: Hrothgar, Hrethric, Hrothmund.

"Father! Brothers! What is wrong? It's Freaw—I'm coming!"

I found myself on my feet, arms outstretched. Several around me jumped up as well.

"My lady, what have you seen? Tell us!" Ana was at my side, clasping my hands in hers. Mine felt icy in her warm grasp.

"I—I cannot tell. Faces in the fire ... it may be only my fancy."

"Ah, my lady Freaw, I saw them too."

Startled, I looked around for the speaker. It was Ragnhild.

"What ... who did you see?"

"Thorkel," she said in wonderment. "and he said ... he said he's still waiting for me."

She ducked her head in embarrassment at this personal revelation, and our group shared a hearty laugh. This seemed to break the spell of the night and the firelight, restoring us to ourselves.

"Wait." I held up my hand for silence. "Ragnhild, you said 'them.' Who else did you see?"

Her voice changed. "That ... that Unferth. And your cousin Hrothulf, though why I should think of them I do not know. Two nastier men would be hard to find."

Surprised at such vehemence, I questioned her further.

"I know Hrothulf can be ... mean, but what do you have against Unferth?"

She shrugged. "He frightens me—I don't know why. I only hope Thorkel hasn't fallen under his spell, like some of the other thanes." She glanced at the men in our circle, but got no overt reaction.

Shivering, I wrapped my cloak closely around me and then sank back down to ponder her words and review what each of us had seen. Faces in the fire: Were they only our own thoughts and desires reflected by the firelight? Or something else? Spirits? Ghosts? If ghosts, they'd have to be ...

I closed my eyes, summoning up the three pale faces. Their lips were blue, and no light shown from their eye sockets. I shivered again. With an effort, I tried to summon the images of Unferth and Hrothulf as well. Again they came—the eyes like coals of fire, the lips twisted. Shuddering, I opened my eyes.

"Time to sleep, my lady. I have prepared your bed."

Rising stiffly, I allowed Ana to lead me to the tent we would share for the night.

True to their word, Wulfgar and the men had our ship ready to sail within a day's time. After one more night on the beach, we rose early to break camp and stow our belongings on board. It was a tight fit with the horses, but at least we had no livestock sharing the hold.

With a smaller crew, we women helped row out to deeper water where we could catch the wind and currents. It was good to lean into the work, focusing on each lift and fall of the oar. But soon my thoughts drifted: I thought of Sven, left behind, sleeping in a mound at Wulfhaus, and of Gyda, presumably still alive and working to find her place among the women there. Ingeld's face loomed before me, and I felt tears salting my lips. I licked them off, shook my head, and rowed on.

"Sail up!"

Wulfgar, standing at the tiller, ducked as the great sail billowed aloft.

"Oars down."

We women eagerly secured our oars and then rose and stretched, shaking out muscles unused to such labor.

"How do you feel, my lady?"

Ana, ever watchful, spoke softly in my ear.

"Like a bird—like flying!"

Exultant, I lifted my arms to the sky. As my hood fell back, my hair came undone and streamed behind me. We picked up speed, heading north … toward home.

Variable winds lengthened our journey, causing us to sail at angles as we worked our way up the coastline. Finally, after two more days on the water and one overnight encampment, we entered territory more familiar to me.

"Look, everyone! The chalk cliffs where Unferth and the men once captured falcons. Brita and I went inland there to gather herbs for Wealtheow."

As my companions gazed in awe at the great white headland, my thoughts turned to Brita and her hopes of marriage.

"I wonder if Ivar has taken Brita to wife in our absence?"

The women exchanged glances, but only Ragnhild spoke.

"Though not the first to do so, she was carrying his child when we left Heorot."

"What? Do you mean he beds all the women?"

"Only those with two legs," observed Ragnhild dryly.

When I became aware that my mouth was hanging open, I shut it abruptly. An anxious thought began working its way to the front of my brain: bedding the servant girls … Hrun's woman … a stillborn child … who had fathered it? I desperately did *not* want to know.

"Here, my lady, take some ginger. You look pale."

"Ginger? Where did you get ginger?"

Ana smiled broadly."I found it among Hrun's stores, not even unwrapped. She must not have known of its uses for morning—I mean for motion sickness."

I took the proffered morsel on my tongue and let it permeate my senses.

"This baby—Brita's I mean—would she keep it? Would Ivar marry her if it were a son?"

"Not likely—marriage, I mean. Why should he? He could choose any free woman if he wanted a wife. It's my guess that Ivar is like most men: he takes his pleasures where he finds them—mostly drinking, fighting, and wenching, in that order."

"Why Ana, Aeschere was never like that—was he?"

"Ah, Aeschere was a good man, a good husband, but he was a man like all the others."

I turned to the younger women. "What do you think? Is Ana right about the drinking, fighting, and … wenching?"

Estrid coughed and cleared her throat. "Yes," she said simply.

Ingeborg laughed outright. "I say thank the gods for it! Where would we be without our men?"

Ragnhild now spoke up. "I know Thorkel's ways, and I can live with them—if we do marry—but this talk puts me in mind of one man who seemed different from the rest. Do you remember that Geat, the one who killed the Grendel?"

"Beowulf? Of course! We all owe him our lives …"

Beside me, I saw Ana's shoulders drop and her face change.

"Oh, Ana, forgive me," I cried, as the image of Aeschere's bloody head and staring eyes rose before me. For a moment we were silent, reliving that time of horror.

"Beowulf, yes. He did seem different—almost like a god." Ana's voice was so low we had to bend forward to hear her. "So courteous to all, so willing to sacrifice himself for us … strangers. A strange man himself, that one. I wonder what happened to him after he got back to his home? We'll probably never know."

We nodded, holding up his image before us like a vision. A shout from the bow broke our reverie.

"Heorot ahead. A half-day's sail. We should make it by dark."

We lifted our heads, breathing in scents of spring wafting from the land. Home was near at hand

We sailed into the fjord just as the sun dipped below the horizon. Hrothgar's coast guard had spotted us from afar and evidently reported our arrival, for a cluster of thanes awaited us in the harbor. At their head stood … Hrothulf.

He seemed taller and thinner than when I'd last seen him, but still dark as a sea crow, with a scowl on his face as our ship came to rest at the dock. He stepped on board immediately, pretending not to notice me as he hailed Wulfgar.

"We were expecting you sooner. What took so long?"

For a moment, Wulfgar had no words. I rose and addressed Hrothulf haughtily.

"We come in the time of our own choosing."

He stared at me in silence; at first, his eyes seemed to soften, but then his lips curled.

"So, the failed peace-weaver comes limping home to Mother, just as I predicted. You're too late for Hrothgar. He's dead—almost."

"What? Where is he? I must see him at once!"

He jerked his head in the direction of the mead hall. "Laid out in the women's house, our temporary headquarters. Wealtheow is with him— and the cubs—they know you're here but were told to stay put."

I scarcely noticed his dismissal of my brothers' stature in my haste to disembark. As I climbed out, my foot slipped on the wet planks. Hrothulf grabbed me instantly, his fingers digging into the soft flesh of my arm.

"You don't know yet how much you will need me," he hissed in my ear. Then he released me and set me firmly on my feet. I did not speak or look at him, but hurried up the path toward Heorot.

When something long familiar is gone, no longer exists, it takes the senses a while to come to terms with the loss. I fancied I saw the last rays of sunlight glowing off the golden face of Heorot. But no, only clouds … disappearing in the growing darkness. A great blank space occupied the spot where Heorot had once dominated the settlement. Only a few charred remnants stood as mute evidence of its former existence.

Stricken at the sight, I paused and then hurried on to the women's house. When I burst in, panting from the rapid climb, my eyes darted to a still figure laid out atop a pile of furs on a serving table.

"Father!" Rushing forward, I flung myself across the body. It moved!

"Freaw? They said you … coming. I did not … believe them."

He opened one eye and then closed it. I felt arms around my shoulders and turned into my mother's embrace. Two more sets of arms encircled me from behind—my brothers. We clung together fiercely. Wealtheow was the first to disengage.

"Welcome home, my daughter. You have returned at the waning of the day—and the waning of your father's life. It is good to have you here."

"Freaw, Freaw, we have so much to tell you—" Hrothmund began, but Hrethric shushed him.

"Not yet, our stories can wait. We have important decisions to make right now."

Hrethric seemed to have grown taller too, though his cheeks were still plump and his voice cracked at intervals.

"First, what happened to Father? Was he wounded in the battle, or—"

Mother laid a finger on her lips and drew us away from the makeshift bedside. As we moved toward a bench, I noticed for the first time what appeared to be two guards posted inside at the single door.

"What does this mean?" I nodded in their direction. "Are you prisoners in your own house?"

"Nay, nay," Mother answered lightly. "They are messengers, charged with reporting to Hrothulf any change in the king's condition."

"Hrothulf? Is he in charge now?"

"At the moment—yes. Hrothgar was stricken the day after the battle: he has been unable to speak much since then. Perhaps your arrival will give him the heart to recover."

Her somber tone of voice belied the hope in her words.

"Stricken? How? Was he wounded?"

"Not in body, no, he bears no mark of the Heathobard weapons. In the heat of battle he was magnificent—the Hrothgar of old!" Her face glowed. "Would that the gods had taken him in that moment—and me with him!"

The vehemence in her voice caught me off guard.

"No, Mother! We all need you—especially now." Reaching out, I took her hand and placed it on my belly. Our eyes locked, but the bitterness in hers did not die. She shook her head.

"You are a woman grown, Freaw, more than able to take charge of your own affairs. My duty now is to champion the interests of my sons."

Shocked, I dropped her hand.

"Is their position in danger?"

A low laugh, almost a sob, escaped her lips. "Look about you. What do you think?"

Suddenly the absence of an important figure occurred to me.

"Unferth—where is Unferth? What part is he playing in all this?"

Wealtheow recoiled as if I had struck her.

"Do not speak of him! He has been playing a dangerous game—more traitorous even than ... Ingeld!"

There—the name had been spoken. Setting aside Unferth for the moment, I asked the question that had lain on my heart since Ingeld's return, blinded and bloody.

"Did my father kill my husband?"

Mother sank down on the bench, pulling me with her. Hrethric and Hrothmund backed away, as if unwilling to hear the story.

"It was his spear, yes, guided perhaps by the gods as Unferth maintains—though he sees Odin's hand in everything!" She did not seem to notice that she herself had spoken the once-forbidden name. She continued. "You said 'kill.' I presume from your return that Ingeld is dead?"

I nodded, my head bowed.

"Hrothgar will soon join him in Valhalla. I wonder—will the feud end there?"

She turned her face away from me, but I had more questions to ask.

"What of the other Heathobards, the ones who burned Heorot? There was one man in particular—a huge, grizzled man, almost Father's age—named Starkartherus. It was he who drove Ingeld to attack."

Mother sat quietly for a time.

"I know not. Unferth could give you the details. He took charge of the bodies. The Heathobard weapons were broken and cast into the sacrificial pool as a tribute to the gods."

"Where is he now? Unferth, I mean."

"With Hrothulf, no doubt. They've become such close friends; they are seldom apart."

"They were not together when we arrived. Hrethric, do you know?"

He shook his head, but Hrothmund came forward.

"I can tell you where to find him—in the old granary. You remember, where he kept Aeschere's head?"

I nodded with a shiver of remembrance.

"Unferth can wait. I must attend Father for whatever time he has left."

Rising, I went to his still body and took his cool hands in mine.

"Father, it's really Freaw. I'm here beside you. I will not leave you again."

Hrothgar lingered one more day and then died in his sleep. He had spoken no more. Mother sat dry-eyed, her grieving internal. I too had no tears to shed. After so many deaths, I did not believe I could ever cry again. Hrethric and Hrothmund paced like caged animals, arguing over what to do next. My two little brothers were little no more, but not yet men. Unferth still had not appeared.

Aelric, our old harper, came in to touch his master's body. Softly he began to sing a lay about the Scylding line, about the great kings of the past. His words sparked an idea.

"Hrethric! Hrothmund! I know what must be done!"

They rushed forward, curious at my eagerness.

"Call an assembly of Father's thanes. Announce your plans for his burial: a full ship burial with cremation at sea! The glory and reputation of Heorot must be clearly asserted and maintained if you wish to be powerful rulers!"

"Will Hrothulf allow that? He has the backing of the majority here." Hrethric looked doubtful.

"Do not give him a chance to object! You are the king's sons and rightful heirs to his throne. Act as if you already have the power!"

Mother now joined us. "Freaw is right. Confidence is needed now … and action."

"Yes," I continued, excited by my own vision. "And after Father's farewell we will begin the rebuilding of Heorot!"

Aelric approached and took my hand in his. "The gods must have sent you, king's daughter, to bring light into our darkness."

I looked into his watery eyes and realized with a shock that he was blind.

"When did you lose your sight, old man?"

"Over time, my lady. I did not see the burning of Heorot, though I felt its heat. Now I see with my fingers."

I squeezed them gently and released him. "There are yet songs to be sung, Aelric. Take heart."

"I will, my lady, I will." He shuffled slowly out the door.

At the assembly next morning, held in the open air for lack of a suitable building, Hrethric took the lead in outlining our plan. Hrothulf was strangely cooperative, agreeing to everything proposed. This should have aroused my suspicion, but I was carried away with the grandeur of the plan. Such a ritual sendoff had never before taken place in our settlement. As news of the idea passed from mouth to mouth, excitement spread.

"They'll be talking about this for generations to come," chuckled Bjorn, the blacksmith.

"Aye, and then we'll rebuild the m-m-mead hall even grander than before!" This came from a young thane whose face I did not at first remember, until he called himself Thorkel.

Everyone seemed eager to take part in the proceedings. Stores were ransacked to equip Hrothgar's funeral ship in royal fashion. Unferth finally emerged from seclusion. He acknowledged my presence with a few cryptic words.

"We were wrong to let you go. Next time I will not fail you."

It was he who chose the ship: one of our newest and most graceful. The dragon head carved high on the prow glared menacingly from huge eyes, a great beast fit to carry a great king out to the depths of the sea.

While the ship lay moored in the harbor, the men sacrificed Hrothgar's warhorse Gullifax, itself too old to go into battle, and two of his favorite dogs. Gold was brought from his hoard, several battle standards, and finely decorated drinking horns and fragile pitchers of blown glass. The women contributed heavy woolen blankets, woven tapestries, and cooking and eating vessels.

We laid Father's body near the mast, dressed in full battle armor, sword in hand, helmet on head, his fingers covered with gold rings. When all was in place, Aelric came forward to lay his harp beside the king, murmuring, "He loved to hear the old stories."

I had not been able to decide what I could add to the riches already heaped around my father. At the last-minute I placed a pouch in his hand containing the rune Thurisaz, symbol of the gateway between worlds, and one white swan feather.

We waited half a day for a favorable wind to help the ship leave the harbor. A dozen of Hrothgar's thanes rowed it out and then abandoned it as fire from Hrothulf's arrow set the sail aflame. Hrethric should have performed this deed, but everyone knew that Hrothulf had the strongest bow arm, so it was left for him to perform this final act, to send a flaming arrow into the heart of the ship.

Everyone in the settlement watched as the ship receded, finally bursting into a ball of flame, red as the setting sun. Hrothgar: my father, a good king, fitly mourned. Now his day was over. Who would rule in his stead?

Hrothulf came to me that night. I had chosen to sleep apart from the other women, thinking to consult the runes before making any decisions about the future. I was still fully dressed when I heard the sound of a door closing. I turned and froze. Hrothulf's dark eyes gleamed beneath his long mop of hair. His lips were curved in what could be taken for a smile.

"You know why I am here, Freaw—for you."

I pretended indifference. "We're all grown up now, Hrothulf. The time for childish games is past." My hand slid under my robe, feeling for the knife hidden inside my clothes, the knife Unferth had given me long ago. As he advanced, I stepped back, gripping the hilt.

"That idiot Ingeld—was he good for you? I can show you what a real man is like!"

"Oh, who do you have in mind? Unferth, perhaps?"

This stopped him.

"Unferth? Unferth?" He began to laugh. "So, she's in love with Unferth! Sorry to disappoint you, but Unferth much prefers his own kind—I know from personal experience!"

My mind reeled, but I fought to suppress rising panic.

"You are joking, of course, but if that were true ... you'd have no interest in me."

He backed away, regarding me sardonically.

"Innocent little Freaw, darling of the court. Can't image the darker pleasures she might be introduced to! Well ... I'm here to teach you!"

As he lunged at me, I brought the knife up, catching him in the belly. Shock and surprise spread across his features. He reached down and brought up a hand dripping with blood.

"The witch bites!" His face turned ugly.

"I can do more than bite ... I can help you, if you'll come to your senses. You don't want me—you want what I know, what I can tell you."

I heard my words, but could not guess where they were coming from.

"What could you know that matters to me?" he snarled.

"Your future!"

For a moment his eyes widened, interest lurking in the corners. Then he sneered.

"If you could really see into the future, you'd never have gone off with that Ingeld. You'd have stayed in Heorot—and become my wife."

"Your wife? But you've always hated me!"

"Hate? Perhaps. Even hate has its passions and its purposes. You would be a fitting queen to serve me the ale cup when I sit on the throne of Heorot!"

"Never!" I raised my knife to strike again.

"Enough! This is a paltry wound, but I want no more. Let us strike a bargain. I will leave you alone for now. In return you will reveal to me what you have promised."

"What did I promise?"

"To tell me my future. Good night, former king's daughter."

He bowed mockingly and backed out of the room. I sprang forward, bolted the door, and sank to my knees. His future? I could not even foresee my own!

During the restless night that followed, I dreamed and dreamed and dreamed again. Or *was* I dreaming? From the swirl of images, I snatched at faces: Hrothulf, Ingeld, Unferth—and awoke with a cry, covered in sweat. Someone was pounding on the door.

"Freawaru! My lady! Let me in!"

How good to hear Ana's voice after the long, dark night. "I'm coming."

Sunlight burst in with her, flooding the chamber.

"Are you all right? It's almost mid-day and you seldom sleep so late. Now ... what's this? Blood on the floor?" She stooped to examine it. "What has happened here? You haven't ... miscarried?"

"No, no, Ana, set your mind at ease. I had a visitor last night, but he found a sharp welcome."

"Not that Unferth!"

"No, again. Why is everyone so suspicious of Unferth? Even Mother has turned against him."

"For good reasons, I'm sure. Your mother is no fool. But if not him ..." She regarded me with questioning eyes as I dressed, unaided.

"Hrothulf. He-who-would-be-king."

She made a face. "That's no subject for sport. Did he ... bother you?"

"Considerably, but not as he intended. That's his blood on the floor. Now don't worry—it was barely a scratch. I had to show him that I am a woman to be taken seriously. I think he got the point."

Ana smiled dubiously. "This could be serious. We are at his mercy here, with your father gone. Who would protect us if he turned … nasty?"

"I think Wulfgar and the men who accompanied us to Wulfhaus. And possibly—Unferth."

"Him again! I don't know how you can trust that man.!"

"I don't either, but I do." I patted the knife concealed beneath my tunic. Ana mistook the gesture.

"The baby—have you felt life?"

"Not yet, but soon. Come. I would speak with Unferth—if we can find him."

"Most of the men were carousing late into the night—drinking toasts to Hrothgar, I'm told, and boasting of how they defeated the Heathobards."

"That's the very subject I wish to discuss with Unferth. Come!"

Reluctantly Ana followed as we searched each building. No one had seen him this morning, nor could they remember if he had been present the previous night. I managed to avoid Hrothulf, reportedly down at the harbor getting construction underway on a new ship to replace the one sacrificed with Hrothgar.

Finally I sent Ana to help with meals and picked my way silently to the granary. Spring had not advanced here as far as at Wulfhaus, but a few patches of green moss cushioned my steps. Inside the dim enclosure I paused, listening for sounds above me. A trickle of grain dust powdered my eyelids.

"Unferth? It's Freaw. I'm coming up."

Getting no response, I put my foot on the lowest rung of the ladder and began to climb. As my head cleared the opening, my nostrils were assailed with a putrid odor. Choking, I was backing down when a bony hand seized my wrist and hauled me up.

"So—we meet again at Odin's altar."

I peered about, trying to make out the objects arranged on a low platform at Unferth's feet. Then I realized what they were: human heads!

"Heathobard heads," he said calmly, as if reading my thoughts. "This one"—he picked it up by the hair—"was their leader."

"Starkartherus!"

"I did not know his name—it was not necessary."

"But Unferth—without proper burial, aren't you afraid he will return to haunt you?" I shuddered and looked away from the grisly object.

"No ... I took the precaution of breaking all his bones and scattering them in the sea."

"Was that the fate of all these men?" I gestured toward the row below us, holding my nose against the stench.

"Yes—as far as I can remember—for I had partaken of the sacred mushroom and entered a berserker state. No one could stand against me and my axe!" He smiled grimly.

"Berserker? I don't understand."

"There is much you do not understand—including the use of your own powers—but I will explain. When I imbibe the flesh of the mushroom, the strength of Odin enters my limbs. I lose all fear and all reason. My only desire is to kill whatever stands in my way."

"But how did you know that Ingeld and Starkartherus were coming to attack Heorot?"

I lifted my gaze to meet his. Unferth's eyes were bloodshot, the pupils large. He looked both crafty and crazed.

"Hrothulf. He had posted lookouts along both coasts, anticipating just such a move. Once we got the alert, we planned a surprise for our guests." He paused, smiling. "Wealtheow helped too. She volunteered to act as a decoy in the mead hall. Oh, I regret that we lost the building—that was not in our plan. Killing the invaders had to take precedence, and by the time we could attend to the fire it was raging beyond control."

"What of Hrethric and Hrothmund? Did they not help defend Heorot? Both have been strangely silent on the subject."

Unferth shook his head. "They tried, but were only in the way. I locked them in the latrine."

"What?" I gasped. "Do the rest of the men know that?"

"No—and I let them out when I came to myself again."

Despite my indignation, I had to chuckle. Poor brothers! No wonder they had avoided giving me any details about the battle.

"Unferth, tell me truly. Who is most fit to be king?"

He did not hesitate. "Hrothulf."

"But then what is to become of my brothers?"

The answer to that question came sooner than expected, but in a form no one could have predicted.

Chapter 14
Heading North

Unable to bear any longer the stench of rotting flesh, I left Unferth to his mad pursuits. On a whim, I made my way to the great oak tree where we had first carved runes together. There I noticed a lower branch that had broken off and now dangled above the stream. It made me think of broken Heathobard limbs—a thought I put behind me. Today I needed to think of the present. Today I needed to recapture the sense of security and freedom from care I had once experienced in this spot, after the Grendel's killing.

The Grendel, Beowulf, Ingeld—all gone, all behind me now. One day soon I would be an old woman like Ana, with flabby breasts and haunches; no man would look on me with favor, not even Hrothulf.

Hrothulf? What was I to tell him? Even if he kept his word and left me alone, I had no vision of the future to reveal. Hmmm. Would I need to enter a trance state to find the answers I needed? What could I use to aid me? Perhaps if I held something of his or obtained a drop of his blood; I'd wiped the knife clean and later burned the rag in the fire. Fire ... fire ... I found myself on my feet heading toward the remains of the mead hall.

Despite the destruction surrounding it, the central hearth remained, clearly outlined with blocks of stone. I nudged a half-burned timber with my foot and felt heat below it. Digging down I found an ember buried beneath. Reaching for splinters of wood scattered nearby, I fed them slowly to the growing flame.

"What are you doing? Playing with fire?"

Hrothulf stood in what had once been the doorway to Heorot.

"Yes."

He stepped forward. "I will help you."

To my astonishment, he began dragging up long pieces of roof timber, blackening his hands in the process. As he handed me the sticks I added them to the flame, carefully building a small framework to hold the fire, almost a miniature mead hall. We worked silently together. When the structure seemed able to maintain itself without further attention, I stood up, wiping my face with a sooty hand.

Hrothulf laughed, the clear, easy laugh of a child. "You look like a crow!"

"So do you!" I retorted "No, more like a *kraki*—a long, thin stick, a pole ladder."

I smiled at the image this created. "Kraki—a good nickname for you—someday as king you will be known by that name, and you will use your ladder to climb higher than any other king of Denmark."

Where had these words come from?

Hrothulf's mouth fell open. "My future? Is that my future?"

"Yes," I nodded, "your future. I have fulfilled my promise."

"Do you really mean it, Freaw? Do you see me as a great king?"

He sounded like a boy, like Hrothmund begging for a bedtime story.

The words came through me, not from me. "It must be so. The gods are with you." I hung my head. "Alas for my brothers."

"Your brothers? Oh, perhaps it's not too late—"

His voice sounded strangled. My head jerked up.

"Too late? For what?"

"Nothing, nothing." His face resumed its mask of adult control. "I'm giving a feast tonight in the men's quarters. I've asked your brothers to attend as a gesture of friendship."

Puzzled, but not wishing to suppress this hint of humanity in my old foe, I spoke sincerely, "You do them honor."

He nodded, staring vacantly at the fire.

"We'd better put this out before someone thinks the Heathobards have returned." He kicked at the mound, scattering burning brands, and then stamped them out with heavy boots.

"There," he shouted. "Hrothulf Kraki has killed the fire."

Despite, or because of Hrothulf's sudden change of mood, I slept with the other women that night, flanked by Wealtheow and Ana. As I started to undress, I noticed Brita on one of the sleeping benches and went to greet her. She responded shyly.

"Oh, my lady, you honor me with your attention."

"Nonsense! I was wondering about your baby: was it a boy or a girl?"

"Neither. That is, I lost it early on."

"Oh, I'm sorry. I did not know." Why had I not asked someone for news before blundering into her pain?

"It's for the best. Ivar's gone, you know."

"No, I didn't know that either! Where did he go?"

"Go? He's dead! Killed by those Heathobards!" Her eyes blazed and then filled with tears. I patted her hand and pulled up her sleeping robe, tucking her in as if she were a child.

"I'm sorry again. Perhaps he'll come to you in your dreams tonight—not as a ghost," I added hastily, seeing her eyes widen in alarm, "but as the Ivar you knew, to comfort you."

She nodded and closed her eyes.

Wealtheow had been watching me and drew me aside when I returned to my bed.

"Something's going to happen. I feel it. Whether for good or ill I cannot tell. Have you ... seen anything, my daughter?"

"Oh, Mother, I have seen too much. I cannot make sense of all I have seen."

I shook my head despairingly and sank down beside her.

"I've been a failure as a peace-weaver, a failure as a wife, and a failure as a seeress. Perhaps Freyja marked me only to mock me!"

"I do not believe that." I felt her hand stroking my hair. "You are still young. Much lies before you."

"But what? And where? Mother, I cannot stay in Heorot with Hrothulf sniffing around me as if I were a bitch in heat, yet where can I go? I won't go back to Wulfhaus!"

Mother closed her eyes and sat quietly.

"Did you ever hear the tale of a woman called Thrith? She too was a king's daughter. She too had unwelcome ... suitors. She had such men strangled for looking at her lustfully."

"What?" I sat bolt upright. "Are you advising me to have Hrothulf killed?"

"No, no, not that. Even were your father alive, he would not allow that."

"Then what?"

Mother took her time before answering. "Thrith found happiness across the sea, in the arms of a young king called Offa. In her new country, she was renowned for her generosity and queenly behavior—or so the stories say."

I stared at Mother. "Was Thrith bearing another man's child—as I am?"

Wealtheow's thoughtful expression did not change.

"That can be dealt with. Your path might be easier if you were ... unencumbered."

"Mother! How can you suggest such a thing? You who were so loving to your own infants? I want to bear Ingeld's son!"

"And if it is not a son, but a daughter?"

"Then I will cherish her and raise her as a gift from Freyja!"

Ana, who had evidently overheard part of our muffled conversation, joined us hesitantly.

"Queen Wealtheow, I will stay with Freawaru—wherever she goes. I will also help care for the babe. It would be good to hold an infant in my arms again," she concluded wistfully.

"Ah, Ana, always an open heart. Freawaru is fortunate to have your friendship."

I put an arm around each woman.

"We are all daughters of the ash tree. As it holds up the world, we hold up each other."

Mother turned to look in my face.

"Daughter, you speak wisely. Now, tell me of your time among the Heathobards."

We spent the night in talk, I recounting all that had happened at Wulfhaus, Ana occasionally adding a detail. I hid nothing from either woman. When we came to the night of my bleeding and the death of my twin sons, Mother stopped me in horror.

"Freawaru, to lose two sons at one time! A heavy blow indeed!"

"Wait, there is more to tell. Hrun switched their bodies for that of a servant's dead baby and told me that I had birthed a single girl child. I believed her, for Ana helped in the deception." I said these words without reproach, for I had no more anger in me. It had been consumed in the funeral pyre with Ingeld and his mother.

"Explain this, Ana!" demanded Mother.

"Queen Wealtheow, Freawaru was close to death. Hrun was afraid the shock might finish her, and besides, Hrun thought … she thought the dead twins were an evil sign from the gods, a sign of disfavor."

Mother pondered Ana's words. "This Hrun—did she worship the goddess?"

Although it seemed a strange question, I answered as truthfully as I could.

"She was old and ill; she had neglected the rituals, though I tried to re-establish them."

"Then perhaps *she* was being punished, not you, Freawaru. The loss of a longed-for grandson and heir would be a bitter draught to swallow."

While I digested this interpretation, Mother spoke again.

"Tell me, did Hrun not know that you were pregnant again?"

I sighed and took a deep breath. "There is more to the story. It hinges on a warrior named Starkartherus."

When the thread of my tale reached the battle of Heorot, I had questions of my own.

"How came you to be inside the mead hall, Mother? Gunter reported that you charged out dressed all in white with your hair down, fierce as a valkyrie."

Mother looked pleased at Gunter's comparison.

"Once we knew that the attack was imminent, we took our places according to a plan drawn up by Hrothgar—with the aid of Hrothulf and Unferth, I should add."

"Were Hrethric and Hrothmund not a part of this plan?"

"Of course, under Unferth's charge, I believe. It was my part to stay in the mead hall with Aelric, who would sing loudly as if entertaining the men inside at a banquet."

I shook my head in wonder at the imagination behind it all, suspecting that Unferth had played a major role in concocting this elaborate plan.

"Were you expecting to meet Ingeld when you burst forth?" I held my breath for her answer.

"I heard his battle cry and knew his voice. I did what had to be done—knowing," she added, looking at my face, "that he had already betrayed his marriage vows by coming to attack us."

I choked back a sob as she continued.

"After he … ran into Hrothgar's spear, I knew our revenge was complete. I went back inside the flaming hall to lead out blind Aelric, and we escaped into the darkness just as the red-bearded Heathobard led his men forward—to be met by Unferth." Here she shuddered.

"Unferth was transformed. He foamed at mouth like a raging bear, attacking everyone in his path, lopping off heads and limbs with a huge axe. The battle was soon over."

I thought back to Unferth's long-ago outburst about the killing of his own brothers and of what I had heard about berserkers. I could almost see Unferth in action, dealing death and destruction in a god-like fury. Then I thought of my cousin.

"What part did Hrothulf play in the battle?"

"He and Hrothgar's thanes pursued all who fled, cutting them down. Only a few escaped." She closed her eyes. "It took many days to clear away the carnage—Unferth saw to most of it. Your father decreed the disposal of enemy weapons and led the final ritual when they were cast into the bog. Heorot had burned, but we had survived. Then Hrothgar collapsed, gasping for breath, and lay on this deathbed—until you came."

She opened her eyes. "You came, bearing life." She placed her hand on my belly and smiled.

The next morning we were all sound asleep when a pounding on the door brought us to consciousness. Brita rose to pull the bar and then shrank back as Unferth burst in, panting.

"Queen Wealtheow, come quickly! Your two sons hover at the brink of death!"

In horror and confusion, we leapt from our beds, grabbing cloaks and shoes. We hurried after Wealtheow, following her to the men's quarters where the door already stood open. Inside a knot of men crouched around three bodies on the floor.

Pushing them aside, we stared down. Wealtheow threw herself on her knees, calling to her sons as she felt for a heartbeat. Hrethric and Hrothmund lay unseeing, their lips and faces blue and ashen. Their clothes were soiled with what looked like vomit.

"I feel a pulse! They still live! Freaw—bring my medicine bag! Ana—fetch boiling water! You men—grab robes and blankets to cover them! We must keep them warm while I search for an antidote." She looked up accusingly. "My sons have been poisoned!"

Uneasily, casting sidelong glances at each other, the men did as she bid. Ana and I ran out and returned immediately with the items demanded.

"What was served at that banquet last night? Has no one else been affected? Where is Hrothulf?"

Mother rained questions at the men. Then her gaze fell on the third body: Aelric. One eyelid flickered in the old man's wrinkled and wizened face.

"Aleric, can you speak? What did you eat?"

His lips trembled as he worked to form one word.

"M ... Mush ... Mushrooms."

The men had been silently drifting toward the door but were stopped when Mother whirled to face them. Her eye fell on Ragnhild's betrothed.

"Thorkel! What happened here? Tell me at once!"

The young thane came forward sheepishly, looking none too well himself.

"We all t-t-tried it, my lady—mushrooms boiled in water—but some felt it more than others. Surely your boys are just s-s-sleeping? They were lively enough last night, shouting and dancing, raging like wolves or bears ... they even climbed up on the rafters and t-t-tried to fly, but Unferth caught them."

"Unferth? Where is he now? I need his help."

"Here, my lady." He lowered his voice as he knelt beside her. "I fear these three ingested something not served to the other men." He laid his palm on Hrethric's forehead.

"Cold. He is shivering, but Hrothmund is sweating. I had already given them thistle and willow bark tea to no avail. When they went into convulsions, I came for you."

Mother rummaged in her medicine pouch, tossing out folded packets of herbs.

"Have you tried tea with honey? Or dandelion?"

Unferth did not seem to be listening. He reached over and plucked something from the corner of Aelric's mouth.

"If this is what they ate, no herb can help them!"

"What is it?" we cried in unison.

"Death cap."

We stared at him in horror as he went on to explain.

"They will seem to recover momentarily, but death cap is fatal. It is only a matter of time before their organs start to fail."

"How much time?" Mother was clinging to Hrethric as if she were drowning.

"Four, possibly five days at the most."

Suddenly Unferth stood up and spoke calmly to the men crowded near the door.

"You may all go your way. The lads are just sleeping it off, as Thorkel said."

Relief in their faces, the men vanished.

"Now, listen to me!" He hissed in a half-whisper. "Whoever wanted Hrothgar's sons to die may not stop there. You are all in danger—especially you, Queen Wealtheow, and you, Freawaru. You should all leave Heorot quickly—tonight, if possible. Flee to some safe haven!"

"And where would that safe haven be?" I cried despairingly.

I felt Mother's hand on my arm.

"With Beowulf—the man who saved us once before—we must go to Beowulf!"

We looked at each other, surprise giving way to acquiescence. Unferth nodded agreement.

"A good choice! That noble lord will surely offer you his protection. Take with you any who are willing to go, but do it quietly. Do not draw attention to your preparations."

"I will not leave my sons while there is any hope!" Mother's eyes flashed as she faced Unferth squarely. "How do we know you are telling the truth? This may be a ruse to get us out of the way so that Hrothulf can take over Heorot with no opposition—it is Hrothulf, is it not, who has poisoned my sons? Or are you responsible, Unferth? You are the one with knowledge of poisonous mushrooms."

Unferth drew back.

"This is not my doing. I had no part in Hrothulf's banquet—until near the end when they first summoned me to control your sons. I admit I have championed Hrothulf's bid to become king, for he is able and ready, but I did not assist him in this dark deed. Do as you like—but I would advise escape while there is yet time."

He stalked toward the door, his back stiff, as we stared after him.

"I think he is right, begging your pardon, my lady."

Ana's voice quivered, but determination shone on her face.

"I think so too," answered Mother, "but I cannot leave my sons like this. Freawaru, gather the people you would take with you as discreetly as possible. Ana, spread word that Hrothgar's sons will recover. That may give us a few days time. Then we will see. Oh, and eat nothing you have not prepared with your own hands."

As we nodded, she turned her attention back to my brothers.

"What of Aelric?" I asked.

"Let me ... let me die here."

"He speaks!"

I knelt beside the old man and took one hand in mine. He tried to smile, but his face sagged in a grimace, his lips working.

"Odin ... Odin may need ... need harper in Valhalla ... as well as ... warriors."

"Indeed, and your songs would delight the gods," I lied. "If you should die, Aelric, you'll be buried honorably. I'll ask Unferth to see to that." I paused. 'If you can, tell me how you came to eat the mushrooms."

He coughed and gagged and then cleared his throat.

"Hrothmund offered—so good, he said—Hrothulf said no, don't waste—Hrothmund—insisted—always generous boy."

These words appeared to exhaust him. I wrapped a fur robe around his thin body and left him in peace.

"I'm going now, Mother."

Wealtheow did not even look up as I joined Ana waiting at the door.

Casually, one by one, Ana and I spoke to all who had returned with us from Wulfhaus, saying that we would not linger in Heorot, but seek a new home among the Geats, Beowulf's people—and enjoined each to silence.

Wulfgar raised an important question: who would guide us to that northern shore? He himself did not know the coastline. Fortunately Ragnhild held the answer: Thorkel was a Swede who knew the country well—if he could be persuaded.

"Ragnhild, I will personally guarantee a handsome dowry if you bring Thorkel with us—tell him so."

She turned bright red, but nodded. "I will, my lady."

That night Brita approached my sleeping bench and spoke in low tones.

"My lady, I know I'm not supposed to know, but I know you're leaving. Take me with you—please. I will serve you well, I swear by the gods."

"Have a care who you swear by, Brita. Some gods are more reliable than others. Yes, I will consider your request. Now go back to bed and do not speak of this to anyone."

"Yes, my lady." She crept meekly away, but her eyes were smiling.

The cargo ship in which we had made our return was not yet fully unloaded, so it was not unusual to make trips in that direction. We posted Thorkel—who had agreed to join us—as a guard at the ship itself, and he stowed the chests and bundles brought down after darkness.

Hrethric and Hrothmund appeared to rally on the second day. They sat up and were even able to walk a bit. Mother continued to ply them with cleansing herbal teas. She had them moved to the women's quarters, along with Aelric, to nurse them herself. In front of Hrothulf's men—for so we now regarded them—we feigned embarrassment, saying that the queen must be indulged in coddling her sons.

Aelric was the first to die. We drew a blanket over his face and told no one outside the "inner circle" of those planning to flee. Hrothmund was next. As I held him close, rocking him like a baby, he whimpered, relaxed, and then grew cold in my arms. Hrethric held out for one more day, fighting for his life, but he too could not escape. As Mother and I stood on either side, our hands on his body, he gave a final shudder, his teeth clenched, and he lay still. Wealtheow buried her face in his hair, weeping silently.

Outside the house of death, we spoke bravely, assuring any who asked that the boys had experienced a setback, but were recovering, slowly. No one seemed to doubt our words.

Five days had now passed since Hrothulf's deadly banquet. With spring advancing and the weather warming we could not hide the smell of three dead bodies for long, despite the herbs used to mask it. Thus we decided to leave early the next morning. Wulfgar and Thorkel would lead our horses down to the ship during the night, and the rest of us would slip away by twos and threes, initially heading for the latrine.

I did not sleep that night, nor did Wealtheow. Ana lay snoring, as she often did. Somehow I had managed to avoid Hrothulf for days, spending most of my time inside the women's quarters. Not for the first time I wondered how he would react once he discovered our departure. Would he allow a proper funeral for our loved ones?

Unferth had sworn to arrange a funeral pyre worthy of their status, and I trusted his word. Mother was still ill at ease, pained to leave her sons without the mourning and ceremony they deserved.

To settle my mind, I tried to focus on Beowulf. What did he look like? Tall, yes, with massive arms and shoulders. His eyes—a piercing blue. His lips—what were those words he had so graciously spoken as he took his leave of us? The sound of his voice came back to me, ringing clearly: "Someday, if your oldest son comes visiting our court, he will find a host of good friends among the Geats. No one who goes visiting far-off lands is more welcome than a strong noble warrior."

Ah, Beowulf, not the king's son but the king's daughter comes visiting your court. Will she be as welcome there as he? Will the Geatish court be anything like Heorot? Who is king there? Hrothgar had once predicted that Beowulf himself might take that role one day. If so, might he also have taken a queen? My thoughts drifted.

"Freaw! Wake up! We may have been discovered! We must go!"

I bolted upright. Wealtheow and Ana stood before me, fully dressed. I had slept in my clothes, so it took only a moment to don slippers and grab my cloak.

"What's the matter? What has gone wrong?"

"Brita is missing. We fear she may have given away our plan."

"Brita? Nay, she wants to come with us. She's probably gone to the latrine first, as we planned."

Ana shook her head. "I just came from the latrine, my lady. Brita is not there."

"Then—down at the ship? She was so eager not to be left behind—"

"Perhaps too eager?"

We whirled toward the voice at the doorway. Hrothulf! He held Brita with one hand over her mouth and the other twisting her arm behind her back. Her eyes were rolled back in terror, like an animal being led to sacrifice.

"So—leaving, were you? I don't think so—at least not the way you planned." He looked around the room and nodded toward the figures draped on the table. "I see that some of you have already ... left. I also see that we'll need a funeral pyre big enough to hold all who wish to join their kin—in death!"

Fascinated, we stared at him, trying not to lift our eyes toward the heavy axe that seemed to hang, hovering over his head. When the axe swung up, I shut my eyes and screamed. Instead of the sound of a skull splitting, as I'd expected, I heard a dull thud. When I opened my eyes, Hrothulf lay sprawled on the floor, Brita struggling to crawl out from beneath him. In the doorway towered ... Unferth.

"Go!" he hissed. "You should have left days ago—then this would not have been necessary! Go!" He waved the axe toward the opening.

Suddenly released from our paralysis, we sprang forward. Brita scrambled to her feet.

"Wait, don't leave me—I'm coming!"

As we passed Unferth, I looked into his eyes.

"Thank you for saving my life—again!"

"Someday perhaps you'll return the favor. Now go!"

We went.

The men, horses, and other women were already on the ship. Wulfgar stood at the helm as we scrambled aboard.

"The gods are with us—the wind will be favorable. Oars out! Row for the fjord and Geatland! Row for your lives!"

My heart still pounding from our narrow escape, I joined the rest fitting oars to oar-holes and thrusting them out into the dark water. I glanced over to see Brita on the other side.

"Together again—have you practiced your rowing lately?"

We choked back hysterical laughter, still fearing pursuit, but none came. Dawn tinted the horizon with pale light as we pulled out to sea, exultant. By the time we raised sail and shipped oars, my arms were trembling, and my whole body began to shake.

"Here." Ana was holding out something wrapped in a fine cloth. Ginger.

"Nay, I'm not sick. It was just—the shock."

"Take it. You have the babe to think about."

"Oh, yes, of course."

Obediently I broke off a small chunk and slipped it in my mouth. Ingeld's baby. What would Beowulf think of that? As the light strengthened, I looked about, counting heads. One in particular was missing.

"Mother? Mother! Where is the queen?"

Ana turned an anxious face toward me.

"Wealtheow stayed behind, my lady. She stopped at the dock and told me to tell you later. She said she could not leave her boys alone, unmourned. She said she had no fear for herself."

"May the gods be with her," I gasped. "No, may Unferth stay beside her!"

Shaken to the core by this fresh loss, I sat frozen. At that instant, I knew I would never see Mother again. A wave of anger surged through me. What needless sacrifice! Of course it was right to honor the dead, but something is also owed to the living. Did she not know how much I needed her? Seeming to read my thoughts, Ana covered my cold hands with her own.

"You may be the last survivor of your family, my lady. As the daughter of such a queen—and such a king—you must act as befits your station. Be proud and hold your head high."

I jerked my hands from hers.

"Words—cold words! What good is a word-hoard that contains no better comfort!"

Ana was silent and moved away, leaving me to my angry thoughts. In the hours that followed, I mourned inwardly for all the members of my family: Father, two brothers, and now Mother—all gone. What did the future hold? Perhaps it would be better to shed the life in my belly after all, rather than bring it into a world of dark uncertainty. Brita broke my reverie.

"My lady, I can tell you're with child, having been pregnant myself. I'll be glad to help with the baby when it comes."

I stared at her so long that she finally dropped her head.

"Yes, Brita—if it lives."

Thorkel turned out to be an invaluable member of our crew. I sought him out when we ate our first meal on board, to learn more of his background.

"How did you come to know this coastline?"

He stopped chewing and hastily wiped his mouth with a grimy hand.

"I hunted s-s-seals along here when I was a boy, with my uncle."

"Did you live with him?" I asked, "like Hrothulf lived with Hrothgar?"

"No, not the s-s-same, not the same. My mother and father were both k-k-killed in a feud—part of the Swedish wars, in a way—so I was r-r-raised by my uncle and his wife. Good people." He fell silent.

"What is it like, Thorkel, this Geatland?"

"Rocky mostly. Heavy forests. Colder than Denmark with heavy s-s-snows in winter and fierce gales from the sea, but a good land— plenty of fish and g-game. Peaceful, mostly."

"You spoke of Swedish wars. Are the Geats involved?"

"Hard to say. We'll soon find out. If all the Geats are l-l-like Beowulf, we'll have nothing to fear."

"Fear?" I echoed. "No, Thorkel, I do not fear for our future. We have treasure enough to buy our place in any court and trusted men like you and Wulfgar to rely on. I foresee a grand new life for us all!"

I rose and stretched, noting that the sun had broken through the clouds high above us. Lifting my arms I called aloud: "May the gods be with us! North to Geatland! North to Beowulf!"